THE
WALKING
DEAD

Other Books in the Walking Dead Series

ROBERT KIRKMAN'S

THE WALKING DEAD

DESCENT

JAY BONANSINGA

Thomas Dunne Books
St. Martin's Griffin
New York

This is a work of fiction. All of the characters, organizations, and events portrayed in this novel are either products of the author's imagination or are used fictitiously.

THOMAS DUNNE BOOKS.
An imprint of St. Martin's Press.

ROBERT KIRKMAN'S THE WALKING DEAD: DESCENT. Copyright © 2014 by Robert Kirkman LLC. All rights reserved. Printed in the United States of America. For information, address St. Martin's Press, 175 Fifth Avenue, New York, N.Y. 10010.

www.thomasdunnebooks.com
www.stmartins.com

The Library of Congress has cataloged the hardcover edition as follows:

Bonansinga, Jay R.
    Robert Kirkman's The Walking Dead: Descent / written by Jay Bonansinga, based on the series created by Robert Kirkman. — First edition.
        p. cm. — (The Walking Dead ; 5)
    ISBN 978-1-250-05717-4 (hardcover)
    ISBN 978-1-4668-6077-3 (e-book)
    1. Zombies—Fiction. 2. Horror fiction. I. Kirkman, Robert. II. Title. III. Title: Walking Dead: Descent. IV. Title: Descent.
    PS3552.O5927R63 2014
    813'.6—dc23

                                                                    2014029970

ISBN 978-1-250-06790-6 (trade paperback)

St. Martin's Griffin books may be purchased for educational, business, or promotional use. For information on bulk purchases, please contact the Macmillan Corporate and Premium Sales Department at 1-800-221-7945, extension 5442, or write to specialmarkets@macmillan.com.

First St. Martin's Griffin Edition: June 2015

10 9 8 7 6 5 4 3 2 1

In Memory of Jane Catherine Parrick
December 3rd, 1928–March 21st, 2014

ACKNOWLEDGMENTS

I owe an enormous debt of gratitude on this one to the Man, the Myth, the Mensch, Mr. Robert Kirkman, for giving me the keys to the family sports car; special thanks to David Alpert for magnificent macro-management, to Andy Cohen for worldly wisdom and wise cracks, to Brendan Deneen for spectacular editing and explaining the differences between "farther" and "further," to Nicole Sohl for traffic control, to Justin Velella for fabulous PR, to Lee Ann Wyatt of The Walker Stalkers for rock star treatment, and to Kemper Donovan of Circle of Confusion for granular editing genius. Additional muchas gracias to Jim Mortenson and Joe Chouinard of Comix Revolution Evanston, Charles Robinson of Eagle Eye Books Atlanta, Eric and James from Walker Stalkers, Stephanie Hargadon, Courtney Sanks, Bryan Kett, Mort Castle, Jeff Siegel, Shawn Kirkham, all the good folks at Skybound, and my two hipster sons, Joey and Bill Bonansinga (I love you, gentlemen). Last but not least, I'd like to send a huge shout-out to the love of my life, an amazing artist, friend, and partner in crime, Jill M. Norton (*Io to amero' per sempre*).

PART 1

Lake of Fire

The days of punishment have come, the days of retribution have come; Let Israel know this! The prophet is a fool, the inspired man is demented. And there is only hostility in the house of God.

—Hosea 9:7–8

ONE

On that quiet morning, two separate and troubling problems lie just beneath the surface of that burned husk of a village—both issues, at least initially, going completely unnoticed by the residents.

The drumming of hammers and rasping of saws fill the air. Voices rise on the wind in busy call-and-response. The congenial odors of woodsmoke, tar pitch, and compost infuse the warm breezes. A sense of renewal—maybe even of hope—thrums beneath the surface of all the activity. The oppressive heat of summer, still a good month or two away, has not yet wilted the wild Cherokee roses growing in profusion along the abandoned train tracks, and the sky has that high-def, robin's-egg brilliance that skies around these parts get in the fleeting last weeks of spring.

Spurred on by their tumultuous regime change, as well as the possibility of a new democratic way of life amid the ruins of the plague, the people of Woodbury, Georgia—a onetime railroad burg fifty miles south of Atlanta, only recently reduced to scorched buildings and battered, scarred, littered roadways—have reconstituted themselves like strands of DNA, forming a sturdier and healthier organism. Lilly Caul is a big reason for this renaissance. The slender, comely, battle-bitter young woman with the dishwater auburn hair and heart-shaped face has become the reluctant leader of the village.

At this moment, in fact, her voice can be heard from every quarter, carrying on the wind with authority, drifting over the tops of live oaks and poplars lining the promenade west of the racetrack. From every open window, every alley, every convolution of the arena, she can be heard selling the little settlement with the verve of a Florida real estate agent peddling beachfront property.

"Right now the safe zone is small, I'll grant you that," she is commenting candidly to some unidentified listener. *"But we're planning to expand that wall over there another block to the north, and this one over here, maybe another two or three blocks to the south, so what we're eventually going to end up with is a town within a town, a safe place for kids, which will one day, if all goes well, be totally self-contained and totally self-sustainable."*

As the lilting sound of Lilly's monologue echoes and penetrates the nooks and crevices of that dirt-track stadium—the place where madness once reigned in the form of bloody death matches—the dark figure trapped underneath a drainage grate jerks its charred face toward the sound of the voice with the mechanized abruptness of a satellite dish rotating toward a signal from space.

Once a lanky farmhand with ropy muscles and a thick crown of wheat-straw hair, this burned, reanimated corpse tumbled through the broken grating during the chaos and fires that engulfed the town not long ago, and now it has gone unnoticed for practically a week, wallowing in the airless, reeking capsule of darkness. Centipedes, beetles, and pill bugs crawl hectically across its pallid dead face and down its tattered, faded denim—the fabric so old and distressed it can barely be distinguished from the thing's dead flesh.

This errant walker, once a captive member of the inhuman gladiators that graced the arena, will prove to be only the *first* of two very worrisome developments that have gone completely undetected by every resident of the town, including Lilly, whose voice now rises with each footstep as she approaches the racetrack, the shuffling of other footsteps audible beneath her own.

"Now, you might be asking yourselves, 'Am I seeing things, or did a gigantic flying saucer land in the middle of town when nobody was looking?' What you're staring at is the Woodbury Veterans Speedway—guess you could call it a leftover from happier times when people wanted nothing more on a Friday evening than a bucket of fried chicken and a track full of men in stock cars sideswiping each other and polluting the atmosphere. Still trying to figure out what to do with it . . . but we're thinking it would make a great public garden."

Inside the festering enclosure of the sewer culvert, the dead farm-hand drools at the prospect of living tissue closing in. Its jaws begin to ratchet and grind, making a papery creaking noise as it scuttles toward the wall, reaching blindly up at the daylight filtering through the grate. Through the narrow iron slats of the overhead grating, the creature can see the shadows of seven living humans approaching.

The thing accidentally wedges its right foot in a divot in the crumbling masonry.

Walkers have no climbing skills, no purpose other than to devour, no sentient awareness other than hunger, but right then, the unforeseen foothold is enough for the thing to almost inadvertently lift itself up to the busted grate through which it had previously plummeted. And as its white shoe-button eyes reach the lip of the manhole, the creature locks its feral gaze on the closest figure: a little girl in rags approaching with the group, a child of about eight or nine years old, walking alongside Lilly with an earnest expression on her grime-smudged face.

For a moment, the walker inside the sewer culvert coils itself like a spring, letting out a low growl like an engine idling, its dead muscles twitching from innate signals sent by a reanimated nervous system. Its blackened, lipless mouth peels away from mossy green teeth, its eyes like milky diodes absorbing its prey.

"You're gonna hear rumors about this sooner or later," Lilly confides to her malnourished clientele as she passes within inches of the sewer grate. Her tour group is made up of a single family, the Duprees, which consists of an emaciated father of about forty years old who goes by the name of Calvin, his waiflike wife, Meredith, and their three ragamuffins—Tommy, Bethany, and Lucas—twelve, nine, and five years old, respectively. The Dupree clan wobbled into the Woodbury town limits the previous night in their beat-up Ford LTD station wagon, near death from starvation, practically psychotic with hunger. Lilly took them in. Woodbury needs bodies—new residents, fresh people to help the town reboot itself and do some of the heavy lifting of community building. "You might as well hear it from us," Lilly says to them, pausing in her Georgia Tech hoodie and ripped jeans, her hands on her Sam Browne gun belt. Still in her early thirties but bearing the visage of a much older soul, Lilly has her ruddy brown hair pulled back in a tight ponytail, her hazel eyes glittering, the spark down in the core of her pupils partly intelligence and partly the hundred-yard stare of a seasoned warrior. She throws a glance over her shoulder at a seventh figure standing behind her. "You want to tell them about the Governor, Bob?"

"You go ahead," the older man says with a plague-weary smile on his weathered, leathery face. Dark hair pomaded back across a corrugated brow, ammo bandolier canted across his sweat-stained chambray shirt, Bob Stookey stands over six feet in his socks, but he slumps with the perpetual fatigue of a reformed drunk, which is what he is. "You're on a roll, Lilly-girl."

"Okay . . . so . . . for the better part of a year," Lilly begins as she stares at each Dupree one at a time, emphasizing the importance of what she's about to say, "this place, Woodbury, was under the yoke of a very dangerous man named Philip Blake. Went by the name of the Governor." She lets out a flinty little breath, half chuckle, half sigh of disgust. "I know . . . the irony's not lost on us." She takes a breath. "Anyway . . . he was a pure sociopath. Paranoid. Delusional. But he got things done. I hate to admit it, but . . . he seemed to most of us, for a while, at least, a necessary evil."

"Excuse me . . . um . . . *Lilly*, was it?" Calvin Dupree has stepped forward. A compact, fair-skinned man with the hard gristly muscles of a day laborer, he wears a filthy windbreaker that looks as though it has doubled as a butcher's apron. His eyes are clear and warm and open—despite the reticence and the lingering trauma of being out in the wild for God knows how long. "Ain't sure what this has to do with us." He glances at his wife. "I mean . . . we appreciate the hospitality and such, but where y'all going with this?"

The wife, Meredith, stares at the pavement, chewing her lip. A mousy little woman in a ragged sundress, she hasn't said more than three words—other than "Hmm" or "Uh-huh"—since the Duprees arrived. The previous night, they were fed, given first aid by Bob, and allowed to rest. Now the wife fidgets as she waits for Calvin to practice his patriarchal duty. Behind her, the children look on expectantly. Each child seems stunned, loopy, gun-shy. The little girl, Bethany, stands only inches away from the broken sewer grate, sucking her thumb with a shopworn doll in the crook of her tiny arm, completely oblivious of the shadow moving inside the trench.

For days, the stench emanating from the sewer—the telltale rancid-meat odor of a biter—has been mistaken for the reek of old sewage, the faint growling noise misidentified as the reverberation of a generator. Now the moving corpse manages to squeeze its clawlike hand through a gap in the broken grate, the moldering fingernails jerking toward the hem of the little girl's dress.

"I understand the confusion," Lilly says to Calvin, locking gazes with him. "You don't know us from Adam. But I just thought . . . you know. Full disclosure. The Governor used this arena for . . . bad things. Gladiator fights with biters. Ugly stuff in the name of entertainment. Some folks around here are still a little jumpy because of all that. We've taken the place back now, though, and we're offering you a sanctuary, a safe place to live. We'd like to invite you to stay here. Permanently."

Calvin and Meredith Dupree exchange another glance, and Meredith swallows hard, looking at the ground. Calvin has a strange look on his face—almost a longing—and he turns and starts to say, "It's a generous offer, Lilly, but I gotta be honest—"

All at once he is interrupted by the rusty shriek of the grate collapsing and the little girl squealing in terror, and then everybody is jerking toward the child.

Bob reaches for his .357 Magnum.

Lilly has already crossed half the distance of scarred pavement toward the little girl.

Time seems to hang suspended in the air.

Since the plague broke out nearly two years ago, the change in the behavior patterns of survivors has been so gradual, so subtle, so incremental as to be almost invisible. The blood-drenched early days of the Turn, which at first seemed so temporary and novel—captured in those yammering headlines THE DEAD WALK and NO ONE IS SAFE and IS THIS THE END?—became routine, and it happened without anybody ever really being aware of it. Survivors got more and more efficient at lancing the proverbial boil, lashing out without fore-thought or ceremony, destroying the brain of a rampaging cadaver with whatever was handy—the family shotgun, a farm implement, a knitting needle, a broken wineglass, an heirloom from the mantel—until the most ghastly act became commonplace. Trauma loses all meaning, grief and sorrow and loss are all stuffed down the gorge until a collective numbness sets in. But active-duty soldiers know the truth beneath the lie. Homicide detectives know it as well. Emergency room nurses, paramedics—they all know the dirty little secret: It doesn't get any easier. In fact, it lives in you. Every trauma, every horrible sight, every senseless death, every feral, blood-soaked act of violence in the name of self-preservation—they all accumulate like silt at the bottom of a person's heart until the weight is unbearable.

Lilly Caul isn't there yet—as she is about to demonstrate over the next few seconds to the Dupree family—but she is well on her way. She is a few bottles of cheap bourbon and a couple of sleepless nights away from total annihilation of spirit, and that's why she needs to replenish Woodbury, she needs human contact, she needs community, she needs warmth and love and hope and grace wherever she can find it. And that's why she pounces on that reeking corpse of a farmhand with extreme prejudice as it bursts from its lair and grabs hold of the little Dupree girl's tattered hemline.

Lilly crosses the fifteen-foot gap between her and the girl in just a couple leaping strides, simultaneously yanking the .22-caliber Ruger SR from the miniholster on the back of her belt. The gun is a double-action rig, and Lilly keeps it decocked with the safety off, a single-stack magazine in it with eight rounds ready to rock and one *always* in the chamber—not a huge-capacity weapon but big enough to get the job done—which Lilly now aims on the fly, her vision coalescing into a tunnel as she charges toward the shrieking little girl.

The creature from the drainpipe has one skeletal hand tangled up in the gingham hem of the child's dress, which has thrown the girl off balance and sent her sprawling to the cement. She screams and screams, trying to scuttle away, but the monster has her dress and bites at the air around her sneaker-clad feet, slimy incisors clacking like castanets, moving ever closer to the tender flesh of Bethany's left ankle.

In that frenzied instant before Lilly unleashes hellfire—a dream-like suspension of time to which plague folks are almost growing accustomed—the rest of the adults and children jerk back and gasp in unison, Calvin fumbling for the buck knife on his belt, Bob reaching for his .357, Meredith covering her mouth and letting out a little mewl of shock, the other kids backing up wide-eyed and stunned.

By this point, Lilly is already in close proximity to the biter, with the Ruger raised and aimed. Lilly simultaneously nudges the child out of harm's way with the toe of her boot while she brings the muzzle down to within centimeters of the monster's skull. The walker's hand stays hooked inside the hem of the child's dress, the fabric ripping, the little girl scraping across the concrete.

Four quick blasts like dry balloons popping penetrate the biter's cranium.

A clot of blood-mist hits the portico behind the creature while a cookie-sized skull fragment jettisons. The ex-farmhand sinks instantly to the ground. A surge of black blood sluices out in all directions from beneath the ruined head as Lilly backs away, blinking, catching her breath, trying not to step in the spreading pool of spoor as she thumbs the hammer down and puts the safety back on.

Bethany continues keening and caterwauling, and Lilly sees that the walker's hand is still clutched—rigor mortis seizing up its tendons—around a hank of the torn gingham dress. The little girl writhes and gasps air as if unable to summon tears after so many months of horror, and Lilly goes to her. "It's okay, honey, don't look." Lilly drops the pistol and cradles the girl's head. The others gather around them, Meredith kneeling, Lilly slamming her boot down on the dead hand. "Don't look." She tears the dress away. "Don't look, honey." The girl finally finds her tears.

"Don't look," Lilly repeats under her breath, almost as though speaking to herself.

Meredith pulls her daughter into a desperate embrace and whispers softly in the child's ear. "It's all right, Bethany, sweetie, I got you . . . I got you."

"It's over." Lilly's voice has lowered, as though she's talking herself into something. She lets out an agonizing sigh. "Don't look," she utters once more to herself.

Lilly looks.

She should probably stop looking at the walkers after destroying them, but she can't help it. When the brains finally succumb and the dark compulsion goes out of their faces, and the empty slumber of death returns, Lilly sees the people they were. She sees a farmhand with big dreams who got maybe an eighth-grade education but had to take over an ailing father's farm. She sees cops, nurses, postal carriers, shop clerks, and mechanics. She sees her father, Everett Caul, tucked into the silk convolutions of his casket, awaiting burial, peaceful and serene. She sees all the friends and loved ones who have passed since the outbreak swept across the land—Alice Warren, Doc Stevens, Scott Moon, Megan Lafferty, and Josh Hamilton. She's thinking about one other victim when a gravelly voice breaks the spell.

"Lilly-girl?" Bob's voice. Faint. Sounding as though it's coming from a great distance. "You okay?"

For one last fleeting instant, staring at the dead face of that farmhand, Lilly thinks of Austin Ballard, the androgynous, long-lashed, rock-star-handsome young man whom she saw sacrificed on a battlefield in order to save Lilly and half the people in Woodbury. Was Austin Ballard the only man Lilly had ever truly loved?

"Lilly?" Bob's voice rises slightly behind her, tinged with worry. "You all right?"

Lilly lets out a pained breath. "I'm good . . . I'm fine." Suddenly, without warning, she lifts herself to her feet. She gives Bob a nod and then picks up her handgun, shoving it back into her holster. She licks her lips and looks around the group. "Everybody okay? Kids?"

The other two children slowly nod, looking at Lilly as though she has just lassoed the moon. Calvin sheaths his knife and kneels and strokes his daughter's hair. "She okay?" he asks his wife.

Meredith gives him a terse nod, doesn't say anything. The woman's eyes look glassy.

Calvin lets out a sigh and stands. He comes over to Lilly. She is busy helping Bob drag the corpse under an overhang for later retrieval. She stands up, wiping her hands on her jeans and turning to face the newcomer. "I'm sorry you folks had to see that," she says to him. "How's the girl?"

"She'll be okay, she's a strong one," Calvin says. He holds Lilly's gaze. "How about you?"

"Me?" Lilly sighs. "I'm fine." She lets out another pained breath. "Just tired of it."

"I hear ya." He cocks his head a bit. "You're pretty handy with that firearm."

Lilly shrugs. "I don't know about *that*." Then she looks around the center of town. "Gotta keep our eyes open. Place saw a lot of upheaval over the last few weeks. Lost an entire section of the wall. Still a few stragglers. But we're getting it back under control."

Calvin manages a weary smile. "I believe you."

Lilly notices something dangling on a chain around the man's neck—a large silver cross. "So what do you think?" she asks.

"About what?"

"Staying on. Making a home here for your family. What do you think?"

Calvin Dupree takes a deep breath and turns to gaze at his wife and daughter. "I won't lie . . . it's not a bad idea." He licks his lips pensively. "Been on the move for a long time, been putting the kids through the mill."

Lilly looks at him. "This is a place they can be safe, happy, lead a normal life . . . more or less."

"I ain't saying no." Calvin looks at her. "All I'm asking is . . . you give us time to think about it, pray on it."

Lilly nods. "Of course." For a brief instant, she thinks about the phrase "pray on it" and wonders what it would be like to have a Holy Roller in their midst. A couple of the Governor's men used to pay lip service to having God on their side, and what would Jesus do, and all that 700 Club nonsense. Lilly has never had much time for religion. Sure, she's prayed silently on a few occasions since the plague broke out, but in her mind that doesn't count. What's that saying? "There are no atheists in the foxhole." She looks into Calvin's gray-green eyes. "You take all the time you need." She smiles. "Look around, get to know the place—"

"That won't be necessary," a voice interrupts, and all heads turn to the mousy woman kneeling by her trembling child. Meredith Dupree strokes the girl's hair and doesn't make eye contact as she speaks. "We appreciate your hospitality, but we'll be on our way this afternoon."

Calvin looks at the ground. "Now, honey, we haven't even discussed what we're going to—"

"There's nothing to discuss." The woman looks up, her eyes glittering with emotion. Her chapped lips tremble, her pale flesh blushing. She looks like a delicate porcelain doll with an unseen crack down its middle. "We'll be on our way."

"Honey—"

"There's nothing more to talk about."

The silence that ensues makes the awkward moment turn almost surreal, as the wind buffets the tops of the trees, whistling through the gantries and trestles of the adjacent stadium, and the dead farmhand festers silently on the ground only a few feet away. Everybody in close proximity of Meredith, including Bob and Lilly, looks down with mute embarrassment. And the silence stretches until Lilly mumbles something like, "Well, if you change your mind, you can always stay on." Nobody says anything. Lilly manages a cockeyed smile. "In other words, the offer stands."

For a brief instant Lilly and Calvin share a furtive glance, and a tremendous amount of information is exchanged between them—some of it intentional, some of it unintentional—without a single word spoken. Lilly remains silent out of respect, aware that this issue between these two newcomers is far from resolved. Calvin glances over at his jittery wife as she tends to the child.

Meredith Dupree looks like a phantom, her anguished face so ashen and drawn and haunted she looks as though she's gradually disappearing.

Nobody realizes it then, but this frumpy, diminutive hausfrau—completely unremarkable in almost every conceivable way—will prove to be the second and far more profound issue with which Lilly and the people of Woodbury will sooner or later have to deal.

TWO

By midday, the mercury rises into the seventies, and the high, harsh sun blanches the color out of the West Central Georgia farmland. The tobacco and bean fields south of Atlanta have all gone to seed or have grown into jungles of switchgrass and cattails, the fossilized remains of farm machinery sunken into the foliage, rusted out and stripped, as desiccated as the skeletons of dinosaurs. Which is why Speed Wilkins and Matthew Hennesey do not notice the secret crop circle east of Woodbury until well into the afternoon.

The two young men—sent out that morning by Bob, ostensibly to find fuel from wrecked cars or abandoned gas stations—had started their journey in Bob's pickup truck but now have gone off-road after getting stuck in the mud and lighting out on foot.

They cross nearly three miles of wagon-rutted access roads before pausing on a ridge overlooking a vast meadow riotous with wild sedges, deadfalls, and a profusion of prairie grass. Matthew is the first to see the deeper circle of green in the far distance, nestled amid the leathery jungle of untended tobacco plants.

"Hold the phone," he mutters, shooting a hand up and becoming very still on the edge of the precipice. He gazes out at the distant tobacco fields wavering in the heat rays, shielding his deep-set eyes, squinting against the glare of the sun. A lanky laborer from Valdosta, with an anchor tattoo on his sinewy forearm, Matthew wears the garb of a bricklayer—sweat-stained wife-beater T-shirt, gray work pants, clodhopper boots pasty with mortar dust. "You got them binocs handy?"

"Here ya go." Speed digs in his rucksack, pulls out the binoculars, and hands them over. "What is it? Whaddaya lookin' at?"

"Not sure," Matthew murmurs, fiddling at the focus knob, scanning the distance.

Speed waits, scratching his muscular arm, the row of mosquito bites a new development, his REM T-shirt sweat-plastered to his broad chest. The stocky twenty-year-old has withered slightly from his playing weight of two hundred and ten pounds—most likely due to a plague diet of foraged canned goods and scrawny rabbit stew—but his neck still has that steel-belted thickness of a lifelong defensive end.

"*Whoa.*" Matthew stares through the lenses. "What the fuck is—?"

"What is it?"

Matthew keeps the binoculars pressed to his eyes, licking his lip judiciously. "If I'm not mistaken, we just hit the jackpot."

"Fuel?"

"Not exactly." He hands the binoculars back, then grins at his comrade. "I've heard it called many things but never 'fuel.'"

They make their way down the gravel slope, across a dry creek bed, and into a sea of tobacco. The odor of manure and humus engulfs them, as thick and redolent as the inside of a greenhouse. The air is so humid it lies heavy on their skin and in their nostrils. The crops are mostly in their flowering stage, rising up at least five feet tall among the tufts of wild grass, so each man has to crane his neck and walk on the balls of his feet in order to navigate. They pull their pistols and thumb the safeties off—just in case—although Matthew saw little or no movement other than waves of khaki green blowing in the breeze.

The secret crop lies about two hundred yards beyond a gnarled grove of live oaks sticking out of the tobacco like palsied sentries. Through the jungle of stalks, Matthew can see the security fence surrounding the contraband plants. He lets out a little giddy giggle and says, "You believe this? I don't fucking believe this . . ."

"Is that what I think it is?" Speed marvels as they approach the fence.

They emerge into the clearing and stand there gaping at the long, lush tines of leaves spiraling up rows of mossy support timbers and rusty chicken wire. A narrow path has been dug out beyond the east corner of the clearing, now overgrown with weeds, no wider than a laundry chute—probably once the province of minibikes or off-road ATVs. "Fuck me," Matthew comments reverently.

"Holy shit, we are going to have a hot time in the old town tonight." Speed paces along the row of plants, looking them up and down. "There's enough here to keep us going until the next fucking ice age."

"Amazing stuff, too," Matthew says, pausing to smell a leaf. He rubs a piece between his thumb and forefinger and breathes in the musky scent of citrusy-sage. "Look at that hairy fucking bud up there."

"Fucking a, Bubba—we just won the lottery."

"Got that right." Matthew pats his pockets, shrugs off his pack. His heart races with anticipation. "Help me rig something we can use as a pipe."

Calvin Dupree holds the tiny sterling silver crucifix with the coiled chain nestled in his palm as he paces the cluttered storage room in the rear of the Woodbury courthouse. He walks with a slight limp, and he's so gaunt he looks like a scarecrow in his baggy chinos. He feels light-headed with nerves. Through the grimy glass of a single window he can see his three children playing in a little community play lot, taking turns pushing each other on a rusty swing set. "I'm just saying"—he rubs his mouth and lets out a sigh—"we gotta think of the kids, what's best for them."

"I *am* thinking of the kids, Cal," Meredith Dupree counters from across the room in a voice taut with nervous tension. She sits on a folding chair, sipping bottled water and staring at the floor.

They each had a can of Ensure the night before in Bob's infirmary to treat their malnutrition, and this morning they had a full breakfast with cereal, powdered milk, peanut butter, and crackers. The food has helped them physically, but they're still grappling with the trauma of near starvation on the road. Lilly gave them the private room a few minutes ago, as well as all the additional food, water, and time they might need to get their bearings. "Best thing for *us*," Meredith mutters into her lap, "is the best thing for *them*."

"How do you figure that?"

She looks up at him, her eyes red rimmed and wet, her lips so chapped they look to be on the verge of bleeding. "You know when you fly, how they show you that safety film?"

"Yeah, and . . . ?"

"In the unlikely event the cabin loses air pressure, you should put the oxygen mask on yourself before you help your kids?"

"I don't understand. What is it you're afraid of if we stay here?"

She shoots him a hard look. "C'mon, Cal . . . you know very well what happens if they find out about my . . . my *condition.* Remember the KOA camp?"

"Those people were paranoid and ignorant." He walks over to her, kneels by her chair, puts a tender hand on her knee. "God brought us here, Mer."

"Calvin—"

"Seriously. Listen. This place is a gift. God has brought us here and He wants us to stay. Maybe that older man—Bob, I think his name is—maybe he's got medication you can use. This is not the Middle Ages."

Meredith looks at him. "Yes, it is, Cal . . . it *is* the Middle Ages."

"Honey, please."

"They drilled holes in the heads of the mentally ill back then—it's worse than that now."

"These people aren't gonna persecute you. They're just like us, they're just as scared. All they want is to protect what they got, make a safe place to live."

Meredith shivers. "Exactly, Cal . . . and that's why they're gonna do exactly what *I* would do if I was them and I learned somebody in their midst was a mental defect."

"Now stop it! Stop talking that way. You ain't no defect. The Good Lord has helped us get this far, and He's gonna see us through—"

"Calvin, please."

"Pray with me, Mer." He takes her hand, cups it in his weathered fingers, bows his head. His voice softens. "Dear Lord, we ask for your guidance in this difficult time. Lord, we trust in you . . . you are our rock and protection. Lead us and guide us."

Meredith looks down, her brow furrowed with pain, her eyes welling up again.

Her lips are moving, but Calvin is not sure whether she's mouthing a prayer or mumbling something far more cryptic and personal.

Speed Wilkins sits up with a start, stirred awake by the overwhelming stench of walkers. He rubs his bloodshot eyes and tries to get his bearings—racking his brain to remember how he had managed to drift off out in the open, without a lookout, alone in such a deserted rural area. The sun is hotter than a blast furnace. He's been asleep for hours. He is soaked in sweat. A gnat hums around his ear. He shivers and bats it away.

He looks around the immediate vicinity and sees that he apparently drifted off on the edge of the overgrown tobacco field. His joints ache. Especially his knees, still weak and brittle from old football injuries. He never was a great athlete. His first year of playing Division III football for the Piedmont College Lions in Athens had been a bust, but he had high hopes for his sophomore year—and then the Turn happened, and it all went up in smoke.

Smoke!

All at once it comes back to him—what he was doing here earlier when he nodded off in the wild grass—and he feels the simultaneous yet contrary waves of shame, embarrassment, and hilarity that often grip him when coming down off a major high. He remembers discovering the clandestine marijuana field just to the north, a treasure trove of sticky, fragrant heaven hidden within the larger acreage of tobacco—a botanical nesting doll—ingeniously concealed from the outside world by some enterprising stoner farmer (just before the Turn harshed everybody's buzz).

He looks down and sees the makeshift pipe that was once a fountain pen, and the matchbook and dark crumbs of ashes lying around it.

Speed lets out a burst of dry laughter—a pothead's nervous chuckle—and immediately regrets making the noise. He can smell the stench of multiple biters lurking somewhere nearby. Where the fuck is Matthew? Scanning the clearing, Speed cringes at the throbbing headache now threatening to split his skull open.

He struggles to his feet, dizziness and paranoia washing over him in equal measures, his Bushmaster assault rifle still slung over his shoulder. The walkers have yet to reveal themselves, but the smell is everywhere, as though it's coming from all directions.

The terrible black odor of the undead has become a bellwether of imminent attacks—the stronger the reek, the greater the number. A faint hint of spoiled meat and feces usually indicates only a single creature, certainly no more than two or three, but the infinite variations that herald larger groups have become as cataloged and articulated as an elaborate wine list. A truckload of cow manure marinated in pond scum and ammonia indicates dozens. An ocean of spoiled Limburger cheese, maggot-infested garbage, black mold, and pus suggests hundreds, maybe a thousand. Right now, judging by the intensity of the stench, Speed is guessing at least fifty or sixty roaming nearby.

He raises his gun, walks along the edge of the tobacco field, and calls out in a loud whisper, "Matt! Hey, Hennesey—where you at?"

No reply. Only the faintest of rustling noises to his immediate left—behind the wall of green—where the untended crop rises at least five or six feet high, consisting of old tobacco, ironweed, and wild bush. The enormous wrinkled leaves make a ghostly noise in the breeze, the whisper of papery friction, like match heads striking. Something moves sharklike out in the sea of khaki green.

Speed jerks toward the shadow. Something is moving slowly this way, the dry stalks and husks snapping in an arrhythmic tattoo as the clumsy footsteps approach. Raising the muzzle, Speed puts the crosshair on the dark mound skimming over the tops of the plants. He sucks in a breath. The figure is twenty-five yards away.

He begins squeezing the trigger when the sound of a voice makes him freeze.

"Yo!"

Speed jerks toward the voice and sees Matthew standing in front of him, out of breath, holding his Glock 23 with its silencer attached. Only a few years older than Speed, Matthew is taller and lankier and so weathered, wind-burned, and tan in his faded denims he looks like a walking piece of beef jerky.

"Jesus," Speed utters, lowering the rifle. "Don't fucking sneak up on me like that—just about shit my pants."

"Get down," Matthew orders softly yet firmly. "Now, Speed, do it."

"Huh?" Still slightly woozy from the weed, Speed stares at his friend. "Do what?"

"Duck, man! *Duck!*"

Blinking, swallowing hard, Speed crouches down, realizing there's a figure directly behind him.

He glances over his shoulder, and for a single instant, right before the dry pop of the Glock, he sees a blur of putrid flesh lunging at him. The female walker is an old woman in tatters with blue-rinse hair like a fright wig, breath that smells of the crypt, and hacksaw teeth. Speed jerks down. The muffled blast snaps, and the old woman's head erupts in a fountain of black spinal fluid and brain matter, the flaccid body sagging to the ground in a heap. "Fuck!" Speed springs to his feet. "*Fuck!*" He scans the adjacent tobacco field and sees at least half a dozen more ragged heads moving convulsively over the tops of the weeds and tassels, coming toward him. "FUCK! FUCK! FUCK!"

"C'mon, homey!" Matthew grabs a hunk of Speed's T-shirt and pulls him toward the trail. "Something else I want to show you before we head back."

The highest point in Meriwether County is located in the rural hinterlands, not far from the intersection of Highway 85 and Millard Drive, just outside a deserted farm town called Yarlsburg. Millard winds up a steep hill, cutting through a thick copse of pine, and then skirts the edge of a mile-long plateau that overlooks a patchwork of farm fields.

At one point along this scabrous road, near a wide spot used for blowouts and piss stops, a rust-pocked, bullet-riddled sign proclaims, without a trace of irony, SCENIC VISTA, as though this impoverished hillbilly farmland were an exotic national park (and not some backwater barrens smack-dab in the middle of nowhere).

It takes Matthew and Speed about half an hour to reach this turnoff.

First, they have to circle back to where Bob's pickup is stuck in the mire along Highway 85 and then maneuver discarded cardboard boxes under the massive tires to provide traction. Once they get the vehicle moving, they have to cross five miles of wreckage-strewn blacktop macadam in order to reach Millard. They see small phalanxes of walkers along the way, some of them shambling out into their path. Matthew has no qualms swerving toward the creatures and knocking them to kingdom come like so many blood-filled bowling pins. This slows them down a bit, but they finally see Millard looming in the dusty heat waves ahead of them.

Then it's a quick shot north into the hills above Yarlsburg.

Speed keeps quizzing Matthew about what the hell is so important that they have to go twenty or thirty miles out of their way. Matthew plays it coy, explaining that it'll all make sense soon enough. Speed gets angry. Why the fuck can't Matthew just tell him why they're going on this wild-goose chase? What the hell is it that he wants Speed to see? Is it some fuel source they didn't think of? Is it an untapped retail outlet? Another Walmart they missed? Why all the mystery? Matthew just keeps nervously chewing the inside of his cheek, driving north and not saying much.

As they approach the overlook, Speed realizes all at once, in a sick, stomach-churning bolt of recognition, that this is the same place the Governor staged all the military vehicles in the moments before the battle for the prison. Gazing out across the woods, Speed realizes then that they are within a mile or two of the vast gray-brick complex known as the Meriwether County Correctional Facility, and an unexpected jolt of dread travels down his spine.

Post-traumatic stress comes in many flavors. It can steal sleep and spark hallucinations. It can sublimate itself sneakily into destructive behaviors, drug abuse, alcoholism, or sex addiction. It can be subtly debilitating—chronic panic attacks, an intermittent pinch of the nerves of the solar plexus at odd, inexplicable times. Speed feels this vague, inchoate dread right now in his bowels as Matthew pulls the truck over onto the dusty apron of weed-whiskered gravel and kills the engine.

This area was the sight of profound mayhem—many deaths, some of them Speed's close friends from Woodbury—and the miserable vibrations still strum at the air. The prison was where the Governor made his last stand—Custer-like, psychotic, megalomaniacal to the bitter end. It also was where Speed Wilkins first registered the natural leadership capabilities of Lilly Caul.

Now Matthew climbs out of the truck with the binoculars already in his hands.

Speed kicks his door open with a rusty shriek of hinges and hops out. The first thing he notices is the overpowering scent of dead flesh hanging in the air, mingling with the acrid tang of smoke. He follows Matthew across the wide spot in the road toward the woods. The tire tracks from the Governor's massive convoy still scar the dirt—even the waffle-shaped imprint of the Abrams tank can be seen—and Speed tries to avoid looking at the tracks as he joins Matthew at the edge of the forest.

"Here, take a look down in the meadow." Matthew points toward a clearing in the thick veil of pine boughs and wild scrub and hands over the binoculars. "And tell me what you see."

Speed steps across the clearing to the edge of the precipice and gets his first good glimpse of the prison in the distance.

The two-hundred-acre lot is still bound in a faint fog of smoke. Some of the caved-in cell blocks still smolder, and will probably continue to do so for weeks. The complex looks like the ruins of some strange Maya temple. The odor is stronger now, and Speed's stomach flips with nausea.

With his naked eye he can see the collapsed cyclone fence wreathing the property like torn ribbons, the scorched husks of guard towers, and the blackened craters punched into the cement from grenade blasts. Abandoned vehicles litter the surrounding lots, and broken glass glitters everywhere. Like ragged phantoms wandering a ghost town, walkers lumber here and there without purpose or direction. Speed puts the binoculars to his eyes. "What am I looking for?" he asks while scanning the outer lots.

"You see the woods to the south?"

Speed swings the binoculars over to the left and sees the hazy green edge of the pine forest lining the property. He sucks in a breath.

The incredible stench of maggot-infested meat and human shit makes his gorge rise and his mouth water sourly. "Jesus H. Christ," he utters, gaping at the multitudes of undead. "What the fuck?"

"Exactly." Matthew lets out a sigh. "All the commotion of the battle must have drawn more of them out of the woodwork than we ever knew. This is just the tail end. Who knows how fucking many of them there are."

"I remember the herd," Speed says, licking his lips. "But I don't remember anything like *this*."

Speed realizes the implications of what he is seeing just as the rancid air gets the better of him, and he doubles over, falling to his knees. It dawns on him—exactly what this means—right as the hot, burning bile stirred by the stench rises up his esophagus. Still slightly high from all the dope, he roars vomit across the coarse, gravelly earth of the precipice. He hasn't eaten much that day, and most of it is yellowish bile, but it sluices out of him with gusto.

Matthew watches solemnly from a few feet away, staring down at his upchucking pal with mild interest. After a few minutes it becomes clear that Speed has spewed every last ounce of stomach acid within him, his right hand still clutching the binoculars, and he sits back with a gasp, wiping the cold sweat from his brow. Matthew waits for the younger man to get his bearings. At last Matthew lets out a sigh and says, "You finished?"

Speed nods and tries to take deep breaths. He doesn't say anything.

"Good." Matthew leans down and snatches the binoculars away from him. "Because we gotta get back ASAP and do something about this."

THREE

Lilly Caul hears the doors of the Dodge Ram slam just as she is crossing the town square in her patched jeans and ratty sweatshirt, a roll of amateur blueprints under her arm. The sun has begun its long, slow descent into the palisades of black oaks on the other side of the railroad tracks, the shadows lengthening, the light softening into golden motes shot through with whorls of gnats. The hammering and rasping noises of the repair crew have ceased for the day, and now the odors of dinner—Sterno pots filled with root vegetables, field greens, and instant broth—waft across the safe zone, mingling with the grassy scent of a late spring evening.

Walking briskly toward David and Barbara Stern's building at the end of Main Street, Lilly finds herself distracted by the nervous shuffling of footsteps coming from outside the massive gate, which is currently blocked by an enormous semitrailer. Bob's pickup is visible through the cab's windows, as are two figures now reduced to blurs as they hurry around the trailer toward the chain-link entrance. Lilly knows who they are. The blueprints will have to wait.

All afternoon she has been sketching ideas for the racetrack gardens—her neophyte knowledge of landscape architecture offset by her energy and enthusiasm—and now she is dying to show her ideas to the Sterns for feedback. But the truth is, she's more interested in hearing about Speed and Matthew's fuel run. The town's generators and propane-powered motors are running on fumes. The tanks need to be replenished soon, before the perishables start spoiling and the construction equipment stops running and the candles get used up and the streets plunge into darkness at night.

She crosses the road just as the young men are squeezing through the gate. Lilly immediately notices that neither is carrying a fuel tank. "No luck finding juice?" she asks as she walks up to them.

Speed glances around the square to see if anybody is listening. "Hate to tell you, but we got worse problems than a fuel shortage."

"What are you talking about?"

"We just saw—"

"Speed!" Matthew steps in between them, putting a hand on the younger man's shoulder. "Not here."

Inside the courthouse, the gloomy hallway smells of must and mouse droppings, the yellow cone of light chasing cockroaches back into the seams of the ramshackle walls. At the end of the corridor sits the community room—a cluttered rectangle of parquet tile, boarded windows, and folding chairs.

They enter the room, and Lilly sets the lantern and the blueprints down on the long table. "Okay, start talking," she says.

In the dim, flickering light, Matthew's boyish face looks positively owlish. He sullenly crosses his arms across his barrel chest. His whiskered cheeks and chin—and the look in his eyes—make him look far older than his years. "There's a new herd forming, we saw it outside the prison." He swallows. "A big one—biggest one yet—biggest one I've ever seen."

"Okay. So." She looks at him. "What do you want *me* to do about it?"

"You don't understand," Speed chimes in, looking into Lilly's eyes. "It's heading this way."

"What do you mean? Prison's like—what?—twenty miles away?"

"Twenty-three miles," Matthew informs her. "He's right, Lilly. It's moving in a northwesterly direction. That'll take it straight through Woodbury."

She shrugs. "At the rate walkers move, all the variables, it'll take it days to get here."

The two men share a glance. Matthew takes a deep breath. "Couple days, maybe."

Lilly looks at him. "But that's if it keeps moving in the same direction."

He nods. "Yeah, right. What are you saying?"

"Walkers don't move like that. They're all fucked-up, they're all over the map."

"Normally I would agree with you, but a herd this size, it's like—"

He stops himself. He looks at Speed, and Speed looks back at him, searching for the right word. Lilly watches them for a moment and then says, "Force of nature?"

"No . . . that's not what I was going to say."

"Stampede?"

"No."

"Flood, brushfire? What?"

"Fixed," Matthew says at last. "That's the only word that I can come up with."

"Fixed? What do you mean, *fixed*?"

Matthew looks at Speed, then glances back at Lilly. "I can't explain it exactly, but this one, this herd, is so huge—so fucking huge—that it just keeps gathering up momentum. If you saw it, you would know what I'm talking about. The direction is fixed. Like a river. Until something or some*one* fucks with it, the direction ain't changing."

Lilly stares at him and thinks about it for a moment. She chews a fingernail and thinks some more, and she stares at the boarded windows and thinks about all the other herds she's encountered—the most recent one the wave of walkers descending upon the prison during the Governor's last stand. She tries to imagine a bigger one, a monolithic herd made up of many herds, and it makes her head hurt. She makes a fist, and her nails dig into her palm, the pain bracing her. "Okay, here's what we're gonna do first . . ."

An hour later, darkness pushes into town while Lilly rounds up her newly established council of elders—most of them *literal* elders—gathering everybody in the lantern-lit community room. She also invites Calvin Dupree in the hope that he'll be swayed into staying when he hears what's heading this way. Being on the road with such a manifestation unfurling slowly toward them is not the safest option—especially for a family with small children—and on top of that, Lilly's going to need as many able bodies as possible to stanch the tide.

By seven thirty that night, the elders have all taken their places around the battered conference table, and Lilly has dropped her bombshell on them as gently as possible.

For most of her presentation, the listeners sit stone still in their folding chairs, remaining silent as they absorb the grim narrative. Every few moments, Lilly asks Matthew or Speed to elaborate on what they saw. The others soak it all in, their faces dour. Stricken. Crestfallen. The unspoken feeling in the room is, *Why us? Why now?* After all the dark days of living under the influence of the Governor, after all the tumult and violence and death and tragedy and loss, they have to deal with *this*?

At last, David Stern speaks up.

"I understand that this is a big herd." Perched backward on a folding chair in the corner, the trim sixty-something man sports short-cropped hair and an iron-gray goatee, and in his silk roadie jacket he gives off the air of a hard-ass professional nearing retirement, a road manager for a band on their last tour. But underneath the surface, he's a softie. "It's gonna be hard to stop, sure—I get that—but what I'm wondering is—"

"Thank you, Captain Understatement," interrupts the middle-aged woman in the faded floral-print muumuu next to him. An earth-mother type with long, unruly gray curls and a soft, round, zaftig figure, Barbara Stern is outwardly cranky but, not unlike her husband, tender underneath. The two of them work together with grudging efficiency.

"I beg your pardon," David says to her with faux politeness. "I'm wondering if I may possibly speak for just a second or two without being interrupted?"

"Who's stopping you?"

"Lilly, I understand what you're saying about this herd, but how do you know it won't just fizzle?"

Lilly sighs. "I guess we don't know for sure *what* it's going to do. I hope it *does* fizzle. But for now I think we have to assume it's going to hit us in a day or two."

David scratches his goatee for a moment. "Maybe if we sent scouts out there to keep tabs—?"

"Way ahead of you." Matthew Hennesey speaks up from the front of the room. "Speed and I are going out early tomorrow morning." He gives David a brisk nod. Throughout most of the presentation, Matthew has been standing like a wooden cigar store Indian behind Lilly, but now he gets animated, and his burly laborer's shoulders bob and weave as he paces across the front wall with its cracked and obsolete portraits of the U.S. president and the former governor of Georgia. "We'll be able to gauge how fast it's coming, whether it's on course, or whatever. We'll use the walkies to radio updates back to y'all."

Lilly notices Hap Abernathy, the seventy-five-year-old bus driver from Atlanta, standing across the room near a boarded window, leaning on a walking stick, looking as though he might drift off to sleep at any moment and start snoring. Lilly starts to say something else when a voice interrupts.

"What about weaponry, Lilly?" Ben Buchholz sits on one side of Lilly with his gnarled hands folded on the table as if he's praying. He is a broken-down man of fifty-some years with pouches under his eyes and a tattered golf shirt buttoned up to his wattled neck. The loss of his entire family the previous year has never truly left his rheumy, watery eyes. "If I'm not mistaken, we gave up a lot of the arsenal in the assault on the prison, so where do we stand now?"

Lilly looks down at the scarred tabletop. "We lost every single fifty-caliber machine gun and most of the ammo. We fucked up. Plain and simple." An audible moan—mostly rhetorical—ripples through the room as Lilly tries to wrestle the mood back in her favor. "That's the bad news. But we still have a lot of explosives and incendiary devices that didn't go up in the fires. And we got that stuff from the Guard depot that the Governor left behind in the warehouse."

"That ain't gonna cut it, Lilly," Ben murmurs, shaking his head with dismay. "Dynamite's a blunt instrument from a distance. We need high-powered rifles, automatics."

"Excuse me," Bob Stookey chimes in. He sits on the other side of Lilly, his Caterpillar cap pulled down low on his wrinkled brow. "Can we at least *try* to stay positive here? Maybe focus on what we *got* rather than what we *ain't got*?"

"We still have all our personal guns, right?" Barbara ventures.

"There ya go," Bob urges her on. "Plus we can pool whatever ammo we each got stashed away."

Ben shakes his head, unconvinced. "If what these young fellas are saying is true, you ain't gonna make a dent in a herd that size."

"Okay, here's my two cents," Gloria Pyne interjects from the corner. The stout little woman in the tinted visor hat and Falcons sweatshirt chews gum incessantly, her pug-nosed face as tough as a stevedore's. "Maybe we're looking at this the wrong way."

Lilly gives her an encouraging nod. "Go on."

Gloria wrings her rough hands for a moment, choosing her words. "Maybe there's a way to . . . what's the word? *Divert* it? Change its course?"

Lilly keeps looking at her. "Actually, what you're saying isn't that crazy."

Bob is nodding. "The lady's got something. It would be a way to fight back without burning through a lot of ammo."

Lilly looks at the others. "We need to figure out a way to lure them off course. Put something in their way, change the landscape they're tromping over. Maybe get their attention somehow, dangle something."

"Now you're talking about using somebody as *bait*?" Ben gives a skeptical shake of the head, his mouth turned down in a sour expression. "Don't everybody volunteer all at once."

"Hey!" Bob scowls at Ben. "What is your *problem*?"

Lilly rolls her eyes. "Calm down, Bob. Everybody has a say in this."

A beat of tense silence.

Ben shrugs, keeps looking at the table. "Just trying to be realistic for a change."

"Realism we got plenty of right now!" Bob shoots back. "What we need is answers. We need to stay positive, think outside of the box."

Another stretch of silence follows, and the tension passes like a microbe from one person to the next. Nobody in the room thinks Gloria's idea is all that terrific, but no one can come up with anything better, and nobody is more acutely aware of this than Lilly. Her first true test as a leader has come sooner than she expected, and the sad fact is she has no idea what to do. Deep down she's starting to have second thoughts about stepping up. She loathes being responsible for other people's lives, and she dreads the possibility of getting more people killed. The scars of losing her father and Josh Hamilton and Austin Ballard are still festering inside her, eating away at her sleep at night.

She is about to say something else when she notices Calvin Dupree sitting alone against the back wall next to a battered, bankrupt vending machine. He looks like a little boy who's been grounded. Lilly wonders if he rues the day he and his family inadvertently stumbled upon this little township. He stares back at her, his eyes narrowing into a worried, furrowed look of concern. "Lilly, I don't want to interrupt," he says, "but when we're done here, I'd like to speak to you in private, if that's okay."

Lilly looks around at the others with a shrug. "Sure. Of course."

Everybody looks awkwardly down at the table, at their hands, at the floor—as if the answer is down there somewhere among the cracked, filthy ceramic tiles. But no answer is forthcoming.

Only more skeptical silence.

Lilly meets with Calvin in the railroad shed out behind the courthouse. One of the only buildings on the west side of town untouched by the fires of the previous week, the shed is the size of a two-car garage and lies within the safe zone, protected by surviving sections of the wall. Inside the dark, ransacked structure, the windows are boarded and the air is musty, with bags of cement mix and potting soil stacked to the cobweb-clogged rafters.

"Does your offer still stand?" Calvin asks Lilly after she has latched the door behind them and lit a lone kerosene lantern near a stack of ancient railroad ties. The pale yellow light flickers off Calvin's lean, angular features, making his intense gaze even *more* intense.

"What offer is that, Calvin?"

"The offer to take my family in, let us stay and join the community."

"Of course it still stands." Lilly cocks her head at him. "Why wouldn't it?"

"You need strong backs, right? You need healthy bodies, people to pitch in? Like me. And my boy Tommy. I mean, he's only twelve, and he's a handful—gives me grief at every turn—but he can lift his own weight in hay bales."

"Yes. Absolutely, Calvin. I already told you, we need you and your family. What are you getting at exactly?"

"A deal."

She stares at him. "What do you mean, a deal? What are you talking about?"

Calvin looks pained all of a sudden, his gaze softening in the lantern light. "Lilly, I believe the Lord has brought us to your town for a reason. Maybe the reason will be revealed later, maybe never. I don't know. It's not for me to say. He works in mysterious ways. But I believe with all my heart and soul that He has guided us here."

Lilly nods. "Okay . . . fair enough. So what do you have in mind?"

"You seem like a good person." Calvin looks as though he's about to cry. His eyes well up with emotion. "Sometimes you trust someone simply because your heart tells you to trust them. Do you know what I mean?"

"Not really."

"My wife is ill."

Lilly waits. Something important is about to be transacted. "Go on, I'm listening."

"To be honest, it's an invisible illness. Most of the time. But these days, it's very dangerous—a dangerous liability."

"I'm not following, Calvin."

He swallows air, a single tear tracking down his gaunt, whiskered face. "We've been kicked out of two other settlements. People don't have the luxury to be Christian about it nowadays, they don't have the luxury to be sympathetic. It's survival of the fittest, and those who are weak, who are damaged somehow, they get shunned . . . or worse."

"What's the illness, Calvin?"

He takes in a girding breath, wipes his face. "She's had a couple of different diagnoses—bipolar disorder, clinical depression. Before the Turn, she was in the care of a psychiatrist who was helping her. Now she's . . . she's . . . she tried to take her own life a couple times."

Lilly nods sadly. "I get it." She licks her lips and tries to ignore the heavy feeling pressing down on her, squeezing her heart. "I'm sorry." She looks at him. "You mentioned a deal?"

Calvin looks at her. "Back in Augusta, before things went bad, she was taking lithium, and it seemed like it was helping." He takes a deep breath. "You got a solid group of people here, Lilly. Good people, decent people. You got this fella Bob and you got this infirmary—you got medicine, people with medical training—"

"Calvin, Bob is a far cry from a psychiatrist. He was a medic in the first Gulf War. And as far as I know, we don't have anything even remotely like lithium."

"But maybe you could find it. Some of the same places you found the other medicine—this drugstore Bob was talking about earlier—maybe they got some there."

Lilly slowly shakes her head. "Calvin, I wish I could promise you that we'll find some . . . but I just can't do that."

"I'm not asking for promises, Lilly. Just that you'll try."

Lilly nods. "Of course we'll try."

"If you do that for me, if you try and find this medicine for Meredith, I will talk her into staying. She'll listen to me, she doesn't want to be out there any more than I do. What do you say, Lilly?"

Lilly lets out a sigh.

She never was much good at saying no.

The next twenty-four hours bustle with a grim sort of purpose—inside and outside the walls of Woodbury—as Lilly delegates and directs. She assigns Gloria Pyne to work with Matthew and Speed throughout the night on a way to alter the course of the herd. By the first light of dawn, they have come up with a strategy: They will use incendiary devices along with any other flammable liquid they can spare to start a controlled fire line across the eastern edge of the herd, in essence blocking the path to Woodbury. It's not an infallible plan, but nobody has a better one.

At the same time, Lilly asks Bob to put together a small team of men to go on a run to find lithium at the derelict drugstore that lies just beyond the wall on the east side of town.

It takes a few hours for Bob to prepare his team, showing them a map of the area surrounding the You-Save-It Pharmacy, priming them to watch for the danger areas in the adjacent ruins, and familiarizing them with the layout of the drugstore. During past missions, Bob has discovered an unexplored lower level beneath the store—previously inaccessible due to padlocks—which may or may not contain untapped reservoirs of medicine and supplies. Bob plans to make an assault on the building later that morning with Hap and Ben.

Meanwhile, Matthew, Speed, and Gloria set out at dawn to put the fire line into play.

They use Bob's pickup on back roads and uncharted trails to get as close as possible to the trajectory of the herd. Matthew calculates the herd's position by extrapolating the speed with which it was traveling and plotting their course along a straight line through the farmland directly west of the prison.

At eight thirty, they see the first signs of the herd in the woods west of Highway 85, about twelve miles outside of Woodbury. Gloria sees it first from the jump seat in the back of the pickup as the truck roars up a steep grade of blacktop. "Yo! Gentlemen!" she says, pointing at the distant forest. "Look at the treetops!"

In the rays of early-morning sunlight, the primordial mists clinging to the ancient oaks are stirring and shivering like jittery ghosts, the tops of gnarled limbs trembling with the pressure of the unseen swarm below. Matthew takes the next side road, a winding serpentine of asphalt, up into the hills immediately to the south.

Fifteen minutes later, they find a vantage point along the edge of the two-lane. Matthew pulls the truck over, parks and gets out, the others following, the air festering with the noxious, maggot-infested odors of the dead. They use the binoculars to see down into the thicker trees.

In twenty-four hours, their number has grown. Now a wave of undead the size of a vast flood tide oozes through the shadows of the forest, more than a thousand strong. Emitting an eerie humming noise, hundreds and hundreds of low growls forming an atonal chorus, they slowly stumble into each other, bumping and scraping tree trunks, tripping over themselves, but somehow, *somehow,* in their haphazard and wooden march, they continue in an eastwardly direction, slowly but steadily, maybe a mile or two an hour.

It doesn't take a genius to do the math.

FOUR

It takes an hour to lay down the fire line. They choose a parched low-lying, rocky area just north of Roosevelt State Park. The long, flat meadow of scrub grass lies about two miles northeast of the herd's current position and spans a section of land directly across its path. The area is maybe eight miles or so from the outskirts of Woodbury, which allows enough of a safety buffer in case the fires spread. Georgia has weathered a series of horrible droughts since the plague broke out, and now the wetlands across the south part of the state are like tinderboxes just waiting to be set off by the next well-placed lightning bolt.

Matthew, Speed, and Gloria work quickly and silently, communicating mostly with hand gestures, following the plan set forth by Lilly and Bob. They hurriedly lay down a chalk line—using a hand-operated contraption found at the elementary school soccer field—to ensure that the fire is surgically precise and burns in a straight line. Then they unfurl nearly a hundred yards of thick rope to absorb the flammables. Last, they hurriedly pour various accelerants along the line, carefully keeping them from splashing their clothing or seeping into the earth.

Pulling one huge plastic container after another from the pickup's cargo bay, they use isopropyl alcohol from Bob's infirmary, ethanol from the abandoned farm and fleet shed, gallons of old liquor from the tavern on Flat Shoals Road, kerosene from the storage warehouse, and even the guts of old fireworks found in one deserted home on

Dromedary Street. The final step involves covering the line with kindling in the form of railroad ties and building timbers gathered around the periphery of town.

By nine forty-five, they're ready. They take their position on a nearby hill—less than a hundred yards to the north—and crouch in the shadows of enormous hickories, swatting mosquitoes.

After a few endless minutes, they smell the first hints of the herd coming, the telltale odor detectable long before anyone actually glimpses the leading edge. The air vibrates with that infernal symphony of moaning and snarling right before Speed gets his first visual of the distant ragged figures materializing on the horizon, emerging from the trees like an army of defective wooden soldiers.

"Right on time," Matthew whispers, gripping the small radio controller and crouching behind a massive tangle of deadfall logs.

His heart races as he prepares to ignite one end of the fire line with his makeshift detonator—a device jerry-rigged from a remote-control airplane found in a ransacked Woodbury hobby shop.

The black tide of undead approaches the fire line, and Matthew waits until they are right on top of the booby-trapped timbers. He thumbs the ignition button, and the end of the line sparks hot and magnesium bright in the sun.

"Burn, you sons o' bitches," Gloria utters under her breath as she watches the flames lick across the hundred-and-fifty-yard-long line, the fire catching the leading edge of walkers unawares, gobbling up their moldering clothes, enrobing their pallid faces in cocoons of flame. The fire builds. Within seconds, the entire front rank of walkers goes up in ribbons of brilliant flame.

The maelstrom flags up into the sky as the fire spreads through the herd. Apparently walkers are as flammable as any fire hazard, with their methane rot radiating off gore-soaked garb and maggot-infested innards. The maelstrom rages brighter and hotter than expected as the entire vast army of undead goes up.

"Oh no . . . no, no," Gloria moans after witnessing the unexpected phenomenon, ducking and pulling her visor down to shield her face from the shockwave of heat and light. "No, no, no, no, no, fuck no. FUCK!"

Matthew just stares through watery eyes, aghast at this unforeseen development.

They have made a huge mistake.

Bob and his team rifle through shelf after shelf of empty pill boxes and unmarked cartons of pharmaceuticals in the derelict drugstore on Folk Avenue and keep coming up with nothing. They're working in the dark, in more ways than one, Bob with a miner's light on his dented metal helmet, Hap and Ben with penlights lodged between their teeth.

All they can find are acne medications, hemorrhoid ointments, and cryptically named medicines long ago left behind by looters. All the juicy central nervous system drugs are long gone. They search for another ten minutes or so until Bob finally holds up his hand. "Okay, time out, fellas. Hold on."

Hap and Ben pause. They pull their penlights from their mouths and look at Bob.

"I'm thinking it's time we try the cellar." Bob's miner's light casts a yellow beam that shrouds his leathery features in silhouette.

The other two men shrug, looking neither pleased nor displeased with the idea. Finally Ben says, "You sure you want to go to these lengths?"

"What lengths? What are you talking about?"

"Risking our lives so some nutcase housewife can get her meds?"

"We don't know she's a nutcase, Ben. Believe me, it's best for all of us, we get her stabilized."

Ben shrugs again. "Lead on, Macduff."

Minutes later, after Bob has broken the padlocks and the men have descended service ladders, Hap Abernathy struggles to see through his half-assed Walgreens eyeglasses. Engulfed in the moldy darkness of the drugstore cellar, turning in a half circle, trying to focus on the movements of the other two men, Hap realizes right then and there he never should have insulted that young optometrist back at the LensCrafters in Belvedere Park a month before everything went to hell. But that smug little shit in that stupid white lab coat kept making cracks about "men of a certain age" as he examined Hap's eyes, and it made Hap so crazy he finally shoved the instrument tray over and walked out. But now, almost two years later, he's trying to survive Armageddon with dime store specs and it's driving him crazy.

"Slow down, gents," Hap calls out to the others, aiming his measly little penlight into the pitch-black ahead of him. Through the filthy spectacles he can see blurry beams of light sweeping across cluttered metal shelves and an octopus of soot-filmed furnace conduits snaking up into the stalactites of exposed plumbing. He hears Bob's gravelly voice through the darkness.

"Follow the sound of my voice, Hap—looks like they got cartons of old medicine stacked up on these shelves, probably expired back around the Clinton administration, but you never know." Hap starts shuffling toward the voice and the blur of silver light. "Holy crapola!" Now Bob's voice sounds off in a higher register. "What in the fucking wide world of sports is *this*?"

"Whaddaya looking at, Bob?" Hap shuffles closer, the silhouettes of two men materializing in the gloom. They stand in the corner of an ancient brick-walled chamber strewn with packing straps, old lumber, mouse turds, and dust as thick as fur on every surface.

Hap shines his penlight down at the spot in the corner toward which the two other men now gape, mesmerized, fascinated. Hap blinks and stares. The wall is a blur, and he has to adjust his eyeglasses for a moment to see what they're looking at. At last, he registers the ancient seam running up the herringbone brick at least five or six feet high, with rusty, congealed hinges sunk into the grout, barely visible along one side. "Judas *Priest*," Hap utters breathlessly as he realizes just exactly what he's staring at. "Is that a *door*?"

Bob nods slowly.

Hap stares. "Where do you reckon *that* goes to?"

Typical! Lilly sets her walkie-talkie down for one second to go to the bathroom and all hell breaks loose. Damn thing is silent as a brick all morning, not a word from Matthew and company—regardless of the fact that Lilly has been doing air checks every fifteen minutes or so while she's been supervising the fortification of the town—and now the thing starts squawking as she's pissing in the lone Porta-Potti outside the construction site.

She reaches for the roll of toilet paper when she hears another burst of Matthew's tinny, anxious voice outside the door of the enclosure. *"Lilly, you copy? You there? Hello? Where are you? Something . . . something really fucked-up happened . . . Hello? Hello! HELLO!"*

Lilly hurriedly finishes her business and pulls up her pants. Since her miscarriage three weeks ago, she has suffered a persistent bladder infection, and even this morning, she notices a certain tenderness in her abdomen as she kicks open the plastic door. "Coming, for Chrissakes," she grumbles under her breath. "Keep your panty hose on."

The walkie-talkie sits on an oil drum fifteen feet away, and Lilly crosses the distance in a few leaping strides, snatching the two-way off the drum. She thumbs the Send button. "Matthew? Lilly here . . . go ahead."

The voice crackles: *"Oh, Jesus . . . um . . . Lilly . . . something really . . . something really messed up has happened!"*

Lilly thumbs the switch: "Calm down, Matthew. Tell me what happened. Over."

The voice: *"It's my bad . . . I didn't . . . didn't see it coming . . . aww SHIT!"*

Lilly speaks up: "Matthew, take a breath. Is everybody all right? Did somebody get bit?"

After a burst of static, the voice returns, breathless, hysterical, coughing: *"We're fine, we're all okay . . . but the herd, Lilly, the goddamn fucking herd . . . we didn't stop it. We just . . . made it worse."*

Lilly transmits: "What are you talking about, Matthew? Did you do the fire line?"

From the little speaker hisses the eerie sound of Matthew Hennesey's humorless, hyperventilated laughter: *"Oh we did it, all right . . . we lit the fucking place up."* Pause, a rustling noise, the sound of heavy breathing. *"The problem is . . . surprise, surprise . . . these goddamn things are dead . . . they're already fucking dead . . . !"*

Lilly listens to the voice deteriorating into more breathless laughter. She thumbs the button: "Matthew, listen to me. I need to know exactly what happened. Just calm the fuck down and tell me what happened."

After a long beat of crackling silence, Matthew Hennesey's voice settles and drops an octave, like a child who's been caught red-handed: "We lit the fire line . . . and . . . and . . . Jesus, I never would have dreamed . . . Lilly, they went right through it . . . like it wasn't even there . . . The front row went up first . . . it was like some kind of fucked-up stunt . . . the walkers in front just lit up like candles . . . just burst into flames . . . the gasses from all the decaying flesh . . . I don't know what it was . . . it was like each one erupted . . . and pretty soon the whole fucking herd was going up . . . It was like that old film of the Hindenburg blowing up . . . remember that? The fire just poured through the swarm . . . until pretty much every last one of them was blazing . . . They were blazing like walking torches, but Lilly . . . the thing is . . . they didn't stop . . . they kept on . . . kept on trudging along like they didn't even have a fucking clue they were burning." He pauses to catch his breath. Lilly, still processing it, stares down at the hard gray earth, as powdery as moon dust. The sound of Matthew's voice crackles again: "They're still heading for Woodbury, Lilly."

Lilly squeezes the Send button: "Wait. Okay. Hold on. I don't understand. Won't the fire destroy them? Most of them? Or at least a good chunk?"

The voice, now reduced to a low murmur, crackles and fizzes through the static: "Yeah . . . in time, I guess . . . some of them . . . I don't know." Dry, husky laughter again. "If the fire destroys the brain . . . or makes the body unable to walk . . . at this point, your guess is as good as mine . . . but there's one thing I can tell you for sure . . . There's so many of them, a good portion will make it to Woodbury by tomorrow morning . . . and it ain't gonna be pretty."

Lilly stares at her watch, thinking about it, slowly shaking her head. The fact is, *nothing* is pretty anymore.

"Shine your flashlights on the right side of the door—right there— yeah, perfect." Bob crouches and muscles the claws of the hammer into the dusty, cracked mortar between two bricks, sending a shower of particles to the floor. He grunts with effort. "This brickwork is over a hundred years old if it's a day," he says, struggling with the hook, wedging it in and then prying as hard as he can.

"Bob—"

The door suddenly gives.

Hap jerks back with a start. Too old to react quickly, too damn blind to see what's happening, he gets bombarded with a series of impressions—the first of which is a cool draft of noxious air puffing out of the seam, as though the seal on a giant mason jar has just been broken. This is followed by the rasp of ancient hinges squeaking as Bob swings the door open, followed by a blur of movement.

At first Hap identifies the thing that bursts out of the doorway as a raccoon. It's dark and low to the ground, and in Hap's bleary eyesight, the only thing that truly registers is a small mouth full of sharp yellow teeth. The thing clambers spiderlike across the floor toward Hap. He lets out a startled gasp as the creature clamps onto his right ankle and sinks its fangs into his flesh.

Now things start happening very quickly—far too quickly for Hap to track—the worst of which is the hot pain that travels up his leg. He loses his balance and falls backward onto his ass, his penlight flying out of his hand and rolling across the floor. The light shines at the thing chewing his ankle.

For one horrible instant before the other two men intercede, Hap stares into the face of a waking nightmare.

The monster that has locked its jaws around his leg barely resembles anything that was ever human. Presumably the time it has spent in the darkness behind the door has desiccated it beyond recognition, its flesh earthworm-gray and so sunken around the angles of its skull and sternum as to look vacuum formed. Jagged, misshapen knots of bone protrude from the corners of its limbs, giving it a ghastly puppetlike appearance. Perhaps once a child or a dwarf, the miniature humanoid stares through luminous, lidless eyes as it gnaws at Hap's arthritic joint, sucking the blood and marrow with the fervor of a starving castaway suckling the last drops of moisture from a coconut husk.

Hap sees a flash, and the blast pops in his ears as Bob blows the thing away with a single head shot that sends gray shards of tissue stippling Hap's face. Gasping for breath, holding his leg, Hap feels the monster release its grip and sag to the floor in a puddle of dark fluids. Hap moans—his ankle burning.

Ben's silhouette fills the doorway in the wall, his Glock up, gripped in both hands, aimed and ready, but only that gelid draft of toxic air puffs out of the darkness on the other side of the door. No movement, no sound, only the ringing in Hap's ears as he lies back in agony, holding his aged, varicose-veined, rheumatoid shin, the warm wet lifeblood seeping out of it, mingling with the rotten fluids spreading across that filthy concrete deck.

"Okay, breathe, Old Hoss, just breathe," Bob is saying now, kneeling by Hap, cradling his head. Hap blinks and sucks breaths against the tsunami of pain coursing over him. He tries to breathe. He tries to speak. He tries to focus on Bob, who continues to softly encourage. "Gonna be okay, gonna get you outta here."

"No . . . no you ain't." Hap has to marshal every last shred of energy to speak, to formulate words and sentences. The pain burrows into him, spreads through every capillary. Some people succumb slowly to the shock of a bite; for others it's a matter of minutes. Hap feels his essence leaking out the bottom of his feet. "You ain't moving me."

"Hap, shush now, we're gonna—"

Hap manages to shake his head. "No, you ain't gonna move me because I'm . . . I'm done. I expected it to happen . . . s-sooner or later. It was a . . . good . . . good run I had in this world."

"Hap—"

"F-finish it now."

"Hap, shut up—"

"Bob," Ben's voice interrupts softly. "You know what you gotta do, there ain't no—"

"SHUT UP!" Bob bats away the sound of Ben's voice behind him as though swatting at a wasp. He inspects the bite wound soaking Hap's pant leg. Frantically, breathlessly, he puts his gun down and tears a hank of cloth from his shirttail, hurriedly making a tourniquet and winding it around the old man's leg. "Now, don't argue with me, Old Hoss. We're gonna—"

Hap gets his trembling fingers around the beavertail grip of Bob's .357 pistol.

Bob looks down.

It happens so abruptly, so quickly, that Bob has no time to prevent it, let alone even *register* what is occurring. He sees something move in the darkness beneath him and realizes that Hap's crooked old fingers have wrapped around the grip of the revolver. Bob shouts a garbled cry as Hap quickly turns the barrel around and presses it against his liver-spotted temple.

Bob reaches for the gun at the same exact moment Hap squeezes the trigger.

Another inarticulate shout from Bob as the blast rings out, flashing and roaring in the darkness. Bob rears back as Hap whiplashes, the back of his skull blowing off, the blood-mist spraying a load-bearing post behind him. Hap flops backward in a cloud of cordite, landing with his eyes pinned open. The gun clatters to the cement—a dark pool spreading.

"NO! FUCK, NO!" Bob lurches toward his friend, acting on instinct. "FUCK! FUCK!" Bob tries to lift the old man's head off the floor, the blood making Bob's hands greasy. Hap slips back to the floor. Bob gibbers to himself as he feels the back of the man's head, feels his neck for a pulse. "Fuck-fuck-fuck!" Bob's eyes fill up and he can't see very well as he pulls Hap's lifeless body into an awkward bloody embrace. "Goddamn it, you stupid old fuck, what did you do? What did you *do*?"

"Bob, c'mon." Ben's voice comes from the shadows behind Bob, sounding as though it's coming from a million miles away. "Bob, he's gone. He—"

"SHUT THE FUCK UP, BEN!" The force with which Bob's gravelly voice pours out of him takes even Bob by surprise, and the unexpected emotion welling up in him makes him dizzy. For some reason, this one hits him hard—this death, this senseless loss, as casual and sudden as a sneeze. He loved old Hap Abernathy, loved his stories, loved his curmudgeonly personality, loved his stubborn bullheadedness that reminded Bob of some of his old army buddies. Hap had done a stint in the navy back in the Korean War and had been a good cook, a typical swabbie, and he made Bob laugh. Now Bob feels the waterworks threatening as he hugs his friend's limp body to his chest, the blood baptizing Bob in misery. He begins to weep softly.

"It was his doing, Bob," Ben's voice murmurs from the darkness, only inches away now but coming from a great, great distance. "He was a good old soul, and he went out like a man."

"I could've . . . I could've . . . FUCK!" Bob puts his face down against the side of Hap's ruined head. "I could've saved him."

"No, you couldn't have."

"I could've . . . *amputated* it."

"No, Bob. There was nothing you could've done. He went out like a man."

Bob tries to say something else but instead closes his eyes and lets the rest of the crying jag travel through him. It takes a minute or so. Then Bob is silent, rocking the flaccid body back and forth. Then he stops rocking the body and just sits there, desolate, empty, drained. He looks up at Ben and says softly, "We're gonna take his body back, give it a proper burial."

"Of course."

"C'mon . . . help me make a stretcher."

The two men gather scraps of wood and rope and packing tape.

They fashion a crude conveyance on which to drag the body back to town. It takes another few minutes to secure Hap's corpse on the stretcher, and when they're done, and they've got the body tied down, and they're wiping the sweat from their brows and preparing to leave, Bob takes one last look at the second body—the mangled cadaver on the floor with the desiccated flesh and the bones sticking out of every joint—and he spits at it.

Then Bob notices something else: On the other side of that cadaver, behind that secret door in the basement wall, a tunnel stretches into the dark.

Bob blinks, wipes his eyes, and stares at the tunnel for a long moment. The passageway is lined with bricks and mortar, and from the condition of the lining it appears to have been hastily constructed many, many years ago. It seems to extend into the darkness for hundreds of yards, maybe even miles.

In fact, the more Bob gazes at it, the more an invisible hook sinks into the deepest recesses of his brain: *Who the fuck built this thing, and why did they build it, and most important, how far does it go?*

At last Bob turns to Ben and says in a drained, exhausted voice, "Let's get out of here."

FIVE

Calvin Dupree bursts into the administrative office on the second floor of the courthouse building with his heart racing and mouth dry with panic. He pauses just inside the door and quickly scans the anteroom, which Lilly has offered to his family as temporary quarters until they are healed up enough to leave. Illuminated by a single skylight, the space has been swept, the desks and filing cabinets pushed against one wall, and the boarded windows hung with moth-eaten drapes.

Now the children sit morosely on one side of the room, mostly keeping to themselves. Bethany sits in a shopworn swivel chair, reading a dog-eared storybook, while Tommy and Lucas sit facing each other on the floor, playing a board game.

"Darlin'?" Calvin calls to Meredith, who sits alone on the other side of the room, staring out a crack in one of the boarded windows, rocking gently on a folding chair, silently mouthing her obsessive-compulsive litany—some of it garbled and inaudible, some of it the phrases 'don't you' and 'say a word'—as the world goes on unabated around her. "Sweetheart, everything okay?" Calvin says as he approaches, clenching his fists nervously.

She doesn't say anything.

"Darlin'?" Calvin kneels down next to her. "Talk to me—what's wrong?"

Still nothing but that disturbing silent mouthing of some talismanic prayer.

"Listen, sweetie. Remember I told you about that herd forming west of here? Well, they tried to stop it and something went wrong. It's still heading this way. We have to stay here now. We're safer within the walls of this place. At least for the time being. Do you understand?"

She doesn't look at him, doesn't respond, simply continues murmuring to herself, softly humming off-key, as a thin shard of light leaks through the boarded window and strikes her face, making her narrow, sculpted features look even more severe than usual. Barely a whisper, more of a moan than a song, her voice sounds as though it's coming from the bottom of a well as she utters the words to an old lullaby: "Hush, little baby don't say a word . . . Papa's gonna buy you a mockingbird."

Calvin realizes this is what she's been mumbling for days, maybe weeks. He touches her shoulder. "Darlin'? Did you hear what I said?"

All at once, she pulls away from his touch as though from an electrical shock. She looks up at him, blinking, scowling. "I heard what you said, Calvin, I'm not comatose!" She frowns. "What happened with the herd?"

"What?" He cocks his head. "Oh. I don't know. They tried to block its path but it backfired somehow." He tenderly strokes her arm. "We'll be okay. Don't worry." He squeezes her arm. "Why don't we pray on it? What do you say? Let's pray together." He bows his head. "Lord Jesus, please hear our prayer—"

From behind him, a quavering voice interrupts: "Can you *please* do something other than *pray* all the time?"

Calvin whirls around and sees his eldest son, Tommy, standing with clenched fists, sweat-soaked hoodie, and veins bulging in his skinny neck. He is a boy on the brink—of adolescence, of violence, of tears. "Mom's totally gone crazy, totally sick in the head, and all you can do is pray?"

"You hold your tongue!" Calvin feels anger flare in his gut. The boy has a way of pushing buttons, and Calvin has a lot of buttons lately. "We are dealing with a life-and-death situation here."

"I know, Dad. That's the problem. You can't protect us with prayers."

"Go sit down! Right now!"

"But Dad—"

"Now!"

The boy lets out an enraged groan, spins, and storms back across the room. He kicks the board game across the floor, startling his younger brother.

Calvin turns back to his wife. "It's gonna be okay, I promise," he says to her, gently stroking her arm.

She pulls away again. "Your son's right, Calvin."

"Don't say that."

"Your wife's a mental defective."

"Meredith—"

"Nuttier than a soup sandwich."

"Stop it!"

"*YOU* STOP!" The sheer volume and timbre of her voice startles everyone in the room. The kids abruptly look up from their scattered game pieces. Meredith's slender face has turned livid, the cords in her neck pulsing. "Stop pretending you can pray your way out of this, and stop pretending everything is peachy keen with this family, and stop pretending this is not the End Days and we're not all screwed!"

"Okay, that's enough—" He goes to touch her again, and she slaps his hand away.

"And stop lying to me!"

He looks at her. "What are you talking about?"

"Tommy heard you were going out to that National Guard depot later today to help these people look for weapons. Is that true?"

"Okay, that's not—"

"IS IT TRUE OR NOT?"

He nods. "Yes, it's true."

She takes a deep breath, her eyes glassy with rage and madness. "I'm going with you."

"Meredith—"

She looks up at him with the strangest mixture of emotions twisting her features: anguish, desolation, sorrow, but mostly white-hot anger. "I'm not going to curl up in a ball and die. Not without a fight. I want to destroy these monsters as much as anybody else. I'm going with you."

The ashes of the former National Guard Depot Number Eighteen encompass a ten-acre plateau of scrubland overlooking Elkins

Creek—about a mile and a half east of Woodbury. A narrow access road of sun-bleached pavement splits off from Highway 18 and winds up the west slope to the front gate, which now resembles a charred skeleton of mangled iron bones torn asunder by the shock-waves of a firebomb.

As Bob pulls the rust-pocked Dodge Ram up to the blasted wreck-age of the entrance, the rest of the passengers silently take in the vast ruins of the property. What was once a fortress of chained-link, thick-walled buildings and heavily guarded armories now resembles a child's discarded play set, the toys scattered across the razed land-scape. Tanks lie scorched and upended like dead tortoises in the dis-tance. Burned-out shells of Humvees and Bradley battle vehicles sit strewn across the lot. Half the buildings are missing doors and win-dows, some of them with entire floors gaping open, ravaged by fire and now exposed to the elements. The crater at the epicenter of the explosion that destroyed the depot now resembles a brackish pond filled with toxic rainwater, the blast radius still apparent to the naked eye in great concentric rings of soot radiating across the pave-ment.

"What in God's name happened here?" Calvin asks from the nar-row backseat, which is a tight fit for three adults. He is squeezed in between Meredith and Lilly, craning his neck to see through the win-dow, while David rides shotgun, an AR-15 assault rifle propped ten-uously between his legs.

David stares out his window at the ruins. "Folks that tangled with the Governor burned it down as a sort of preemptive act."

"When did this happen?"

David shrugs. "I don't know—about a month ago, something like that."

"Who *were* these people?" Calvin asks almost rhetorically, shocked by the devastation.

"Just people," Lilly speaks up, rubbing her legs as though trying to get feeling into them. Her slender body is wedged against the rear door. The traumatic memories of the last month still flare up within her without much warning. Hap Abernathy's death this morning has touched off her old feelings of panic. She feels like a fraud. Who the hell does she think she is? She tries to drive the doubt from her mind.

Gazing out the window, she sees the scorched remains of biters on the ground, littering the property, and the sight of all those blackened corpses puts a squeeze on her midsection. There easily could be burned walkers still moving around inside these derelict buildings. She pulls out her Ruger, checks the clip, and says, "Regular people. Just like us. People just trying to survive."

Meredith, on the other side of the rear seat, fidgeting with nerves and adrenaline, at last speaks up. "You ask me, we're never gonna find anything just circling in this flippin' pickup . . . Gonna have to get out and search on foot at some point."

After an hour of futile searching—each building either scoured clean by looters or burned beyond recognition by the blast—they find a narrow, low-slung Quonset hut in the far corner of the property, next to the parking garage. Either due to the steel exoskeleton, or the vagaries of the blast's shockwave, the hut is still intact, padlocked from the outside.

Bob breaks the lock with a ball-peen hammer, and the whole team pours into the darkness of the hut, which smells of machine oil and mold.

Flashlights snap on. In the slender beams, huge crates are visible, stacked to the ceiling, covered with cobwebs. Block letters stenciled across the sides of the crates read UNEXPLODED ORDNANCE, 100 .50-CAL BROWNING ARMOR-PIERCING AMMUNITION, HIGH EXPLOSIVE COMPOSITION C, and 50 25MM HIGH-PERFOMANCE SIGNAL FLARES. Finally Bob's flashlight beam pauses on one labeled INCENDIARY MUNITIONS/WHITE PHOS. "Son of a buck," he utters under his breath.

"What is it, Bob?" Lilly shines her light on the label. The words mean nothing to her.

"I've heard about this shit," he says, kneeling in front of the crate, blowing dust off the slats. "White phosphorous. Army used it in Kuwait."

"What is it?"

"Nasty, nasty stuff. Like napalm only brighter and faster."

"Firebombs?"

"Kinda."

"Didn't we already try that?"

"This stuff is different—believe me." Bob looks over his shoulder at her. "Like fire on steroids."

She thinks about it for a second. "Can we use this stuff?"

He gives her an enigmatic look and then turns to the others. "Somebody give me a hand, we need a dolly or something to carry all this stuff back to the truck."

Late that afternoon, Lilly and the others return to Woodbury and find that Matthew, Speed, and Gloria have already beaten them back to town.

Shaken, sweaty, and covered with soot, looking like they just narrowly escaped a coal-mining disaster, Matthew and company meet with Bob and Lilly in the infirmary, where Bob treats the team for minor burns and mild smoke inhalation, and Lilly questions them about the rate at which the herd is now closing in on Woodbury.

"I'd say we have about twelve hours at the most," Matthew says, sitting on the edge of a gurney, wiping grime off his face with a towel. Gloria and Speed sit across the room, sipping bottled water, looking bedraggled and haunted.

Lilly paces and probes. "What the fuck happened? I've seen walkers get *spooked* by fire, *recoil* from it. Right? But nothing like this. What made them impervious to it?"

Matthew shrugs and looks across the room at his comrades. "I'll be damned if I know. It happened so quick I wasn't even sure what I was looking at."

Speed pipes up. "It's gotta be slowing them down—some, at least—but most of them, I don't know, it's like they don't even fucking know they're on fire."

This stops the conversation cold for a long moment, the ensuing silence excruciating.

Lilly looks at Bob. "How long before we get that corner of the west wall beefed up?"

"Should have it done by nightfall." Bob clears his throat nervously. "I realize time is tight. I know we don't have time for a proper burial service. But what if I went ahead and said a few words later, before we plant old Hap." Bob sounds like he's got a frog in his throat—he keeps clearing it—but Lilly knows he's actually fighting tears. "He was a good old cuss. Saved a few lives in his day. I feel like we owe it to him. Whaddaya think?"

"Of course, Bob." Lilly studies his deeply lined face. His ancient eyes are buried in webbings of wrinkles. He has the tics and shakes of a dry drunk. For a fleeting instant, Lilly wonders if he might be close to falling off the wagon. She has no idea what she would do without this man. "As soon as we get the wall reinforced," she says to him, "and we get everybody situated . . . we'll meet in the square, and then bury him next to Penny."

Bob nods and casts his gaze at the floor, partly in gratitude, partly in shame. Nobody knows how bad he wants a drink right now.

Across the room, Gloria takes her visor off, runs fingers through her thinning dishwater-gray hair. "You would think the fires would thin the herd eventually. Half them things were going up like Roman candles." She looks at Lilly. "By the time they get here—with any luck—there ain't gonna be many left."

Lilly nods and rubs her eyes. "What's the old saying? From your lips to God's ear?"

"Speaking of God," Speed says, "I saw that dude—that Jesus freak dude—working with y'all earlier, working the wall. Have they decided to hang around?"

Lilly lets out a sigh. "I guess . . . I don't know." She thinks about it. "Calvin's cool, by the way. He doesn't impress me as a zealot or anything." She thinks some more about the Dupree family. "Kids are sweet, too. It's the wife I'm worried about. She's really wired tight. I want everybody to keep an eye on her. She's got that look about her—I've seen it before—she's been out there too long. She wants to help with the explosives, but I'm not sure that's a good idea. This lady is dangerous. I think she wants to single-handedly wipe this herd off the map."

After a long pause, Gloria comments softly, "Who doesn't?"

SIX

Ten minutes before eight. Darkness setting in. Night crickets roaring. Something putrid on the wind. A distant humming noise like high-tension wires buzzing—or maybe an army of the dead closing in. Clock ticking. Each and every resident of Woodbury, Georgia, hustling to get things done before the deluge.

Under the racetrack, Barbara Stern leads a gaggle of children ranging from ages three to twelve years old down a series of steps into the subterranean labyrinth of service bays. The yelping and barking hyena noises of the eight kids bounce off the tile walls of the central corridor as the middle-aged woman in the muumuu hurries toward the last office on the left. "Don't push, Robbie," Barbara admonishes one of the younger dervishes. "Take your fingers out of your mouth, Alyssa. Keep moving. Nathan, help your sister."

Barbara has only a vague memory of the service office. She saw it once while accompanying the Governor's goons down here, and as she ushers the kids past battered garage door after battered garage door—each door drawn down and locked—she gets a queasy, uneasy feeling in her gut. Here is the place where pit crews once repaired or stored their machines, where men in greasy coveralls futzed endlessly under the hoods and chassis of muscle cars, rolling around on dollies, ratcheting and hammering. But it is also the place where Philip Blake, aka the Governor, tortured his prisoners—the screams of the condemned blending with the shriek of drills and the laughter of the inquisitor—a place that became a real-life house of horrors. Barbara once saw a documentary on CNN about Saddam Hussein's palace, raided and put under marshal law after the U.S. invasion. For some reason she remembers the creepily *ordinary* quality of that evil place—the photos of hunting trips on the refrigerator magnets and the porn on the bedside tables—and right now she is reminded of exactly that as she passes a pinup calendar on the wall showing a nude woman on a mechanical bucking bronco.

"Last door on the left, Tommy," she calls out to the boy in the lead.

A miniature version of his father, Tommy Dupree is a wiry, fair-haired kid with a ruddy face that displays emotions readily, openly, his huge brown eyes full of intelligence and vigor. He looks like a little soldier right now in his denim overalls and Caterpillar cap as he marches toward the office, dragging his younger sister along by the neck of her sundress. From the moment she met the boy, Barbara felt an immediate kinship with the feisty twelve-year-old. Childless and unaccustomed to the insatiable neediness of most kids, Barbara resonates strongly with Tommy's old soul. The boy is a pisser, a real wiseacre who suffers fools poorly, and Barbara identifies with that.

"I'm not blind," Tommy calls back to her. "I can see the sign." Like a dog sitter herding puppies, he grabs the sleeves of his younger siblings and urges them toward a glass door marked PIT AND SERVICE ADMIN in faded stenciling. Five-year-old Lucas stumbles slightly in his corduroy jumper and saddle shoes, dropping a little knapsack full of papers on the stained floor.

Coloring books flop open, crayons spilling across the floor, papers fluttering here and there. "I'll get it, Luke, it's okay, you go in," Tommy comments sourly, but also with a trace of long-suffering patience in his voice, as though he has become a martyr—a parent by proxy—as he gathers up the contents of the knapsack.

Barbara whisks the rest of the kids past Tommy and into the room.

She returns a moment later to help the boy pick up the art supplies. Kneeling next to him, she stuffs errant crayons back into the sack while Tommy picks up individual sketches hastily drawn in black marker and pencil by the shaky hand of a five-year-old. One of them catches Barbara's eye. "Not to be nosy," she says to the twelve-year-old, "but who's that supposed to be?"

"Oh, this?" He holds the paper up, and Barbara gets a closer look at the strange misshapen humanoid figure with the horns, cadaverous face, and huge forked tongue flagging out of its fang-lined mouth. "That's the Aunty-Christ."

"Really."

"Yep. My little brother has visions. Most of the time he sees visions of the Rupture. Or at least that's what my dad calls it."

"The Rapture, you mean?"

"Yep," the boy says with a casual nod, putting the picture back in the knapsack. "My dad says we're in the Triboolation times when some of us get lifted up into heaven and some of us have to stay behind and fight the Aunty-Christ. That's where all these monsters come from. They're signs of the Triboolation times."

"Oh." Barbara cannot muster much of a response other than a tepid, "I see."

"I think it's all bullshit," the boy goes on. "But I don't say anything, it would hurt my dad's feelings. He's not a bad father, he just gets so annoying sometimes with the Jesus talk and the praying and the God stuff." He zips the knapsack and rises to his feet. "I'm an atheist myself. Don't tell my mom and dad, though—it would kill them."

Barbara chuckles as she rises and ushers the boy into the office. "Now see, we have something in common. I'm not a Jew, but don't tell David's parents—it would kill them."

They close the door behind them, drawing the shade down, the sound of the latch slamming home echoing down the empty passageway.

In the hours before the first sighting, Lilly supervises the last-minute tasks required to fortify the town and prepare for the attack. She has six women and fourteen men working continuously on reinforcing the west wall, allocating ammunition, placing arc lamps, positioning the gunners, installing Matthew's makeshift catapult, distributing explosives, and handing out equipment such as scopes, night-vision goggles, tracer bullets, flares, and ammo magazines. After scavenging what they could from the ruins of the Guard depot, and combining their private stashes, they have a grand total of sixteen live grenades, a few hundred .45-caliber rounds, about sixty .38-caliber rounds, a hundred and fifty high-velocity .30-caliber armor-piercing bullets, and about a hundred .22-caliber slugs in ten separate magazines for Lilly's two Ruger pistols. It's not a very impressive arsenal—especially considering the variables here—but they'll have to make do. The explosive ordnance from the Guard depot could be their trump card. Lilly advises those with assault rifles to fire controlled bursts since the weapons will spray eight hundred rounds a minute if the trigger is continuously tripped.

Around eleven o'clock that night, they pause to have a brief memorial ceremony in the square for Hap Abernathy. By torchlight, the twenty adults huddle in a semicircle around the stone statue of Jeb Stuart, heads bowed, as Bob stands before a pine box wrapped in rope and duct tape, speaking in low tones about Hap's days shuttling middle-school kids to and from school in his yellow bus. Hap was a curmudgeon, but he was also well liked, and several survivors have stories they want to tell. Everybody gets a chance to speak, but the ceremony is short-lived, as the unmistakable odor of walkers begins to drift on the wind, an offense to the proceedings. Everybody gets jumpy when they detect a new aspect to the stench. Just beneath the telltale scent of rancid meat and festering shit, like a dissonant musical counterpoint, is the black, acrid, oily odor of charred flesh.

The mourners disperse, taking their positions on the rooftops of cars and truck cabs parked along the barricade. Matthew sets his jerry-rigged catapult on the top bucket of a cherry picker near the west gate. A conglomeration of bungee cords, wooden dowels, and the guts of a wheelbarrow, the catapult features a slingshot apparatus that fires projectiles weighing up to ten pounds. Beside the catapult he piles a stack of C-4 explosive, bundles of dynamite, and one-pound squares of white phosphorous.

Next to Matthew, on the bonnets of two semicabs, the self-proclaimed sharpshooters in town set up their equipment, including tripods, ear protection, sighting scopes, and metal boxes of high-velocity armor-piercing bullets. Ben learned long-distance target shooting back in ROTC at Vanderbilt and claims to be able to take down a head shot at a hundred and seventy-five yards. Lilly can't decide whether she believes him, but it doesn't matter. Somebody has to operate the M1 Garand rifle. The other sharpshooter is David Stern. With very little experience, as well as a bum right eye, he lacks Ben's credentials but makes up for it with his even temper. David has impressed Lilly as being unflappable—a trait that goes a long way in the heat of battle.

Sometime after midnight, Lilly decides to have one last powwow before the arrival of the herd. She gathers everybody by the trucks parked across the west gate. By this point the stench is unbearable, so pervasive it suggests that the herd is even bigger than they thought. But no one has yet sighted any walkers. The worst part, perhaps, is the unmistakable odor of burned meat. Lilly has never encountered any fatal house fires close up, or witnessed any deaths by immolation, but she has certainly smelled bacon grease burning in an iron skillet, a common result of her father Everett's attempts at making breakfast. *This* odor smells like Everett's burning bacon multiplied by a thousand, mixed with scorched animal fur and charred human hair. It keeps Lilly's guts levitated throughout the last-minute pep talk.

"Okay, so, here's the deal," she announces to the group in the wee-hour darkness. They have extinguished the emergency sodium-vapor lights, killing the generators and plunging everything into moonlit gloom, the resulting eerie silence broken only by the wind warbling over the distant humming of undead. The noise—growing and intensifying with agonizing slowness and certainty—sounds like a monsoon coming, like a squall building behind the trees. The faces gathered around Lilly reflect the cold moonlight and thinly veiled terror. "I want everybody to take your positions and don't get too comfortable—obviously the herd's gonna be here ahead of schedule."

"How do you know that?" Ben Buchholz wants to know, his gaunt face shaded by his John Deere cap. The other faces—Calvin, Meredith, Speed, Matthew, David, Gloria, and the rest of them—look on with intense, wide-eyed alertness. Adrenaline flows through the group like an electric current.

"You smell that?" Lilly gives Ben a hard look. "Just take a whiff."

"All right, I get it," Ben grumbles.

"No matter what happens, stay at your positions." Lilly scans the group. "Don't stare at the herd, don't get mesmerized, don't pick out a single walker and waste ammo trying to take it down. Just fire controlled bursts toward the tops of the bodies." Lilly pauses to let this sink in. The wind carries a chorus of moaning from the west. Lilly feels a shiver coming on but hides it. The clock ticks. Even though Lilly isn't even remotely close to being an experienced leader, either military or otherwise, she finds the words coming out of her mouth now almost unbidden, innate, automatic. "I'll be roving with the twenty-two-cal pistols and the walkie-talkie. Matthew will have the other radio. If something goes wrong, or if you see something you think needs to be addressed differently, then go ahead and—"

"Lilly!"

The voice calling out her name—familiar and raspy and whiskey cured—interrupts her spiel in a sort of Shakespearean stage whisper.

"What is it, Bob?" The older man is kneeling on the crown of a semitruck, the binoculars in his hand at his side, his chiseled features creased with nervous tension in the darkness. He looks as though he has just witnessed a deadly accident.

"You gotta see this," he says, holding up the binoculars, teeth gritted, struggling to hide his terror for fear of alarming the others.

"Everybody take your positions!" Lilly calls out over her shoulder as she darts toward the cab. She climbs the service ladder two rungs at a time and reaches Bob's perch within seconds.

"Just on the edge of the trees," he says with a sort of grim finality, handing over the binoculars.

"Oh, Jesus." Lilly sees exactly what he's talking about. "Bob, I'm going to need you to fire off a few signal flares."

The common wisdom among plague survivors is that a herd is the personification of Armageddon—the ten plagues of Egypt wrapped up in a single wave of rotting flesh and gnashing black fangs— and its presence spells doom for any living creature within miles. Lilly has seen a few of them firsthand—each one living on in her nightmares—but up until now they have been, if nothing else, *consistent* in their behavior patterns. Up until this moment, all herds have behaved in an almost identical fashion—a uniform flock of walkers crowded together and moving as one, pushing ever forward, a reeking flood tide of cadavers migrating lemminglike toward some inchoate destination. Eventually all herds have dissipated either in time or after a natural obstruction impeded their progress. But *this*—this abomination emerging from the tree line west of Woodbury at one fifty-three A.M. Eastern Standard Time and starting across the litter-strewn vacant lot adjacent to the railroad tracks—defies analysis, transcends past performance, and boggles the mind of anyone still breathing who lays eyes on it.

Three flares in quick succession arc over the meadow, flickering magnesium daylight down on the horror.

Lilly attempts to comment as she peers through the binoculars, but no words will formulate themselves, no salient thought will coalesce in her mind, and all she manages to do is gape and move her mouth in an approximation of words. But no words will come. Her flesh rashes with icy goose bumps, her sacrum tingling with horror, her scalp crawling with a million pinpricks. She stares. The herd has pushed out into the open now and is fully visible in the cold radiance of the flares.

At roughly two hundred and fifty yards, the front line can be seen with the naked eye, writhed in a vast low-hanging haze of smoke, but only those with binoculars can truly behold what is coming this way. Scores and scores—perhaps hundreds—of burned corpses shamble in formation toward the town. Still smoldering, their eyes like cinders, their tattered clothing fused to their charred skin, they shuffle as one reanimated army of burn victims—as though a nuclear holocaust has swept through their rank and left behind only ghostly husks in its wake—now propelled by the invisible puppet strings of their ceaseless, relentless, insatiable instinct. A few of them crunch and crackle as they lumber along, as though they're about to crumble apart at any moment. Others in the back rows still burn slightly, the winnowing flames curling up from their hairless skulls and mingling with the miasma of smoke and stench that now hangs like a storm cloud over the meadow. The odor emanating off the horde is practically indescribable—a mixture of rubbery, burning-chemical fumes, scorched proteins, and acrid, greasy, bitter tar bubbling off a hot skillet. The stench permeates the air and makes Lilly cough even as she stands paralyzed by the sight of it all.

Gaping, staring, she presses the binoculars so tightly against her eye sockets that they shoot pain down the bridge of her nose. Her free hand instinctively moves down to the miniholster on the corner of her left hip and clasps the grip of her .22. She feels the killer instinct rise within her. She feels her mouth watering with both nausea and latent violence.

In that awful instant before the first shots ring out, Lilly feels a sudden, unexpected, and overwhelming wave of sorrow coursing over her. The effect of this vast army of immolated corpses—somewhat reduced in number from the original superherd—is different from the standard swarm of rotting reanimated cadavers. The flames propelled by the methane and rot and degradations of flesh have blasted away all remnants of individuality. No longer can an onlooker make out the distinctions among the walkers—a former nurse, an auto mechanic, a child, a housewife, a farmer. Now there is no delineation among the burned, only a great mass of blackened, smoldering revenants shuffling endlessly forward, moving without purpose, without hope, without God or mercy or logic, simply moving.

Lilly jumps as the first bark of a sniper rifle flashes in the darkness to her left.

Through the binoculars she sees one of the lead corpses whiplash in a puff of smoke and blood-mist, then fold to the ground—a crisp pile of scorched remains for the buzzards—as its brethren slowly and obliviously trample it as they continue in their dog-whistle march across the field. More shots ring out from the platforms to Lilly's left and right, and more charred cadavers pop their corks and collapse in fountains of sparks. The gunfire snaps Lilly out of her daze, and she lowers the binocs and draws her Ruger and grabs the walkie-talkie off her belt.

Thumbing the switch, she yells, "Matthew, I want to hold off on the incendiaries until they're close enough to do damage! Do you understand? Matthew? Tell me you understand! Matthew, do you copy?"

Through crackling static, Matthew's voice: "Copy that! One question, though!"

Lilly thumbs the button. "Go ahead!"

The voice: "Did you take the big boys?"

Into the mouthpiece, Lilly says, "What? Did I take what?"

Through the tiny speaker: "The big bundles of dynamite. They're missing!"

"What do you mean, they're missing?!"

Matthew's voice: *"They're not fucking here—what the fuck happened to them?"*

Lilly glances over her shoulder at the cherry picker fifty yards away. In the darkness she can see Matthew's hunched form rifling through the canisters of explosives and stacks of phosphorous. Lilly is only partially aware of the implications—her mind swimming, sparking with adrenaline in the darkness. She quickly turns back to the slow-motion onslaught.

Already the herd has made significant progress across the meadow. It is now a hundred and fifty yards away, the odor as thick as a pall.

"Okay, everybody, fire at will!" She thumbs back the hammer on the Ruger. "FIRE AT WILL! FIRE AT WILL! FIRE AT WILL!"

Crouched on the roof of a semitruck next to the cherry picker, Calvin hears Lilly's voice cutting through the crackle of gunfire just as he reaches for his .357 Magnum.

The gun, given to him by Bob Stookey, weighs a ton and feels awkward in his hand. He's not a sportsman, not former military, not a gun guy—although the small Kentucky town in which he was born and raised was a haven for gun nuts. But now, with the advent of the Tribulations, he has forced himself to learn firearms.

He brings the front sight up and draws a bead on a reanimated bundle of scorched flesh shuffling along in a halo of smoke about a hundred yards away. He fires. The roar makes his ears ring, and the recoil jerks his shoulder blade as he sees the walker stumble but not go down. The blast has taken a chunk of burned flesh from the creature's ribs, leaving a gaping hole through which the moonlight shines in a beam of smoke and swirling dust, but it's not enough to destroy the thing, and Calvin sniffs back his frustration.

He senses something wrong. "Mer? Darlin'?" he calls down to Meredith.

She had been standing down below, next to the cab, only a second ago. Calvin had talked her into wearing his thick leather jacket, high boots, gloves, duct tape around her wrists, and a couple of *shemagh*-style scarves around her neck, just in case—God forbid—she got too close to a walker. Only a minute ago Meredith had been complaining about the stiffness of the get-up, handing spare ammunition up to Calvin, grumbling that she should have a gun, too.

Now she's gone.

"Oh, no," Calvin utters under his breath. He turns and scans the shadows inside the barricade, gazes up and down the west wall, and sees only the other men and women blasting away at the oncoming horde. Muzzle flashes spark in the darkness, turning all movement into the surreal slow-motion of a silent movie. "MEREDITH!"

Calvin quickly descends the cab's emergency ladder. He drops to the ground and runs north through the darkness with his .357 still gripped in his right hand.

"MEREDITH!"

He stops at the end of the barricade, where the wall meets Canyon Road. Heart racing, he turns in a circle, racking his brain to come up with an answer. She could have returned to the underground tunnels beneath the racetrack to be with the kids. But why wouldn't she tell him? It wasn't like Meredith just to vanish without saying anything. His mouth goes dry with panic, his flesh crawling. Something is very, very wrong. He hears the first charge of explosives going up across the meadow, launched by Matthew's catapult, and the sonic boom makes him practically jump out of his skin.

For a brief instant, the darkness turns to day as Calvin screams, "MMMMEEERREDITH!"

On the far northwest corner of the barricade, behind the gargantuan old oak tree that has stood for over a century at this lonely street corner, Meredith Dupree wrestles with a padlock. Nobody sees her. At this end of town, all the power is down and all the streetlights are out, and the only illumination comes from either moonlight or the flicker of distant gunfire and explosives, so she has plenty of time.

She works in the darkness, humming her lullaby and gazing through tears as she tries to wrest the lock off the handle of a screen door pilfered from the nearby Walmart. The door is reinforced with burglar mesh and hastily nailed up between a narrow gap in the seven-foot-high wall. It is a remnant of the old order—the Governor's men put the door in a year earlier for quick emergency egress—and now it has rusted and burned and practically fused to the wall panels.

Meredith's hands do not shake as she works, despite the fact that she can hear her husband calling out for her above the gunfire and explosions. She keeps her attention focused on the door. She works at the padlock with a crowbar she found last night in the toolshed behind the deserted railroad depot. She's not a strong woman— broad in the hips but flat-chested and scrawny in the upper body— however, considering the momentous nature of the occasion, she puts everything she has into the bar and finally it snaps the lock.

The padlock falls to the ground with a faint thud. She drops the crowbar and tries to push the door open, but it sticks. She kicks it with the heel of her boot—once, twice, three times—until the screen finally detaches and the door rasps open.

For a moment, she is virtually paralyzed by the wide-open darkness on the other side of the door—the landscape at night unexpectedly beautiful—and she just stands there staring for a long beat.

Then she picks up her satchel, takes a deep breath, and lugs the heavy cargo through the doorway and into the flickering night.

PART 2

The Labyrinth

No one knows, not even the angels in heaven, nor the Son, but only the Father. Be on guard, keep awake. For you do not know when the time will come.

—Mark 13:32

SEVEN

Outside Woodbury's barricade, beyond the derelict post office, You-Save-It Pharmacy, and rows of modest aluminum-sided buildings lining Jones Mill Road, lie the thick pecan groves and tree-lined paths of Nolan Woods. At this time of night, with the sky this clear and the moonlight this bright, the landscape turns almost primordial, mystical, bound in night mist and fireflies, the swaying, windswept treetops stretching as far as the eye can see, silhouetted against the riot of constellations spangling the sky.

Meredith shoulders the enormous canvas satchel as she moves across this shadowy landscape.

For a long while it's almost as though the hordes of walkers have spared this side of town, the gunfire and screams and choruses of moans fading into the back of her consciousness as she heads north. Meredith remembers first driving into Woodbury from this direction, she remembers passing the lake, and she remembers the fireflies—like God had sprinkled fairy dust down from the heavens, like the Spanish moss had been dripping magical sparks. She smells the horde—the scent of evil, of weakness and sin—and she hears the shuffling footsteps behind her.

Some of the dead have spotted her with bird dog intensity. The rabbit has been roused from its hole, and now the chase is on, the walkers are coming for her, a huge contingent of the herd splitting off and pursuing her. She starts to sing as she picks up her pace. "Hush, little baby, don't say a word, Papa's gonna buy you a mockingbird . . ."

The sound of her voice—so alien to her own ears in the bullet-riddled air—begins to draw more and more of the walkers away from the town.

In her peripheral vision, Meredith can see their shadowy forms silhouetted against the far sodium arc lights, blackened, empty cocoons in the shape of people, slowly turning toward the sound of her singing, awkwardly changing course, one by one, coming for her.

Crossing the thick weeds of a vacant lot, stepping over deadfalls and stone, Meredith lifts her voice and sings louder, "And if that mockingbird won't sing, Papa's gonna buy you a diamond ring!"

The walkers come en masse now, scores of them trudging stupidly after Meredith, only their eyes visible like reflectors buried in their charred faces. The plan is working. Meredith feels the mob closing in on her like acid bathing the back of her neck. She turns east and heads down a narrow footpath. She can't see the lake through the trees yet, but she knows it's close, she can smell its swamp gas and mossy odors mingling with the horrible stench of the horde rising in the darkness around her. She can hear their collective moaning and ululating, the noise spurring her on. She peers through the thick undergrowth ahead of her and sees the first glimmers of a stagnant body of water shimmering in the moonlight. She practically screams the song now. "AND IF THAT DIAMOND RING TURNS BRASS, PAPA'S GONNA BUY YOU A LOOKING GLASS!"

She reaches the edge of the clearing and descends the bank of the tiny crescent-shaped lake.

Not much to speak of as lakes go—more of a glorified pond, if she were to be honest about it—it reminds Meredith of the secluded fishing holes her brother Rory used to find in the backwoods of East Kentucky. She glances north and south, and sees the cypress trees dangling down into the scummy water, the little inlets glistening in the darkness, the ancient boat docks here and there with long-forgotten dinghies like stray pets, still moored, awaiting sportsmen and families who will never come.

The walkers close in behind her, snapping branches and vibrating the undergrowth like great tectonic spasms shaking the woods, making treetops tremble. Meredith realizes she has little time left. She descends the bank, opening the satchel, and singing softly now, more to herself, as she sinks into the muck. "And if that looking glass gets broke, Papa's gonna buy you a billy goat . . ."

Timing is everything.

The first line of the walkers bursts through the tree line like disfigured babies being born, charred faces working, masticating, the feeding frenzy in full swing. Some of them are already reaching their scorched, burned arms toward the woman in the water.

Meredith stands knee-deep in the mire as she hurriedly opens the satchel to reveal the twenty-five pounds of ordnance that she snatched from Matthew's arsenal—the cords of dynamite tucked into bundles, wrapped in fuses, the white phosphorous chunks like massive bars of soap, smelling of turpentine, taped to the incendiary devices—and she works quickly in the dark and the stench. The methane from the pond is so thick it practically overpowers the reek of the dead as more and more emerge from the woods and clumsily descend the muddy bank.

Searching the bottom of the satchel for the Bic lighter, Meredith remembers a buried memory of her brother telling her about the flammable nature of methane. "Some of them ponds up to Green River, you could light the top of the water like a Sterno pot," Rory had marveled. "Some of them swamps could burn till the twelfth of never." Her heart races suddenly. She can't find the lighter.

The first walker splashes toward her, a black shell of a monster. The smell is beyond terrible, a living thing wheedling up into her sinuses. She frantically searches the pit of the satchel and finally she gets her hand around the small plastic node. She pulls the lighter out and sparks the fuse.

"And if that billy goat don't pull," she murmurs softly, pushing the satchel out into the middle of the pond, "Papa's gonna buy you a cart and bull."

The first one pounces on her, a blur of putrid burned flesh and exposed teeth. Meredith goes limp in the water, sinking into the silt as slimy incisors penetrate her neck. She continues to sing softly to herself, comforting herself, a coo of a mother to a child, a soft cold rag on the forehead of a sick little girl. "And if that cart and bull turn over, Papa's gonna buy you a dog named Rover . . ."

More walkers reach her, and the feeding frenzy intensifies. She sinks deeper into the silt. The noise is tremendous—a turbine engine of watery gobbling sounds—rising around her as blackened canine teeth bury themselves into her neck. She can smell her own coppery blood, feel the wet sensation of her life draining down in cold rivulets into the dark, murky water. Slimy bicuspids clamp down on the fleshy parts of her thighs, her shoulders, her nape, even the left part of her face, tearing into the gelatinous grist of her left eyeball, snapping off her vision as a television would go to a test pattern, and the pain erupts in her, but she doesn't struggle.

The explosives have floated twenty feet away, the canvas satchel glowing with the flickering fuses as it begins to sink, a Chinese lantern casting a warm glow over the gently rippling water now gilded with a shimmering membrane of scum like liquid gold in the dying light.

She softly sings to herself in the final moments before the meat of her neck is torn completely away, along with her vocal cords, "And if that dog named Rover won't bark, Papa's gonna buy you a horse and cart."

In her last blip of consciousness—her body completely torn and quartered now in the swamp, all the feeling gone, the catastrophic pain replaced by cold darkness—she thinks of her children. She thinks of the good things, the quiet hours, and the love, as the burned corpses swarm her, at least fifty, maybe more, consuming her in a feral orgy of drooling and gobbling and smacking and chewing. More come shambling down the bank. Hundreds. Maybe a thousand all told if you count the regiments of dead pressing in now from those thick woods bordering the lake.

Meredith sings one last line, unsure if she is singing it aloud or in her mind or not at all: "And if that horse and cart fall down, you'll still be the sweetest little baby in town."

The white heat of the blast abruptly cuts off Meredith's final thought.

The night sky turns to day as three successive explosions rock the woods northwest of the Woodbury city limits. The final eruption—

the biggest of them all—shoots a mushroom cloud of blinding magnesium-hot phosphorous up into the heavens, spreading outward in tendrils of cleansing white fire, sending flaming particles in every direction. A massive sonic boom breaks windows, sets off car alarms, and chimes in the rafters of the speedway a mile to the east— the aftershock mowing down trees across a blast area of ten square acres, immolating at least three hundred reanimated corpses in its wake.

The conflagration is so sudden and massive, the reverberations are felt as far east as Highway 19, as far west as LaGrange, and as far north as Peachtree City and even some of the outer suburbs of Atlanta. But it's the dark thickets of pine and old-growth oak to the south of Woodbury in which the aftershock reaches an unexpected listener.

A couple of nanoseconds after the initial fireball lights up the sky, the resounding boom that ensues makes a figure crouching in the deepest part of those woods jerk with a start. A young man in his middle twenties, clad in work boots and a faded, patched chambray shirt, he has the feral gaze, filthy face, and matted hair of a lone survivor.

He twitches at the noise and light, and he instinctively ducks behind the deadfall logs next to which his nominal campfire still smolders. He has been in the wilderness for nearly three weeks now, searching for help, never giving up hope or abandoning the cause that propelled him here. Now, for the first time, he believes there may be others out there who can perhaps help him—as well as the family he left behind—and the thought of it makes his heart beat faster. Explosions of this magnitude rarely happen on their own. Whoever detonated this thing could be the savior he is looking for. On the other hand, that light in the sky could also spell doom.

The progenitors of this explosion could be emissaries of the devil, just waiting for someone like him to wander into their web of violence and sin.

He shivers and wraps the tattered blanket from his pack around his slender form. He gazes up at the orange bruise of light on the northern horizon and wonders if he should follow that light . . .

. . . or avoid it like the plague.

"NO! JESUS, NO!" Calvin Dupree, on his belly now, just outside the blast area, on the ground at the edge of the vacant lot along Dromedary Street, screams into the dirt. Plumes of his dusty breath are visible in the fading radiance of the blast.

Only minutes ago, when he had realized with horror what was happening—the missing ordnance, the AWOL wife, the sudden and unexpected shift in the herd's course, and the echoes of Meredith's lullaby drifting ghostlike over the trees—he had frantically squeezed his way through a gap in the wall, charged across town, and had almost made it to the woods. But Lilly had chased him down, and at the last moment, before the sky lit up, she had made a leaping dive and tackled him to the ground. Calvin had struggled mightily in her grasp when the explosion finally shook the earth and rained debris down on them.

Now Lilly struggles to sit up next to him, her ears ringing so severely she can hardly hear his sobbing.

"SWEET JESUS!" he cries into the earth. "MEREDITH, OH, GOD! NONONONONONONONO!"

The light of the blast has faded already to a dull orange glow behind the trees, the air stinking of cordite, burned circuits, and brimstone. A few surviving walkers scatter across the vacant lot in front of them, on the edge of the woods, stunned by the blast, moving now as though punch-drunk. Calvin rises to his feet and lunges toward the glowing fires through the trees.

"No, Calvin—wait! WAIT!" She leaps to her feet and grabs him. "There's nothing you can do! You'll get yourself killed!"

A stray walker approaches, with blackened flesh crackling and mouth creaking open and shut—a former adult male, burned beyond recognition now—reaching its scalded arms for Calvin, who stumbles when he tries to sidestep the creature. Calvin falls to the ground, sobbing with grief and horror, yelling something about not caring whether he lives or dies, as Lilly draws her Ruger from the back of her belt, swings it up, and squeezes off two pinpoint shots into the cranium of the troublesome walker.

The thing lashes back with the impact of the blasts, the top of its head flinging off into the night, trailing a comet tail of brain matter.

The creature collapses five feet from where Calvin hunches in a heap on the ground, weeping, slobbering inarticulately about Meredith being sick and this didn't have to happen and why, God, *why*? Lilly sees more walkers coming and kneels next to Calvin and reaches out for him, but then something happens that takes Lilly aback—even in the midst of all this carnage and horror—to the point where she stiffens suddenly.

Calvin wraps his arms around her. He hugs her tightly, sobbing, trembling, murmuring now, only a few of his words audible in Lilly's ringing ears: "This was bound to happen, I should have seen it coming, I should have known, I could've—I could've—oh, Lord, I could've stopped it!"

"Sssshhhhhhhhh," Lilly utters softly in his ear, her body stiff and awkward in his embrace. She pats his back. Out of the corner of her eye she can see more walkers skulking along the tree line, silhouetted by the dying glow of the fires. They have to get out of there soon, or they could easily be overwhelmed. But her attention is wrenched from the here and now to some other time. She thinks of Josh, and she thinks of Austin, and the very thought of them—her former lovers, saviors, partners in crime, lost forever—sends a zing of sympathy, even *empathy*, bolting down Lilly's spine. Her eyes well up as she pats the trembling back of this poor man. "It's not your fault," she whispers to him, "just remember that."

"Look what she did . . . she saved us," he manages, his sobs stealing his air, his breath hot in Lilly's ear. "Look how she . . . how she went out."

"I know." Lilly takes the man by the shoulders. "Look at me now, Calvin. Can you look at me?"

"She didn't deserve to go out this way, Lilly," he says, almost moaning the words as though gut-shot. "She never meant anyone any—"

"Hey!" Lilly shakes him. "Look at me, Calvin. Look at me."

"What?" He gazes at her through liquid eyes. "What do you want from me?"

"Listen to me. We have to get back. There's too many of them out here."

He nods. "I understand." He wipes his mouth and his eyes. Another nod. "I'm ready." He rises to his feet, feels for his gun. "My gun . . . what happened to it?"

Lilly gazes off at a cluster of smoldering, blackened corpses dragging toward them.

She grabs a handful of Calvin's shirtsleeve and yanks him gently backward. "Leave it, Calvin," she says. "Leave it . . . c'mon . . . *now*."

He doesn't have to be told a third time.

For the rest of that night, and well into the next morning, Lilly and the people of Woodbury go about the business of cleaning up the mess. Fortunately, the explosions that razed the adjacent woods took the steam out of the herd, reducing the throng to a manageable fifty or so shell-shocked walkers still shuffling about the periphery of town. It's a simple matter of picking off the remaining corpses with sniper rifles from positions above the wall. The process takes longer than one might expect, however, due to the lack of training among most of the shooters, as well as the questionable aim of David Stern in particular.

By noon the next day, they have destroyed practically every remaining walker in the general vicinity—the burned cadavers, dubbed Krispy Kremes by Speed, much to the annoyance of Lilly, who's trying to keep things quiet and respectful considering the tragic events of the night before—until there are only a handful of unburned dead dragging back and forth across the wall. Lilly assigns a team to remove the corpses from the immediate area with a pickup truck equipped with a front shovel. They use the contraption to dig a trench on the other side of the railroad tracks for the mass burial, which takes a good part of that afternoon.

Throughout the cleanup operations, they manage to keep the details of the previous night from the Dupree children—for the time being, at least—instead telling them that their mother is off on a run with some of the other residents. Calvin has asked Lilly to give him time to figure out how to break the news to the kids.

Late that afternoon, Calvin, Lilly, and Bob have a brief and private memorial for the heroic, troubled woman. They have the impromptu service on the edge of the woods, with Bob keeping watch behind them for any walkers that might be drifting by. Calvin speaks of his wife's generosity, her love for her kids, and her deep, unshakable faith.

Standing in the shade of a giant black oak, head bowed, gnats humming around her ears as she listens to Calvin's liturgy, Lilly is impressed by the man's command of Scripture—he recites the entire Litany for the Souls of the Faithful Departed without missing a beat. Although Lilly has never been a big fan of religious types, she's now coming around to a different conclusion. Perhaps because of the apocalyptic nature of the world around her, or maybe *in spite of it*, she feels a deep and abiding and somewhat unexpected respect for this man. He's gentle and kind and steadfast—traits that are becoming increasingly rare these days.

When he finishes his eulogy, Calvin walks across the leprous ground to the edge of the scorched crater formed by the blasts—a vast and ravaged swampland of ruined trees and shreds of inhuman remains still faintly smoking in the breeze—and bows his head and cries softly for several minutes. Lilly and Bob give the man his space, standing back outside the tree line for a spell.

At last, Calvin digs in his pocket and pulls out a small piece of jewelry.

From her vantage point fifty feet away, Lilly can see that it's a gold ring, perhaps a wedding ring—it's hard to tell at this distance—which Calvin tosses ceremonially into the crater. The sense of finality, of closure, is apparent now on the wiry man's face as he turns and walks slowly back to where Bob and Lilly are standing. Lilly can see a sense of relief on the man's gaunt features as well. Maybe Meredith Dupree had come to weigh heavily on her husband, like a yoke, pressing down more each day. Maybe the burden of her mental illness had taken its toll, and no matter how sad her exit from this world had turned out to be, it was probably, when all things were considered, for the best.

"You okay?" Lilly studies the thin man after he returns from the crater.

He gives her a nod, wiping his eyes. "I'll be fine," he says.

"She was a hero in every sense of the word."

Another nod, his gaze intense. "I think I'm ready, Lilly."

"Ready for what?"

He looks at her. "Ready to tell my kids the truth."

The sun sets that day on a clear sky, leaving behind very little trace of itself other than a deep indigo-red glow on the horizon. The golden hour that follows settles down on the backwaters and forests of Central Georgia like eiderdown, turning the light all gauzy and amber. The stillness that sets in causes sounds to travel farther than usual, echoing and reverberating over the hollows and valleys and chains of lakes. At this time of night, the ghostly moaning of walkers can be heard from great distances.

In a nest of weeds under a thicket of tall pines approximately eleven miles southeast of Woodbury, the lone survivor tries to block out the echoing sounds of walkers on the wind by covering his ears. He winces, his boyish face so covered with grime he looks like a chimney sweep in some Dickens tale. A high-strung young man with a collection of nervous tics and obsessive-compulsive habits, Reese Lee Hawthorne has his meager provisions now arrayed upon the surface of a mossy stone in front of him, a pathetic inventory of a starving man: a Swiss Army knife, a candy bar that's already been sectioned into pieces, half of it gone, a .38 Police Special pistol with a single speed loader and six rounds, a Roy Rogers autographed canteen, and a small Gideon Bible. Not much in the way of survival tools. If he doesn't catch a rabbit or a fish soon, it looks like another night of Milky Way crumbs and sips of tepid well water.

Who is he kidding? He's not some Delta Force grunt survivalist—he's just an uneducated mall rat from the suburbs of Jacksonville. What gave him the idea he could single-handedly save his family? Why did they send *him*—Reese, the youngest adult male—to find help, to find somebody willing and able to rescue the entire group? What were they thinking? What was *he* thinking?

He jerks at a gust of wind carrying another horrible warbling chorus of moaning—probably the vocalizations of the same swarm that surrounded his family. The collective noise of the undead—especially scores and scores of them—takes on an eerie, atonal, chiming sound out here in the wide-open spaces of rural Georgia, like countless broken church bells heralding some hellish black mass.

Reese covers his ears tighter, trying to block it out. He needs to get moving again. He feels paralyzed in this warren of cattails and wild juniper. If only he could think of a way to navigate toward that flash of light in the sky he saw last night.

That controlled explosion means people are out there, and the existence of people means the potential for help, maybe even the saving grace for his family. If only he could figure out a means to navigate. He looks up at the sky. Already a faint sliver of a moon is visible overhead in the luminous indigo heavens. The stars will be coming out soon.

Reese blinks, a revelation striking him, coursing through his marrow. Of course . . . *the stars.* He remembers it was clear last night—looks to be the same tonight—and then he stares at his candy bar wrapper. He stares and stares, the realization turning in his gut like a cold fist: *Milky Way.*

The North Star is part of the Big Dipper constellation in the Milky Way galaxy—he remembers *that* much from grade school—and that means he can keep moving at a ninety-degree angle to its vector, which is west . . . or something like that.

He starts packing up his scant supplies, oblivious of the fact that there are now seven dark figures moving through the undergrowth less than a hundred yards away.

"Got some very sad news to tell y'all," Calvin says to his children after closing the door to the administrative offices of the Woodbury courthouse. The three kids all sit on a threadbare sofa pushed against the boarded windows, a small bookcase beside it with about a dozen children's books and a few board games lining its shelves, a rocker against the opposite wall. The furniture had been brought in to make the place more homey for the Duprees—Lilly had offered up the courthouse's second floor as a temporary quarters for the family—and Meredith had been in the process of making it a little more convivial.

Now the father of the family paces in front of his kids with his hands in the pockets of his filthy chinos. "There ain't no easy way to say this so I'm just gonna come out and say it . . . your mama is . . . well, the fact is she's with the Good Lord in heaven now."

"What?!" Tommy Dupree scowls at his father as though the man just passed gas. "What are you talking about?"

Calvin lets out a long, agonized sigh and slowly nods at his son. "Your mom got in a tight situation with the walkers last night, and she didn't make it." He looks at the younger kids. "Your mama went and got herself killed last night and went to heaven."

The brief beat of silence is excruciating as the faces of the three children register what he's saying. The younger ones crumble immediately: Nine-year-old Bethany stares at her father as though the world has begun to melt in front of her eyes, her cherubic face stretching into a mask of agony, tears spontaneously tracking down her cheeks. The youngest—five-year-old Lucas—makes a valiant attempt to be strong like his big brother but can't stop his lower lip from jutting out miserably, nor can he prevent his huge doe eyes from welling up with enormous tears. Only Tommy reacts with a complex series of expressions and postures. It's unclear to Calvin how much the twelve-year-old knew about his mother's condition, but now the boy stands with clenched fists and paces to the other side of the room and stares at the wall. His lips are pressed together so tightly they look as though they were drawn on with an eyeliner pencil. He blinks and scans the room as though someone might jump out at any moment and say, "April fools!" At last, he looks at his father with a baleful frown full of scorn and recrimination. "What happened, Dad?"

Calvin looks at the floor as the younger kids' crying builds up steam, gradually at first—just hitching, gaspy breaths—but then Bethany starts to wail. Calvin can't take his eyes off his work boots, the same paint-spattered steel-toed Timberlands that served him well for the last fifteen years as a general contractor in Fayetteville, Alabama. Now the flecks of gray paint are stippled with deep reddish-brown droplets of dried blood. "She was helping out with the explosives that we was using to ward off the herd, and she got too close to the . . . she had a . . . she had an accident with the . . . she . . . she couldn't . . . aw, *screw it*!"

Calvin looks at his kids, then glances across the room at his oldest boy. Fists clenched, jaw set, teeth gnashing, Tommy burns his little hormonal twelve-year-old scowl like a laser into Calvin's soul. What is Calvin supposed to do? Lie to his son? About something this important? Swallowing back the agony, wiping his eyes, Calvin goes over to the rocking chair. He flops down with a grunt and a sigh, the weight of the world on him now. "Okay . . . the truth," he says. He looks at each kid. One at a time. He looks at them with the love of a father as well as the hard realities that good fathers do not hold back from their kids. "The truth is, your mama was a hero."

"Did she get bit?" Bethany speaks through her sobs, her small hands wringing the fabric of her skirt. "Did them walkers eat her up?"

"No, no, no . . . darlin', no." Calvin leans forward, reaches out for the two little ones, and pulls them gently off the couch and over to the rocker. He sits one on each of his skinny legs. "It's the other way around. Your mama didn't get bit at all." He tenderly squeezes their shoulders. "Your mama got the better of them monsters. She saved this town. She saved the lives of each and every man, woman, and child in this town."

The kids are sniffing back the tears, nodding, listening intently as Calvin tells the truth.

"She did something amazing. She took a bunch of dynamite and led the walkers away from town, and when she got them all in one place at a safe distance, she blew them bastards up." Calvin's voice breaks then, and he feels the grief unexpectedly bubbling up. He begins to cry. "She . . . she blew 'em up . . . and she . . . she saved us all. Just like that. Saved this town. Your mama. She's a hero and always will be. Probably build a statue of her someday." His sobs tumble into hysterical laughter. "What do you think of that? A statue of your mama right next to the one of General Robert E. Lee!"

The kids look down, sniffling and trying to process it all, as Calvin reins his emotions back in. He strokes their hair. His voice softens. "She led them monsters like the Pied Piper all the way out of town so nobody would get hurt." Calvin looks across the room at his oldest son, his problem child, his black sheep.

Tommy looks at the floor, lips pursed tightly, trying not to cry. He scrapes the toe of his Chuck Taylor high-top sneaker across the dusty checkerboard tile. At last he feels the sorrow resonating off his father's words, and he looks up, and the two of them—father and son—meet each other's gaze.

"Your mama was a stone-cold, bad-ass hero," Calvin says to the little ones.

But it's obvious now he's talking to Tommy.

Slowly nodding, turning to the wall, Tommy closes his eyes and finally allows himself to silently sob.

EIGHT

Contrary to the old saying, time does not heal *all* wounds. With some wounds, it makes no difference the amount of time that passes, or how much one drinks, or how many therapists one sees. Glaciers could cleave continents, and the pain would still live somewhere in the secret chambers of the heart. For the lucky ones, scar tissue forms, and the passage of time builds more and more tissue until the pain is simply part of a person's makeup, part of who he or she is—the grain in the wood. Lilly knows this from experience, and she knows that Calvin and his children will experience it in their own ways in the coming weeks and months and years.

For the Dupree family, the scar tissue begins to form the very next day.

Lilly puts everybody—including the Dupree kids—to work cleaning up the town, for both practical and psychological reasons. Lilly figures it's best to keep people moving, keep minds and bodies occupied, to not give anybody time to ruminate, a rolling stone gathers no moss, idle hands are the devil's workshop, a moving target is hard to hit, and all those other hoary old clichés that cross Lilly's mind that day as she keeps things buzzing along.

The wall needs more work. There are still the charred remains of walkers to clear. And the long-gestating idea of planting crops in the racetrack arena needs the next stage implemented—gathering the seeds to be tilled into the ground.

Bob asks Lilly if he can go on another run outside the barricade to the derelict drugstore. Bob has become obsessed with that mysterious tunnel in that cellar under the store, and he explains to Lilly that it could be a gold mine—figuratively, at least—leading to hidden caches of valuable resources. Woodbury is getting dangerously low on fuel, drinking water, batteries, soap, lightbulbs, propane, ammunition, candles, matches, and any edible protein other than dried beans. It's been weeks since somebody bagged a deer, waterfowl, or even the scrawniest rabbit. Not that Bob is planning on doing any big-game hunting under the You-Save-It Pharmacy, but one never knows what one might find in such a place. He remembers reading about coal and salt mines in these parts that occasionally get bought off by large companies and turned into vast subterranean storage facilities. Lilly agrees that it's a good idea to investigate further and suggests that Bob take along Matthew and Speed. Bob decides to head out the next morning at dawn.

He has a feeling about that place. Bob rarely has feelings like this. He doesn't take them lightly. Of course, it could be nothing.

But then again . . . one never knows.

"Yo, Bob! You gotta see this!" The voice booms in the fetid, clammy darkness of the tunnel, coming from the abyss fifty feet ahead of where Bob crouches in the dust, his miner's lamp casting a circle of light on the cracked dirt floor. The air smells of old roots and ancient bottom soil and the flinty musk of eons passing in the dark. For the last fifteen minutes, Bob has been hunkering down in the four-foot-wide passageway, doing tracings of strange fossilized impressions in the walls and across the floor with the pages of onionskin paper he found upstairs strewn behind a counter. The tracings have been serving as a note-keeping device in lieu of a digital camera. All the cameras in Woodbury are out of battery power or stolen or simply too much of a luxury on which to waste precious energy—AC *or* DC. Now Bob has gathered at least twenty of these sheets of tracings, neatly folded and stuffed into the inner breast pocket of his jacket, most of them bearing pencil impressions of footprints, wagon-wheel ruts, and strange chainlike shapes embedded in the walls and hard-packed earth of the tunnel. "You ain't gonna believe this!"

"Keep your shirt on, I'm comin'!" Bob rises to his feet and carefully makes his way down a main conduit of plaster and earth walls reinforced with wooden planks and load-bearing timbers, the dim yellow beam of his miner's lamp leading the way. He can see Matthew up ahead, his flashlight shining down at the tunnel floor, forming a silver circle the size of dinner plate. Beyond the point at which Matthew crouches, the tunnel seems to go on forever into the void of darkness. The sound of Bob's boot steps, crunching in the grit, echoes eerily.

After nearly an hour of exploration, Bob and his two comrades have concluded several things about the tunnel: (1) There are far more tunnels than they first thought—in fact, a *labyrinth* of tunnels, the main pipeline intermittently crossed with tributaries—most of the secondary tunnels barely wide enough for an adult to pass on hands and knees. (2) The main conduit seems to extend for miles, the limits of which Speed Wilkins, with his high-powered flashlight duct-taped to his AR-15, is currently testing. And (3) Bob keeps discovering odd little pieces of evidence that may very well suggest a human presence many years earlier.

"Get a load of this," Matthew intones gravely as Bob comes up behind him, crouching to take a look at what the younger man is babbling about. Matthew's Bushmaster rifle is dangling from a shoulder strap, and a few toothbrushes still in their blister packs stick out of his jeans pocket. The toothbrushes, also from the ransacked pharmacy, are Bob's idea, as are the dental mirrors, tracing paper, floss, magnifying glass, cotton swabs, hand wipes, and rubbing alcohol. He sees this mission as a sort of archaeological dig—a very important experiment that could easily have a direct impact on the lives of everyone in Woodbury.

"Holy fucking Christ," Bob utters softly as he stares at the oval of light. "How the hell did I miss that?"

The human skull is sticking sideways out of the ground, as burnished with age as old ivory. The teeth lining the jawbone look like Indian corn. A rusty iron band, so oxidized it looks barnacled, is also partly visible, wrapped around the muddy stalk of a neck where the cervical vertebrae poke through like a strand of yellowed pearls.

"It was totally buried," Matthew says almost reverently, not taking his eyes off the skull. "I stepped on something brittle, heard a crack." He shines the light farther down the edge of the path. "Check *this* out."

Bob feels his scalp crawl as he gazes at pieces of a spine gleaming dully in the flashlight beam, a femur, and what looks like a half-buried foot with a partial ankle. But what truly captures Bob's imagination is the shackle—the same kind of ancient iron as the collar piece, same patina of age like plaque on an old tooth—clearly bound around the ankle of whoever perished here God knows how many years ago.

"Holy Christ," Bob mutters as he notices the crumbling links of a chain snaking off in the dirt.

"What do you make of all this, Pops?" Matthew shines the light in Bob's face.

Bob blocks the beam with his hand. "Take that light out of my face, Junior." The beam sweeps away. "And don't call me 'Pops.'"

"Oops. Sorry." Matthew grins, playing along with the curmudgeon routine. The two men have been teasing each other good-naturedly for weeks, ever since Matthew asked Bob's age, and Bob told him "old enough" and advised him to mind his own fucking business. "But seriously, what do you think this shit means?"

"Hell if I know," Bob says, and then he hears a noise and looks toward the farthest reaches of the main tunnel. He sees a bruise of light flickering in the center of the darkness, like a candle flame, and hears a faint series of footsteps, as well as a huffing noise. "Hopefully Joe College here will be able to fill in some gaps."

They both stand and face Speed's silhouette as the young bull of a man emerges from the depths of the tunnel, coming this way with the AR-15 at rest across his chest, the flashlight beam bouncing with each stride. He looks winded, as though he just covered a great distance. "Gentlemen," he says as he approaches.

"Find anything?" Bob asks.

"Just more tunnel." He stops in front of them, leans his rifle on his shoulder.

"How far did you go?"

He shrugs, wiping the grime from his face. "Shit, I don't know. A mile? Three miles?"

Matthew looks at him. "You're shitting me! Damn thing goes that far?"

Speed shrugs again. "Farther, man. I gave up finding the end of it."

Bob asks if he noticed anything odd, anything in the ground, anything out of the ordinary.

Speed shakes his head. "Ran across a walker about a half an hour ago. Didn't fire at it, though, didn't want to draw any more of 'em."

"What'd you do?"

"Caved its head in with the butt of the rifle—no big deal."

Bob lets out a sigh. "Was hoping we'd find something we could use down here." He looks around. "So far it's just these weird remains." He gestures at the bones and tells Speed about the shackles.

Speed seems disinterested. "Whatever, man. Only thing I found back there is fucking tunnel and more tunnel. Not sure how a walker would get down here but . . . whatever." He licks his lips and looks at Bob. "What now, Pops?"

Bob lets out an annoyed sigh, turns, and heads back toward the hatch, silently wishing they would stop calling him that.

"Lilly!"

Lilly hears the voice right after she turns the corner at Dromedary Street and starts toward her condo. She pauses in the late-afternoon sun and wipes the sweat from her brow. Exhausted from a full day of supervising all the crews, getting the soil plowed in the arena, and starting on the extension of the barricade, she feels damp and sore and light-headed as she sees Calvin jogging around the corner and coming toward her with a friendly wave. She is in no mood to counsel anybody right now, but she puts a smile on her face, waves back, and says, "Hey there, Calvin."

"Glad I caught you," he says, panting slightly as he trots up to her.

"What can I do for you?"

He swallows hard and catches his breath. "I think we're gonna stay, Lilly."

She stares at him for a moment while this sinks in. "That's . . . fantastic."

He nods, proffering a sad smile, eyes softening around the edges. "Wish the circumstances were different but . . . there ya have it."

"I think you and the kids will be happy here."

"I think you're right." He gazes out at the wall in the distance. "Places like this are few and far between."

Lilly nods and studies the man. "I'm really sorry for your loss."

He looks at her. "Thanks, Lilly. I appreciate that, I surely do."

"How are the kids hanging in there?"

"They're doing pretty dang well. Tommy's as surly as ever. Bethany's sleeping better, and little Luke thinks all this was prophesied."

Lilly cocks her head. "Prophesied?"

"Long story."

"You're talking about all *this*?" She makes a sweeping gesture meaning the whole town. "Woodbury . . . and everything that's happened?"

Calvin sighs. "The little duffer has visions. At least, that's what he tells us. Dreams, visions . . . I'm not sure exactly what's going on in that little noggin of his."

"Wow." Lilly stares at him. "Seriously?"

Calvin shrugs. "Good Lord works in mysterious ways."

"I've heard that before."

Calvin gives it some more thought. "Who am I to dismiss what the child says—anything's possible, I guess . . . right?"

Lilly gives him another polite smile. "You got that right."

"Be that as it may." He looks at her. "I want to thank you for your patience with us, your kindness. You've really accepted us as equals."

Lilly looks at the ground. She feels a strange flutter in her midsection. Maybe it's nervous tension. She's not sure. She feels vaguely self-conscious around this man. "It's the Christian thing to do, right?" She looks at him and smiles. "I mean . . . that's what I hear."

Calvin chuckles—a warm, clean chuckle—perhaps the first time he has laughed at anything since he arrived here. "Very good, Lilly . . . not bad for a heathen."

"You mean I'm not going to hell after all?"

His smile widens. "That ain't for me to decide. But I'd say you were pretty safe."

"That's a relief."

His grin fades as he gazes out at the wall and the dark, swaying treetops beyond it. The air has been almost completely free of walker stench since the day before yesterday, when Lilly and company finally cleared away the last of the burned corpses from the adjacent lots and woods and buried the remains in the mass graves along the railroad tracks. Today the breeze carries the smells of summer on it—green grass and clover and rich, fecund soil—but also a faint, troubling noise drifting occasionally across the sky, scraping the clouds. Like the call of an exotic bird that doesn't belong in this eco-system—a ghostly, primordial warning signal to all its prey—the distant choir of moaning can be heard intermittently above the wind. It's enough to raise the hackles of every resident of Woodbury and cause gooseflesh to ripple down the backs of the less robust souls in the vicinity. Calvin seems to take it all in before turning back to Lilly and saying in a lower register, "Or maybe *this* is hell . . . maybe we all got damned without even noticing it . . . damned to huddle inside walls like these or wander this hell on earth for eternity."

Lilly stares for a moment, then blinks away the sudden pall of doom. She gives him a look. "No offense, Calvin, but remind me not to invite you to any parties."

Another weary chuckle from the man. "Sorry about that." He pulls a bandanna from his back pocket and wipes the moisture from his neck. "Guess I get carried away sometimes." He gives her another warm smile, and just for an instant Lilly sees the good and simple artisan that Calvin had been in preplague days. She could just imagine him making a chalk line and carefully planing wood with those calloused hands, a cigarette dangling from his lips. "You gotta watch me constantly," he says to her finally, "or I'll go all Pat Robertson on ya."

Lilly laughs. "That's okay, I can take it." She offers her hand to him—a spontaneous gesture that takes even *her* by surprise—and says, "I guess I should make it official. Welcome to Woodbury."

He shakes her hand with a firm grip. "I thank y'all for that."

"We're glad to have you, Calvin."

"Thank you."

They release their grip, and Lilly says, "If you're interested, I'd like to invite you to be a permanent member of the committee."

"The what?"

"Group of people that meets regularly—you met them last week when we were discussing what to do about the herd. The purpose is basically to make decisions. We need clear-headed people."

Calvin chews the inside of his cheek as he turns it over in his mind. "I guess I could do that."

"Good. It's settled, then."

"One thing, though."

"What's that?"

"You mentioned this gentleman, used to run things around here, called himself the Governor . . ."

Lilly nods. "That's right. What about him?"

Calvin looks at her. "I just want to be clear. I know this guy was a bad apple. And you got more of a democracy around here now. But I just want to be clear about something so I understand."

"Understand what?"

He looks as though he's parsing his words. "Are you sort of . . . well . . . the new Governor?"

She lets out a long, anguished breath. "Not even close, Calvin. Not even close."

Late that night. The moon high in the sky. The forest east of Woodbury as quiet as a chapel. Crickets droning down in the velvety shadows of pines along Elkins Creek. The air stitched through with errant sounds—warbling, plaintive moaning, twigs snapping, and a series of hyperventilated breaths as an emaciated figure in tattered clothing stumbles along the banks of the stream looking for a way across.

Reese Lee Hawthorne has been weaving clumsily through the trees all evening, following the creek south, looking for a footbridge or a cluster of deadfall logs over which he can cross the wide channel of murky water. He needs to head due west, but the creek—at this point more of a river, its currents running swift, cold, and deep—has prevented him from crossing. Now he's beginning to hallucinate from lack of food. He sees tiny luminous eyes watching him from behind the trees. He sees motes of stardust floating in the shadows. His legs are about to give out. He can smell walkers nearby. He can hear the rustling footsteps, awkwardly shuffling through the leaves behind him. Or maybe he's imagining it. He knows he shouldn't be traveling at night. Too dangerous. But it's the only way he can navigate and stay on course.

He pauses to catch his breath, leaning against the trunk of a massive oak, silently praying to the Lord, asking for guidance, asking for strength, when he sees a strange apparition about thirty-five yards away. He blinks and looks away, thinking it must be another hallucination. He looks back at it.

Sure enough, in the middle distance, it rises up above the treetops and spans the river: a modest little wood-frame cottage floating ten feet or so above the water with no visible means of support, a magical, fairy-tale home for some leprechaun or water sprite. Reese swallows the fear and shakes his head at the impossibility of it, but there it is.

The darkness and the shimmer of moonlight on its gabled roof give it an almost ethereal quality as Reese approaches it cautiously from the woods. If this is a mere hallucination caused by starvation, stress, sleeplessness, or low blood sugar, it is absolutely the most detailed hallucination in the history of man. Reese can see the worm-eaten siding as he draws closer, the traces of chimney-red paint long faded and burnished away in the Georgia sun.

Fever chills crawl down Reese's nape as he approaches and sees the shadow of the house cast by the moonlight across the water beneath it. Sure enough, without reason or logic, the cottage levitates in the air above Elkins Creek like some perpetual magic act. Reese abruptly stops. He freezes and stares at the weather-beaten cottage. Wait a minute. He stares at the huge maw of an opening at one end of the edifice, a passageway big enough to accommodate a horse-drawn carriage or a small pickup truck. He sees the rough-hewn road leading into the structure.

"Stupid . . . stupid *idiot*," he chides himself under his breath, realizing that it's a covered bridge.

This part of Georgia is lousy with covered bridges, some of them dating back to antebellum days. Most of them are modest enclosures of barn siding and shingles, but a few are elaborate Victorian gingerbreads so festooned with trim and other embellishments they look as though they were fashioned by elves. This one is a simple affair of clapboard and shingles, with a single decorative dormer on each end. Kudzu vines cling to one outer wall, and a runnel of slimy water flows down one corner into the brackish currents beneath it.

Reese takes a deep breath, scales the slope leading up to the east entrance, and enters.

Inside it's all darkness and foul-smelling rot, like a wine cellar in which all the bottles have broken and the wine has turned to vinegar. The air is so fusty and dank it seems to have weight to it. Reese considers running to the other side—the length of the bridge is less than thirty feet—but for some reason he walks. His boot steps on the boardwalk crunch loudly in his ears; he can feel his pulse in his jaw.

His gaze fixes itself on a pile of rags near the opposite opening.

At first glance, in the shadows, it looks like a mound of earth, but as Reese draws closer and closer, he sees that it's a pile of old discarded blankets and unidentifiable clothing, filmed in moss and filth, so weathered and distressed the pile has congealed and adhered to the floor of the bridge. Reese doesn't even look at it as he passes it on his way out the other end.

He is halfway through the opening when a blackened arm shoots out of the pile as though it were spring loaded. Reese yelps and stumbles to the ground, a walker's hand clamped around his ankle. He twists in its grip, fumbling for his gun. He keeps a bullet in the chamber for these very emergencies but the viselike pressure of the fingers and the startling condition of the attacker have him paralyzed.

Barely visible, the thing from the rag pile is a surreal sight in the moonlit shadows—a creature whose gender has become unrecognizable. Desiccated by the weather into a shriveled corpse of scabby flesh and bone, its hair like seaweed matted to its skull, it opens half a mouth and chews at the leather instep of Reese's boot with the vigor of a wood chipper. The vibration and sound of it—for one frenzied instant—registers in Reese's frantic thoughts as a chain saw on its slowest speed digging into a particularly stubborn root.

Reese manages to get his .38 Police Special out from behind his belt and halfway aimed, with his thumb snapping down on the hammer and his finger around the trigger pad, before the thing's mossy teeth puncture the shoe leather now standing between Reese and eternity. Reese squeezes off three shots in the general direction of the creature's cranium—the series of flashes like lightbulbs exploding in the night—the radiance flaring brightly in the walker's copper-penny eyes.

Half its sunken face is blown off, along with part of its scalp and an enormous chunk of its shoulder—the wound so profound that the head detaches from the body, the rotted tendons like waterlogged vines—and the body falls away to the ground.

Reese lets out a spontaneous scream that echoes up across the dark firmament when he sees the head still furiously chewing on his boot. The brain intact, the teeth still latched on to Reese with the Zen-like fervor of a praying mantis, the head goes at him more vigorously than ever. Reese kicks at it—again and again—until just before the teeth penetrate the capsule of boot leather and break the skin, the skull snaps off and rolls.

Clambering to his feet in the darkness, drunk with terror, mind swimming, Reese Lee Hawthorne scuttles after the rolling head.

The cranium has gathered speed on the downward slope and tumbles toward a ditch. Reese chases it—grunting and hyperventilating and yelling garbled, inarticulate cries—until he finally catches up to it and stomps on it as though putting out a fire. The cranial bones collapse as the thing caves in. He stomps and stomps. The skull flattens with the pulpy wetness of an overripe melon.

Reese doesn't even realize that he's crying until the pain of his repeated stomping shoots up his leg and cramps in his thigh and hip.

He falls to his knees, and then collapses onto his back. He sobs and sobs, lying on the hard-packed road, staring up at the night sky. He weeps without shame or inhibition, sobbing noisily and wetly for several moments—much of it saved up over the last few days of relentless foraging—until he literally runs out of breath. In a weakened state from early-stage starvation, he can hardly move now. He just stares up at the star-riddled heavens, taking shallow breaths, lungs hitching painfully.

A long moment passes. Reese thinks of God the Father up there in the glittering sky. A childhood spent in the Pentecostal church has taught Reese that God is an angry, stern taskmaster. God is judgmental and vengeful. But maybe Reese's God will have mercy on him. Perhaps *this* God—the same deity who visited this hell on the earth—will pause in his acts of vengeance to give Reese Lee Hawthorne a break. *Please, God*, Reese thinks, *please help me find the people who ignited those explosions.*

No response is forthcoming . . . only the vast and impassive silence of the black sky.

NINE

Lilly can't sleep. But instead of lying in bed, staring at the plaster whorls in the ceiling of her apartment on Main Street, ruminating on all the things she has to do, she decides to get up and fix a cup of instant coffee and make some lists. Her father, Everett, always used to say, "You get overwhelmed by life, Little Missy, you make a list. It's always a good first step, and even if you don't get a single thing on it done, it'll make you feel better."

Which is why, for the better part of two hours that night, Lilly sits by the front bay window—boarded on the outside and blocked on the inside by rows of spindly houseplants that Lilly is trying to nurse back to life—and scrawls to-do lists on a legal tablet with a pencil she keeps sharpened with her pocket knife. Many of the items that she initially writes down she hastily erases, realizing there is no hardware store in which to purchase the required nuts and bolts for the task, or the item is impossible without replenishing the dwindling fuel supplies. After an hour or so, she ends up with a workable list of undertakings:

TO DO

1. Put together fuel search team
2. Find more fuel
3. Put together seed search team
4. Find seeds for arena gardens
5. Finish plowing arena infield

6. Plant arena gardens
7. Establish rotating barricade builder teams
8. Work on extending barricade to Dromedary St.
9. Have Bob do house-to-house health check
10. Do agenda for steering committee meeting
    Tutor for kids
    Health center
    Food-sharing co-op
    Solar heaters
    Compost
    Biofuel
    Sustainable technologies
11. Meet with steering committee
12. Stay positive
13. Find somebody else to be the leader of Woodbury

Scanning this last item, she can't hold back a wicked smile.

Lilly knows there's nobody dumb enough to assume the leadership role of this little ship of fools, but she keeps on fantasizing. She keeps on thinking about it. What if she were just a citizen, an ordinary resident of an ordinary town? Wouldn't that be amazing? She pushes her chair back and levers herself to her feet, rubbing her sore neck. She's been sitting at the front window for nearly two hours now, going through half a dozen pencil leads, mostly scratching out the items on her wish lists, and now she feels like she just might be able to get some much-needed sleep.

She goes back into her bedroom and pauses in front of the makeshift mirror that's canted against the wall behind her door. She looks at her reflection. The girl staring back at her is almost unrecognizable.

In her baggy sweatpants and Georgia Tech sweatshirt, Lilly looks androgynous, even boyish, her wan, sun-tinted auburn hair pulled back tight and scrunched with a rubber band, which only serves to draw attention to her severe, angular features. It's literally been two years since she wore makeup. But it also looks as though there's something new behind her hazel eyes, something behind her stare that Lilly hasn't previously noticed. In normal circumstances she might chalk it up to age—at the moment, the single kerosene lamp in her bedroom throws an unforgiving light on her face, making the crow's-feet around her eyes look even more prominent than usual—but in this environment it suggests darker changes than simple wear and tear. The original softness in her face has been sandblasted away by the savagery of these times, and Lilly isn't sure how she feels about this.

She lifts the loose fabric of the tattered sweatshirt and looks at her scrawny tummy. A slender girl for most of her life, Lilly has gone from skinny to downright withered in the past few months—her ribs poking through the flesh of her sides like vestigial fins. She pinches a tiny amount of flesh around her nonexistent belly. She wonders what she would've looked like if she hadn't gone through the miscarriage last month. She looks at herself and imagines her midriff growing plump, her breasts filling out, her nipples darkening, her face becoming round and full and ripe. All at once a dagger of emotion stabs her midsection, and she turns away from the mirror, tamping down on the sadness. She drives the melancholy thoughts from her mind and crosses the room.

Exhausted, she flops down on the bed with her clothes still on. She drifts off to sleep without even being aware of it because it seems almost as though the knocking noises come an instant later. Lilly sits up with a jerk as though she dreamt the noise, but the knocking continues, hard and fast, somebody impatiently banging on her door.

"Jesus, what now?" she grumbles as she drags herself out of bed. She considers grabbing her pistol but decides not to and instead shuffles out into the living room in her bare feet, yawning and scratching her sore tummy.

"Lilly-girl, I'm sorry to bug you at this hour," Bob Stookey says when Lilly finally pulls the front door open. Dressed in a wife-beater and paint-spattered work pants, the older man is breathless. His grizzled face blazes with excitement. "I think when you see what I got to show you, you'll understand."

Lilly yawns again. "Can you give me a hint?"

"Okay . . . hint. It'll change the way we live our life here in Woodbury."

She looks at him. "Is that all?"

"Okay, hardy-har-har. C'mon, get your shoes and grab a flashlight."

They cross the silent town square, the darkness and chill of the predawn hours at their deepest, the sky moonless, the air as stagnant as that of a tomb. Only their footsteps can be heard echoing in the stillness.

"Not too many people been in here lately," Bob comments as he climbs the stone steps of a small two-story brick edifice. "Guess folks are more interested in survival than enriching themselves." They pause at the entrance. Bob points at the shattered windowpane in the door. "Somebody broke in and ransacked the place not too long ago but probably didn't find much use for old encyclopedias and broken-down mimeograph machines."

The door squeaks open, engulfing Lilly in a memory scent as strong as antique potpourris: steam heat and bookbinding glue; musty pages and old floor wax. She follows the beam of Bob's flashlight across the littered lobby, pausing to take in the shadowy forms of bookshelves, file drawers, library carrels, and empty coatracks where grade-school children once hung their rain slickers on field trips to research the national flower of Nicaragua.

"Watch your step, Lilly-girl," Bob says, sweeping the beam of light across a heap of overturned chairs and spilled books, their ancient spines broken open like the remains of dead birds on the floor. "It's just down this aisle."

It takes some maneuvering—they have to weave through a junk heap of fallen shelves, scattered books, and broken glass—but Lilly finally sees Bob approaching a reference table arrayed with large documents illuminated by a pool of yellow kerosene lantern light.

"What the hell is all this?" she wants to know, looking over Bob's shoulder as he stands over the table, opening a huge leather-bound register of some kind. The book is the size of a car door.

"Meriwether County survey maps, historic registries, property line plats, and such." Bob turns the massive pages of the register to the place he's bookmarked, sending puffs of dust through the cone of kerosene light. "First thing you need to know: The You-Save-It pharmacy? Little place over on Folk Avenue? Where you found that pregnancy test kit way back when? You have any idea what that property once was?"

"Bob, it's late, I'm freezing . . . just tell me, cut to the chase already."

"Do the words *Underground Railroad* ring any bells?" He points to an arrangement of onionskin pages on which his tracings are scrawled. Lilly notices chains, bones, human skulls, and what looks like a femur with a thick band around it. Bob nods at the sketches. "I made these tracings down there the other day, and I'll put money on the fact that these are fossilized remains of runaway slaves. Here, look at this." He turns to the register and runs his finger down a column of historic places. His grimy fingernail stops on the last entry:

1412 Folk Avenue, Woodbury, Georgia 30293
Former Site of the South Trunk Museum
Underground Railroad Safe House

Lilly studies the entry. "Okay, so that's good to know, but how the hell does this affect—?"

"Hold your horses." He closes the register and pulls a faded parchmentlike plat survey into the light and carefully unfolds it until it practically covers the entire table. "Lemme show you something else." He runs his finger along a series of lines—some of them solid, some dotted—crisscrossing property lines from here to the border of Alabama. "You see them squiggly lines?"

With an exasperated roll of her eyes Lilly says, "Yes, Bob, I see the squiggly lines."

"You know what them dotted ones are?"

She starts to give him another snarky, impatient answer but stops herself. She feels a tingling sensation along the back of her scalp as she realizes what she's looking at. "Holy fuck," she mutters, staring at the survey. "Those are the tunnels."

"Bingo," he says with a nod. "In them days, some of the routes were aboveground, of course, but some of them were actually underground."

"Truth in advertising," Lilly murmurs, gaping at all the dotted lines fanning out across the state like a Medusa tangle of braids. She stares at one of the longer serpentine lines. "Looks like some of them go on for miles and miles."

"Yup."

She looks at him. "I know that look," she says, grinning at him.

"What look?"

"Like you swallowed a canary."

Bob smiles, closing the massive register with a thump, sending a faint dust cloud through the dim light of the lantern. He shrugs. "Okay, look at this." He turns the parchment at an angle and points at a tiny X with a circle around it. "You see that? I'm thinking that's a point of egress."

"An escape hatch?"

"Exactly." Bob stares at the survey. "I know it's a little early to un-cork the champagne bottle, but by God it looks as though we could use some of these tunnels."

"For what?"

"Just think about it for a second." His old hound dog eyes smolder with embers of excitement. In this light, his face looks positively spectral, the deep creases and lines accentuating his enthusiasm. Lilly has never seen him like this. Even when Megan Lafferty was alive, and old Bob was harboring the secret crush of his life, traips-ing around town like a lovelorn teenager, he didn't look like this. The potential of this discovery has taken years off him. "We can move back and forth, travel for miles without risking exposure—without ever setting foot aboveground until we get to where we're going."

"I thought you said there were walkers down there, like the one that got Hap."

"A few, yeah, but hell, we can clear them out, maybe reinforce some of the tunnel walls and whatnot. You ask me, this is definitely worth the effort."

Lilly thinks about it for a moment, chewing a fingernail. "What would you need—manpower-wise, equipment-wise?"

Bob purses his lips. "I'm thinking maybe two or three other men, and if I could figure out a way to get power down there without hav-ing to run a three-mile-long extension cord or asphyxiating us with carbon monoxide from the generators . . . it would make life a hell of a lot easier."

Lilly sighs. "Extension cords and generators we got, it's the goddamn fuel issue that's killing us."

Bob runs fingers through his dark, greasy hair. "Walmart filling station is pretty much S-O-L . . . and them wrecks along Eighty-five and Eighteen are picked clean."

"What about the loading dock at Ingles Market?

"Ran dry ages ago."

"What about the farm implements at Deforest? Don't they keep those gassed up?"

"We'll check it again, I ain't sure, maybe out back there's a few that we haven't sucked dry."

"There's gotta be a source we haven't tapped."

Bob looks across the ancient document on the table, his gaze playing over the network of tunnels. "Gotta move farther outside the neighborhood."

Lilly gazes beyond the shadows of the overturned bookshelves. "Still got those crates of cooking oil in the warehouse."

"Yeah, great . . . if you want to make a slew of hush puppies for the Friday night fish fry, you're in business."

"What about biodiesel, though—?"

"What about it?"

"Don't you make that shit from cooking oils?"

Bob lets out a ragged sigh. "Yeah, if you got the recipe, the know-how."

Lilly looks around the ransacked library. "I'll wager we can research it right here."

Bob gives her a grin. "Not a bad idea, Lilly. You're getting this leadership thing down."

She lets out a grunt. "I don't know about that."

Bob gazes at the document. "Something tells me the answer to a lot of this stuff is right in front of our noses." He looks at Lilly. "Sooner I get back down there, the sooner we figure out where this thing's gonna take us."

After a long beat of silence, Lilly says, "Just make sure you know how many walkers you're dealing with when you go spelunking down there again."

Bob doesn't offer any response, only a quick, furtive glance back at the survey map.

The next day dawns muggy and overcast, the late spring weather starting to give way to the oppressive heat of a Georgia summer. By seven o'clock the mercury has already reached seventy-five degrees, and the woods and hollows to the east of town buzz with insects. Soon the drone of crickets, frogs, sparrows, and thrashers rises to a dull roar.

The ambient noise is so all-consuming that the lone figure stumbling through the deep woods along Riggins Ferry Road thinks he's hearing things.

He bangs into trees, his balance thrown off by exhaustion, terror, and starvation. He splashes through swampy patches and nearly stumbles, at one point falling to his knees, nearly going face-first in the mire. But he gets back up. He keeps moving. At all costs, he keeps moving. Sunburned, dehydrated, in the early stages of shock, Reese Lee Hawthorne hears voices in the din of the woodland fauna around him, the sounds of preachers hollering fire-and-brimstone sermons, the low rumble of the earth rending apart.

When he reaches the clearing adjacent to Riggins Ferry and sees the string of abandoned cars along the scorched asphalt two-lane, the wreckage piled up and stretching as far as the eye can see—a frozen, eternal traffic jam—he nearly collapses, but somehow, moving on sheer adrenaline now, he keeps staggering forward.

In the distance he sees the signs of a town. In his bleary vision, the objects materializing like those of a dream, he sees the outskirts of a once tidy little farming community: the landscaped parkways and boulevards now overgrown with weeds, littered with unidentifiable detritus and human remains, concertina wire tangled around some of the street signs—a typical postplague landscape. A few scattered walkers roam the city limits like the forgotten homeless, another common sight outside survivor settlements. Like ubiquitous moths drawn to the flames of human life, a certain number of walkers can always be found in close proximity to people.

Reese sees the wall. About three hundred yards away now, the center of the town tucked behind it, the scarred planking of a giant barricade stretches for about a block and a half in either direction. There's an opening at the southeast corner, blocked by a grime-covered semi-cab. Some of the planks look stained with soot, as though a fire raged through this area not long ago. Some of the rooftops behind the wall look scorched and fire damaged. Even the weed-whiskered roads and vacant lots look burned.

Reese hears the sudden growl of a walker off his right flank.

Reaching for his .38—he has only one bullet left in the chamber—he loses his balance again and falls. He lands hard on his left shoulder, the pain shooting down his arm and ribs. The sudden agony takes his breath away as he rolls onto his back and two-hands the gun. The walker approaches—a large female, obese and feminine in life, with a lopsided bouffant and a tattered sundress—her mouth a blackened divot in her skull. Reese waits until she's within point-blank range and then fires at her scalp, blowing a hole in her head the size of a small saucer.

The hole gushes black brain matter and murky fluids with the force of a fountain, as the fat woman collapses into the weeds.

Reese struggles to his feet—his last bullet gone, his head spinning from pain and fear—and he makes one last-ditch effort to outrun the other walkers drawn by the noise, now coming toward him from all sides. He charges across the railroad tracks, past the train sheds, and across the vacant lot outside Woodbury's main drag. He gets close enough to the wall to see a single individual—a middle-aged man—with some kind of military-grade rifle.

"WHOA, KEMOSABE!" The sound of a second man calling out to Reese echoes across the lots. "THAT'S FAR ENOUGH!"

Reese falls to his knees on the edge of Folk Avenue, a hundred yards east of the very same derelict drugstore where Lilly found her pregnancy test kit last month, the same property under which Bob and his team now creep through the subterranean darkness. "P-please," Reese huffs and puffs, gasping for breath on his hands and knees in the dirt. "P-please l-let me in, I n-need—"

"ARE YOU ALONE?"

In the rising sun, the face of David Stern becomes visible peering over the top of a cherry picker abutted against the wall, his wrinkled visage gray and drawn in the harsh light. But even amid the tension now reverberating between the two men, there's a certain gentle quality to David's manner, apparent in his baggy eyes and rich baritone, even at this distance. Reese Lee Hawthorne now gasps for breath on the ground, sensing the other walkers closing in on him. He has only a minute or two to convince this older gentleman with the rifle that he means no harm. "Yes, sir!" Reese calls out. "I'm all alone and n-need help . . . not just for me but for my family, too!"

A tense beat of silence passes as David lowers his weapon.

Thousands of feet down the main conduit, at least a mile and a half of tunnel behind them, the stagnant air getting exceedingly cold and clammy and malodorous, the four men encounter their first cave-in.

"Aw, shit, look at this," Bob says to the others, pausing to wipe his sweaty brow with a snotty bandanna. His flashlight illuminates the wall of dirt about fifty yards away, drifted against the tunnel wall, blocking their path.

They join each other in the center of the tunnel, their torch beams sweeping the gritty darkness, the odor of decay as strong as the inside of a dirty sock. Ben pushes his Caterpillar cap back on his balding, sweat-damp scalp and narrows his pouchy eyes as he takes in the obstruction. "Looks like the roof of the tunnel caved in."

"Fuck . . . I thought we had this thing licked," Speed complains with a crestfallen tone in his voice. The first mile of their combination reconnaissance and cleanup mission had gone off without a hitch—no walkers in sight, the tunnel clear and dry, and only a few remnants of campfires and rest stops here and there from a century and a half earlier. Each man had brought along a gunnysack filled with tools—shovel, pickax, crowbar, hammer, pruning sheers, nails, spare two-by-fours, batteries, brushes, and white paint for leaving geographical marks and notes.

"Miners call that a bounce," Matthew comments absently, glancing down at his pedometer. He found the device in the drugstore and decided to keep it clipped to his belt in order to help them keep track of not only how far they were penetrating the tunnel but also, in conjunction with a compass, their location up top. "Sometimes a small tremor will do it, something that goes undetected aboveground." Matthew comes from Blue Ridge, Kentucky—coal country—his daddy a lifelong miner, as well as his daddy's daddy. Which is probably what made him so antsy to get the hell out of Blue Ridge. His tradesman's license was his ticket out. The real estate bubble in Lexington gave him enough work as a tuck pointer and brick man to start a pretty decent life before the bubble burst. "Might be all she wrote," he mutters, staring at the readout on the pedometer, "especially if the tunnel beyond it has caved."

Bob starts toward the cave-in. "Matt, do me a favor and give me an exact footage count over here." Bob approaches the sloping wall of earth that rises up to the ancient stalactites of limestone and roots hanging from the ceiling. He kneels by the obstruction.

Matthew joins him, pulling out the pedometer and reading the display. "Looks like . . . exactly eight thousand two hundred and eleven feet."

Bob gazes up at the ceiling of roots. Then he takes a closer look at the earthen obstruction. He reaches out and feels the wall of loose earth. It's granular and dry, some of the tiny crumbs of earth scuttling down the slope when Bob takes his hand away. "I'm no expert, like Mr. Hennesey here," Bob says, "but this looks recent to me." He pulls a folded map from his pocket as the other two men join them. He looks up at the ceiling again. "Eighty-two hundred and eleven feet is what?" He spreads the map out on the hard-packed earth of the tunnel floor. "If I'm not mistaken, that's over a mile and a half?"

"About a mile and three-quarters due east of town," Ben surmises.

"Shine that light down here, Ben." With a grimy thumbnail, Bob traces the route. "As the crow flies . . . we should be right under Elkins Creek, maybe even all the way to Dripping Rock Road."

"How far you think this thing goes?" Speed chimes in.

Ben lets out an incredulous grunt. "Sure as hell doesn't go all the way to Canada."

"It does make sense that they would head east," Matthew surmises. "The slaves, I'm talking about."

"East to the border states, maybe, Maryland, D.C." Bob studies the map. "My guess is, this hooks up with another—"

A noise cuts him off, a slight tremble in the wall, a trickle of loose earth rolling down. Each man goes for his weapon. Muzzles snap up, front sights on the wall. Bob has a .357 Magnum with a four-inch barrel, which he has instinctively drawn from a short holster.

"Get away from the wall, Bob," Ben warns suddenly, backing off, his Bushmaster rifle raised and ready to rock and roll.

Bob folds up the map with one hand, holding the revolver with the other, but he doesn't see the dirt wall shuddering down by his leg until it's too late.

The men hear the muffled shuffling noise before they see the object protruding from the earth. Bob feels pressure on his leg, looks down, and sees the blackened hand that has just burst through the dirt wall and latched onto his pant leg like a grappling hook.

"FUCK!" Bob jerks with an involuntary start, pulling his leg back.

The walker forces its way through the wall, a large male with mossy hair dangling down across its sunken, filth-encrusted face. The remnants of an orange construction worker's vest still cling to its ragged body. The thing opens its mouth to expose a row of wormy gray teeth, and it snaps cobralike at Bob's leg.

"Duck down, Bob—NOW!" Ben's voice gets Bob moving, and Bob hits the deck right as the first controlled burst flares hot and bright out of Ben's AR-15. Four blasts connect with the top of the thing's skull.

The former construction worker instantly collapses as the top of its head shatters and its skull fountains black fluids all over Bob's lower half. It feels like greasy bile soaking his pants. "Goddamn it," Bob complains as he scoots back on his ass, fumbling for his gun. "Fucking piece of shit puss-bag cocksucker!"

"There's more of 'em!" Speed indicates the upper part of the dirt wall. "Look!"

Like contorted plants sprouting in time lapse, more arms burst through the dirt. Some lanky and long, others emaciated and withered, they push their way through the loose earth and claw at the air. Fingers blackened from decay, some of the hands clench open and shut with such puppetlike vigor they remind Bob for a single crazy instant of Venus flytraps. The men raise their weapons, cocking mechanisms snapping back, flashlight beams sweeping up, Bob taking aim from a sitting position.

Matthew lets out a bellowing cry: "BLOW THEM FUCKERS AWAY!"

For several moments, the fusillade fills the tunnel with tremendous light and noise as innumerable rounds are emptied into the wall. Ricochets spark off rocks, ping off stalactites, and penetrate calcium deposits, the cordite smoke gathering, the booming reports making ears ring, the clatter echoing down the length of the passageway. Soon, Bob can't hear a fucking thing, and he can barely see through the haze as the thunderous barrage continues unabated, strafing the wall of earth, until the volley of gunfire causes a small avalanche, tearing a giant doorway in the dirt wall, revealing the half dozen walkers on the other side now popping like blood-filled balloons. Heads erupt and gush, bodies jitterbugging, blood-mist pulsing and flinging off into space. After another excruciating moment, the giant maw in the dirt obstruction reveals that all of the half dozen or so walkers have folded to the ground, and the tunnel beyond the wall is now all clear and ringing with the echoes of high-powered gunfire. Beyond the carnage, which is now strewn across the hard pack, glistening in the gloom and faintly steaming, the tunnel extends into the darkness for an undetermined distance before it curves off to the right.

"HOLD YOUR FIRE!" Bob screams at the others, his ears ringing so severely he can hardly hear his own voice. Another noise crackles nearby, tugging at his attention, as the last blast roars out of Matthew's AK-47, ricocheting with an enormous ping off the tunnel wall on the other side of the gaping cavity in the dirt.

"GODDAMN IT, STOP FUCKING SHOOTING!" Bob struggles to his feet. He hears a tinny voice crackling out of his radio. He reaches for the walkie-talkie clipped to his belt and fumbles for the volume knob. He turns it up and hears Gloria Pyne's voice: *"Bob . . . you copy, Bob? Can you hear me? Hello, Bob!"*

Bob thumbs the button: "Gloria? It's Bob, go ahead."

"Bob, we got a situation here, you might want to come on back."

Bob looks at the others. Matthew ejects a spent magazine, the clip bouncing off the earth floor. Ben and Speed stare at him, waiting. Bob presses the switch: "Negative copy on that, Glo . . . say again."

Through the crackle of static: *"I said we got a bit of a situation brewing here, and Lilly wanted me to round you guys up and get you back here."*

Bob blinks, thumbs the button: "What's going on, Gloria?"

Through the speaker: *"I think it's better you just come back and check it out."*

Bob sighs. "Can't Lilly handle this herself? We're making progress down here."

"I don't know, Bob. I just work here."

"Can you put Lilly on?"

"Bob, come on. She told me to get you back, now get your fat, hairy ass back here!"

The click echoes down the tunnel as the other three men stare at Bob.

TEN

In the makeshift infirmary under the racetrack, the young man sits shirtless on the edge of a gurney, hugging himself with his spindly arms, his midsection wrapped with thick gauze bandages where he had fallen and broken two ribs. His skin is mottled with the abrasions and scars of exposure. His ferretlike face stays downturned as he breathlessly speaks. "Never seen a herd like the one came at us that night, never seen that many in one place. Lost five of our people that night. Like I said, it was bad . . . real bad. Got pinned down in a place called Carlinville, about ten, fifteen miles from here."

The overhead lights flicker and buzz. Lilly stands across the room, listening intently with a paper cup of coffee going cold in her hand. The air smells of metallic chemicals, blood and ammonia. Lilly's scalp prickles as she puts the puzzle pieces together in her mind. "Can I ask when this was, Reese? Can you remember how many days ago this was?"

The young man swallows hard and blinks as he tries to calculate the passage of time. "Guess it was . . . what? Maybe a week ago now?" He looks at Lilly with bloodshot eyes and a trembling jaw. "I kind of lost track of time out there, to tell ya the truth. Still sortin' things out."

"It's okay . . . can't say I blame you." Lilly glances across the room at the others now listening closely to the young man's story. Bob stands near the steel sink basin, his arms crossed judiciously across his chest, a stethoscope around his neck. Barbara and David Stern sit side by side on the edge of a desk. Matthew, Ben, Gloria, and Calvin stand on the other side of the room near the equipment hutch, each of them silently chewing on every word.

When the young man arrived a couple of hours ago, he was so dehydrated and malnourished he could barely move or speak. With Bob off in the tunnels, Gloria and Barbara provided the best emergency medical care they could muster under the circumstances. They gave Reese electrolytes, hooked him to a glucose drip, dressed his wounds, and gave him water and instant soup in small doses until he seemed stable enough to tell his story. When he got to the part about his group being pinned down in Carlinville by the mysterious horde, and then revealed why he risked his life to come all this way alone with meager supplies and no idea how to navigate the wild, Lilly decided to call in the committee.

Lilly looks at Bob as she says, "I might be wrong about this, but I'm thinking what we're dealing with here is a part of the superherd."

Bob gives her a nod. "The one that formed outside the prison."

The young man on the gurney looks up as though awakening from a dream. "Superherd?"

Lilly looks back at Reese. "I think we dealt with a part of this same herd. Saw it forming not far from here a week ago."

Ben interjects, "Goddamn herds are like amoebas—growing, separating, splitting off into multiple herds. Can't get a goddamn break with these things. Getting worse every day."

"I don't know nothing about that," the young man utters, his glazed stare riveted to Lilly now, the terror behind his eyes burning brightly. "But I do know that herd that pinned us down is still there, trust me. Once they surrounded Carlinville, they just stayed there . . . like, like, like . . . like bees swarming a hive."

"How do you know the herd's still there, though?" Gloria asks from the other side of the infirmary. The room is lit by halogen lamps on a single generator, and they flicker every few moments, giving the space a jittery quality. "Were you in contact with your people? In the woods, I mean? By radio or whatever?"

The young man shakes his head. "No . . . I just . . ." He looks up. "I was in contact with God."

This causes almost everybody in the room to simultaneously look at the floor. The newcomer has been saying things like this every few minutes, and it's getting a little awkward. Nobody has a problem with God around here—a little good-natured Bible thumping or Scripture quoting is part of the fabric of plague life—but right now, Lilly needs to focus on the practical, stay on-message, keep to the facts. Especially in light of what the young man is asking of them. She parses her words now. "This group you're with, Reese," she says. "It's a church group?"

Reese Lee Hawthorne takes a deep breath. "Yes, ma'am . . . but we really don't have no bricks-and-mortar church to speak of. Our church is pretty much just us and Reverend Jeremiah and the open road." He looks down and swallows thickly again. "Before the Turn, we used to have a big old bus, carried our tent on the roof . . . Brother Jeremiah would do revival meetings up and down the eastern seaboard . . . baptisms and such." His face twitches with grief, the horror causing tics at the corners of his mouth. His eyes well up. "That's all gone now, though . . . all gone." He looks at Lilly, wipes his eyes. "Satan's army of walkers took it from us."

A beat of silence presses down. Lilly watches the young man. "How many of you are there?"

He looks at her. "In Carlinville right now? Counting me? There's fourteen of us."

Lilly licks her lips and measures her words. "This Reverend Jeremiah? Is he . . . pinned down in Carlinville with the others?"

Reese nods. "Yes, ma'am." Another flinch, another twinge of agonizing memory. "He saved our lives that night the river turned red."

Lilly looks at Bob, and Bob gives her a look, and the others exchange a series of uneasy glances. Lilly turns back to the young man. "You don't have to tell us what happened, Reese, if it's too painful for you."

The young man gets a dreamy look in his eyes, his expression going slack as though suddenly plunged under hypnosis. "Jeremiah always says the best way to deal with this plague is just to keep on going . . . keep on preaching and saving souls . . . It's the best way to fight the devil." Reese gets very still, gaping at the far corner of the room, as though some far-flung horror is kindling there in the shadows. "I remember it was hot that night . . . so hot and humid you had to work just to take a breath. Chattahoochee was like bathwater. We had our bus parked just north of Vinings . . . and we set up the tent about a quarter mile north along the river." He pauses and with great effort swallows a mouthful of agony. "We started with some local men. Brother Jeremiah would take them down to the water, a part of the river that was maybe four, five feet deep . . . pretty deep for a baptism but that's how the reverend likes to do it . . . like John the Baptist . . . total immersion, man." Another pause. "He didn't see them things moving around under the surface . . . they was upriver a ways, in the deeper part of the water." He bows his head again as though his cranium now weighs a thousand tons. His voice is reduced to a whisper. "He didn't see them things until it was too late."

Lilly waits a respectful moment before licking her lips and saying, "It's okay, Reese, you don't have to—"

"He took a group of women down next . . . there was maybe five or six of 'em . . . all ages, a couple teenagers, an older woman, a few mothers." Silence. "He was baptizing them one at a time, and they was singing 'The Old Rugged Cross' . . . and they was praisin' and singin' and fillin' up with the spirit." Silence. " 'Heavenly Father, in your love you have called us . . . to know you . . . to trust you . . . to bind our life with yours.' " Silence. "And Jeremiah would take each gal in his strong arms like he was dancin' with her . . . and he would dip her backward into the warm waters . . . *splash, splash.*" Silence. "And he would say, 'Sister Jones . . . may God pour out his blessings upon your life today . . . so that you may walk in His abundance.' " Silence. "Then he'd dunk her in . . . *splash* . . . and . . . and . . ." Silence. "And then he'd take the next gal, and do the same thing . . . *splash.*" Silence. "It was the third or fourth woman." Silence. "I think it was the fourth." Silence. "When . . . all of a sudden . . . the reverend dipped her in the water . . . and . . . and . . ."

"Okay, Reese. That's enough." Lilly walks over to the young man, puts her hand on his shoulder. He jumps. "It's okay, we get it."

The young man looks at Lilly with an expression on his face that will likely live in Lilly's nightmares from this moment on. "She didn't have no head." His face tightens, the tears coming. "The blood . . . it was . . . it was everywhere . . . Them things had been under the deep end moving around like sharks . . . and they came up from the deep . . . and there were screams . . . and Brother Jeremiah dropped the woman's body and he tried to fight back with his silver cross . . .

but now the water was moving like crazy with them things and the river was turning beet red . . . and . . . and . . . I tried to dive in and help . . . and then more women were getting pulled under . . . and the water was turning the darkest shade of red you ever saw."

Silence.

Not a single person in that infirmary moves or speaks or makes eye contact with the young man.

Reese drops his head and tears track down his face, his voice crumbling. "Reverend Jeremiah . . . he got most of them things with his big sterling cross . . . got many of us out of that water in one piece . . . He saved my ass, I'll tell you that . . . but that river turned the deepest shade of red . . . The water . . . I never seen anything like that . . . so red . . . deep, deep red . . . like in the Bible at the End Days."

Silence.

Lilly looks down at the floor, figuring she might as well let him get it all out.

"Them poor women that got ate that night . . . they was praying as they went down . . . I heard 'em praying . . . them things devouring them . . . the river running red . . . I heard their voices under the screaming . . . 'The Lord is my shepherd . . . He makes me to lie down in green pastures . . . He leads me beside quiet waters . . . He refreshes my soul.'" Silence. Snuffling. Silent tears. "'Even though I walk through the darkest valley . . . I will . . . I will fear no evil.'" Silence. Shoulders slumping now, head lolled forward as though about to pass out. "And then . . . and then . . ." Silence. Broken sobbing. "We s-saw them coming out of the water . . . like the centurions . . . ragged, bloated . . . faces the color of fish bellies . . . shark eyes . . . they were coming for *us* . . . we were backing away toward the bus . . . Satan sent them after us . . . and we . . . we . . . got out of there . . . We left our sisters and we got out of there and . . . and . . . oh . . . *ohhhhhhnnnnngghh!*"

The young man finally lets the convulsions of grief and horror rock through him until he can no longer speak. He slips off the edge of the gurney. Lilly lunges toward him, and he falls into her arms and weeps. He weeps and weeps into her midsection as she holds him in an awkward embrace for a few agonizing moments.

She turns and starts to say something to Bob when she notices that Bob is already fumbling with a sterile needle and small vial of sedative across the room. He preps the hypo while the others watch in stunned silence. Lilly gives a nod, and Bob comes over and administers the drug.

The young man named Reese Lee Hawthorne gazes up at Lilly once before sliding out of her arms and collapsing to the floor in a state of semiconsciousness.

Bob calls out over his shoulder, "Ben! Matthew! Gimme a hand here!"

They converge on the body of the young newcomer, lift him off the floor, and carry him across the room to a padded gurney pushed against the wall. They gently set him down on the bed, cover him with a sheet, and watch his eyes go to half-mast . . . and then close. For a moment, nobody says anything. The group huddles around the bed, watching the young man's chest softly rising and falling.

At last, Lilly turns and fixes her gaze on Barbara Stern. "Stay with him, Barbara, watch for any changes." She looks at the others. "The rest of you, let's talk outside in the corridor."

Lilly has never believed in ghosts. As a little girl, she enjoyed her father's "spook stories," many of them told on the porch of their house in Marietta, usually on autumn nights with the scent of woodsmoke and burning leaves on the breeze. Everett Caul would tell tales of vanishing hitchhikers and disappearing cabinets and mysterious seagoing vessels doomed to eternally circle the ocean, and Lilly would lap it all up. She also adored the delicious shudders she would get when reading the twist ending of a Shirley Jackson novel, or watching the denouement of an *X-Files* show, or devouring books from the school library such as *Strange but True Tales of the Supernatural*. But she never truly believed in such a thing as a haunting. Until now.

With the Governor a mere memory, dead and gone now for several weeks, the subterranean labyrinth beneath the racetrack arena still vibrates with his presence, as haunted as any drafty Victorian mansion. His brutal interrogations in the cinder-block-lined service bays still echo in Lilly's midbrain, and the smell down here—that gritty, chalky, moldy odor of ancient axle grease and old rubber—

still evokes the dark machinations of a madman. Even the faint stench of walkers, as pungent as the insides of a discarded garbage can, still emanates from the cells in which they were kept hungry and at the ready for the gladiatorial games. Lilly finds all this swirling through the back of her consciousness as she tries to focus on the challenges at hand, and the drawn, nervous faces of her peers gathered around her . . . waiting.

"Okay, obviously this kid is messed up from his time alone in the sticks." Lilly rubs her eyes, leaning against the wall outside the infirmary, feeling the feverish gazes of the six other committee members. "I'm thinking we wait until he's healed up before we make any moves."

Ben Buchholz speaks up, his droopy eyes glittering with tension. "So this means we're seriously considering a rescue mission here?"

"What are you saying, Ben?" David Stern chimes in. "You don't want to go after these people? You just want to let them die on the vine?"

"I didn't say that." Ben flashes a glowering look at David. "All I'm saying is, we're really going out on a limb if we try and find these people."

"I have to agree with Ben." Gloria Pyne looks at Lilly. "We have no idea how much of this herd is still out there—it could be replenishing itself, growing again—and we just don't have the people to spare here."

"Everything we do comes with a calculated risk," Lilly counters. "We're talking about fourteen people here, we're kind of obligated to try. Right? I mean, unless I'm mistaken, these people would most likely do the same for us."

"I'm sorry, Lilly." Matthew Hennesey has a sheepish look on his face. "I gotta go with Ben and Glo on this one. How do you know these people would do the same for us? I mean, really. I believe in the goodness of humanity as much as the next guy, but come on. For all you know, these people are fucking assholes."

"Thank you." Ben gives a satisfied nod to Matthew. "That's exactly what I was thinking." He looks at David. "Fucking preachers—nine out of ten of them are fucking pedophiles."

"Are you serious?" David stares Ben down, and the corridor seems to constrict in the slipstream of their anger. "That's the reason you don't want to go after them? On moral grounds?"

Ben gives a shrug. "You can spin it any way you want."

"You sure it's not a more personal reason? Self-preservation, maybe?"

"Why don't you just say it?" Ben takes a provocative step toward David. "Why don't you just say what you're thinking—that I'm a chickenshit coward, maybe?"

"Whoa, gentlemen—" Lilly starts to get between them, but David moves to within inches of Ben.

"I didn't say you were chickenshit, Ben. Paranoid, maybe. Surly, perhaps."

"Get away from me." Ben shoves the older man back a few inches. "Before I wipe that smug smile off your face."

"Hey!" Lilly raises her voice, pushing Ben back. "Back it down, both of you!"

The two men fix their gazes on each other as Lilly turns to address everyone in the corridor.

"We've been down this road before—bickering and quarreling over every decision. I won't have it!" She pauses for emphasis. "Here's a news bulletin for you: Our lives are on the line here. You want to turn this town into the Wild West, you keep on doing this macho sixth-grade playground bullshit! Oh, and by the way, you can find somebody else to run things, because I'm about this far from giving fucking notice!" Another pause. She has everybody's attention now. She looks at every face as she softens slightly, her voice dropping a register. "All I'm asking you to do is take a deep breath, step back, and look at this logically. What we have here is a risk-reward situation. Yes, it does involve crossing dangerous territory, putting ourselves out there for these people, but you gotta calculate the rewards. We need more people to survive. I'm not sure we can keep this town safe with only twenty-five, thirty people. We barely have enough people for three shifts on the wall each day. We need strong backs, sharp eyes, people who are willing to pitch in. I don't know from church groups—I'm an agnostic—but I do know these people are basically not going to survive if we don't go get them. So I need everybody to be together on this."

Ben stares at the floor. "That's a great speech, Lilly, but you can go without me."

Lilly's chest tightens with anger, her fists clenching. "You got a short memory, Ben. If I'm not mistaken it was only ten days ago—"

"Lilly, I'm sorry," Gloria interrupts in a low voice, a voice tempered with shame. She looks at Lilly with wet eyes. "I appreciate all you done for us. Really, I do. Stepping up and all. But I just ain't got it in me to put my ass on the line for these people."

Lilly can hardly breathe, the fury rising up her gorge and strangling her. "Really? Seriously? That's your legacy? That's how you honor the memory of people like Austin Ballard? Austin put his ass on the line for *you*, Gloria. And *you*, Ben. And you, Matthew! He lost his life for his trouble!" Lilly swallows her rage, a red filter drawing down over her eyesight, her throat going dry. "Go ahead! Stay behind the wall! Stay safe! Tell yourselves you're safe behind these walls! But you're *not*! You're not! Because we are all part of the same war! It's a war with ourselves! And if you hide from it, you will die! YOU WILL DIE!"

All at once Lilly realizes she is out of breath, and the others are all looking down at the floor like children who have been sent to bed without dinner, and a low, gravelly voice has said something behind her and Lilly has only partially heard it in one ear. She sees Bob Stookey leaning against the door to the infirmary. He's been there all along, calmly listening to the shouting match, and now he's finally said something that Lilly has only half heard. "What was that, Bob?"

Bob looks at her, looks at the others. "I said, what if I could seriously cut down the risk involved here?"

This is met with stone silence, the strange statement hanging in the air.

Lilly looks at him. "Okay, I'll bite. What the hell are you talking about?"

Bob's deep-set eyes, nestled in pockets of wrinkles, almost twinkle as he begins to explain.

The rest of the day passes without incident or altercation. The children play kickball in the square while most of the adults help Lilly till the arena infield. Lilly has drawn up plans for rows of vegetables as well as sturdy crops like soybeans and corn from which both food and energy sources can be harvested. She has big plans for the future of Woodbury in terms of renewables and has already found diagrams in the library for homemade solar cells and heaters.

That afternoon, in the infirmary under the racetrack, Bob nurses the young man from the church group back to health with forced fluids, vitamin B_{12} injections, and old war stories from the Middle East. The newcomer takes to Bob, which is ironic, since Bob has never been too fond of people with evangelical tendencies. But Bob is a born medic—a good soldier first and foremost—and he treats patients with equal-opportunity care.

By dusk that night, this odd couple has become inseparable. Bob shows Reese around town and even gives him a peek at the tunnels. Walking with a pronounced limp, and still groggy from exposure and malnourishment, Reese is eager to rescue his brethren, but Bob tells him that he'll have to heal up a little more before accompanying the rescue team to Carlinville. The young man wants to know when they can leave, and Bob guesses it won't be until the end of the week, in three or four days, and the kid should rest until then, get his strength back, prepare himself for the long journey. This seems to satisfy Reese, for the time being, at least.

That night, the sun sets behind the jagged spires of ancient live oaks to the west along Elkins Creek, turning the daylight amber and filling the air with a haze of cottonwood fluff in the lengthening shadows.

Inside the arena, most of the workers have departed, leaving behind only two souls, who now crouch together in the dying light, planting the first of the zucchini seeds. The task is a simple one, but not without symbolic meaning. Lilly is well aware of this fact as she kneels on makeshift kneepads with a small trowel, notching out a narrow trough in the black Georgia clay.

Calvin hunkers next to her with a handful of small gray seeds.

He drops them one at a time, in a neat little row, as Lilly carefully covers them with loose earth, patting lightly. Squash plants have long taproots that enable zucchini to do well in dry climates. The growth cycle is about a month, so the yield is also good throughout the summer. Lilly digs another trough and Calvin drops in more seeds, and they repeat, again and again, until Lilly notices Calvin mumbling under his breath every time he opens another package and drops a handful in the ground.

"What did you say?" Lilly asks him finally, sitting back to wipe the perspiration from her brow.

"Excuse me?" Calvin looks at her for a moment as though she's lost her mind.

"You've been mumbling something every time we plant more seeds."

He chuckles. "Oh, sorry. You got me. Little prayer for the harvest. I was praying."

Lilly loves this. She gives him a sidelong glance. "You sure it's a good idea to bother the Almighty for something this . . . small?"

"It's a habit I picked up from my grandpa. Old codger was a to-bacco farmer down in Calhoun County, used to grow watermelons in his backyard the size of Winnebagos. Always told people he had a secret formula. When I was twelve he finally took me out back and gave me my first plug of Red Man tobacco and showed me the se-cret formula."

"He prayed when he planted."

Calvin nods. "He said a Hail Mary over every row he planted— even though he was a lifelong Baptist. My grandma Rosie used to give him guff about it."

"Hail Mary . . . seriously?"

"Gramps always said there was something about the Italians he knew up to Jasper, had a vineyard up there, and they was always beat-ing the pants off Gramps at the Georgia State Fair with their prize tomatoes." Calvin shrugs. "Started hearing Gramps mumbling all the time, 'Hail Mary, full of grace, the Lord is with thee, blessed art thou among women, and blessed is the fruit of thy farm . . . *watermelons.*' "

Lilly laughs, and it feels spectacular, it feels liberating.

"He always said it like that," Calvin marvels with a chuckle, "like it was some kind of magical incantation . . . *watermelons . . . watermel-ons!* I thought he was so cool. When I was a kid, I wanted to be just like him. He always had a plug of Red Man between his cheek and gum, and of course I had to try it."

"Didn't he give you some that day?"

"Yep."

"Did you like it?"

"Lord, no. I puked my guts out all over the seat of his John Deere tractor."

Lilly chortles. She hasn't laughed like this for what seems an eternity, maybe not since the plague broke out. In the grand scheme of things—in the history of humor—Calvin's little story isn't that funny. But Lilly *needs* to laugh right now.

He looks at his watch. "I better be getting back to the courthouse. Kids are probably eating the sofa cushions right about now."

"I'll walk you home."

They finish up and throw their tools in a nearby wheelbarrow.

The air has cooled significantly from the full-on sun of the afternoon. The breeze smells of lilac and clover and wet hay molding in the fields. On their way back to the courthouse, Lilly and Calvin discuss the young man from the church group and Bob's master plan of using the tunnels to get to Carlinville. Nobody knows how far the main circuit runs—the town is a little over ten miles away—but Bob assures everybody that they can safely clear the passageway and get to their destination via the tunnels.

Lilly can't imagine the tunnel extending that far—nor can she fathom traveling that distance down a filthy, subterranean channel—but Bob claims that the historic surveys have so far been accurate up to three miles in every direction. Apparently the runaway slave culture back in the nineteenth century was bigger and broader in scope than most modern historians had conceived in their wildest extrapolations. And Bob is confident that, with the young newcomer's help, he can get the rescue party close enough to the place where the church group is now under siege. The plan is to then dig up through layers of sediment to the surface, rescue the people, and use the tunnel to get back to Woodbury.

"On paper it makes sense," Lilly says as they cross the deserted town square and approach the courthouse building. "But it seems . . . I don't know . . . like a stretch. I trust Bob. But on the other hand, nobody knows what the hell we're going to find under there . . . or if we're just going to hit a dead end."

They pause at the stone steps leading up to the courthouse door. Calvin turns and touches Lilly's arm. His hand is work scarred, rough on her skin, but also tender. "It's in God's hands, Lilly. You were right. We have to do it. It's the right thing to do."

She looks into his eyes. "Maybe I should say a Hail Mary over it."

"Couldn't hurt." He smiles at her. His hand remains on her arm. "The Good Lord will watch over us."

She touches his cheek. "Thank you." A flutter in her heart, a spark of electricity traveling down her spine. Has he moved closer? She can smell his scent—Old Spice, chewing gum—and she feels a tremendous urge to bury her face in his neck. His eyes are so clear, washed clean by his grief and humility and deep, deep faith. "To be perfectly honest," she whispers to him, "I wish I had your faith."

He leans in closer. His hand moves to her cheek. "You're a good woman, Lilly." He reaches up to his collar and pulls a small crucifix on a chain from around his neck. He carefully opens the clasp and puts it around Lilly's neck. "Here, this has served me well."

She swallows a surge of emotion rising up in her. "Oh, my God, I can't take this," she says, taking a closer look at the tiny gold cross.

"Yes, you can. I just gave it to you." He smiles. "Wear it in good health."

"Thank you . . . thanks."

He touches her hair. "My pleasure."

Has he moved closer still? Lilly can't tell. Her heart is racing. Knowing it's wrong, knowing it's too soon, knowing the town will disapprove, she moves in, her eyes closing.

Their lips come to within a centimeter of each other when a child's scream rings out from the second-floor window above them.

They freeze like animals in the wild confronted with the headlight of an oncoming train.

ELEVEN

Calvin and Lilly slam through the door of the second-floor administrative office and lurch into the room. Quickly scanning the space for any sign of danger, rampaging walkers, or some kind of struggle, they see only a lone little girl standing in the center of the outer office, where all the desks have been shoved against the wall, and the moth-eaten drapes now shroud the boarded window.

"It's Luke," Bethany says when Calvin rushes over to her, kneels, and takes her by the arms.

"Are you okay?"

"I'm fine, Daddy," she says. She wears her footie pajamas and holds a Maurice Sendak storybook, and she yawns as she explains. "Tommy was reading to Luke and Luke fell asleep and had a nightmare."

"He's in here, Dad."

The voice draws Calvin's attention over his shoulder to the door leading into the inner office, which is currently being used as the children's bedroom. Tommy Dupree stands in the doorway in his Falcons T-shirt, jeans, and bare feet, looking sheepish and exhausted. He, too, holds a book of fairy tales. "He fell asleep and started screaming."

Calvin springs to his feet and rushes into the inner room, Lilly right on his heels.

She feels as though she's intruding all of a sudden as she plunges into the cluttered world of the Dupree children—the dog-eared picture books strewn across the floor, the clothes piled in one corner, the candy wrappers, the smell of bubble gum, liniment, and baby powder. Bob had brought back a carton of comic books from the You-Save-It Pharmacy the other day for Tommy Dupree, and now Lilly's feverish gaze lands on the curiously neat and orderly stack of comics on the far windowsill, right next to a coffee can filled with paintbrushes, a drawing tablet, an immaculate eraser, and a perfectly symmetrical row of a wallet, a pocketknife, and keys.

Tommy's little obsessive-compulsive domain—the defense mechanism of a sensitive boy in chaotic times—now seems doubly poignant to Lilly.

"Baby boy . . . baby boy!" Calvin kneels by his youngest child's bedside—a broken-down little futon that Lilly found while digging through the town's warehouse. He gathers the little boy up in muscular, wiry arms, strokes the kid's sweaty, matted brow with gnarled workman's hands. "It's okay . . . Daddy's here."

"I saw Mama!"

The voice that comes out of little Lucas Dupree is barely a squeak—the mewl of an injured kitten—as the child clings to his father with simian force. The child looks deeply and thoroughly spooked. His cherubic face glistens with night sweat, his Thomas the Tank Engine jammies soaked through. "I saw Mama again, Daddy."

Calvin glances across the room at Lilly, who stands next to Tommy. The twelve-year-old keeps staring at the floor, chewing the inside of his cheek. Calvin clears his throat nervously. All at once Lilly gets the idea that this is not the first time this has happened since Meredith Dupree passed, and it's not something the family wants to share with outsiders, and maybe it would be best if Lilly excused herself. "Calvin, I'm going to leave y'all to this and head on down to—"

"No." Calvin meets her gaze. "Please. It's okay. You can stay. Luke likes you." He turns to his little boy. "Right, Luke?"

The boy tentatively nods.

Calvin gently brushes a strand of ginger-colored hair from the child's eye. "You can tell us about the dream, Luke. It's okay."

The boy sits back against the futon's armrest and stares into his lap. He mumbles something. Lilly has to strain to hear it.

"Was it like the other one you had?" Calvin asks his son.

Luke nods. "Yes, Daddy."

"Was she in the backyard?"

"Yes." Another nods. "This time it was at Grammy and Papa's house."

Calvin strokes the boy's hair. "You remember what I told you about nightmares and visions?"

Luke nods again slowly, staring at his hands in his lap. "We're supposed to talk about 'em because talking about 'em makes 'em less scary."

"That's right."

"Mama was there by them rosebushes . . . only she was dead . . . but she was there anyway. She wasn't no walker or anything. She was just all white and dead and stuff. It made me sad."

The boy lets out a little cough, distorted by a moan, and for a moment Lilly thinks he is about to cry again. Instead, he looks up into his father's eyes with a gaze as sharp and hot as an arc welder. "You know how Mama always said the end of the world is comin'?"

"Yes, sir, I remember." Calvin shoots an awkward glance at Lilly, then looks back at his son. "Was Mama telling you that in the dream?"

The boy nods. "She was crying. I didn't see the Aunty-Christ yet. He was behind the bushes but I didn't see him yet. Mama was on the swing set and she was swinging and crying and singing."

"What was she singing, Luke? Do you remember?"

The boy presses his lips together and thinks hard before softly singing in a little off-key voice, " 'Hush, little baby, don't you cry . . . Mama's gonna sing you a lullaby.' "

Calvin nods sadly. "Yeah, she always sang that song when she was puttin' you to bed, didn't she? Sang it real pretty, too."

"That's not what was happenin' in the dream, Daddy. She wasn't puttin' me to sleep."

"Okay," Calvin says with a cock of his head, a little reluctant to go farther. Lilly can feel the tension in the room ratchet up. Calvin says, "You want to tell me about it, buddy?"

The boy presses his lips together, and offers no response.

"That's okay, Luke. We don't have to talk about this no more."

The boy looks down, a tear dropping from one eye. His lips move now, but no words come out. He looks like a toy doll that has slipped its spindle.

"Luke?"

In the beat of silence before the child replies, an invisible Rubicon is crossed. Luke looks up at his father through wet eyes, and he musters up the words. "She said I could never ever go to sleep again . . . none of us could or we would end up like her."

In the coming days, long after Lilly has forgotten the exact details of that night with the Dupree children, a vague, undefined, inchoate feeling of dread lingers in the back of her mind like a shark swimming just beneath the surface of her thoughts. Lurking there, just out of sight, a dark impenetrable presence, the feeling of doom weaving through every moment, every task, every meeting and conversation and encounter, it buzzes in the back of her mind as she helps Bob and David gather maps, survey charts, tools, supplies, and weapons for the trip underground. It reverberates in her nebulous, fragmented dreams as she struggles through restless nights alone in the airless, musty apartment at the end of Main Street. It thrums in her bloodstream as she counts down the hours until the moment of their departure.

By the time Friday rolls around, Reese has fully recovered, and all the preparations have been made for the journey through the tunnels. Lilly tries her hardest to put the feeling of trepidation out of her mind. She decides to leave the town in the capable hands of Barbara Stern, Gloria Pyne, and Calvin Dupree. These three seem able to handle any emergency that might come up, and more important, Calvin's kids are best served having their father stick around rather than go gallivanting off on some dangerous, Quixotic mission. Resources have gotten dangerously low in Woodbury—for the town as a whole, as well as the provisions for the rescue team—so everybody feels things are being stretched as thin as they can be stretched without breaking. The battle with the herd has chewed up much of their ammunition—most of the weapons that are being taken down into the tunnels are handguns with speed loaders or eight- and ten-round magazines—and most of the nonperishable food items that are being taken along on the trip are of the canned variety. Just before dawn on Friday morning, the team assembles in the town square loaded down with rucksacks that feel as though they weigh a ton.

"What the hell did you put in these things, fucking boulders?" Speed grumbles to Bob in the gloomy half-light of the square as the older man helps the younger man shoulder the enormous backpack. The air snaps with tension and the chill of predawn, the horizon just beginning to bruise with orange daylight.

"Stop your bellyaching," Bob scolds as he hefts his own pack onto his shoulders. "You're supposed to be the big football stud, what are you complaining for?"

"Come see me after eight or ten miles under there, Pops, see how *you* like it." Speed snorts distastefully, his close-cropped sandy hair wrapped in a bandanna, his U2 T-shirt already spotted with perspiration. He adjusts the straps around his broad shoulders with a grunt and shoots a glance across the square at Matthew Hennesey, who sits on a nearby bench, loading an ammo magazine with fresh rounds.

Matthew looks up at Speed with a grin. "Don't be a pussy, Speed-O."

Lilly watches all this nonsense from the other side of the square as she secures her own knapsack, trying to ignore the hollow, anxious feeling in her bones that has been plaguing her all week. She has both her .22-caliber Rugers with her, one holstered on each hip, gunslinger-style, and a miner's hat over her ponytailed hair, secured with a makeshift chinstrap. She feels like a paratrooper about to be plunged into endless free fall. Just this morning, in fact, she awoke in the darkness of her apartment with a realization as sudden and unexpected as a firecracker going off behind her eyes: *the reason for her vague sense of doom.*

Now she feels it pressing down on her heavier than the straps of her overstuffed backpack, which are already digging into her shoulders. In addition to the canned goods, they have packed every last spare battery in the town, medical supplies, digging and mining implements, extra flashlights, signal flares, coils of rope, duct tape, walkie-talkies, and various and sundry gadgets that may or may not be useful in the unknown territory of the underground.

"Are we ready?" David asks somewhat rhetorically, standing behind Matthew's bench, the single streetlight shining down on the square putting a sodium-vapor halo around David's flyaway gray mane. In addition to his heavy pack, assault rifle, and bandolier of bullets, the gray-bearded man wears a motorcycle helmet rigged with a halogen light. He looks like an aging spelunker preparing to descend into the chasms of hell. "Bob, we all set?"

"As set as we'll ever be," Bob mutters, tightening his belt. "Let's do it."

They follow Bob across the square, down Jones Mill Road, and through the gap at the southwest corner of the barricade. Lilly feels the flesh on her neck crawling as they light out across the wasted vacant lots. The predawn stillness is broken only by the jangle of their footsteps, the rattling contents of their packs, and the thumping of Lilly's heart, so loud in her own ears that she begins to wonder whether the others might be able to hear it as well. She's not sure how long she can keep her little secret from them. It gnaws at her now as they cross the littered streets south of the wall, take a turn at Folk, and head single file down the scarred walkway that lines the boarded-up storefronts.

Lilly learned of her affliction—the reason for the poisonous burning fear now stewing in her gut as they close in on the drugstore—when she was just a kid, eight or nine years old, during a game of hide-and-seek with her cousins, Derek and Deek Drinkwater.

The Drinkwaters were old money from Macon. The father, Everett's stepbrother, Tom, was involved in overseas oil trading, and was rolling in it. The Drinkwaters' enormous antebellum Tudor mansion in Warner Robins was a chockablock monstrosity brimming with nooks and crannies and innumerable little side rooms, dumbwaiters, pantries, and water closets in which a disgruntled child could hide for days with a sack lunch and some board games.

One Sunday afternoon, while Everett was visiting Tom and his sister-in-law, Janice, the kids launched into a marathon game of hide-and-seek. With the adults sequestered in the breakfast nook, working their way through a pitcher of gin rickeys, Lilly and the twins had their run of the house. Lilly was good at the game and usually went undetected long past *Ollie ollie oxen free.*

On this particular day, she found an old storage closet beneath the third-floor staircase and crawled in, closing the rickety old door with a resounding *click,* the finality of which put gooseflesh on her arms and legs. She curled her knees against her chest and burrowed into the corner behind the mothball-redolent fur coats and musty boxes marked JANICE HATS AND MUFFLERS and TWINS BABY THINGS, and she began to sweat. That was the first indication of her condition—undiagnosed and undetected until this moment—an odd and sudden hot flash that spread over her spindly body like a brushfire. In seconds she was drenched. She tried the door and found the thing stuck. Maybe it had jammed or automatically locked from the outside or something. All Lilly knew at that moment was that she had to get out.

The sensation, as most sufferers of this condition will attest, is not unlike suffocation. Lilly couldn't breathe in that little closet as she backed into the corner, her scalp prickling, her flesh crawling, the coats hanging down in her face seeming to close in on her, threatening to strangle her. Her heart was racing faster than it ever had before. She felt the walls pressing in, the darkness deepening.

It was a few minutes later when the screaming started. Lilly shrieked and keened and sobbed in the darkness of that tiny prison until one of the twins found her, prying the door open and letting her lurch out into the air and light of the hallway.

The incident in the Drinkwater house was soon all but forgotten by everyone present but Lilly, who realized—either through the trauma of the experience or some innate brain chemistry—that she had indeed acquired the disorder and would have it the rest of her life. It certainly was not paraplegia or cancer or anything fatal or debilitating, but it was definitely there within her, as palpable as color blindness or flat-footedness. And it would rear its demonic head within her at the most inopportune times.

She feels it now as the team approaches the drugstore. She feels her heart thrumming in her slender chest as they pause outside the entrance. Bob steps up to the shattered glass door and peers into the ransacked pharmacy for any sign of disturbance, any evidence of walkers. The cluttered aisles, broken displays, and overturned shelves lie in absolute stillness and darkness, the burgeoning purple light of dawn behind them not yet penetrating the convolutions of the You-Save-It Pharmacy.

"Lights on, everybody," Bob murmurs as he snaps his miner's light on and pushes the door open with the barrel of his shotgun. Bob carries the cut-down pistol-grip 12-gauge whenever he's expecting close quarters as well as unknown walker quotients.

Lilly's chest seizes up with terror as she follows Bob into the pharmacy, the others crunching through the broken glass behind her. The pharmacy seems to bristle and react to her presence—even though it's all in her mind, and she knows it—the walls closing in as slowly and surely as glaciers shifting. Her mouth goes dry as they cross the empty store and each take their turn scaling down the service steps of the elevator shaft. Her joints stiffen and her spine goes icy-cold as she reaches the bottom of the steps.

The basement level is bigger than she expected and infested with moving shadows, as the slender beams of light from the helmets and flashlights sweep across the gloom. Bob locates the gaping hole in the wall—as big as a submarine hatch and exuding wafts of musky air from the darkness on the other side—and he waves everybody over. "This way, folks," he says, lighting the way with his torch, "ladies' lingerie and sportswear."

Lilly's throat closes up as she follows David into the tunnel, ducking to avoid hitting her head on the crown of the doorway.

For a moment, she pauses just inside the door, her body immobilized with fear as the others pass her, one by one.

The terror seizes her limbs, freezes her tendons, and closes her throat until she can hardly breathe as the last of the five other team members trudge past her and continue down the tunnel, their silhouettes melting into the darkness, their narrow beams of light dancing off the earthen walls and evenly spaced load-bearing timbers.

She can't move, can't breathe. The tunnel has morphed into the closet under the stairs, the stalactites of roots and calcium deposits now becoming the hanging fur coats and plastic-covered rain slickers that engulfed her as a child. The walls of the passageway begin to press in. She wobbles for a moment, the dizziness threatening to knock her down. One of the silhouettes in front of her pauses, turns, and glances worriedly back at her.

Bob's deeply lined face is barely visible in the spill light from his miner's hat, the glow revealing his vexed expression. He trudges back toward her, his pack jangling.

She looks up at him. "Sorry, Bob, I'm—" She wheezes and gasps for her breath, as though suffering an asthma attack. "I'm not—" She can't form the words.

"What's the matter, Lilly-girl?" He puts an arm around her and squeezes. "What's going on?"

She inhales and exhales, inhales and exhales, until she's calm enough to speak. "Bob, I got some bad news."

"Tell me, honey, what's wrong?"

She looks at him, licks her lips, lets out a pained sigh, and finally works up the nerve to explain. "I got a nasty case of claustrophobia."

For a moment, Bob just stares at her, and then, as though a circuit breaker has blown, starts laughing, and his laughter echoes down the ceaseless passageway—a ghostly sound that makes the others abruptly halt, turn, and gawk.

It takes only a minute or so for Bob to finish having his little laugh and then dig in his medical kit for a couple tabs of Xanax. He gives them to Lilly, apologizing for his laughter, assuring her that he didn't mean to belittle or diminish her condition and he knows how horrifying claustrophobia can be. In Kuwait, he saw a soldier choose the battlefront over a behind-the-lines job just so he could avoid the tight quarters of his Quonset hut office. But Bob goes on to explain that sometimes the shit piles up so high in this god-awful world that you just have to laugh. Besides, claustrophobia is the *least* of their problems right now. If the walkers don't get them down here, the likelihood of methane poisoning, cave-ins, or a chemical leak asphyxiating them is far greater than dying from some panic attack.

The Xanax does the trick in about fifteen minutes, after which time Lilly feels good enough to walk in the lead (after apologizing to everybody for her freak-out). She's embarrassed by her momentary paralysis, but, in a way, it had a strange girding effect on her. It braced her for the journey ahead.

They make incredibly good time that day, tracking their progress with Matthew's pedometer. The first hour, they put two miles behind them without encountering a single walker or cave-in.

In this early stage, the tunnel seems fairly uniform, with a crossbrace timber embedded in the ceiling every hundred feet or so and the hard-packed earthen walls reinforced with ancient chicken wire. The air smells oily, fecund, and musky, heavy with the odors of black earth and mold. Every few moments, Lilly's miner's light flickers across the bleached bones of human remains partially buried in the sediment. It makes her uneasy but also strangely ennobled by the purpose of their mission. Or perhaps it's just the momentary euphoria of the drugs. Who knows?

Bob tracks their progress and current position aboveground with the survey map.

At the end of the second hour, their progress has slowed a bit due to the passageway narrowing around mile five. They pass a bizarre accumulation of calcium and limestone deposits hanging from the ceiling, which resemble massive ornate chandeliers of slimy iridescent icicles. The walls are fringed in moss at this juncture, and the air is exceedingly clammy and fetid, as though they're moving through a rain forest.

Then the tunnel bends slightly to the right, which Bob assures everybody is south, and they run into a few partial cave-ins. Lilly starts to notice a change in the infrastructure of the tunnel—the shape becoming more squared off, with a greater number of braces and support beams—as well as intermittent gaps in the walls, which look like tributaries or secondary tunnels now boarded over and leaching gelid breaths of musty air.

When Lilly points out one of these tributaries to Bob, the older man keeps walking, mumbling casually, "Zinc mines . . . mostly zinc. Some of them lead, coal, maybe." He points to the cross bracing and adds, "My guess is, the Underground Railroad linked up with defunct mines now and again, hopping from mine to mine like stepping-stone all the way to the Mason-Dixon Line."

Lilly just shakes her head in awe, nervously fingering the beavertail grip of her Ruger, as they trudge onward for another two or three thousand feet, sidestepping enormous drifts of earth that have sifted down across the path over the decades, as well as the remnants of campfires, until they see a massive obstruction in the distant shadows.

At first it looks as though they've reached the end of the line—as though an aged brick wall has been erected to mark the tunnel's terminus—but the closer they get to the obstruction, the more the true nature of the object is revealed in the flicker of their flashlight beams. "What the fucking Sam Hill is this?" Ben mumbles as the group reaches the massive piling.

It looks as though an immense mortar cylinder, covered with a patina of age like tiny barnacles on its wormy gray surface, has been driven into the earth directly through the middle of the passageway. With a diameter of five or six feet, it nearly blocks the path—with only a narrow gap on either side—but it remains unclear whether the thing's involvement with the tunnel is by design or accident.

Lilly sticks a hand through the gap on one side. "Looks like we might be able to squeeze one at a time through either side." She shakes off her pack. "Might have to empty some of the bigger loads."

"That's just fucking great," Matthew grumbles. "More packing and unpacking."

Reese Lee Hawthorne stands in the shadows behind Speed, chewing his fingernails. "Sorry to tell ya, but I'm pretty sure Carlinville's still a long ways off.

"Hold your horses a second." Bob has already crouched down by the thing and pulls out his topographical map. He shines a penlight on the page and mutters, "I think I know what this is." He looks up at David, who is gazing over Bob's shoulder with a furrowed brow. "David, gimme some more light down here."

Lilly comes over to Bob. "You want to tell us what the hell this thing is?"

"I'll tell you exactly what this is." He glances back at the map, studies it, runs his thumbnail down a tributary. He glances up. "This here's a load-bearing piling—a big one—the kind they sink into the ground for skyscrapers."

Everybody processes this for a moment, all eyes and ears focused on Bob's calculations . . .

. . . which is why nobody notices the faint sound of shuffling footsteps coming down the dark tunnel behind them.

TWELVE

In the sticky, opaque darkness underground, noises are tricky—especially one as faint and fleeting as this—but at the moment, if anyone actually bothered to listen closely to it, they would hear the riffling sound of footsteps coming from the darkness that the rescue party had just traversed, as if some clumsy, intoxicated, forgotten member of their group were hurrying to catch up. Further masking the noise is David's incredulous, high-pitched voice: "Bob, I'm no cartographer, but unless we made a major wrong turn somewhere I'm pretty sure we aren't standing under the streets of Atlanta right now. Am I missing something?"

"Didn't say we were anywhere near there . . . and I didn't say this is part of a building." He rises to his feet on creaking knees, letting out a little sigh of pain. He points back down the tunnel, indicating the darkness from which they came. "That limestone and moss hanging down from the ceiling a mile or so back there—remember that?"

Everybody is nodding, and David says, "There's a connection?"

Bob folds his map, puts it back in his shirt pocket. "Calcium deposits and mossy walls are from seepage. We were under Elkins Creek back there."

Lilly calculates the distance, and remembers the countryside to the east of Woodbury, and realizes what Bob is getting at. "This is part of an overpass," she enthuses breathlessly, turning back toward the massive piling, which now looks almost luminous in the darkness, as cryptic and haunting as wreckage from the *Titanic*. "We're standing underneath a highway."

"Best I can tell, somewhere near mile eleven, something like that." Bob pats his breast pocket. "Which gives us a landmark to really pinpoint where we are."

"Highway Seventy-four?" Reese speaks up. "Is that the one y'all are talking about?"

"That's the one," Bob says. "My guess is, we turned south a ways ago, probably right after we crossed under Elkins Creek, and now we're following the highway."

"We're closer than I thought," Reese observes, running fingers through his hair. "This is good, this is fantastic. Carlinville's right next to the highway. We're almost there! God is good."

Another voice behind him: "Yeah, well . . . I hope God can help us with something else right now."

"Huh?" Reese whirls toward the sound of grave, low words that just came out of Ben Buchholz. "Excuse me?"

"Wait for it," Ben says with a voice full of dread. "Anybody else hear that?"

Lilly's heartbeat kicks up a few notches. Less than a hundred yards away, the bend in the tunnel is visible behind a low-lying phosphorescent mist—most likely caused by methane—glowing now like purple gauze through moonlight. The sound of awkward shuffling footsteps rises, as a faint shadow appears on the outer wall of the bend, and all at once the ringing of hammers clicking on pistols and cocking mechanisms jolting back on assault rifles surrounds Lilly as she draws her own gun and aims the front sight at the ghostly shadow, which is getting bigger, and bigger, and bigger, until suddenly Lilly says in a hissing stage whisper, "Wait! Everybody wait! Hold your fire!"

"Fuck that," Ben snaps back at her, pressing the rear sight of his AR-15 to his eye. In the distant shadows, the lone walker staggers into view. Ben hisses, "I'm not gonna get pinned down by these fucking goddamn biters."

"There's one! Ben, there's just one!" Lilly's voice is stretched taut with nerves, but also authoritative enough to make Ben release the trigger pad. "Wait and see if we got any more coming!"

She doesn't have to explain how stupid it would be to unleash a thunderous barrage of gunfire in these tight subterranean quarters. Not only would they draw every walker within hearing distance, they would very possibly set off that ethereal purple mist. Better to take the solitary stragglers down quietly.

The walker, drawn by their voices and their scent, starts shambling toward them with a pronounced limp, reaching out with that trademark stiff-armed lumber, as though angrily demanding to be hugged. Lilly and the others just stare at it and let it come to *them*—zero emotion, no fear, very little affect, just the impatient waiting of fishermen preparing to spear a salmon—and the closer it gets, the more Lilly ponders it with forensic interest.

Apparently a former middle-aged man of indeterminate race, its clothing reduced to tattered strips, the thing is so filthy with grit and mud it looks like some kind of bog creature, a mummy or a pharaoh pickled in primordial goo. But it's the leg that catches Lilly's eye and imagination. "Bob, look at its left leg."

"Nasty break, ain't it?" Bob studies the creature through the scope of his stainless steel .357 Magnum with the care of a jeweler inspecting the facets of a gemstone. The creature has closed the distance between them to fifty yards, and now the severity of the broken leg is evident—a polished knob of bone sticking through the rotting flesh of its thigh—a debilitating injury that causes the creature to move with a profound dragging motion like a car missing a wheel. "Makes you wonder."

"Yes, it does." Lilly contemplates the awful, shuffling gate of the mud walker as it approaches, closing the distance to twenty-five yards. At this close proximity, the blackened teeth are apparent working inside its maw of a mouth, the rusty snore of a growl coming out of it like an engine. Lilly turns to Speed. "You want to do the honors?"

"Love to," the thick-necked former football hero responds with cold indifference as he reaches for a crowbar wedged down the side of his backpack. The others watch calmly as Speed starts toward the oncoming creature. "Nice outfit," he says to the thing as he walks up to it and rams the sharp end of the iron crowbar up through the roof of its mouth and into its frontal lobe.

The point of the crowbar bursts through the top of the thing's skull.

For a moment, the thing merely stiffens, remaining upright, gaping emptily at its assailant as rivulets of black fluids pour down its forehead and over its face. Speed pulls the crowbar free with a ghastly smacking noise as the creature finally collapses in a heap of wet tissues.

Lilly and the others gather around it with the mild interest of pathologists. "Is it me, or is that from the herd that burned?" she says, gazing down at it, poking its papery, blackened garb with the toe of her boot. The tattered clothing is charred crisp.

"Looks like it, yeah," Bob murmurs, staring at the abomination, thinking.

"So that means . . . what?" David ponders the gruesome thing on the tunnel floor while holding a handkerchief over his nose and mouth to ward off the stench, muffling his voice. "It found its way down here just recently?"

"Yep." Lilly kneels by it, taking a closer look at the catastrophic break wrenching its left leg and hip, the protrusion of bone like a misshapen ivory tusk. "My guess is, the thing fell." She looks up at the ceiling, the roots and icicles of limestone hanging down. "Which doesn't exactly give me a warm, secure feeling."

Bob is already inspecting the stalactites near the top of the giant piling.

Matthew and Ben watch him. Finally Ben asks him what he's looking for.

"Not sure," Bob murmurs, pondering the intricacies of the ceiling.

He shines his flashlight up at the twists and tangles of roots, the fossilized beams, the calcium deposits shimmering like fool's gold. Lilly joins him, and they exchange a look. She knows what he's thinking.

"Maybe this is a blessing in disguise," Bob mumbles as he regards the ornate constellation of roots.

Ben stares at him. "How the hell do you figure that?"

"There's a million different ways that thing could have fallen down here—culverts, sewer manholes, weak spots in viaducts."

"Yeah . . . so?"

Bob looks at Ben. "I was planning on digging our way out when we get there, but if there are ways to fall in . . . that means there are ways to get out."

They travel another three and a half miles before Reese starts seeing signs that they're closing in on Carlinville. The first clue appears like a phantom in the beams of their flashlights and lamps: a thin curtain of dust sifting down through the silvery beams of light, and Lilly walks under it, shielding her face. The Xanax has worn off and she feels brittle and shaky as she shines her lamp up at the tunnel ceiling. The roots are vibrating with the weight of many, many, many shuffling feet.

"Oh, fuck," she mumbles, the sinking feeling tugging at her innards.

The others gather around her, Bob shining his light up at the stirring whirls of dust. "Looks like the goddamn Seventh Infantry marching around up there." He lets out a sour, exasperated breath. He pulls out the survey map. "According to the map, we're right smack-dab in the middle of the town." He shoots a glance at Lilly. "Gotta admit I was hoping the goddamn things would've cleared out by now."

Lilly pulls out one of her Rugers, checks the clip, snaps it back in. "Nothing we can do about it." She checks her other pistol, shoves it back in the holster. "When we get up there, everybody remember: safeties off and watch your backs."

"We can get closer!" Reese's voice comes from the shadows farther down the tunnel, where water has gathered. "I found another landmark!"

The others stride toward the sound of his voice, checking their weapons, splashing through two or three inches of greasy standing water. Ahead of them, in the flicker of their flashlight beams, Reese Lee Hawthorne comes into view standing next to an antique iron stepladder embedded into the mortar wall.

"What is it?" Lilly asks him as she approaches, drawing her Ruger, holding her flashlight next to the barrel. She aims the light up the steps to the circular iron object set into the roots of the ceiling.

Reese explains, "This here has to be the manhole cover at the corner of Maple and Eighteenth."

Lilly looks at him as the others gather around them, slamming magazines into pistols, yanking levers on the sides of assault rifles. "How close is that to the heart of town?"

"Less than a block." Reese takes a deep breath. In the darkness, his lean, emaciated features shimmer with flop sweat.

"And where's the chapel they're pinned down in? It's a chapel, right?"

A quick nod. "Yes, ma'am . . . it's on the other side of the street."

"How far?"

Reese chews his lip, thinking it over. A thin wisp of dust suddenly drifts down through their light beams, the vibrations still resonating through the ground. Reese swallows hard. "From the manhole cover? I don't know exactly. I think it's just across the street, little wood-frame place, white picket fence."

"Okay, everybody, listen up." Lilly turns to the others, who push in closer, their eyes glinting with adrenaline in the shadows. "Who's got the AR-15? Ben? Okay, you and I are going to go first, one at a time, followed by Reese, who's going to identify the place for us."

"All right, got it, got it," Ben Buchholz mutters nervously, gripping the rifle with white knuckles. All his bluster, all his macho posturing, all of it is gone. Evaporated. He looks like a little boy now trapped in the body of a loudmouthed redneck. "Ready when you are."

"Conserve your ammo as much as possible." She looks at the others. "Use your bladed weapons whenever you can. That goes for everybody."

Nods all around, straps being tightened, belts secured, the handles of knives, machetes, and pickaxes at the ready. Their faces gleam with tension.

Lilly turns to Reese. "There's thirteen people up there, correct?"

Reese nods.

Lilly thinks about it. "Did you say six men and seven women?"

"The other way around."

"Okay, everybody, time is of the essence here." She goes to the bottom of the stepladder. Some of the flashlights around her are switched off, the tunnel getting darker. She pulls off her miner's hat and tosses it to the tunnel floor. "In and out, quick and clean, that's the best way to avoid getting swarmed. Find the chapel, get them out, get back here. Nothing to it." She looks at Speed. "You think you can pry the thing open?"

"You got it, Lilly." Speed trots over to the ladder, climbs up, brushes aside roots and weeds, inhales dust, coughs, pulls his crowbar from his pack, and then starts working at the congealed, oxidized edges of the ancient manhole cover. "Look out below," he warns.

"Don't let it fall," Lilly calls up to him. "When you feel it give, hold it in place so that Ben and I can get back up there."

"Got ya."

After another minute of grunting and groaning from Speed—a span of time that feels to Lilly like a million years—the manhole cover creaks, and Speed holds on to it. "Okay, Lilly, got it." He looks down. "Come on up."

Lilly climbs up next to Speed, and Ben clambers up halfway, pausing just a few inches below Lilly. The others gather around the base of the ladder, bracing themselves to spring into action.

Lilly looks down at them. "On my signal, guys. You ready?"

Nods all around, their eyes hot, air being swallowed nervously.

Lilly takes a deep breath and turns back to the manhole cover. "Let's hope they've thinned out a little bit up there," she mutters, almost under her breath, essentially talking to herself. "Okay, here we go." She swallows hard. "Ready, everybody." Another breath. "NOW!"

She pushes the manhole cover open, and daylight streams into the tunnel.

Lilly climbs out and instantly lets out an involuntary, spontaneous gasp.

Time stands still as Lilly finds herself engulfed in a swarm of walkers so thick and densely packed, the mere odor of it takes her breath away—most of them so close to her as to be indistinguishable from each other—a nebula of blackened faces, yellow teeth, and luminous eyes flashing in a blur, making a hellish racket of groans and slobbering, garbled gnashing noises. Only a fraction of a second passes before Lilly has the Ruger up and roaring, but in that horrible instant, the span over which a single synapse fires in her brain, she makes several observations.

Through the milling throng of undead, she catches a fleeting glimpse of the little country chapel across the street, two doors down, windows boarded, timbers nailed across the entrance, maybe a hundred feet away, it's hard to tell—the Cape Cod–style clapboard building with its weathered whitewashed cross rising up against the cornflower-blue sky, sandwiched between a boarded barbershop and a ramshackle play lot—the edifice too far away to judge the distance. But Lilly has no time to consider the options or abort the mission or even breathe because clawlike hands have already tangled themselves up in her sleeve, the left leg of her jeans, and the tail of her denim shirt. That's when she manages to draw a Ruger .22 pistol with each hand and starts shooting.

The first six blasts, three and three, come in quick succession, so loud they pierce Lilly's left eardrum, the rounds driving the closest creatures back in eruptions of brain matter, rotting faces coming apart at point-blank range.

"STAY IN THE TUNNEL!" she wails down at Ben and the others. "TOO MANY OF THEM! DON'T COME UP HERE!"

She fires again at the next wave that presses in—three large males in ragged camo pants and hunting vests, and a gangly female in a tattered hospital gown—the blasts shearing the tops of three skulls and sending fountains of blood-mist into the clear air above the horde, the fourth one a direct hit between the eyes, the skull coming apart and exploding from the noxious gasses within.

At the same time, Lilly manages to shove the manhole cover with her boot back across the opening, the iron disc dropping back in place with a dull, clanging thud. The last thing she sees in the darkness down there before the cover settles over the opening is Ben's horror-stricken face, gaping up at her, pale and drawn, lips moving but no sound coming out, eyes raging with terror.

Then Lilly's moving, lurching toward the street, lowering her shoulder and ramming into about half a dozen of the things, knocking them over like bowling pins. The stench is tremendous, a miasma of human bile slow cooking in shit, and it nearly steals what's left of Lilly's breath. There are so many of them pushing in now that they tumble backward like dominoes as Lilly cuts a swath toward the church, firing as she goes, ears ringing, eyes watering with panic.

These shots are less accurate—some of them going high into the sky, others punching holes in dead shoulders and necks but leaving heads intact. With nine rounds in each pistol—eight in each mag, one in each chamber—she goes through the remaining dozen bullets in short order. But by the time her pistols start clicking impotently, she realizes she's halfway there.

Through the tumbling, staggering bodies, she sees the chapel only forty or fifty feet away, and she sees that the boarded entrance has been pushed open slightly, and she sees a face peering out the gap— a man, middle aged, fair skinned, silvery-blond hair, dressed in a stained suit coat and pants, is motioning to her. He's yelling something, but Lilly can't quite make it out.

More walkers close in on her, and she has no time to reload, so she jams the guns back in her belt and reaches for her collapsible shovel. The thing is thrust down a zippered pocket in her rucksack, and she has to work it free; she gets it out and up and swinging just as a rotting skeletal male lurches at her neck. The sharp edge of the shovel embeds itself in the thing's temple, causing a clot of brain matter to spew out of its cranium before it falls. Another wave of attackers moves in, but Lilly doesn't hesitate, she keeps swinging and moving toward the white clapboard building with singular purpose.

She takes down another half dozen biters, and she gets to within thirty feet of the chapel, when she sees the fair-haired man in the filthy charcoal suit lurch out the door with a large sterling silver crucifix. The cross is the size of a small ax and gleams in the sunlight as the man lashes out at the mob in front of his church. "THIS WAY, SISTER!" he calls to Lilly. "YOU'RE ALMOST HOME FREE!"

He impales the forehead of an older female walker as Lilly makes one last-ditch, heroic bid to reach the church in one piece.

"C'MON, SISTER—*ALMOST THERE!*"

In the tunnel, only minutes earlier, when the resounding thud of the manhole cover came slamming down on the opening, and the clang pealed through the dark passageway, it was Bob who went a little berserk.

"Fuck! Fuck! NO! NONONONONONO!" He comes running over to the bottom of the steps, his miner's light bobbing and its beam jumping in the faces of the others. "THE FUCK ARE YOU DOING?"

Ben hops off the lowermost rung and lands hard on the floor, breathless, a little confused. "She—she said to—I was just—she said to get back down."

"Who the fuck put the manhole cover back?"

"She did, Bob! She said to get back down!" Ben wipes his mouth with the back of his hand, his eyes wet with dread. "It happened real quick."

"FUCK! FUCK! FUCK!" Bob pulls his .357 from his hip and starts toward the ladder. The gun is unfamiliar in his hand—a newer model than the one he's used to—a replacement for the one Calvin left in the field. "I'm gonna go get her, goddamn it! We can't leave her out there!"

Bob is halfway up the steps when Speed grabs his leg and pulls him back. "Pops, wait!" Speed's grip feels like an iron vise. "We go together!" He gently pulls the older man back down the steps. "She's a big girl, she's handy with them Rugers, we should all just—"

The sound of dust sifting down interrupts, a shuffling, thudding parade going on up above.

Bob whirls and sees the thin swirl of powdery particulate in the beam of his miner's light. The ceiling vibrates with the pressure of countless shuffling feet, all that dead weight milling about the streets of this doomed little village, and it gives Bob an idea. He sees another tendril of dust falling off to the right, and then another off to the left, and he says, "Wait a minute, *wait*."

"What?" Speed looks at him, and the others come over and press in.

"I got a better idea." Bob snaps his gnarled fingers and starts looking around the floor. "Somebody find something we can use to punch a hole in the ceiling."

Lilly reaches the chapel doorway at the last possible instant, a cluster of ravenous moving corpses right on her heels, and she reaches out. The man in the doorway has moved to the edge of the front portico. He reaches out to her.

The two hands clasp, and the man gently but firmly pulls Lilly across the threshold.

Lilly stumbles through the doorway into a squalid vestibule lit by flickering kerosene lanterns, the malodorous air heavy with BO and rot. The man in the gray suit quickly pulls the double outer doors shut behind her, slamming them in the faces of the oncoming swarm.

"You all right, missy?" The man turns to Lilly, who is trying to catch her breath, hunched over, hands on her knees.

"Is she bit?"

The voice comes from the other side of the foyer, a heavyset woman in a stained Braves T-shirt, Capri pants, and high-top sneakers peering out from an inner door. There are others behind her, crowding in and looking on—grimy, haunted faces in the shadows of a ruined sanctuary.

"Take it easy, Sister Rose," the man in the suit says. He shoves his enormous crucifix into a sheath on his belt, as though it's a saber or medieval mace. "Bring our friend here some water."

"I'm good, thanks." Lilly gets air into her lungs and looks around the cluttered vestibule, her left ear ringing unmercifully. Hymnals, trash, and blood spots cover the floor. The walls—once displaying bulletin boards with the dates of upcoming bake sales—now appear scourged, riddled with bullet holes and Rorschach patterns of dried blood as black as onyx paint. "Haven't been bit, as far as I can tell." Lilly looks up at the man. "Thanks for giving me a hand."

The man proffers a little gallant bow and a smile. "It's entirely my pleasure."

In the lantern light Lilly gets a better look at the guy and sees that he's a man in his forties, maybe younger, a boyish face that's just beginning to age around the corners. With his lantern jaw, clear blue eyes, and big mop of Kennedy-esque hair just beginning to pepper with gray, he looks like a former child actor maybe fallen on hard times. His suit is well worn, shiny in the seat and shoulders, but the way he carries himself—his clip-on necktie still knotted neatly against his throat despite the flecks of blood and grime on the material—gives off an air of a leader, a man to be reckoned with.

Lilly extends her hand. "I'm Lilly Caul." She manages a smile. "Reverend Jeremiah, I presume?"

The man's smile fades slightly, his eyes narrowing and his big chiseled head cocking suddenly at the unlikely fact that she knows his name.

THIRTEEN

It takes Bob and the others several precious seconds to find a suitable spot in the tunnel ceiling through which to punch their hole. These are seconds that they would have preferred not to waste—they have no idea how Lilly is faring up there in the mob of walkers, whether she has made it to the chapel—but at the moment they need to be proactive and nobody has a better idea. In a series of hasty extrapolations, consultations with Reese, and glances at the survey map, Bob chooses a spot four-hundred-plus feet back down the tunnel, around a bend, and under a convoluted phalanx of stalactites—about the length of a football field between this spot and the heart of the swarm—in order to give them the optimum amount of room but still be close enough to get the horde's attention.

They use the square-edged spade that Matthew brought along, and Speed—probably the strongest of all of them—does the honors. The former defensive end weighs a hundred and ninety-five pounds, and Matthew and Ben have to get down on their hands and knees, elbow to elbow, directly underneath the spot, in order to give Speed something to stand on. They work quickly, communicating with very few words—Bob doing most of the talking—as Speed climbs onto their backs and begins to cut a divot in the ceiling with the shovel, his AR-15 dangling on a shoulder strap.

"How do we know there ain't pavement directly above us?" Ben wants to know, still on his hands and knees on the floor, his voice strained with effort, the weight of Speed's clodhopper boots pressing between his shoulder blades. "How do you know it'll break through?"

"I don't," Bob mumbles as he turns to David. "Look in the front flap of my backpack, see if that dental mirror we found at the drugstore is still in there."

While all this is going on, the thumping sound of Speed slamming the blade into the roots overhead continues, a loud drumbeat, each impact sending a fresh load of dirt sifting down into the darkness. The hard Georgia clay is unyielding, but Speed puts his estimable shoulder and neck muscles into the job.

A few feet away, in the darkness, looking on nervously, Reese chews his fingernails.

An invisible stopwatch ticks in Bob's brain as he waits for Speed to break through. A couple of minutes have elapsed now since Lilly was plunged into the herd, alone, exposed, fighting her way through the throngs. The sound of her gunfire has ceased. Good news if she made it to the chapel; very, very bad news if she ran out of ammo or got engulfed—and now Bob's heart begins to race.

"Whoa!" Speed jerks back when a huge spadeful of dirt cascades onto the backs of Matthew and Ben. Daylight streams into the tunnel—a blazing yellow nimbus—diffused by all the dust. The walker stench is immediately evident as though somebody just opened a garbage can. "We're through! We're through!"

Bob steps closer. "Okay, now blast a few controlled bursts out the hole, not too many, don't waste a lot of ammo, just enough to get their attention."

"You got it." Speed tosses the shovel aside and swings his AR-15 up at the gaping hole in the ceiling. He sticks the barrel out. "Here goes!"

The roar of the assault rifle ignites the darkness with light and noise.

Reese and David cover their ears, Bob still fidgeting. The two men on the ground yell something at each other that nobody else can hear. At last, after the third short burst, Speed ejects the magazine. The metal clip falls directly onto Ben's back. "Ouch! Goddamn it, do you mind?"

"Sorry, sorry . . . coming down."

Speed awkwardly hops off the trembling backs of the two men on the ground, slamming a fresh mag into the rifle's receiver breach.

"Can we fucking get up now?" Ben has run out of patience, his voice quavering with rage.

"No, stay there for one more second," Bob says, and then looks at the others. "All together, everybody, make a big fucking racket!"

Bob starts screaming and whooping and hollering under the hole in the ceiling, and the others follow suit. Soon the tunnel fills with the riotous sound of their voices bouncing around the fossilized walls, a wild party in full swing, a strange hullabaloo in such a grim, crypt-like space. At last Bob shoots a hand up to cut them off. "Okay, lemme take a look."

He climbs up onto Ben and Matthew, and he sees that the hole in the ceiling is bigger than he thought—about the size of a hubcap—and he carefully prods the dental mirror up into daylight and angles it so he can get a glimpse of the street.

The reflection in that postage-stamp-sized mirror is horrifying.

A tiny cameo portrait of hell on earth.

"Brother Jeremiah, look! Look what's happening outside!" The fat woman in Capri pants peers through a narrow gap in the boarded window.

The rest of the people in the room—stunned only moments ago by the sound of automatic gunfire in the distance—fall silent immediately and watch the preacher rush over to the window.

He looks out and sees what the lady is talking about. He becomes very still, steps back, turns, and looks directly at Lilly. Then he does something that not only fascinates Lilly but will live in the back of her thoughts, haunting her, for days. The man adjusts his clip-on tie. He does this as though he's about to go on stage or deliver a sermon. He fiddles with it for just an instant, and if Lilly had blinked she would have missed it, but it is so odd and out of place and anachronistic that it burns itself into her brain. Then Jeremiah says, "We don't have much time. Your friends have coaxed the horde away from the building."

Lilly looks at him. "Is there a straight shot to the manhole on the other side of the street?"

"There is indeed." He turns to the others. "Everybody grab whatever you can carry on your backs. We have been given a second chance by the Good Lord as well as these fine people—hurry up, now, just the bare essentials."

The others spring into action, tearing open knapsacks, tossing unnecessary items onto the cluttered floor. Makeup mirrors, extra shoes, paperback books, keys, and coffee cups go spinning across the parquet tiles. Lilly watches for a moment, mesmerized by the dynamic between the preacher and his people. The seven men and six women—all ages and sizes—follow the man's instructions with the guileless obedience of nursery school students—despite the fact that it's a motley, heterogeneous assemblage of former housewives, laborers, matrons, and old codgers from the deepest backwaters of the Old South.

In addition to the plump lady in the Capri pants, named Rose, the others have managed to hastily introduce themselves to Lilly, and now Lilly's brain swims with names and hometowns and brief tales of how none of them would be alive right now if it weren't for Reverend Jeremiah. Oddly, the preacher had more questions for Lilly than she had for him. He wanted to know what kind of community she was building in Woodbury, what kind of resources she had, and most important, why she had come all this way just to save them. Folks are careful nowadays not to just blithely go off with the first sentient human that happens along. Lilly is no different. From the moment she set foot in the chapel, she had been giving the minister and his flock the once-over, judging faces, measuring handshakes, scrutinizing the look in their eyes.

For the most part, these people seem normal, albeit road scarred and traumatized by loss.

At one point, Lilly had noticed moving shadows and noises coming from a side room along the sanctuary and asked Jeremiah about it. After all the heads had bowed, Jeremiah had rubbed his eyes sadly and said in a soft voice, "Them are the less fortunate of our group, the ones who . . . fell to the beasts." At that point Lilly had peered around the corner of the doorway and got a glimpse of two males and one female bound to the wall with makeshift chains and cables around their necks, their milky eyes fixed on the void before them, their puckered mouths moving impotently.

Now Lilly puts all these considerations out of her mind as she rushes across the room to the window, peers out, and sees the intersection of narrow streets outside slowly clearing as if some magic dog whistle were beckoning the horde away from the chapel. In just a few more seconds, the street corner will be completely clear. Lilly pulls out her pistols one at a time, checks the magazines as if the empty cartridges might have magically regenerated more bullets. She sees that they're still empty, replaces them, and shoves the pistols back into their holsters.

Jeremiah comes over to her. "Alas, Sister Lilly, we have only a couple weapons." He hurriedly waves a pair of his male congregants over. "This here is Brother Stephen." He motions to a gangly young man in his midtwenties with a tattered short-sleeve dress shirt, bow tie, and black trousers. He looks like a worn-out Mormon missionary who has rung too many doorbells. He holds a single-barrel pump-action shotgun and gives Lilly a nod.

"It's a Mossberg, ma'am, loaded with deer shot," he says to her, as though this explains everything. "Ain't as accurate as a rifle, but it'll do quite a bit of damage at close range."

Lilly nods nervously. "Okay, stay close to the front of the group."

"We got one more firearm," the preacher says, and turns to another man—older, weathered, wearing a Caterpillar tractor cap and chewing a plug of Red Man—who had already introduced himself to Lilly as a traveling Bible salesman. "You already met Anthony here."

The older man holds up an ancient revolver, so old the blue steel has turned gray. "It ain't much to look at but it got my daddy through Korea and forty-seven years under the counter at his hardware store."

"Okay, okay, good, good . . . we'll hope these guns won't have to be fired right now." She looks at each man. "Do you understand what I'm saying? It's really important that you do not fire unless it's absolutely necessary."

The men nod, and Reverend Jeremiah gives them a stern look. "You boys listen to this lady, do exactly as she says. You got that?" He turns to the rest of the group. "That goes for everybody. With the help of our Lord and Savior, this woman here is gonna save our behinds."

By this point, all essential items have been secured into knapsacks, and the congregants have pressed in toward the front door. Lilly can smell old sweat leaching out of their skin, body odor under their filthy clothes. Starvation and chronic terror have taken a toll on their faces. Reverend Jeremiah compulsively fingers the knot of his tie as he turns to Lilly and looks her in the eye. "Where do you want me, missy?"

"You okay with bringing up the rear?"

"Absolutely." He lays a hand on the top of the enormous steel crucifix on his hip, as big as a baseball bat. On closer examination, Lilly can see that the thing has been sharpened on the end—perhaps on a whetstone or sharpening wheel—where Christ's feet are nailed. "If we encounter a stray," Jeremiah says wearily, without pleasure, "I will administer the old rugged cross to it without making too much noise."

"Fair enough." She takes one last look through the gap in the boarded window. The intersection has completely cleared. Only a few wadded pieces of trash blow across the pavement. The manhole cover is clearly visible a hundred feet away. "Okay, folks, on my signal I want everybody to walk quickly—do not run—walk quietly and quickly across the street to the sewer entrance." She glances over her shoulder at all the pinched, feverish, terrified faces. "Y'all can do this. I know you can."

"Listen to the lady," Jeremiah urges. "God is with us, brothers and sisters, yea though we walk through the valley . . . our Lord and Savior walks beside us."

A few scattered *amens.*

Lilly nervously fingers the grips of her empty Rugers and looks at Brother Stephen, who clutches his shotgun as though it were a rip-cord on a parachute. "Stephen . . . on three, I want you to very quietly push the door open. You understand?"

He nods furiously.

"One, two . . . *three!*"

The sound of their footsteps—fifteen pairs of feet charging across a hundred feet of wasted cement, each person huffing and puffing, weighed down by a heavy knapsack—would normally draw the attention of every human and walker alike within a half-mile radius.

But at the moment, the noise of this sudden exodus from the chapel is drowned out by the wave of garbled moaning and snarling emanating from the horde, which has now drifted a block or so away, drawn to the booming noises issuing out of the ground. Lilly runs out in front of the church group, her gaze fixed on the manhole cover dead ahead. The closer she gets to it, the more she becomes convinced it's moving. Like an enormous bottle cap opening, the seal on one side has broken, a gap forming, a face visible in the maw of shadows beneath it.

"Watch out!" Bob's leathery features peer out from the opening, his square head silhouetted by a beam of flashlight. "Straggler! Behind you!"

Just as Lilly reaches the manhole, she glances over her shoulder and sees Reverend Jeremiah lagging behind the group, lashing out with his sacred bludgeon at a dark figure lurching toward him. The large female in ratty dungarees has pounced at precisely the same moment the sharpened end of the Savior's bound feet strikes the creature's temple, hacking through a huge portion of its skull and half its rotting brain, sending a loopy segment of tissue flying through the air on a cushion of blood-mist.

"KEEP MOVING, BROTHERS AND SISTERS!" the preacher calls out as he staggers after the group.

Meanwhile Bob has pushed the manhole cover all the way off and has begun to help the congregants—older women first, then younger women, then men—down into the dank, shadowy bosom of safety. Lilly is second to last to plunge down the hole, followed closely by the well-dressed minister. Once Jeremiah has plummeted out of sight, Bob pulls the cover back over the opening. The dull metallic thud rings through the darkness of the tunnel, drowned out by the ringing in Lilly's left ear as she lands on the small of her back on the floor, and sees stars.

The sudden lack of daylight and clean oxygen is jarring—it feels to Lilly as though she has just plunged underwater—the air so fetid and damp and greasy it feels like a membrane over her face. She brushes herself off and levers herself to her feet.

"Brother Jeremiah!" Reese Lee Hawthorne stands a few feet away, wringing his hands, beaming at his mentor and father figure, trying to play it cool, trying to hide his tears and be the macho Christian soldier. He swallows his emotion. "Thank the Lord you're all right!"

Jeremiah starts to reply when, all at once, the younger man loses his cool and lurches toward Jeremiah and practically collapses into the older man's arms in a swoon. "Thank God, thank God, thank God . . . you're okay," Reese murmurs, burying his face in the preacher's coat. "I prayed every chance I got that you'd make it out of there."

"My brave, brave young scout," Jeremiah mutters, taken aback by Reese's unexpected display of emotion. He shoves the massive cross back down into its sheath and returns the embrace, patting the young man between the shoulder blades with the tenderness of a long-lost father reunited with a son. "You done good, Reese."

"I thought for sure we'd lost y'all," Reese says softly into the threadbare fabric of Jeremiah's coat.

"I'm still standing, son. We're all still here by the grace of God and these good people. Wasn't our time yet."

The preacher gives a nod to Lilly and the others, as the rest of the church group gathers behind Lilly, brushing themselves off and checking their belongings. Everybody is still breathless and jittery from their mass exodus across the street, some of them looking around the narrow tunnel as they catch their breath, getting acclimated to the drastically different atmosphere down here. They managed to convey an impressive amount of cargo in their overstuffed backpacks and knapsacks, and now they stand roughly two abreast, the tunnel too narrow for them to huddle in one place. There are half a dozen women of ages ranging from teens to sixties, a single black man, and men in various states of agitation and physical fitness, and they all face Jeremiah and Lilly, as the two leaders begin to make introductions with the aplomb of chieftains, Lilly motioning to Bob Stookey first, introducing him as the brains behind this tunnel.

"Good to meet you, Reverend," Bob says to the man in the suit.

"Call me Jeremiah," the preacher says, returning Bob's handshake with a twinkle in his eye. "Or Brother Jeremiah—or just Brother— like the Good Samaritan of yore."

"Sounds good." Bob gives the man a look. Lilly sees it from across the tunnel—it's subtle, and it's missed by everybody else in the shadows of that passageway, but Lilly makes note of it in the back of her mind. She can tell immediately that Bob doesn't like this guy. Bob plasters a smile on his grizzled features. "You can call me whatever you want, just don't call me Pops." He looks pointedly at Matthew, who merely smiles.

Jeremiah returns Bob's gaze with a faint smile and flicker of something in his eye. Lilly wonders if she's watching some kind of chemical reaction between these two old lions.

While all this is going on—most of the members of the church group still catching their breath and checking their gear and gazing around the tight quarters—the faint noise emanating from the shadows five hundred feet down the passageway is missed by everyone.

At first, the noise is so soft as to be almost inaudible, but if anyone strained an ear, he or she would hear the faintest sound of cracking. Initially very muffled, watery, and indistinct—like the rending of a green branch—it drifts down the tunnel in the darkness, unheard, unheeded, unnoticed . . . until it reaches Speed's ears.

Speed stands at a point in the tunnel that's almost completely engulfed in darkness, about fifty feet away from Lilly, the closest person to the source of the cracking noises, which now rise in fits and starts, as though a great pressure is being applied to a stubborn root. For the last few minutes Speed has been checking his ammo mags, counting out his remaining rounds, but now he becomes very still, listening to the noise. "Hey," he whispers to Matthew, who kneels nearby, digging through his pack, looking for something. Speed tries to stay calm. "You hear that?"

"Hear what?"

"Ssshhh . . . listen."

"I don't hear anything."

"Keep listening."

Now the noises rise to the point that a few of the others—David, Ben, the plump lady in Capri pants—begin to turn toward the cracking sounds, cocking their heads in consternation. The noise has grown to the point of bringing to mind a sailing vessel creaking in a storm or a massive tree slowly keeling over—that deep, rending crack that makes a person's flesh crawl—and it rises and rises until the others pause in their conversations.

By the time Speed realizes the source of the sound, it's too late.

It happens in what seems like slow motion, although Lilly isn't sure whether it's actually occurring with syrupy slowness or it's simply her state of shock: Hundreds of feet away, in the dark, around a bend, out of sight, at the point the shovel had augered its hole in the tunnel roof, weakening the structure's integrity, the ceiling has begun to collapse from the weight of the herd aboveground.

As the tunnel reverberates with the horrific noise—rotting bodies plummeting down through cascading earth, a sound so alien it's like subterranean thunder—Lilly backs away instinctively. She clenches her teeth and reaches for her guns, although she knows deep down—as all those around her know deep down in the fiber of their beings as they back away from the noise—that they have nowhere to run, nowhere to hide. One of the church people—the fat lady named Rose, who is also backing away—starts keening, "*No no no no no no nonononono . . .*"

The first thing they see is a mushroom cloud of dust curling around the bend in the tunnel, punching through the air with the force of a battering ram, coming toward them in the darkness like a tidal wave. Several people have their flashlight beams trained on the thing, and the surreal quality of that flickering light reflecting off the moving dust storm is dizzying.

At this point, no one has turned away or started to flee, as everybody is still in that stunned, paralytic terror of registering the implications of this dark nebula rolling toward them. The thunderous noise emanating from behind the dust cloud continues unabated as more and more walkers plunge into the tunnel. Lilly can't tear her gaze from that dust wave as it closes in.

Bob's voice cuts through her trance. "Okay, all the folks with firearms out front!"

"Bob, we can't take this many on!" Lilly's hands instinctively clutch the grips of her Rugers. "There's too—!"

"We got no choice!"

"There's too many of them!"

"How do you know how many there are? We don't even know how big the—!"

Bob falls silent. The others freeze in their tracks. Lilly stares.

It takes only a fleeting moment for her eyes to register what she's seeing, and another nanosecond for that visual information to zap across her brain and travel through her cortex and down into the rest of her body where it spikes her heartbeat and makes her mouth go dry and rages through her tendons with the brushfire of fight or flight.

Reverend Jeremiah pushes his way between Speed and Matthew, and then walks slowly to the front of the group. The preacher stands next to Lilly, and at first Lilly doesn't hear the man's hushed voice as he mutters, "And there was war in heaven, and Michael and his angels fought valiantly against the dragon . . ."

A hundred feet away, the rolling cloud of dust has abruptly dissipated, and from the nucleus of the dust, like phantoms birthing themselves from the ether, a column of undead has begun to emerge, shuffling practically shoulder to shoulder, some of them clumsily brushing the earthen walls of the tunnel. More and more of them materialize in the flickering coins of flashlights, a ghastly clown car issuing innumerable clowns, the rank and file of moving corpses extending so far back into the darkness their number is incalculable.

They keep coming and coming . . . until Lilly's simple prescriptive shout is the only thing tethering the living inhabitants of the tunnel to reality.

"FUCK THIS!" Her voice has gone high and thin, the voice of the primal Lilly—the teenage, fucked-up, wild-ass Lilly Caul.

"RRRRUNNNN!"

All at once, they're running—either single file or side by side—a group of twenty souls now. Some of them stumble but somehow manage to stay on their feet, others sideswipe the scabrous walls of the narrow tunnel, letting out yelps of pain, tripping and falling, quickly lifting themselves back up (or allowing themselves to be hoisted up by one of the stronger members of the group such as Speed, Matthew, or Ben, and then continuing headlong in the darkness. A few of them peel off from the group and try to scurry up the service ladder and escape through the manhole cover at the corner of Eighteenth and Maple Streets, but Lilly quickly intercedes, yanking them back down the steps, rebuking them as she urges them onward down the south branch of the tunnel, breathlessly explaining that there's not enough time to get everybody out of the manhole, and besides, the town is overrun with walkers and there's no place to hide, and they'll just end up getting pinned down again. Nobody knows how far the tunnel extends to the south. Miles? Hundreds of feet? For that matter, nobody knows exactly where the tunnel is leading them, but such considerations are secondary now to the simple imperative of evading this hideous rolling tide. The herd is moving slowly yet relentlessly as it shambles and lumbers after the smell of humans, the stench of the dead as well as the dust kicked up by the collective shuffling of lifeless feet permeating the air. Soon, each and every one of the fleeing humans begins coughing convulsively as they run—their pace, which started as a full-bore sprint, now reduced to a wounded, gimpy jog. They find themselves turning another corner, hacking and wheezing in the airless darkness—only a few of them armed with flashlights to illuminate the path in front of them—when all at once the two people in the lead suddenly scuttle to a stop. Some of the runners behind them stumble into each other, a domino effect that sends a few of them sprawling to the floor, while others brace themselves against the tunnel wall, and soon the entire group of twenty people has collectively frozen in the shadows, staring at the same thing the two people in the lead are now gaping at a mere twenty-five feet away in the darkness.

"Oh, fuck me," Lilly utters without even being aware of her own voice as one of the flashlight beams slowly sweeps the width of a brick wall forming a dead end.

FOURTEEN

At Georgia Tech, Lilly once wrote a paper for Psych 203 called "The Mother of Invention," which was a scholarly study of how the snap judgments of people in stressful situations—cops, soldiers, paramedics—often led to ingenious solutions, which occasionally become standard operating procedure in places like emergency rooms and modern battlefields. "It is an undeniable fact of all human existence," the young Lilly Caul wrote in her typically hyperbolic nineteen-year-old style, "that all great inventions of the human imagination are totally pumped up and enhanced by life-and-death situations." Sadly, over the course of the last two years, Lilly has learned that this concept does not necessarily hold true in the hellish pressure cooker of the plague. Over and over again, she has seen people walk directly into traps, lose all common sense amid swarms of walkers, make deadly mistakes, and generally become either sheep or monstrous versions of their true selves in the name of survival. But Lilly has also noticed that she may very well possess a kernel of prodigious skill in this area—turning catastrophe into creative solutions—which calms her in times of great peril. In fact, she feels this odd, nameless sensation right at this moment as the dead-end wall registers from person to person behind her in a series of hushed moans and shocked gasps.

"We were doing *so goddamn good*," Matthew opines next to her.

Bob turns away from the wall and snaps the hammer back on his Magnum. In the darkness, his eyes gleam with tension. "I got two speed loaders." He tosses a look at Ben. "How many mags you got left?"

"Two left, ten rounds each." A pearl of sweat drops off the end of Ben's nose. "Ain't much to speak of, situation like this."

"Wait a second, hold on," Lilly says, but right at that moment, nobody hears her. People are frantically loading and cocking their weapons. Some are crying softly, praying to themselves. Everybody is hyperaware of the churning sounds of the swarm coming toward them—unseen at the moment, coming from around the last bend in the passageway, about seventy-five feet away—a grinding, gnashing sound. The walkers' ETA is a minute or two at the most.

Out of the corner of her eye, Lilly sees the Reverend Jeremiah reaching for his tarnished steel cross, and soon he is moving toward the distant bend in the tunnel while softly praying. What Lilly *can't* see is the strange look on the preacher's face.

"What else we got in the way of firepower?" Bob is asking the group as a whole.

"Got about a dozen shells of deer shot left," the young man with the shotgun announces.

"We'll never hold them off!" a younger woman in a faded gingham pinafore wails. "It's our time—and it's not fair! Not like this!"

"Shut up, Mary Jean!" Sister Rose in her Capri pants has transitioned from sobbing to shrieking. "JUST STOP IT. STOP IT!"

David puts a hand on the fat woman's shoulder. "It's okay, sweetheart, we'll figure something out."

Bob turns to Matthew. "How about you and Speed get between us and the herd?"

"I'm low on rounds, man," Matthew warns. "Not gonna be able to hold them off long."

Bob nods. "Gonna have to resort to whatever blades, picks, and axes we got up our sleeves."

"Wait, wait . . . hold on." Lilly has an idea. It just materializes in her brain like a bubble popping. She moves toward the front of the group, shoving her way through the praying, sobbing congregants, moving in the direction from which they have just come, gazing up at the fingers of roots and icicles of limestone hanging down.

Ahead of her, Reverend Jeremiah has lowered himself to one knee, head bowed, softly praying. The wave of upright cadavers closes in, maybe less than a minute away. Lilly nearly chokes on the smell as she approaches the kneeling preacher. She still can't make out the strangely out-of-place expression on the man's face. But she can't think about that now; she's too focused on the task at hand and the process of turning disaster into inspiration.

She pauses and gazes up at the ceiling. In her mind's eye she sees the vectors of the tunnel—the load-bearing beams, the intermittent points of egress, the weak spots, the aging timbers, the worm-eaten supports—and all the noise around her disappears. The praying, the approaching rumble of the swarm, the pathetic sobbing noises, the sound of Bob preparing the shooters, the yelling, the shrieking, the arguing—all of it fades away in Lilly's ringing ears into the white noise of inspiration. She finally sees the stroke of luck for which she was hunting.

"Bob!" She spins toward the others. "Right up there!" Lilly points at the ceiling about thirty feet away from her. "See the broken beam?"

Bob holds his hand up to quiet the others. "EVERYBODY SHUT THE FUCK UP!"

Lilly and Bob make eye contact. The two old friends—who have been known to finish each other's sentences, read each other's minds, and share nonverbal communication of all sorts—now lock gazes. Lilly doesn't even have to say it. Bob knows. He can tell what she's thinking. "That beam is weak, Bob," she says. "Can you see it?"

Bob nods. He nods very slowly at first. Then his eyes widen, and he quickly turns to the others. "Speed! Ben! Matt! Everybody with a bullet left in his gun! FORGET THE WALKERS! YOU HEAR ME?"

For a brief moment, frantic, vexed glances are exchanged among the men with firearms.

"HEY!"

Lilly's booming shout wakes them up. She stands about fifty feet away from them, drawing both her empty Rugers. She aims at the ceiling as if to demonstrate what she wants. "EVERYBODY FIRE INTO THAT BEAM! ON MY SIGNAL! SEE IT?"

Bob shines his flashlight up at the rotten timber crisscrossing the roots and tongues of calcium. The sounds of bolts clanging fill the darkness. Lilly shoves her guns back into their holsters, and then points up at the cross brace. She sucks in a breath. She can hear the leading edge of the walker tsunami approaching, the odor of rancid proteins overwhelming. She screams, "NOW!"

The tunnel lights up with the fury of half a dozen firearms—muzzles flaring magnesium silver in the darkness—the collective roar drowning all other sound.

Everybody blasts away at the general vicinity of the cross brace, and the barrage gobbles through the rotten timbers with the efficiency of a chain saw, the splinters and dust flying in all directions, filling the darkness with a snowstorm of particulates, until the other members of the group begin to cough and back away and hold hands over their mouths. At last, the guns run dry—and the roof begins to cave in.

The enormous creaking noise makes everybody jerk back with a start, the swarm of walkers closing in, their silhouettes looming in the errant beams of flashlights. Their ghastly stench engulfs the tunnel, and their vocalizing rises to the point of a vast out-of-tune symphony swelling in the enclosed space, and Lilly backs against the wall, gaping at the spectacle, unable to tear her gaze from the ceiling as it begins to collapse directly on the front row of walking dead. Five or six of the creatures pause stupidly to look upward as the dirt sifts down on them and then begins to rain down in a torrent of earth and dust and shafts of celestial light slicing through the swirling haze like spindrifts.

People scatter. Lilly grabs the preacher by the collar and pulls him backward. Others dive for cover around the bend, some of them falling to the floor and covering their heads, while a few hobble quickly off into the deeper shadows. Bob shoves Ben away from the cave-in at the last possible moment as the ceiling comes down in a thunderhead of dust, the noise like a three-hundred-foot clipper ship wrenching apart in a storm. For a moment, Lilly closes her eyes and buries her face in the dirt floor as the tunnel becomes a thick undulating cloud.

Oddly, in those briefest of moments before Lilly closes her eyes as the ceiling comes down—just a single millisecond of time—she registers the blurry, indistinct image of a face in her periphery. The preacher Jeremiah has ducked down beside her, only inches away, covering the top of his head, the side of his face pressed against the floor. But in that soupçon of time that it takes the sight of his face to register in her brain, she realizes something strange and unexpected, something that, at first, simply does not compute, and will not make much sense for quite a while.

The man is smiling beatifically.

The dust clears moments later, and it takes another minute or so for Lilly to realize the sun is shining down on her. The chatter of crickets and birds comes from somewhere overhead, and the noise braces Lilly as she struggles to sit up with her back against the tunnel wall, blinking against the harsh daylight. She breathes in the clean air and smells pine—she hadn't noticed the scent of trees when she emerged from the passageways earlier—and now in her peripheral vision she sees the silhouettes of others rising to their feet in the nimbus of dust still flooding the breached tunnel. Lilly stands up. Next to her, Jeremiah brushes off his filthy suit coat and trousers, adjusts his tie, and gazes sadly at the sloping drift of earth before them.

"Poor wretched beasts," he mutters, almost speaking to himself, as he stares at the wall of dirt formed by the cave-in, the dust still clearing. "Certainly deserve a less ignominious death than this."

As the haze dissipates, Lilly sees five walkers sticking out of the massive pile of earth. They look like marionettes being operated by a psychotic puppeteer—their heads shuddering up and down, their blackened mouths working, their diode-white eyes bulging, tragically clueless—and they make the most disturbing noise. Their snarling, spitting growls have been reduced to a chorus of crumbling moans, the mewling of skinned cats, warbly and almost falsetto.

"All of God's creatures deserve deliverance," the preacher murmurs as he strides over to the cave-in, pulling the massive crucifix from its sheath. He pauses in front of the sloping cairn of dirt, some of the walkers reaching impotently for him, biting at the air. Jeremiah glances over his shoulder. "Rose, Mary Jean, Noelle . . . I'm gonna need y'all to turn away for just a second now."

Lilly notices the others have all risen to their feet, gathering in the pool of ashen daylight, looking on, silently transfixed by the cave-in, their matted hair tossing in the breeze. Bob, David, Ben, and Speed stand directly behind Lilly, and Bob mumbles something inaudible—but slightly skeptical—under his breath. The rest of the faces turn away, as if out of respect, as the preacher nods and turns back to his solemn task.

He gets the job done quickly. Each blow comes down hard and decisively, the sharpened end of the crucifix splitting the center of each rotting skull, letting out a bubbling cauldron of noxious gasses and cerebrospinal fluids as creature after creature flops forward, ruined head lolling with finality. The whole process takes only a minute. But that minute is both fascinating and troubling for Lilly.

After the last walker has been put down, they begin the process of climbing out of the tunnel. Bob goes first, scuttling up the forty-five-degree slope of loose earth with his .357 at the ready, Speed and Matthew coming up right behind him, their assault rifles locked and loaded. When they get to the top of the cave-in and peer over the mound of loose earth, they see at least a dozen creatures aimlessly wandering the desolate streets and boarded storefronts of Carlinville.

Among them, the three men have enough ammo to pick off the errant walkers one by one—the creatures going down in distant puffs of blood-mist and flopping limbs—and Bob even manages to conserve a few rounds for the long journey home. When he's satisfied that the outskirts are clear enough to convey all twenty people, he starts bringing people up from the tunnel one at a time.

It takes forever to get all the elder members of the church group—as well as the group's sizable collection of bulging knapsacks—out of the trench and across the patchwork of vacant lots and access roads. Bob has to stay on top of the older ones like an overworked sheepherder.

When everybody is safely hidden within the cover of the forest, Bob takes them single file down a narrow path. Lilly and Jeremiah bring up the rear. Bob can hear them talking—he can't make out what they're saying—and it bothers him. This preacher makes Bob nervous. He tries to put it out of his mind and focus on the journey, with

Matthew and Speed striding alongside him, their assault rifles cradled high against their burly chests.

They remind Bob of those Delta Force types who used to patrol the streets of Kuwait City. Those Special Forces douche bags used to push Bob around, pull rank on him all the time—and don't even get Bob started on how they treated the indigenous personnel—but secretly Bob was glad they were there. Just like now. Speed with his rhino neck and steroidal muscles, and Matthew with his gnarled biceps and barrel-chested laborer's physique, they can be a huge pain in the behind, and half the time they seem like they're on something, weed or pills, but regardless, Bob is still glad that they're on *his* side.

Bob has a strong feeling that, sooner or later, he's going to need them.

They head north through the wooded hills of Upson County, following an old footpath that runs between the tobacco farms and old defunct cotton fields. Once upon a time you couldn't throw a rock down here without hitting a plantation. And as far as Bob knows, this very trail could have been a legacy of the Underground Railroad—now overgrown at points with jungles of sumac, kudzu, and boxwoods—which would be highly apropos considering the mission they are on. Bob uses his survey map and visual landmarks to keep them on course.

At certain points, the path winds up the sides of hills, giving the group an unimpeded view of the Crest Highway on one side and the serpentine tributaries of Elkins Creek on the other. From this vantage point, the stream looks like a ribbon of tinsel weaving through the neglected cotton fields, and the scattered silhouettes of walkers—from this height as tiny and busy as cockroaches—seem to be everywhere, infesting the ruins of old barns, scuttling along deserted roads, treading through the stalks of overgrown farm fields, and hunkering here and there in dry creek beds and valleys, feeding off the remains of some unfortunate human or animal.

Thankfully the high footpath seems to be off the walkers' radar at the moment.

Five miles into the journey, Bob starts wondering about something.

Out of the corner of his eye, he's been catching glimpses of the preacher and Lilly at the rear of the pack, chatting idly, occasionally laughing at some irony or humorous anecdote. Bob notices the heavy duffel bag that the preacher hasn't let out of his sight since he left the chapel. Four or five feet long, made of heavy black canvas, the thing looks as though it weighs a ton. And whatever it holds looks far more substantial than the vestments and accoutrements of a clergyman. What the hell does he have in there? Guns? Gold bullion? The Holy Grail? Or maybe he's carrying a lifetime supply of holy water and wafers.

Again, Bob tries to put it out of his mind and focus on the journey.

He knows that they'll need to turn west at a certain point and find a bridge across Elkins Creek in order to reach Woodbury by nightfall. The older people are already exhausted, despite the fact that Lilly has allowed the group three separate rest stops. Their water supplies are getting low, and they don't have the ammunition to overcome another herd. Bob starts to get worried. The sun has started to sink behind the tree line to the west, and there's still no sign of Highway 18 in the distance—just a continuous, unbroken chain of abandoned fields.

It'll be another hour before Bob will admit to the others—and himself, for that matter—that they are hopelessly, inexorably, dangerously *lost*.

"It ain't something I ever want to live through again, I'll tell ya that much," the good Reverend Jeremiah Garlitz confesses in a low voice to Lilly as the twosome amble along the winding path, the late-afternoon sun blazing down on the backs of their necks. They walk slowly in order to keep enough paces between them and the rest of the church group, mostly to maintain a modicum of privacy—not that they're saying anything illicit or have anything to hide. They simply prefer discretion at this point. "Never saw it coming," he mutters, shaking his big handsome head. He carries his heavy black duffel on one broad shoulder, the strap digging into his suit coat. "We had done baptisms in that river a million times, brought countless of our brothers and sisters to Christ . . ."

He pauses and looks down as he walks. Lilly sees the tears in his eyes.

Jeremiah continues. "I thought it was fish at first, we get catfish down there sometimes the size of Dobermans, but when the water started stirring up, and that poor, poor woman from Hastings got snagged . . ."

Again he stops, adjusting the shoulder strap, and a single tear tracks across the cleft in his prominent chin. Lilly looks away and remains silent out of respect.

"Anyway, with that said, it would be a blessing to settle somewhere." He looks at Lilly. "Somewhere safe, with good folks like yourself." He looks thoughtfully at the backs of his flock, the slumped shoulders and sunburned baldpates of the older congregants as they trudge dutifully along, following Bob up the winding path. "These poor folks have been through hell," Jeremiah says. "They seen things that no decent person should ever have to see." For a moment he gazes off at the horizon as though searching some hidden part of his memory. "One thing this here plague has taught all of us—believers and nonbelievers alike—and that's the immutable fact that there are things could happen to a soul that are much, much worse than dying." He pauses, then looks back at Lilly, his eyes clearing. "What am I saying? You've probably seen things I can't even imagine."

Lilly shrugs as she walks. "I guess you start to get numb to it. I don't know." She thinks about it. "It still gets to me, though." She thinks some more. "I guess I should be thankful for that."

He looks at her without breaking stride. "Whaddaya mean, thankful?"

She shrugs again. "Thankful that I haven't become completely dead inside . . . that I still have the ability to be shocked."

"That's because you're a good soul—a natural-born good person—I can tell. I know we just met, but you can just tell with some folks."

Lilly smiles. "Spend a little time with me and you'll change your mind."

He chuckles. "I doubt that." The wind buffets the flap of his suit coat open, exposing the top of the crucifix sheathed on his belt. He rests his hand on it. "But you know, you're right about one thing. No matter who you are, you lose a little bit of your soul every time you gotta put one of them wretched creatures outta its misery."

Lilly offers no response. They walk a little bit farther in silence. At last, Lilly glances at the top of the crucifix visible inside his coat. "Can I ask you something?"

"Shoot."

"What's with the crucifix?"

"How do you mean?"

Lilly smiles. "It's not exactly standard equipment for a minister."

He lets out a sigh. "True . . . but there ain't much of *anything* in this world that's standard anymore."

"True. But isn't it—I don't know—a little *sacrilegious* using a cross for cracking open heads? Bet there's an interesting story there."

He looks at her. "There's a story, all right, but it ain't all that interesting."

"I'll be the judge of that," Lilly says with a grin, realizing once again that she might as well face the fact that she kind of likes this guy. God help her, she kind of trusts him.

"Couple years ago," he says, "right around the time the whole mess broke out, I was down to Slidell, Louisiana, visiting friends. There was an old Catholic church down there—went all the way back to Lewis and Clark—the minister there was an old friend, and he got bit real bad. I came as soon as I found out, and I found him in the sanctuary, on the floor near the altar, on his last legs. Hadn't turned yet, but you could just tell he was going over any second. He held my hand and he asked me . . ." He pauses, looks down, licking his lips. Lilly can tell this is hard for him, but she just keeps silently walking alongside him and patiently waiting for him to complete the thought. "He asked me to do him in," Jeremiah finally murmurs in a lower register. "I pulled my pea shooter, but he stopped me. And then something very strange happened. With every last ounce of strength he had in him . . . he pointed up to the big old cross above the altar. I knew immediately what he meant. I don't know how I knew, but I just did."

Another pause. Lilly waits for a second, and then she asks him what happened.

"I administered the last rites best I knew them. I found a font of holy water and I apologized for not knowing any of the Latin, but I anointed him and took his confession. He was happy it was me with him in those last minutes. I could tell. Better some old Pentecostal yay-hoo from your backyard sending you off than some stranger in a hospital or some deacon out in the field. Anyway, after that, I did what comes naturally when you see them eyes going yellow like fish eyes . . . and you see them teeth showing. I bashed his head in. Lost my mind a little, I guess. I think I passed out. When I woke up there was some of them creatures in the sanctuary with me, and they was coming for me, and I went a little haywire. Couldn't find my pistol. All I had was this old cross. I took them down one at a time with the thing, and afterward I saw it gleaming in the votive light and I guess I reckoned that was some kind of a sign. Basically, that's how it all came about."

Lilly nods. "Makes sense to me."

"I made a few modifications to the thing," he says. "I don't think the Good Lord would mind too much that I've defaced the image of his only Son, this day and age. Serves me well in tight quarters."

Lilly lets out a little nervous chuckle. "Have to admit, you're pretty handy with—"

She stops when she notices something going on ahead of them on the trail. Apparently Bob, Speed, and Matthew have stopped on the edge of the path about fifty yards away, the people behind them coming to an abrupt stop at the sight of Bob's hand shooting up.

Something is wrong. Lilly can tell. She can feel it. In the elongating shadows of dusk, through the whirling dust devils of gnats, she can see Bob pointing to the north, and then to the west, and the other two men arguing with him, and David coming up to the group to put his two cents in, and then Ben getting involved.

"What now?" Lilly says somewhat rhetorically to the preacher.

FIFTEEN

In the overmedicated, overdisinfected, overprotective years before the plague, nobody over the age of six ever got lost. With GPS devices in everything from cars to phones to key chains—as well as the satellites of Big Brother orbiting the earth—very few journeys were ever undertaken without the digital bread crumbs of tracking devices showing people the way home. Then came the scourge of the reanimated dead, and all around the world the grids, towers, transmitters, cell service providers, routers, cams, drones, and bugs went dark. Making matters worse was the gradual decay of the environment. Like the effects of aging on a human face, the landscape began to gray and sag and appear strangely homogenous. Old men look a lot like old women, and one rural backwater has begun to look a lot like another on an opposite side of a county. Weeds and foliage and opportunistic vines have overtaken farm fields. The weather has turned every structure into the same dilapidated pile of lumber the same shade of wormy gray. The cities have all become overgrown Chernobyls with desolate, boarded buildings swallowed in thick kudzu and brown creeping ivy. Everything has begun to look the same, which is exactly why Bob now stands on a craggy bluff overlooking the deepening shadows of the Central Georgia farmland, scratching his chin nervously as he tries to figure out where the hell they are. He looks at his survey map and then at the horizon. The snaking silver waters of Elkins Creek shimmer inscrutably in the dying light.

"Did you check the compass?" Ben asks from the other side of the trail, where he has dropped his heavy knapsack in the dirt. His voice drips with sarcasm. "Those little gizmos have been known to come in handy when you're lost."

"Put a lid on it, Ben," Lilly says under her breath, keeping the exchange from the earshot of the others. Her heart gallops. Getting lost is not an option, and even though they see only a smattering of walkers off in the distance, on the edges of the desolate bean fields and down in the troughs of dry streambeds, they don't have the resources to spend even one additional night in the wild. "Bob, did we cross Highway Eighteen by mistake?"

"I don't know," he says with a sigh. "Compass says we're heading northwest, but I'll be damned if I can tell how far north we are." By this point, the rest of the church group has gathered around. Jeremiah comes up behind Lilly and slides the enormous duffel bag off his shoulder, setting it down carefully with a weary sigh. The muffled sound of something clinking in the bag gets Lilly's attention for a moment. What the fuck does he have in there? Cases of booze? Sacramental wine? She turns back to Bob and sees him running fingers through his greasy graying hair, squinting into the setting sun, the wrinkles around his eyes deepening to the point of looking like braided leather. He looks at her. "Only thing I can tell you for sure is we should have reached the River Cove overpass by now."

"We're too far north," Lilly says gravely.

"Thank you, Sherlock," Ben wisecracks.

David shakes his head. "Ben, are you just naturally an asshole, or do you work at it?"

Ben grins, maybe for the first time since they left Woodbury. "Somebody's gotta do it."

"Everybody, just shut up for a second and let me think," Bob says, the survey map open to Meriwether County. Lilly watches him trace the winding tributary of Elkins Creek with a grubby fingernail, when the sound of Matthew's voice tugs at her attention.

"Lilly?"

Lilly looks up from the map and sees Matthew and Speed standing side by side behind her, each man looking a bit hangdog, sheepish, maybe even a little anxious. Each holds an assault rifle high on his chest. Matthew says, "Can I suggest something?"

"Go ahead, Matthew."

"The thing is, Speed and I have been scouting this territory for weeks now. Maybe we could go take a quick look-see while the group rests, maybe we'll find a landmark or something."

Lilly thinks about it. "All right, if you make it snappy. We don't want to be out in the open when darkness rolls in. I'll go with you."

Matthew and Speed exchange a glance, and Matthew scratches his lower lip awkwardly, indecisively. "Um . . . we can handle this on our own, you don't have to—"

"I'm going and that's the end of it. *Come on*, we're losing daylight."

A huge sigh from Matthew. "All right, whatever."

Lilly looks at Bob. "If something happens, and we're not back in half an hour, get these people somewhere safe, or at least safer than standing out here in the open on this fucking footpath."

"Will do," Bob says.

Lilly turns to the others and speaks up so the people in the back can hear her. "Ladies and gentlemen, we're going to take a small scouting party out, get the lay of the land before we go any farther."

The big woman in Capri pants steps forward. "Y'all are lost, ain't ya?"

It takes the three of them less than ten minutes to reach the bottom of the wooded hills and start following Elkins Creek south. Matthew takes the lead, with Lilly on his heels, and Speed bringing up the rear with his assault rifle in the ready position, the stock braced on his shoulder commando-style. They traverse at least a quarter mile in this fashion, eyes wide and alert for walkers, sensory organs heightened by the light and space of the farmland. Speed has never been trained in paramilitary protocol or even the most rudimentary handling of firearms. Everything he knows about weaponry he learned from playing video games. But he knows one thing for sure—one indisputable, unassailable, undeniable fact—and it fills his nostrils now as they cross the rocky, matted earth of an arid riverbed and plunge into the thickets of an overgrown tobacco field.

"Matt! You smell that?" Speed breathes in the musky, herby scent permeating the breeze. "Correct me if I'm wrong, but it's getting stronger!"

About thirty feet ahead of him, walking a few paces in front of Lilly, Matthew cuts a swath through the gigantic tobacco leaves with his muscular tradesman's body. He holds his AR-15 against his collarbone, cradled stiffly in his sinewy arms. He reminds Speed of an enormous grizzly on the scent, closing in on a school of trout.

Matthew knows this smell as well as Speed—the telltale sour sage funk that gets into one's drapes and the carpets of one's car and can even invade the fibers of an empty pocket or a ziplock when the cops come sniffing around. To many, it's a fragrance as convivial as that of freshly baked cookies, as sensual as an ocean breeze, as seductive as expensive perfume warmed by the body heat of a beautiful woman. Right at this moment, in fact, even Lilly can detect a familiar odor.

"Is that—?" Lilly pauses and glances over her shoulder at Speed weaving through the stalks and leaves. "That smell, that's not—"

"Yes, Lilly, it is *indeed*," Matthew says with the kind of reverence one reserves for finding the largest truffle in the forest or the biggest golden nugget in the mountain stream or the one holy chalice used by Christ. He lowers his gun and pauses amid the tobacco plants. The sea of enormous kelly-green leaves talk in the breeze, making hollow bongo-slap sounds that drift up into the humid, hazy clouds.

"You guys been holding out on me?" Lilly says to Matthew with a crooked smile. She would never consider herself a stoner, but she used to imbibe on a regular basis with her friend Megan to the point of missing it in the morning if she couldn't have a toke with her first cup of coffee. When the plague broke out, she found herself wanting it more and more to take the edge off, but scoring a bag of weed in these times was easier said than done.

"We were going to share it," Speed assures her with a forced smile as he joins them in a narrow clearing surrounded by a wall of green at least six feet high. The smell of marijuana is so redolent now— mingling with the odors of black earth and decay—that Lilly feels like she's getting a contact buzz.

"In terms of direction," Matthew says, standing on the toes of his jackboots, trying to see over the tops of flowering tobacco swaying in the wind. The buffeting drumming noise of the leaves nearly drowns out his voice. "I'm thinking the stash is that way . . . Speed-O, your thoughts?"

Speed peers over the stalks. "Yeah, definitely, I can see the trees. See 'em?"

"Yep." Matthew looks at Lilly. "Just inside that little grouping of oak trees to the west? See them? There's a plot of land right there, smack-dab in the middle of the tobacco, where somebody was growing the sweetest bud this side of fucking Humboldt County."

Lilly gazes at the trees. "Okay, so I assume this means you know where we are?"

Matthew exchanges a grin with Speed, then turns the grin on Lilly.

"Walk toward the smell, folks," Matthew instructs as he and Speed usher the group down a winding path that skirts the edge of the tobacco fields.

Bob and Lilly bring up the rear, giving each other loaded glances.

A few minutes ago, Lilly had allowed the two young men to harvest a few ounces before returning to the group, and now she has to struggle to keep from grinning. She saw them sneaking a few tokes before taking their places at the edge of the bluff like a stoned Lewis and Clark. Now they're leading the ragtag group with suspiciously grandiose bearings.

The woman in Capri pants frowns as she sniffs the air with the curiosity of a bloodhound. "Is that skunk?"

"Skunk *weed*, is more like it," Bob mumbles under his breath.

Lilly stifles her laughter. "I think it's a family of possums."

Bob coughs to disguise his chuckling. "I believe the plural of possum is *possum*."

One of the other church members murmurs, "Never smelled no possum like that."

The preacher appears to be wise to the ruse. He smiles as he lopes along with his flock, making Lilly wonder if he has imbibed in the herb himself. "It's all part of God's rich bounty, Sister Rose," he says with a twinkle in his eye and a wink for Lilly.

They make it home before full darkness sets in, dragging with exhaustion, spent from the journey. They come from the east, bathed in the blue light of dusk, and they see the outskirts of the town long before the sentries on the east wall see them.

By this point, Lilly has the lead, and she quickens her pace when she glimpses the old ruins of the railroad depot and the burned-out shells of cars in the hazy distance. She sees the broken-down water tower with the faded letters WOO URY stenciled on the side, the boarded engine shed with its charred roof damaged by the fires earlier that month, and the ramshackle barricade with its semitrailer gate north of the shed. Her heart beats faster as she turns and signals the others.

At this very moment, as the group hastens across the wasted outer lots and closes in on the east entrance, a number of revelations strike Lilly. Chief among them is the fact that she never realized how much this place had grown on her. For all its traumatic memories, the deaths of her friends that occurred here, the loss of so many good people, and the horrific reign of the Governor, Lilly has adopted this place as her home. Or maybe it has adopted her. Who would have thought that she—the cool, hipster fashionista from Atlanta—would have come to love such a tiny, backward burg as this? More important, as she hurries toward the wall, waving at the frizzy-haired figure of Barbara on a cherry picker in the distance, Lilly realizes with some measure of chagrin that her heart is racing now for completely unexpected reasons—a powerful set of emotions, some of them contradictory to each other—that are just now bubbling to the surface.

For practically the whole time she's been away on this rescue mission—intermittently and yet sometimes at the oddest moments—she has been thinking about Calvin Dupree. Half-formed images have been flickering in the back of Lilly's mind from that night she almost kissed him. For some reason she hasn't been able to stop thinking about his scent—that soapy combination of Old Spice and chewing gum—and the clear, deep, knowing look in his eyes. For the entire trip Lilly has been continually aware of the delicate chain with the tiny cross around her neck that Calvin gave her. If they had gone ahead and kissed that night in front of the courthouse, Lilly probably wouldn't have been thinking about that moment so long-ingly, so compulsively, so obsessively. But that moment now looms so large in her mind that she feels—as she closes in on the wall—like a child on Christmas morning rushing down the stairs to see what Santa has left her.

"Look what the cat dragged in," Barbara jokes from her perch on the cherry picker, calling down to the weary travelers as they approach. "What are you doing, Lilly, pretending you're Moses?"

David trots alongside Lilly, grinning up at his wife of thirty-seven years. "Typical! We're not even inside the wall yet and already she's giving us shit!"

"You look like hell, David!" Barbara gazes at the others. "Am I supposed to cook for all these people?"

"I love you, too, sweetheart!"

The engine in the semicab fires up suddenly as Bob gives a whistle.

Lilly and the others crowd around the entrance. Bob holsters his .357 and yanks a cross brace away from the gap as the truck cab rumbles, belches black fumes, and then begins to back away from the opening. Ben, Speed, and Matthew pull chains off the breach and motion to the others that it's safe to go ahead and enter.

Reverend Jeremiah looks like a child seeing the big city for the first time, his eyes wide with awe, his gigantic duffel weighing down his shoulder as he gazes with wonder at the scorched, battle-worn, be-leaguered town. He mumbles a continuous stream of *Thank the Lord* as he ushers his flock one at a time through the opening.

By this point, word has spread like a brushfire through Woodbury that the rescue team is back, all in one piece, and the jubilation and surprise show on the expectant faces that appear around street corners and buildings. Gloria comes rushing around the end of an adjacent semitrailer with a rifle in her hand and a huge grin on her face. Tommy Dupree comes scampering up from the speedway gardens still gripping a shovel, his face blazing with excitement. Others come out of doors and around the sides of the courthouse building with euphoric expressions on their careworn faces.

Hands are shaken, hugs proffered, introductions made—the preacher seems to be in his element, bowing, grinning at people with his million-kilowatt smile and blessing everyone within fifty yards, his charisma on high boil—and Lilly watches it all with awkward satisfaction. She keeps scanning the grounds, looking for Calvin. Where is he? She asks Tommy and the boy gives a whistle and calls out for his dad. Lilly's pulse starts to quicken. In the distance across the square, the courthouse door bangs open, and Calvin comes scuttling down the steps in his work pants, clodhoppers, and chambray shirt, rubbing the back of his neck with a bandanna. He looks like a country gentleman, maybe a construction foreman or bachelor farmer, hurrying to work. When he sees Lilly, his face lights up.

"Look who's here, Dad!" Tommy Dupree stands proudly next to Lilly as though he brought her back alive himself. Lilly feels the boy's fingers brush hers for a moment, and then, very naturally, as though he's been doing it all his life, the boy grasps her hand and holds it.

Calvin comes up and gives Lilly a chaste little hug, the kind of greeting a pair of coworkers at a cocktail party might give each other. "God, it's good to see you."

Lilly grins at him. "Back at ya, Calvin. You have no idea how good it is to be back."

"Looks like it's mission accomplished." He makes a gesture toward all the introductions going on around them. "Pretty impressive."

Lilly shrugs. "They would have done the same for us, believe me."

"Barbara said they lost contact with you."

"Walkies were out of range for a while, some of the batteries were low."

Calvin nods. "Wasn't the same without you around here." He puts a hand on Tommy's shoulder. "Tommy's turned into quite a gardener."

The boy beams at her. "I planted the rest of them melon seeds today."

"That's great, Tommy. Maybe tomorrow we can start in on the tomatoes."

The boy nods. "And when them tomatoes grow, can we make spaghetti?"

Lilly lets out a chortling laugh despite her exhaustion. "Oh, my God . . . what I would give for a plate of fettuccini Alfredo."

Calvin is looking at her with an easy, natural smile, but there's a spark of something darker behind his eyes, something more like longing. "Would you settle for some stale dry cereal and powdered milk?"

She returns his gaze. She sees the glint of desire in his eyes. It takes her breath away. She smiles back at him. "Are you buying?"

That evening, Reverend Jeremiah makes a special point to personally introduce himself to each and every one of the twenty-two residents of Woodbury who stayed behind. Dripping with charm and exhibiting a joie de vivre that folks around these parts have not seen in a long while, he holds court in the town square long after darkness has set in and the torches have started to burn down to the nubs in doorways and windows. For hours he lingers under the crooked limbs of ancient live oaks, in the light of a fire pit, lovingly introducing the people of Woodbury to the people of his small congregation, making gentle little jokes about each member's personality quirks. He jokes about Sister Rose in her Capri pants being the fashion icon of the group, and he ribs his eldest member, Brother Joe, for being the closest to God . . . *literally*. He teases his two college-age congregants, Brothers Stephen and Mark, for being Sunday school dropouts, and he introduces his only black congregant, a middle-aged man with a fussy little pen-line mustache named Harold Stauback, as the Voice of Valdosta, a former deejay and famous soloist from the Calgary Baptist Church choir. But for most of the evening, between sips of broth and instant tea, Brother Jeremiah profusely thanks the Woodbury people for saving the lives of his flock and giving them a second chance at survival. He pledges to work his proverbial butt off to make Woodbury safe and prosperous. He promises to be a team member and pitch in and do his part and make sure all his people do the same.

If he were running for something, he would be elected in a landslide.

"I know it's a golden oldie of a cliché," he says late that night, puffing a cheroot, leaning back on one of the rickety Adirondack chairs positioned around the fire pit, the dwindling flames illuminating the faces of the faithful who have remained gathered around him, "but the Good Lord does work in mysterious ways."

"How do you mean?" Ben Buchholz asks from the other side of the pit, the flickering glow of the firelight making his weathered features look almost lupine in the darkness. Perched on a stump, smoking an unfiltered Camel, Ben has been listening intently to the preacher all night long, laughing at the man's jokes and nodding thoughtfully at every homespun piece of wisdom that has come out of his mouth. Those who have known Ben the longest have been highly amused at this phenomenon and the speed with which the preacher has won over the town curmudgeon. Now the other dozen or so stalwart souls who have remained in the town square that night to chew the fat wait attentively for the man's answer.

The preacher yawns. "All I mean is that we were meant to come here and be with y'all." He smiles, and even in the darkness his Ultrabrite grin is dazzling. "This is where our destiny lies, Ben. Y'all are God's people. I might even go as far as saying y'all are the chosen people, and we are blessed by y'all risking your lives to take us in." He pauses to puff on his stogie. "We lost some of our people back there in Carlinville. We pray that their souls are sent home, and they rest in peace in God's loving hands." He looks down, and the others remain silent out of respect. Even Ben looks down out of deference to the preacher. After a moment, Jeremiah looks up at them. "I promise you one thing. We ain't gonna take this act of kindness, mercy, and love for granted. We're gonna earn our way here. I'm gonna roll up my sleeves and help out in any way I can. And so are my people. I can see that Lilly's the one in charge here, so whatever she wants, she's gonna get. We owe y'all our lives."

He tosses his cheroot onto the smoldering embers of the fire as if punctuating his proclamation with this grand gesture.

The others soak it all in. Beside Ben, David and Barbara sit on lawn chairs, nodding pensively, a blanket over their laps. Speed and Matthew lounge on the grass behind the Sterns, absorbing everything that's being said while passing a small pipe back and forth, pretending nobody knows that they're imbibing in the fruits of their secret harvest. On the other side of the fire pit, Gloria sprawls sleepily on a chaise longue, nursing a plastic Solo cup of cheap wine, drifting in and out of a catlike slumber. The half dozen or so other souls relax on the ground around the preacher, hanging on his every word. Sister Rose is still there, hanging in, as is the gospel singer, Harold Stauback, now lying on the grass, propped up on one elbow as he listens. They all silently process the preacher's magnanimous soliloquy and think about how good it is these days for two tribes of people to come together as one, to work hand in hand, to help each other, to love each other.

In fact, beyond the boundaries of that flickering firelight in the square that night, virtually every living soul in Woodbury feels the same way: that the dark days are behind them, that the future of the community has never looked brighter, and that there's hope.

The only one taking exception to all this utopian bliss hasn't been seen for hours.

Bob Stookey has been mostly keeping to himself since returning home from the rescue mission, and he will continue maintaining a low profile—keeping his feelings to himself—for as long as it takes to find evidence to back up his suspicions.

Then he will expose this two-bit flimflam artist who calls himself a man of God.

SIXTEEN

In the wee hours that morning, in the courthouse basement, where a modest cafeteria once served the secretarial pool and midlevel bureaucrats of the Meriwether County government, Lilly and Calvin watch Tommy snoring softly, his head on one of the big folding tables, a few empty Red Bull cans, Styrofoam bowls, empty cereal boxes, and the wadded wrappers of a half dozen Twinkies arrayed around his head like an enormous halo. An ancient sign hangs on the wall behind the boy, showing a friendly bear in a ranger hat asking all who pass to keep Meriwether County free of forest fires. For the last hour and a half, Tommy had been trying to stay up with his dad and Lilly, talking about the day's mission and the adventures in the tunnel, until his head started nodding and lolling forward. A few minutes ago, he nearly went face-first into his Post Toasties. Calvin decided to let him doze right there while Lilly and he discussed private matters.

Now the two of them have moved to the end of the long table, and Lilly sits on the edge of the table while Calvin paces restlessly, murmuring softly, "I won't lie to you, I had my doubts about this whole rescue mission."

"Whaddaya mean?" She looks at him. "You mean whether we would find these people?"

"Yeah, I guess . . . that and whether you could even get all the way to the other side of the county in this tunnel. I could tell *he* was really worried, too." Calvin indicates the slumbering teenager. "He fidgeted and worried the whole time. I tried to keep him busy in the raceway garden, but he's been through a lot lately with his mom's passing and all." Calvin looks down. "He's really sweet on you, Lilly." Calvin looks up at her. "All the kids are."

The briefest pause, with Lilly wanting to ask Calvin if *he* is sweet on her as well, but she controls the urge and just says, "I adore *them*." She licks her lips. "You said it yourself, we had no choice. We had to do it. It was the right thing to do."

"Obviously. Look at all the lives you saved. Woodbury's gonna be stronger for it."

"That preacher's a character, isn't he?"

Calvin chuckles. "He's got the spirit in him, that's for sure." His smile fades. "I've seen a slew of men like him over the years, kind of guy who could sell an ice cream cone to an Eskimo." He thinks about it for a moment. "Usually these guys turn out to be opportunists. You know? But *this* guy, he seems . . . different. I trust him for some reason. Don't ask me why. He just seems like a decent human being who found his calling preaching the Word."

Lilly smiles. "I have to say, I kind of know exactly what you're talking about. He seems honest . . . sincere. Something. Can't quite put my finger on it."

Calvin nods. "I know. Just trust your gut, Lilly. It's served you well up to now. It's served us all well."

Her smile turns bashful as she looks down. "I thank you for that, Calvin."

Calvin chews his lip for a moment. "I keep telling you to call me Cal."

"Sorry . . . Cal it is." She looks at him, wanting to reach out and touch the faint shadow of whiskers on his strong chin. Her midriff flutters suddenly as he comes over and sits on the edge of the table next to her. Now she can smell that trademark scent of soap, Juicy Fruit, and Old Spice. How the hell does he manage to smell so good in this crazy age? Most people smell like wet dog fur and dried urine, but this guy smells like he's about to go on a date. "I'll be honest," he says to her now in a softer voice, "I wasn't exactly cool as a cucumber myself the past twenty-four hours."

She looks at him. "Were you worried about me, too?"

He shrugs and grins. "Well, you know how it is. I'm a worrywart."

A noise from the other end of the table gets their attention. Tommy Dupree stirs, lets out a little cough. Calvin puts his hand over his mouth and gives Lilly an exaggerated *Oops* look. She puts a finger to her lips and tries to quell her giggles. They push themselves off the table and tiptoe across the room, performing a pantomime of two bandits stealing away in the night, trying not to set off an alarm or rouse the bank guards.

They slip out the door and into the cluttered, shadowy main corridor, where a single emergency lamp glows at the end of the hall, lengthening shadows and barely illuminating a floor littered with shell casings, coils of strapping tape, and filthy puddles of muck. Plastic tarps cover the radiators, and a few of the exposed pipes in the ceiling still drip with dirty water backed up for months.

They stand against the corridor wall, facing each other, gazes locked. Calvin touches her chin lightly, mesmerized by the contours of her face. "I *was* worried about you," he says with a smile. "I confess . . . I missed you."

Something changes like a switch being thrown. Calvin looks into her eyes, his smile fading. Lilly's smile fades as well, as she returns his gaze. They stare at each other for an endless moment, the water dripping every few seconds, landing between them, making plinking noises on the floor but hardly registering with either of them. Lilly feels a warm sensation in her midsection rising like a tide, her spine tingling, her flesh rashing with goose bumps. She can barely hear Calvin's voice as he says, "Maybe we ought to go somewhere and—"

She lunges at him and presses her lips on his, and he seems ready for it because he wraps his arms around her and presses his lips back on hers.

The kiss lasts for several seconds, and has a narrative to it, a series of stages, which begins when Lilly opens her mouth and hungrily thrusts her tongue into him, and he responds in kind, probing her with his own tongue, and their embrace tightens and progresses from desperate hugging to mad, intense groping and fondling and caressing and squeezing, and nothing is off-limits now. There is an engine driving both of them. He grabs her breasts and presses his palms against her hardening nipples, and she lets out a little muffled gasp as she presses against his crotch, which has already started to tent outward, and now they move into the second stage as she pins him against the wall, and he starts dry-humping her, and the condensation only adds to the mounting heat between them. The water drips in their hair and on their shoulders as they undulate against each other, their kiss deteriorating into a mad sort of wrestling hold. Their lips are pressing so hard on each other now that they draw blood. Lilly can taste it—coppery and salty on the back of her tongue, gushing warmly—and the flavor of it only fuels her frenzy. She releases his lips and bites his neck, tastes his flesh, and almost inadvertently, like two people who have fallen off a cliff, they career into stage three. It begins with Calvin's hands fumbling downward, pulling off his belt, ripping open his fly, prying open her thighs, yanking her waistband down, spinning her toward the wall and shoving into her, shoving, thrusting, shoving, while Lilly lets out little rhythmic cries and rides the lightning bolt that's building between them. The water has inundated them now, and for one brief, wonderful moment of electric abandon, Lilly has completely lost herself in the liquid lightning, and she doesn't know her own name or where she is or whom she is with, and there is no plague anymore, and no death, and no misery, no space or time, no physical laws of the universe, there is only the lightning . . . the blessed, sacred, cleansing lightning.

At first light the next morning, Lilly wakes up shivering on the floor of the corridor, a shipping blanket tossed haphazardly over her and Calvin, who lies asleep next to her, his brow furrowed and knitted with a nightmare. A thin beam of daylight filters through a boarded window. The small of Lilly's back is stuck to the floor in the grit and moisture. For a moment, she feels like a piece of garbage—on many levels—as she peels herself off the floor and sits up, rubbing her sore eyes and stretching her neck. Calvin stirs. He blinks and clears his throat as he slowly awakens, suddenly sitting up as though startled.

"Oh, wow," he says, rubbing a kink out of his neck and looking at his pants still bunched around his ankles. "Oh, my . . . I'm sorry. I'm sorry."

"Let's not make a big deal out of it," Lilly says as she pulls her clothes back on, swallowing the taste of dried blood and sleep in her mouth. "It happened. It is what it is. You're still the same good person you were before last night. Case closed."

He looks at her. He blinks some more, and he tries to latch onto her words. "Case closed? Does that mean—"

"It doesn't mean anything . . . I don't know what it means, I don't know what I'm saying exactly, I'm not thinking straight." She runs her fingers through her hair and swallows the bitter taste in her mouth. "Is Tommy still in there?"

Calvin struggles to his feet, lurches across the corridor, and peers through the narrow window embedded in the door. "Still sawing logs." Calvin turns to her, wringing his hands nervously. "Dear Lord, I hope he didn't hear anything last night."

Lilly goes to him, puts a hand on his shoulder. "Look, I know you've been through a lot—"

He pulls away from her. "I shouldn't have done this, I don't know what I was thinking. Out in the middle of a hallway like this." He looks into her eyes, his gaze feverish with regret, shame, even terror. "I have a family—a wife of seventeen years—I mean I *had* a wife." His eyes get big and wet. "I can't believe I did this."

"Cal, listen to me." She takes him by the shoulders, bracing him. She speaks in an even tone, locking gazes with him. "World we live in, it's not business as usual. You can't beat yourself up over something like this." He starts to respond, but she grips his shoulders even tighter. "I'm not some lovelorn high school girl. I'm not gonna spread this around if you're not comfortable."

"It's not that, Lilly." He steps back from her, but he holds one of her hands. His voice softens. "I don't blame you one whit for what happened. God gave us all free will. I been flirting with you all along. But it's a sin what I did, in front of God and all. Twenty feet away from where my child is sleeping?"

"Calvin, please—"

"No!" He burns his gaze into her. "Let me finish. Please. What I'm saying is, it *does* matter in these times, these End Days, a person's choices, how a person behaves—"

"Wait . . . slow down . . . what do you mean, End Days?"

He looks at her as though she just slapped him in the face. "I know you ain't a believer, but that still doesn't change the fact that Armageddon is exactly what this is. Look around, open your eyes. These are the End Times, Lilly, and it matters more now than it did before what a person does—*because God is watching*. You understand? He's watching us even more closely than he was before."

Lilly lets out an anguished, frustrated breath. "I respect your beliefs, Cal. I really do. But here's a news flash for you: I'm no heathen. I always believed in a higher power, ever since I was a kid. I believe there *is* a God. But not a God that punishes or keeps score or wreaks havoc on us for not being perfect. I believe in a loving God, and I believe that this loving God had nothing to do with all this."

Calvin's eyes flare with anger. "I hate to burst your bubble, Lilly, but the Lord has something to do with everything in the universe."

"That's fine. We can quibble over philosophy, but there's no—"

"Lilly—"

"No, Cal! Now it's my turn. You listen to me. First of all, we still don't know how all this started. It could be fucking toxic waste, it could be the additives we put in our fucking coffee creamer. But I guarantee you, it's no God-like intervention. It wasn't prophesied in the Bible or by fucking Nostrodamus. It's as man-made as global warming, endless war, and reality TV. Whatever caused it, Cal, I promise you: One day, when they figure it out—and we'll probably both be long gone by then—it'll be traced back to simple human greed. Shortcuts. Corners that were cut by some asshole in some midlevel cubicle in some fucking research lab." She runs out of breath.

Calvin looks at the floor and softly murmurs, as though reciting, "The finest trick of the devil was to persuade mankind he doesn't exist."

"Okay. Fine. Have it your way, Calvin. This is punishment because we're all sinners. It is written. The end is nigh. Consult your local listings. But give me this much." She moves in closer, puts a hand on his arm. Her touch is tender and conciliatory, but her voice still has an edge to it. "We have to give each other a break. Whatever gets people through the day . . . as long as it doesn't hurt anybody, or put anybody in jeopardy . . . fine, whatever. Somebody drinks, so be it. Basket weaving, masturbation, medicate the hell outta yourself— doesn't matter. Have another one on me. Just so we got each other's back. Because that's what this is really about, Cal. It's not about how it all started or even whether God is responsible. It's about survival. It's about whether we can work together, build a community, and be human beings instead of animals. I respect your faith, Cal. I respect the fact that you have experienced incredible loss. But I ask that you respect *my* faith . . . in *people*." By this point, she has his undivided attention. He has gotten very still. He looks into her eyes, and she returns his gaze as she jerks a thumb at the other side of the corridor where her tools and gun belt lie on the floor by the baseboard. "With a little faith left over for those two Ruger twenty-two-caliber pistols."

Calvin lets out a long, tortured sigh. His shoulders sag slightly, his muscles relaxing as though in surrender. He smiles sadly. "I'm sorry, Lilly. You're right. I'm sorry. I guess I just don't know how I'm supposed to feel right now."

Lilly starts to respond when a high-pitched voice comes from behind them, startling both, and making Calvin jerk with a start.

"Feel about what?"

They both whirl around and see Tommy Dupree standing barefoot in the doorway, rubbing the sleep from his eyes, his Spider-Man T-shirt damp with perspiration. "What are you guys talking about?"

"Nothing, buddy," Calvin blurts. "Just talking about . . . *pistols*."

Lilly and Calvin exchange a glance, and Lilly can't help grinning. Her cockeyed grin is contagious and makes Calvin smile, and then he lets out a spontaneous little chuckle—half laugh, half coughing release of tension—and Lilly starts to laugh at the mere fact that Calvin is laughing. The boy comes over and stands before them, a quizzical look on his face. By this point, the two adults have begun to chortle as though losing touch with what made them laugh in the first place, and soon they're simply guffawing at the fact that they've begun to guffaw.

Tommy watches them with a puzzled furrow to his brow, but soon he's begun to giggle himself, and the fact that Tommy is giggling at them—which makes no sense whatsoever—makes the two adults laugh all the harder. Now the three of them have begun to cackle in hysterics over nothing at all—perhaps the mere fact that the laughter has risen to such a volume—and it seems so hilarious that they would chortle with merriment in this day and age, that they hoot and snort even louder. The tears on their faces feel alien to them—tears of release, of delight—and the process of wiping them away finally makes the laughter fade.

At last, they calm down, and both Calvin and Tommy find themselves waiting for Lilly to say something to break the spell.

"Anyway . . ." she murmurs, looking at them, her smile lingering. She has never noticed how much this boy looks like his father—the same jut of the chin, the same sandy hair, the same cowlick—and it sends a bolt of emotion down her midsection. Her smile goes away. The phantom pain in her gut from the miscarriage she suffered only weeks ago now twinges as her mind casts back to those old fantasies of home and hearth and family. In a single instant she sees a parallel life passing before her mind's eye. She sees herself becoming the adoptive mother of Calvin's children, and she sees herself moving in with them, and she sees herself braiding little Bethany's hair, and telling Luke bedtime stories, and taking Tommy fishing, and cooking for them, and caring for them, and sleeping in a huge feather bed with Calvin each night while the skylight overhead blazes with twinkling stars. She sees herself living a normal life.

"C'mon, you two," she finally says. "Let's go see if we can find something other than cold cereal and powdered milk for breakfast."

They gather their belongings, and Lilly leads them down the corridor, out the exit, and into the sultry air of a hot Georgia morning—all the while, the seed of an idea taking root in the back of her mind. It's a concept that will soon occupy her every waking thought, accompanied by the certainty that things are about to change in Woodbury . . . whether the residents like it or not.

In the days before Lilly has her heart-to-heart with Bob, Reverend Jeremiah's people prove over and over again their willingness to pitch in.

Lilly is exceedingly worried about Woodbury's dwindling supplies of fuel—they are down to their last tank of propane, and only a few gallons of gasoline remain in the train shed—so she calls an emergency meeting in the town square to enlist every able body. The preacher shows up for the meeting with each and every member of his congregation poised for action. The men of the church group volunteer to go on supply runs with Speed and Matthew, and several of the women volunteer to help Gloria forage for edibles in the neighboring fields. Some of the church women have backgrounds in child care, and Barbara happily integrates them into the daily chores with the children. A congregant named Wade Pilcher, a former cop with military training, offers to join the nightly walker patrols on the wall. Lilly is delighted to have the help, and she sees the results almost immediately. With the extra sets of eyes and strong backs, Speed and Matthew's search party unearths an untapped fuel storage tank beneath the ruins of a motorcycle dealership about twenty miles south of Woodbury on Highway 85. Meanwhile, some of the women, while out foraging for nuts and berries, discover a previously unknown corn field, the shoulder-high stalks already bearing mature ears of corn. The bounty promises countless bushels of nutritious complex carbohydrates and sugar for the town.

Lilly continues to be impressed by Reverend Jeremiah's willingness to roll up his sleeves and help with the cause. The preacher goes on several supply runs, happily doing the heavy lifting when necessary, cheerfully taking orders from Matthew or Ben, and entertaining everybody along the way with colorful commentary and wily anecdotes. Later, when a walker slips through the cordon of the southeast gate and threatens to go on a rampage through town, the preacher is the first to intercede, dashing out the door of his temporary housing and using his weaponized crucifix on the thing, silently stoving in the creature's head before it has a chance to cause any further mischief. On another occasion, one of the town's children injures himself in the arena working with a trowel, and the reverend single-handedly carries the boy across the gardens and down to the infirmary while simultaneously singing five verses of "Will the Circle Be Unbroken."

One night, Jeremiah asks to see Lilly in the community room of the courthouse, where he presents her with a roster of his people and how they can better be utilized by the existing work crews. Looking over the document, Lilly is amazed at his initiative:

ROLES AND RESPONSIBILITIES
PENTECOSTAL PEOPLE OF GOD, REV. J. GARLITZ, PSTR.

NAME	AGE	OCCUPATION	DUTY
		—WOMEN—	
Mary Jean	17	Student	Foraging team
Colby	32	Housewife	Foraging team
Noelle	19	Student	Foraging team
Rose	47	Housewife	Day care
Cailinn	63	School cook	Day care
Emma	31	Housewife	Supply runs
		—MEN—	
Joseph	73	Retired grocer	Walker patrol
Harold	51	Disc jockey	Supply runs
Stephen	26	Laborer	Wall construction
Mark	28	Bricklayer	Wall construction
Reese	23	Student	Wall construction
Wade	41	Retired cop	Walker patrol
Anthony	39	Salesman	Supply runs

"My compliments," Lilly says after studying the document. The preacher's chart is drawn on stationery with a single gold embossed cross at the top, and the letters *P.P.G.* under it, which Lilly assumes stands for Pentecostal People of God. She is still unclear whether this was once an actual bricks-and-mortar church or simply a traveling ministry or a cult or whatever.

"Just want to pull our weight around here," the reverend assures her from across the table. He cradles a Styrofoam cup of instant coffee in his big manicured hands, his gaze level and fixed on Lilly. He wears his trademark dress shirt and clip-on tie, the cloth shopworn, blood-stippled, and soiled from the rigors of plague life.

"Very well thought-out," she says.

"You inspire us, Lilly. What you have here is real, it's a statement on the enduring strength of the human spirit, and we want to be part of it."

"You *are* part of it. You're just as much a part of it as anybody here."

The preacher looks down at his coffee. "I thank you for saying so, Lilly, but we don't take anything for granted—not in this day and age."

"Our people love you guys. It's as simple as that. We want you to stay here indefinitely."

The preacher smiles. Lilly can see that one of his incisors has been capped in gold. "That's very kind of you." He levels his gaze at her. "We feel God has chosen this place for us to live out our days."

Lilly returns the smile. "Let's hope that doesn't come for a long time."

His expression changes, his convivial smile transforming into an inscrutable mask. "Man plans and God laughs, as they say."

"I guess that's never been truer than it is today." Lilly looks at him. "Is everything okay?"

The preacher finds his smile again. "Absolutely. Reckon I'm just a little tired."

"You deserve a rest, you've been hauling ass over the last week."

He shrugs. "Haven't worked any harder than any of the other good people in this town."

"They do love you, you know. I think you won over half the people in town that second night when you put that walker down inside the gate."

"It's nothing I haven't seen you do *yourself* on occasion, Lilly."

"And you won over the rest of them yesterday when you chopped up that stubborn stump by the post office into firewood."

"Half the men in this town are capable of what I did, I just pitched in, that's all."

"Your modesty is the frosting on the cake," Lilly tells him with a smile. "These people would take a bullet for you, and that's important these days."

He shrugs. "If you say so, Lilly." He looks at her. "You sure everybody feels that way?"

"What do you mean? Yes, absolutely. Did somebody say something?"

The man rolls the coffee cup thoughtfully between his huge pianist's hands. "Lilly, you don't have to be a mind reader to see that the older gentleman—Bob is his name?—he's none too keen on me being here."

Lilly shrugs off the assertion. "Bob's fine, he lives in his own little world." The fact is, nobody has seen Bob in days. He's been brooding in the tunnels, working on the ventilation system and trying to get power down there. He claims it's in case they need the passageways on a more long-term basis someday. But Lilly can tell that Bob is disgruntled and paranoid about the newcomers. "You let me worry about Bob," she adds. "You just keep doing what you're doing. It's a huge help, and nobody appreciates it more than I do."

"All right, Lilly, but I have to ask you something else." Another pause. "Is there maybe a point to all these kind words? Something else you're getting at here?"

She looks at him, her expression changing. She takes a deep breath and clears her throat nervously. "You got me. Yes. There is something I want to ask you." She chooses her words carefully. "I sort of inherited the leadership role here." Pause. "I won't go into the details."

"And you are a *natural*—I've already told you that—anybody can see that."

"I don't know about that," she says, waving off the compliment as though it were a fly buzzing around her. "All I know is, I never wanted the job. I sort of took it on by default." Pause, parsing her words. "Just between you and me, there's nobody around here that's exactly leadership potential—all good people, believe me, but no real leaders in the bunch. And to be honest, I would rather be living a simpler life." Pause. "I know the possibility of leading a 'normal' life is probably out of the question." Another pause. "But I could envision myself having a family."

The preacher's voice softens as he says, "I notice you spend a lot of quality time with that fella Calvin and his little brood."

She grins. "Guilty as charged."

"You're good with them kids, I'll tell you that. And that fella is a good Christian man."

"Thank you, I appreciate that."

"Okay, so . . . what can I do to help?"

She smiles and takes a deep breath. "You can help me by becoming the leader of this community."

SEVENTEEN

That night, much heated discussion follows Lilly's proposal, and Lilly learns that Jeremiah is very hesitant to take on such an important role. He's skeptical that the original inhabitants of Woodbury would accept him—an outsider who's been there only a week—as their official leader. Nor is he certain it would sit well with his flock. They have grown very possessive of him. Lilly is relentless, though, and talks him into a compromise: coleadership. Jeremiah reluctantly agrees, and they shake hands on it.

The decision is all very hush-hush and unofficial at this point, but Lilly feels as though the weight of the universe has been lifted from her shoulders.

The next few days, she walks on air as she supervises the planting of watermelon and cantaloupe seeds on the north side of the arena, helps clean the last of the bloodstains and shackle anchors from the service bays beneath the racetrack, and tills the soil on the east side of the infield for a border of flowers. The flowers are Lilly's idea—some folks are jokingly suggesting lilies—but some of the crankier folks in town think it's a waste of time. Why spend one minute of your time on decorative, nonessential, frivolous things such as flowers? People in this town are in a life-and-death situation. They need to spend every waking moment fortifying the walls, gathering provisions, working on being self-sustainable, and just generally improving their odds of survival. Of course, no one can argue with this logic. Lilly knows it. Jeremiah knows it. Everybody knows it. But Lilly still yearns to have flowers in Woodbury.

The idea begins to obsess her. The memory of her father's rose-bushes looms large in her imagination and in her dreams. Everett Caul used to tend to his prize-winning flower garden with monastic attention, his English roses that bordered their picket fence the pride of Marietta. Plus, Lilly believes that she can convince the others that a flower bed is not completely lacking in purpose. She argues futilely that the flowers will attract bees, which will in turn aid the pollination of the other crops.

She talks to the Dupree kids about it, and they offer to help her plant them in secret at night after everybody has gone to sleep. The children instantly get the whole "flower thing" (which is now the phrase everybody is using for the controversy). Children accept things that adults have had leached out of them by the fast, brutal currents of life. But Lilly doesn't want to go against the tide of opinion among the others, especially during such a delicate process of what she has come to think of as *peaceful* regime change.

The days continue to pass without incident or walker attack. The migratory pattern of the superherd has shifted directions, and the bulk of the walkers in the immediate area now have seemingly drifted to the north, perhaps drawn by the light and fires and noise still seething in the back alleys of Atlanta. Or perhaps it's all desperately random. People are still puzzling over the movements of the undead, the innate behavior patterns, and the impossibility of predicting what they'll do next. In her private thoughts, Lilly believes that they could return at any moment, a thousand times stronger than before, as devastating as an earthquake or tornado. All the more reason to live. Breathe the air. Love each other. Enjoy life as much as possible. And please, please, please—someday, somehow, God willing—*stop and smell the flowers.*

Over the next week, Lilly gets even closer to Calvin and his kids. She reads fairy tales and children's stories—sometimes from memory, sometimes from dog-eared books that Bob had long ago scavenged from the library. She teaches Tommy how to load, fire, and care for a pistol. They practice down by the train yard—the place where the Governor once relentlessly trained himself to shoot with one functional eye—and Tommy develops a mad crush on Lilly, the first real crush of his adolescence. Calvin finds all this bonding wonderful, and little by little he begins to regret some of the things he said to Lilly the morning after they hooked up in the lonely corridor of the courthouse. It is very possible that Calvin Dupree is slowly, steadily, inexorably falling in love with Lilly Caul.

Lilly refrains from immediately jumping back into bed with him. She takes it slowly, treats him with respect, acts platonically around the kids, and generally denies the simmering sexual tension returning with a vengeance between the two. A few times they find themselves alone, at night, on the second floor of the courthouse, the kids fast asleep behind latched doors, and the drone of night crickets roaring outside the boarded windows, when they fall into each other's arms and kiss like there's no tomorrow, but Lilly keeps her clothes on. She's not ready yet. She won't give herself over to him completely until it's time, which will be soon. She might as well face it: She wants to be the mother of his children.

By the end of that week, the church group has been a part of the community for almost a month, and Bob has been seen only a handful of times. The old army medic has been hunkering in the tunnels, alone, living like a monk, working on the ventilation and power, mapping all the myriad tributaries, reinforcing some of the load-bearing timbers, and basically stewing about the growing role Jeremiah is playing in the community. Lilly has decided to essentially leave him alone. She believes he'll come around soon enough, and it's best to let him soften on his own accord. But as Lilly will soon discover, Bob has been doing more than just stewing. He's been spending a good chunk of his time trying to find out what the preacher is hiding in those enormous black duffel bags that are currently stowed under his bed in his apartment at the end of Main Street.

For some reason, which even Bob would be hard-pressed to explain, he is certain those duffel bag hold the key to Jeremiah's true agenda.

High summer officially arrives the following Saturday, the crushing heat and humidity coming up from the Gulf like an invading army. By the afternoon, the asphalt two-lanes bordering town turn to sizzling skillets, and the hickory groves south of the railroad cook in the blazing ashen sun, their cinnamon musk perfuming the dense air of the forest like the sachets of moldy drawers.

Woodbury bakes in the heat until people start coming out of their stifling apartments and bungalows to at least breathe some fresh air. No one has the luxury of operational air-conditioning—the only A/C unit that's still working off generators is a window unit in the back of the warehouse on Dogwood Lane where all the perishables are stored—so the best place to be at the moment is the town square under the generous shade provided by two-hundred-year-old live oaks, which spread their misshapen, aged arms across that single square block of seared crabgrass.

By dinnertime, practically the entire population of Woodbury has gathered under those oaks. Some folks have blankets spread out on the grass. Three of the church ladies—Colby, Rose, and Cailinn—have butchered a couple rabbits and arrive at the square with a long cookie sheet laden with deep-fried rabbit made on a campfire with recycled corn oil. Two of the younger church girls, Mary Jean and Noelle, have made extremely strong punch from canned fruit juice and Ben's horrible homemade moonshine. Speed and Matthew have befriended the younger men of the church group—Stephen, Mark, and Reese—and the five of them break out the weed behind the courthouse building.

Everybody smells the sickly sweet odor of reefer wafting across the property, but now even the church folks seem to have become inured to the forbidden smell. Wade Pilcher, the middle-aged former Jacksonville police officer who has become the self-appointed sergeant at arms for the church group, actually finds it humorous. At one point, he goes around behind the building to play cop and scare the young men, and when they all scramble to hide the corncob pipes they're using to smoke the pot, he lets out a guffaw, chastises them for not "bringing enough for the entire class," and asks for a toke. At this point, the party kicks up a notch.

The sun begins to set around seven o'clock, and the genial light of dusk brings blessed relief from the blazing heat. By this point, the impromptu party has swung into overdrive. The combined population of Woodbury, now numbering forty-three souls, lets off the steam and stress of plague life in a spontaneous celebration. The Dupree children play red rover in the street with the half dozen other kids of Woodbury while Gloria breaks out her ukulele and starts strumming bluegrass tunes. Soon, David has joined her with his harmonica, and Reese has come over with a plastic bucket, which he starts drumming softly in time with the strumming.

Everybody gathers around as the sound of "Amazing Grace" swells up into the purple twilight. Harold Stauback, with the heartbreaking gospel voice, comes over and begins to sing. The kids quiet down, and the hushed air of dusk seems to hold and highlight the beauty of that single plaintive voice.

When Harold finishes, everybody applauds and whoops and hollers, and the Reverend Jeremiah Garlitz rises from his picnic blanket and ambles over to the makeshift bandstand and puts his arm around Harold.

"How about another hand for the pride of the Tallahassee Baptist Combined Choir," Jeremiah booms, addressing the crowd in a joyful voice. "The former voice of WHKX Country, the great Harold Benjamin Stauback!"

Cheers ring out, and Harold takes a suave little bow and waves. "I thank y'all kindly," he says when the cheers die down. He wipes his dapper mustache with a handkerchief and gives another bow toward Lilly, leaning against a nearby tree, carving a crab apple with a pocketknife, who gives him a huge grin. "And I know I speak for all of us when I say thank you to Miss Lilly Caul and the good and decent people of Woodbury." The man's eyes well up. "We knew the Good Lord would take us home sooner or later . . . but we never dreamed it would be . . . in a place as beautiful as this."

Lilly glances across the square—not really registering what the man just said—and she sees the silhouette of a figure way off in the distance. An older man with greasy, pomaded hair and cords of neck wattle, dressed in a tattered wife-beater T-shirt worn gray with dust, he sits perched on a split-rail fence at the edge of a vacant lot. It's hard to tell at this distance, but the man seems to perk up when he hears the preacher's voice return to the breeze.

"If y'all would humor me for just a second," Jeremiah says to the group, patting Stauback on the shoulder as the singer sits back down on a stump with the musicians. "I'd like to say a few words." He grins. "This should come as no surprise to my people, who are used to me spoutin' off about everything from rainbows to the Internal Revenue Service." He pauses to let the chuckles ripple through the crowd. His smile goes away. "Just want to say a few brief words about flowers." He looks at Lilly and gives her a nod. "Now one might make a case that flowers don't serve much purpose in this old world other than for first dates and anniversaries. Maybe once in a while when you been stupid and you want to apologize to your best gal. Or maybe you want to gussy up a table or a room. But certainly nothing practical . . . like food, water, shelter, self-defense . . . or any of the things that have come to mean survival in these last couple of years."

He pauses and scans the crowd now, making eye contact with virtually everyone present *other* than Lilly, playing the silence in the manner of a master orator, a man born to preach. He smiles a tranquil, knowing smile.

"You ask me, though, it's easy to forget the purpose of God's gifts such as music, brotherhood, good food, a fine cigar, and a stiff bourbon once in a while. I'm here to tell you that these things, in some ways, they're more important than food and water, more critical to us as fully formed children of God than oxygen and sunlight . . . because they are all about what it means to truly be alive."

Distracted by the lone figure down the street, Lilly now turns her gaze back to Jeremiah. Something about his words, and the way he's saying them, grabs her, holds her attention. She can see the preacher is tearing up.

"We were *not* put here to merely survive," he is saying, wiping his eyes. "Jesus did not die for our sins so we could merely exist. That's the thing, brothers and sisters. If all we do is survive . . . we have lost. If them things out there cause us to forget God's simple gifts—the giggle of a child, a good book, the taste of maple syrup on a pancake on a Sunday morning—then we have lost our way, and we have lost the war. Them dead things have already beat us . . . because we have turned our back on who we are."

He pauses again, pulls a handkerchief from his pocket, and wipes his face, which is glistening now with sweat and tears tracking down his cheeks.

His voice crumbles slightly as he goes on. "A tire swing over a lake, an old La-Z-Boy tilted back in front of a football game, holding hands with your sweetheart . . . y'all remember these things. We all do." He pauses, and Lilly hears others fighting tears, a few throats clearing, some sniffling going on, and it makes her own eyes burn. "Yep, them are just flower seeds that Lilly Caul wants to plant. Won't feed anybody, heal anybody's wounds, slake anybody's thirst . . . but I submit to y'all, brothers and sisters, them flowers—like a runway at night with lights on for the planes—them flowers are a message to God, can be seen from heaven." He pauses to gather his breath and work through his tears. Lilly can hardly move or breathe; her skin tingles at the power of this man's voice. "Them flowers are telling God and the devil and everybody in between . . . we remember . . . we still remember . . . and we will never forget . . . what it is to be human."

Some of the older men and women are overcome with emotion, their thick weeping sounds carrying up into the treetops on the warm, dusky, pine-scented breeze. It's almost dark now, and the purple light seems to have put an exclamation point on the preacher's words. He bows his head and murmurs, "One more thing I want to say, brothers and sisters." He takes a deep breath. "Lilly has kindly asked me to help out with the leadership duties here in Woodbury." Pause. He looks up. Tears on his face. Complete, utter, naked humility. "With all y'all giving your blessings . . . it would be my honor to stand alongside this good-hearted, decent, brave woman." He looks at Lilly. "Thank you, partner."

A tear tracks down Lilly's face and she wipes it with a smile.

The preacher turns to the little impromptu band. "Y'all know 'The Old Rugged Cross'?"

Gloria grins at him through the tinted brim of her visor. "Hum a few bars, Preach—we'll figure it out."

In a high lonesome voice that's surprisingly delicate and beautiful, Jeremiah starts crooning the same song that Bob Stookey once sang softly to the corpse of a little girl named Penny, the same words now coming out of the handsome minister in a clear, warm, honey-flavored warble: "In that old rugged cross, stained with blood so divine, a wondrous beauty I see, for 'twas on that old cross Jesus suffered and died, to pardon and sanctify me."

Soon some of the others, mostly the older folks, find their voices and sing along. All of which mesmerizes Lilly right up to the moment she notices in her peripheral vision the shadowy figure in the distance push himself off the fence, turn, and march disgustedly away into the night.

"Wait!" Lilly turns and hurries after the figure. "Bob, wait up!"

It takes her a minute to charge across the square, cross the street, and circumnavigate the northeast corner of the vacant lot. She finally catches up with the older man near the barricade.

"Bob, stop! Listen to me!" She reaches out for his arm and pulls him to a halt. "What's wrong with you? What's your problem?"

He turns and scowls at her, the light of a distant torch flickering off his deeply lined face. "Partners? Are you fucking out of your mind?"

"What is your thing with this guy, Bob? He's a good man, anybody can see that."

"This guy is bad news, Lilly, and you've swallowed his bullshit hook, line, and sinker!" Bob turns and storms away with fists clenched.

"Bob, wait. Hold on." Lilly goes after him, gently tugging on his arm. "Talk to me. Come on. This isn't like you to withdraw, acting all paranoid and shit. Come on, Bob. It's me. What's the deal?"

The old medic takes deep breaths as though tamping down his temper. In the distance, voices rise on the wind, the old hymn reverberating in the trees. Bob finally lets out a sigh and says, "Let's go somewhere we can talk in private."

EIGHTEEN

Inside Bob Stookey's apartment on Dogwood Lane, amid the peach crates full of empty bottles and behind the hastily draped windows, Bob drops reams of old yellowed documents and publications on a table, making a loud *thud,* which makes Lilly jerk with a start.

"That little library I took you to last month, the one on Pecan Street," Bob says, staring at the stack of newsprint, Xerox copies, and dog-eared magazines. "It's one of them throwbacks. Dewey decimal system, card files, microfilm . . . remember microfilm?"

"What's the point of all this, Bob?" Lilly stands near the front door with her arms crossed across her chest. She can see an old magazine at the top of the pile called the *Tallahassian*—presumably the slick, breezy, gossipy mag that once ostensibly promoted the Florida capital.

"Not the biggest library in the world, I'll grant you that," Bob goes on, still looking at the pile of publications with the admiration of a proud father gazing upon a gifted child. "But still . . . you don't need the Internet to find stuff in there." He looks at Lilly. "I shit you not—they got old daily newspapers here dating back to the Eisenhower administration."

"Are you gonna tell me what this is all about, or do I have to guess?"

He sighs and paces around his dining table on which an impressive array of documents is stacked and organized. "Your boy has been quite a busy little beaver in his life, made quite a name for himself down to Florida and thereabouts." Bob stares at Lilly. "That's right . . . I got the scoop on your honorable Reverend Jeremiah Garlitz."

Lilly lets out an exasperated breath. "Bob, whatever it is . . . I'm sure it's ancient history. In case you haven't noticed, we don't look at people's résumés anymore."

Bob continues pacing as though he hasn't heard a word she has said. "Evidently he was a military brat as a kid, an only child, shuffled from school to school."

"Bob—"

"Best I can tell, his daddy was an overbearing cocksucker—a chaplain in the army—known for being a hard-ass, paddling his recruits with a metal baseball bat he called the Bethlehem Slugger." Bob shoots a sidelong glance at Lilly. "Cute, huh?"

"Bob, I don't see how any of this—"

"I guess young Jeremiah never fit in, always an outcast, a misfit. Got the stuffing beat outta him on the playground a lot, but it made him tough, resourceful. Became a Golden Gloves boxer, saw visions of the apocalypse, entered the clergy at age eighteen and became the youngest Baptist minister ever to establish a megachurch in the state of Florida." Bob pauses for emphasis. "And then there's a lot missing . . . a big hole in the biography."

Lilly looks at the old medic. "Are you finished?"

"No, I ain't. As a matter of fact, I'm just getting started." He points at the pile of publications. "Best I can tell from the paper trail, he was given the boot by the deacons at the Universal Church of the Pentecost in Jacksonville, stripped of his license, drummed out of the state of Florida. You know why?"

Lilly sighs. "No, Bob . . . I have no idea why he was kicked out of the state of Florida."

"That's funny, neither do I!" Bob's droopy, red-rimmed eyes blaze with the latent buzz and paranoia of a dry drunk. "It's all been redacted by lawyers or the church or whatever. But I guarantee it has something to do with what they're calling the End Days . . . Armageddon. Judgment Day, Lilly. The big kiss-off."

"Bob, I really gotta be honest with you . . . I just don't have the energy for this right now."

"Don't you see the pattern? That's why he was wandering around the South with no church to speak of at the time the Turn came around!" Bob wipes his mouth. He looks badly in need of a drink.

"It's unclear from the public record, but it looks like they found something . . . something in his possessions, maybe a diary, photographs, something incriminating, a smoking gun . . . *something.*"

"What are you saying exactly? You think he's a fucking child molester?"

"No . . . I mean, I don't know . . . maybe it's something else." Bob paces some more. "I just wouldn't trust him farther than I can spit." Bob pauses and looks at her. "You remember them huge duffel bags? The one he was carrying . . . and the other one, kid named Steve was luggin'?"

Lilly shrugs. "I guess . . . yeah, I remember them. So what? They had heavy duffel bags."

"You seen them things since they been staying here with us?"

Another shrug from Lilly as she thinks about it. "I guess I haven't. So what?"

"What's in them things?" Bob stares at her. "Ain't you the slightest bit curious?"

Lilly clenches her jaw and lets out another taut breath through her nose. She knows this salty old medic better than anyone else, maybe better than Bob knows himself. Over the last two years, Lilly and old Bob Stookey have become the closest of friends, sharing their deepest, innermost secrets, sharing their tragedies, their dreams, and their fears. She also knows that Bob—not unlike the preacher himself—grew up dirt-poor, abused as a kid by deeply religious parents. As an adult, Bob developed an abiding hatred of evangelists, which is now coloring his every thought. With this in mind, Lilly finally says, "Bob, I'm gonna cut you some slack here because of your issues with organized religion . . . but I really think you need to take a breath, step back, and dial it down. You don't have to like this guy. Hell, you don't even have to talk to him. I'll deal with him. But I'm begging you to drop the fucking witch hunt."

Bob stares at her for a moment. "You don't even care about finding out what's in them goddamn duffel bags?"

Lilly lets out a sigh, goes over to him, reaches up and tenderly touches the edge of his grizzled chin. "I'm gonna go ahead and get back to the party now." She gives him a tepid smile. "I'm really tired . . . and I need to kick back and put my mind on autopilot. My advice to you is to do the same. Just let it go. Concentrate on the future, the tunnels, the fuel situation."

She pats his cheek, turns, and heads for the door. He watches her. Before leaving, she pauses in the doorway, turns, and looks at him. "Let it go, Bob. I promise you . . . you'll be glad you did."

She walks out, shutting the door behind herself, the dull clunk of the bolt reverberating in the silence.

Over the next week, a casual observer might conclude that the town of Woodbury, Georgia—a place once heralded on water towers and welcome signs as "A Peach of a Place"—has begun to experience the greatest renaissance since the completion of the Norfolk and Southern Railroad trunk line in 1896. For the most part, the walkers leave the town alone, staying well to the west of Elkins Creek, and allowing the people of Woodbury to finish the expansion of the wall. With the added manpower provided by the church group, the barricade is extended north along Canyon Road, all the way to Whitehouse Parkway, and then east to Dogwood Lane. The expansion adds a dozen more freestanding homes, as well as scores of unexplored stores into the safe zone. One of the key windfalls is a small auto parts shop on Dogwood called Cars Et Cetera—previously only hastily scanned by the Governor's men for valuable provisions—now offered up as a gold mine of hidden treasures and supplies.

Reverend Jeremiah James Garlitz takes his place beside Lilly at all town council meetings and brings a refreshing dynamic to the planning sessions. The council institutes new programs to expand farming activities, standardize reconnaissance runs, establish a new political manifesto for the town, draw up a set of rights and responsibilities, create new regulations and curfews, and explore all possible technologies that might bring sustainability to their community. Lilly and the preacher assign teams to build an aquifer to gather rainfall for irrigation and drinking water, build compost heaps for fertilizer, and begin searching the immediate rural area for all green technologies that they might scavenge. By the end of that week, they've discovered a previously unexplored warehouse in the neighboring county filled with mint-condition solar cells and small wind turbines.

The reverend seems to embrace his new role with gusto. He begins having regular interdenominational prayer services and performing baptisms. Calvin Dupree, a lifelong Baptist, has never experienced the old-fashioned immersion ceremony and asks the preacher if he can be the first citizen of Woodbury to be baptized. Jeremiah is delighted to oblige, and Lilly proudly stands with the three Dupree children one evening at dusk along the banks of Elkins Stream—the same place Meredith Dupree took her own life so heroically. They choose a spot under a massive ancient hickory, and Harold Stauback sings a hymn as Jeremiah puts one arm around the white-robed Calvin and slowly, ritually, lowers him backward into the warm, mossy currents. Lilly surprises herself when she realizes, as she watches, that she has tears of deep emotion on her face.

Nobody notices the subtle yet seismic shift in the moods of all the church people. To the uninitiated, untrained eye, they appear as if they have accepted their new home with gratitude and serene satisfaction. Upon closer scrutiny, however, one might begin to question the beatific smiles on their faces, the glassy, almost drugged quality of their gazes. In this brutal era, with death around every corner, nobody ever gets this happy without the assistance of heavy medication. But the members of the Pentecostal People of God—almost to a person—appear to be getting more and more blissful and exultant with each passing day. And not a single one of their fellow residents—including Bob Stookey—even suspects that some great and epochal event in their lives is approaching.

For most of that week, in fact, Bob is too distracted by his obsession with the gigantic duffel bags—if indeed they still exist at all and haven't been thrown out or destroyed—to notice the minute changes in demeanor among the church people.

Most nights, Bob waits until the folks have retired to their bedrooms, then surreptitiously creeps around town, casually peering through windows, stealing glimpses inside tents, and checking the storage areas under the fire escapes and stairways of apartment buildings. They have moved Jeremiah a few times, first putting him up at the Governor's old building at the end of Main Street, then upgrading him to one of the bungalows along Jones Mill Road, finally moving him to the brownstone-style building across the street from Lilly. The other duffel bag—presumably in the possession of the young church member named Stephen—has also vanished. Bob searched the young man's apartment one morning when the kid was away on a work crew and came up empty.

Bob hasn't had a chance to break into the preacher's current digs—but he will, he promises himself he will; when the time is right, Bob will check the place across from Lilly's for any sign of the mysterious bags.

For now, Bob spends his days in the tunnel, reinforcing the walls and refurbishing the dingy passageway into a more livable space. He enlists the help of David and Barbara—the only residents other than Lilly whom Bob trusts unconditionally—and starts experimenting with solar cells and generators in order to get electrical power and, in turn, lights and ventilation into the tunnels. He successfully powers nearly a quarter mile of the main branch with a half dozen cells positioned in trees along the route, an array of batteries and cables cannibalized out of wrecked cars, and three heavy-duty generators that he positions aboveground, waterproofed and rigged to run on biodiesel. Bob concocts his own home-brewed version of the fuel by mixing old cooking oil, a small amount of gasoline, methanol from an antifreeze called Heet (found at the auto parts store), and a few gallons of Drano (which contains sodium hydroxide). By the end of that week, nearly fifteen hundred feet of tunnel have become a clean, well-lighted, and odorless place to hide from the world.

On Friday, late in the evening, Bob is in the tunnel, alone, exploring the farthest reaches of that main branch—using his survey map to notate the points at which the local sewer begins to intersect with the passageway—when he hears a noise. Muffled voices are resonating faintly in the dark, coming from aboveground somewhere, apparently close by. Bob finds a tributary and follows the sound of the voices down a parallel tunnel, which he calculates must be under the woods east of town, right around the swampy creek in which Calvin Dupree was baptized.

He pauses in the dark, the voices clearly audible now, directly overhead. The flesh on the back of his neck prickles when he recognizes the preacher's silky baritone.

"All I'm saying is, when the time comes, make sure we leave no one behind."

Perfectly audible in the tomblike silence and darkness of the tunnel, Jeremiah's voice sounds as though it's coming down through a drain.

A second voice—younger, thinner, reedier—sounds as though it's coming from a pull-string doll: *"I just want to make sure I understand—you're gonna go ahead and take all these nonbelievers with us."* This voice is also instantly identifiable: the young fellow who first stumbled into Woodbury from the wilderness, the one named Reese. Bob's flesh crawls. His gut turns cold. He feels light-headed, his mouth as dry as an ashtray as he listens to the deep twang of the preacher's response.

"We owe it to these people, Brother, we owe them a trip home with us. They are children of God, just like us, they deserve to touch the hem of His garment as much as we do. They are good souls."

A single pearl of sweat tracks down the bridge of Bob's nose.

The voice Bob has identified as Reese's proclaims: *"Praise God, and praise to you. You're a generous man, Brother."* There's a pause, and it makes Bob feel as though he's shrinking, as though he's sinking into the tunnel floor, into the molten center of the earth. *"But what if they resist?"*

"Yessir, some of them are gonna fight it. No doubt about that. They won't want to go, they won't see the glory in it, but we will overcome that. We'll educate them. And if we can't educate them . . ."

"Then what? What do we do then? How do we get them to go home all at once?"

"Gotta be very careful, Brother Reese. And we gotta do it soon. We gotta get on home before somebody takes it the wrong way, tries to interfere."

"Whatever you say, Brother J."

"These are good people, Reese, decent people, God's people. I will do anything to convince them, and the Good Lord will not let anybody stop us from going home. If they try and stop us, we'll just go around them, under them, over them, or through them. Whatever it takes."

"Amen."

"*Glory hallelujah. We're going home, Brother Reese. At last, at last. And there ain't nobody gonna get in our way this time.*"

"*Yessir, amen. Amen.*"

"*It's set, then. We take our leave tomorrow night. Look at me, Reese. Tomorrow night. Twenty-four hours . . . and then we take these good people home.*"

"*Amen!*"

NINETEEN

Later. Wee-hour darkness, like a pall, lowering its membrane of chill silence over the town. A single figure moving through the maze of side streets, a single red blood cell seeking out a diseased organ.

Bob Stookey slips between two buildings on Pecan Street and moves through the gloom with his flashlight off. He knows this part of town almost by feel. He used to hide out here, right here, hunkering down with a bottle of bourbon and bad memories and crashing right on the cement under that same fire escape. Now he passes the spot in a dark blur.

He finds the preacher's quarters on the ground floor of the brownstone at the end of Main, the one across from Lilly's place. He approaches it from the back alley and silently crosses the patio to the rear door. He knows the preacher is away for the night, meeting with his elders in the forest, making his plans, getting everybody on board for whatever it is they're planning. Bob knows that time is not on his side here—the preacher could return at any moment—so he quickly jimmies the back door with a locksmith's tool.

He goes inside and gets to work. Flashlight on now, scanning the cluttered dark, heart beating hard, he looks in the closets, on the shelves, under the sofa, and finally, under the big brass bed in the bedroom, he locates the infamous duffel bag.

He sucks in a breath, girding himself as he pulls the heavy satchel out.

On the second floor of the courthouse building, in the back room, which is now as dark as the inside of a stew pot, fragrant with the body odors of children, a five-year-old boy named Lucas Dupree tosses and writhes in a tangle of damp sheets. His brother Tommy sleeps soundly on a trundle bed on the other side of the room, his sister slumbering on a love seat in the corner. Lucas dreams he's in the backyard of his grandparents' place in Birmingham, Alabama, hiding in his grammy's rosebushes. It is very real. He smells the sour odors of fertilizer and dog shit, feels the matted pine needles prickling the palms of his hands and the pads of his knees as he crawls through the dark, searching for his mom. He knows he's playing hide-and-seek even though he can't remember the beginning of the game.

Dreams are like that. You just know stuff. Like the fact that his mama is dead but she still wants to play, so he crawls toward an opening in the bush and sees his mom crouching on the grass by the clothesline, her back turned to him. She counts to ten in a crackly, robotic voice—"*seven, eight, nine, ten*"—and then she turns.

Her teeth are black, her eyes like the red cinnamon eyes of a gingerbread man, her skin as rough and gray as stale bread dough. Lucas screams, but no sound comes out of him. He freezes as his undead mother strides over to him. She kneels. At first Lucas thinks she's going to eat him.

Then she leans down and whispers something to him. He hears it like water trickling next to his ear—a very important message.

Kneeling next to the old brass bed in the dark bedroom, Bob unzips the enormous duffel bag and sees the bottles. At least a dozen laboratory-grade beakers sealed with plastic lids and scientific labels are tucked in there like milk bottles ready for delivery.

Bob fumbles for his reading glasses. He finds them in the breast pocket of his denim shirt and puts them on. He leans in and shines the flashlight on the label. It says CHLORAL HYDRATE—1000 ML—DANGER—KEEP OUT OF THE REACH OF CHILDREN. Bob's pulse quickens.

He finds other beakers ranging from 50 to 100 mL. These containers are labeled HYDROGEN CYANIDE—DANGER—EXTREMELY POISONOUS.

Bob sits back and lets a thin breath escape his tightly pressed lips.

He hardly notices the other contents of the duffel: cakes of C-4 plastic explosives wrapped in wax paper, detonating cord rolled into tiny coils, and bundles of dynamite sticks packed as neatly as silverware in a drawer.

His gaze remains glued to those glass containers of deadly clear fluids. Bob is a former army medic, a man well versed in basic chemistry and pharmacology. He knows that chloral hydrate is a strong barbiturate and he also knows the devastating effects of cyanide.

Bob gets very still and tries to get air into his lungs. He knows now just exactly where the good reverend's suicide cult will be taking everybody tomorrow night.

"You must never go to sleep, Luke." The hushed whisper of a dead woman penetrates the ear of the young dreamer. "Or you'll end up like me."

Lucas slaps his face in the dream and tries his hardest to wake up. He doesn't like this dream one little bit. He wants so badly to wake up. Now. *Wake up, wake up, wake up, wake up . . . WAKE UP!*

His dead mother just laughs . . . and laughs and laughs. Luke can't breathe.

Maybe he's already dead, like his mom. Maybe they *all* are . . . his brother and sister, his dad, everybody . . . doomed to sleep forever.

PART 3

Last Rites

Behold the day of the Lord comes, cruel, with wrath and fierce anger, to make the land a desolation and to destroy its sinners from it.

—Isaiah 13:9

TWENTY

From the time he was still wearing Red Ball Jets sneakers on his huge feet and braces on his big overbite, Jeremiah James Garlitz has been perpetually obsessed with pleasing his daddy. Even in the years following his old man's death—Daddy went out like a lightbulb in his Barcalounger in front of a Braves game in 1993 from a cerebral aneurism—Jeremiah has dreamed of making Master Sergeant Daniel Garlitz proud of his only child. Not a day goes by—really, not even an hour—without a memory of the old man flicking across Jeremiah's mind screen. Over and over, the preacher casts his thoughts back to the time his daddy made him recite the books of the Bible while kneeling on broken glass in the garage of their old Victorian house in Richmond. Or the time Big Dan Garlitz locked the boy in a footlocker in the basement of their Wilmington home with nothing but a Concordance Bible and in his underwear and didn't let the boy out until Jeremiah had shit himself and had started to scream so loudly his mother heard the noise and interceded. Today, Jeremiah looks back upon these memories with a strange kind of morbid, compulsive fascination—like a man continually picking at a scab. The memories give him a charge, an electric jolt, and make him dream of the day he will finally make Sergeant Dan truly proud.

Which has come at last—the day of deliverance, the day of salvation—praise the Lord.

This realization runs through the back of the preacher's mind as he crouches in the scorched ruins of the train shed on the southwest corner of Woodbury's barricade just before dawn that morning. He feels like a coach before a big game, a manager for Team Jesus, and he speaks softly, furtively, so as not to be heard by any nonessential resident who might be up early for whatever reason. "Remember the two stages of the ritual," he says to the others as he draws in the dirt with a stick. He makes a big circle and labels it *Woodbury*, and then he draws arrows pointing inward from the four corners of the neighboring farmland. Then he puts an X in the middle of town and labels it *Arena*. "Stage one is communion." He smiles, looking at the men as a father would gaze proudly at his prodigal sons. "We take the blood and the body of Christ in the square at sunset. Amen."

The five other men huddling around him—Reese, Mark, Stephen, Anthony, and Wade—absorb this news with great anticipation, like anxious paratroopers, their sweat-damp faces reflecting both joy and nervous tension.

"Stage two, of course, is the summoning." The preacher nods toward the stocky retired cop kneeling next to him. "Which will be your department, Wade."

The former patrolman with the Jacksonville PD smiles, intoxicated with the spirit. The ultimate offering, the definitive sacrifice—to be consumed by the very creatures that have brought about the apocalypse—will be the Pentecostal People of God's greatest moment. "The wall shouldn't be a problem," Wade assures the preacher. "The only thing I've been wondering about is the location of the herd."

The preacher nods. "You're wondering if there's gonna be enough of them."

The cop nods.

Jeremiah's grin intensifies, a light on a rheostat. "God will bring the multitudes to us . . . as he brought the mountain to Mohammed."

Some of them answer with *amen* or *praise Him* as they exchange exultant grins.

Jeremiah feels tears moistening his eyes. They have been waiting eagerly for this great and wonderful moment for years. They came close a few times, but local church authorities and the laws of the state of Florida got in the way. Now there is nothing that can stop them. God has paved the way for this glorious moment.

Harold Stauback is the only member of the group who isn't smiling. The dapper man, dressed in a threadbare golf sweater and torn khakis, stands across the shed near a pile of railroad ties, hands thrust in his pockets, chewing his lips nervously, pensively, kicking the dust at his feet. "I just wish we didn't have to spring this on these people." He looks up. "I've really grown fond of these folks."

Jeremiah levers himself to his feet and ambles across to where Harold is standing. "Brother, I hear you." He touches Harold's shoulder. "I feel the same way. I wish to God we didn't have to be so secretive." Then Jeremiah hugs the man. Harold sniffs as he returns the embrace. Jeremiah speaks softly into the man's ear. "I have prayed and prayed on it, and I can't come up with another way." He stands back, still holding the black man's shoulders, bracing him. "You're a good man, Harold. You belong in heaven, not in this horrible hell on earth." The preacher pauses, thinks about it. "You know that fella, name of Calvin? Good Christian man with the kids?" He sees Harold nodding, and he chews the inside of his cheek, thinking it over. "Why don't you approach him later this morning, in private, just float the idea to him, see if he gets it."

Harold rubs his mouth, pondering the idea. "What if he tells the others? Rebels against it?"

"I wouldn't worry about that, I have a feeling about that fella." Jeremiah turns to the others and aims his high-voltage smile at them. "Think about it. We are doing these good people a favor—the favor of a lifetime—the Christian ones will see that." The men bow their heads, nodding, as if in tribute. Jeremiah wipes tears from his eyes. "This time tomorrow, we'll all be in paradise." He gazes at them through his tears. "No more walking corpses. No more walls. No more grief." He lets out a strange and almost giddy chuckle. "No more powdered milk."

The sun rises that morning at precisely five thirty-two, the exact time displayed on the old wind-up pocket watch that Bob still cherishes from his days in the army running ambulance units up and down Highway 8 between Baghdad and Kuwait City. Despite its tarnished finish, the watch is a beauty, engraved with Bob's unit and insignia, the stem gray from all the winding over the years—the kind of timepiece his mother would have called a "turnip" watch—and now Bob keeps it handy as he crouches on the roof of Deforest Feed and Seed Company at the end of Pecan Street.

The wind tosses Bob's graying, oily, thinning hair across his eyes as he scans the area. With its huge soot-stained chimneys offering cover, and a scenic view of both Main Street and Woodbury's patchwork grid of side streets, the roof is an ideal place for a lone figure to hide and keep tabs, waiting for the town to wake up and go to work. Bob can see the preacher's brownstone a block and a half to the west, and he also has a clear view of the square, the courthouse, Lilly's place, the farthest points of the barricade, the distant woods beyond, and most of the other significant landmarks. Bob knows it's up to him to stop this madness. But he also realizes he has to be careful. If he doesn't do this properly, nobody will believe him. It's almost as though he has to deprogram the original members of the town—including Lilly—who have fallen under the spell of this flimflam artist who calls himself a man of God.

Bob checks his .357, which sits on the tar-paper roof next to his canteen. He has used the Magnum for years now for everything from shooting raccoons to putting down walkers. The revolver has served him well, despite the fact that it holds only seven rounds—six in the cartridge and one in the breach—and it also tends to be bulky and awkward in quick-draw situations. But with its smooth single-action triggering apparatus, as well as a nifty 2X scope with a laser sighting option, the gun offers a big kill ratio and reminds Bob a little bit of what it's like to drive a Buick Roadmaster with a V-8 engine and two-hundred-plus horses under the hood down a long stretch of straightaway, leaving all the other little go-carts in his dust.

God bless General Motors, God bless Clint Eastwood, and God Bless Misters Smith and Wesson: Nobody fucks with a .357.

He checks the gun's cylinder, spinning it with a dull click, and then takes a sip of well water from his canteen. The water tastes foul and metallic, but it's cool and wet so it does the job. Bob found a few cartons of cereal bars at the ransacked Walmart a few months ago and has been living on the things ever since. He pulls one from his pocket and tears into it. Tasteless, dry, and stale, it ain't exactly eggs Benedict—plus, it's his last bar—but Bob doesn't care. He feels like a gambler going all in.

As his unit commander used to say right before a deployment, "It's fuck or walk, boys."

An hour of waiting goes by, with the town remaining fairly quiet, and Bob's legs start cramping and tingling, when out of the blue, a figure suddenly appears on the edge of the woods just beyond the northeast gate. Bob uses the 2X scope and peers around the edge of a smokestack, tracking the figure as he enters the safe zone, turns south, and briskly walks down the deserted sidewalk toward the square. Bob recognizes the only African American in town—the dapper gospel singer Harold Stauback—as the man climbs the steps of the courthouse and knocks on the main entrance.

A minute later, a sleepy Calvin Dupree appears in the doorway, dressed in sweatpants, yawning and scratching his ass. The men exchange a few words, and finally Calvin invites Stauback inside. The door slams, echoing up across the rooftops.

Bob looks at his pocket watch. It is now almost seven o'clock, and he can hear other voices rising on the breeze, most of them muffled behind walls and windows, as people stir and climb out of bed and get on with the business of the day. With no newspapers, TV, radio, Internet, restaurants, bars, show clubs, theaters, or any other form of modern entertainment to keep people out at night, the circadian rhythms of most folks have begun to shift. People have started to retire earlier at night and wake earlier in the morning. Or maybe it's simply a built-in evolutionary adaptation—after all, the darkness brings more hazards. Best to stay inside at night with your 12-gauge next to your bed.

At last, Bob sees the man of the hour—the square-jawed, toothy preacher, resplendent in his anachronistic wool suit and tie—emerging from the back of his brownstone. Walking with his trademark saunter, he joins three other members of his suicide cult in the dusty street. Bob recognizes the skinny kid, Reese, who first stumbled into Woodbury, along with the preacher's two other minions, Wade and Stephen. Bob knows that Wade is a former cop, and Stephen is a clean-cut choirboy from Panama City Beach, Florida, and that's about the extent of Bob's knowledge about these people.

Bob has avoided these folks like a hare at a hound dog convention.

The four men march down the sidewalk toward the raceway arena, greeting some of the other citizens and church members as they come out of their doors with shovels and trowels and sacks of seeds. The group grows as the preacher approaches the racetrack, laughing and patting people on their backs and bidding everyone a good morning—ever the hail-fellow-well-met, ever the politician. Bob thinks that if there were babies present, the preacher would be kissing them.

Bob feels like puking as he watches the citizens enter the arena gardens with the preacher. His stomach lurches, but not entirely from nausea. The nervous tension has returned. Bob knows it's now or never, and for a brief moment he craves a drink. He swallows the sour taste of copper on the back of his tongue and casts the thought out of his mind. He doesn't drink anymore. He may be a drunk, but he doesn't drink. He knows this is the way it has to be.

He gathers his stuff and crosses the back of the roof to the wrought-iron guardrail bordering the fire escape. The wind rattles the steps as he swiftly descends. His vision tunnels and his heart thumps as he reaches the bottom of the fire escape and hops off the last rung.

Then he turns and hurries down the alley, taking the back way to Lilly's place.

When the knocking sounds first start clamoring through the still, silent air of the apartment, Lilly is having a bad dream. She's dreaming that she's lost in a vast warehouse the size of an airplane hangar and dead bodies are lined up on the floor like cordwood, and she has to step over them to get to the exit, but the exit keeps eluding her, vanishing before her eyes, and soon she realizes there's no way out of this place and the human remains on the floor are all the people she has known, who have either died in her presence or have vanished without a trace. She sees her father, Everett, and she sees Josh, Austin, Megan, Doc Stevens, Alice, her uncle Joe, her aunt Edith . . . when all at once comes a loud knocking sound, and she thinks to herself—in the dream—whoever is knocking on the door of *this* terrible place is insane. Who the hell would want to come in here? And the knocking continues until the dream begins to collapse under the weight of the noise like a house of cards in a tornado.

Lilly sits up with a jerk, the brilliant rays of summer sun slicing through a gap in the bedroom drapes. She shakes off the nightmare and looks at the clock: 7:13. The knocking rises and quickens. Somebody out there really, really needs to see her.

She hastily pulls on a pair of gouged jeans and a shopworn Wilco T-shirt, and hurries across the apartment to the front door, pulling her hair back in a knot as she goes.

"We need to talk," Bob Stookey says to her the second she unbolts the latch and cracks open the door.

Bob takes her across the street, around the back of the deserted brownstone, and in through the rear entrance. Lilly keeps making disgusted, annoyed noises as she reluctantly follows him inside the airless shadows, shaking her head and glancing over her shoulder to make sure nobody is watching. Bob has been assuring her all along that everybody is currently at the racetrack arena, working the gardens and having their morning coffee, and she and Bob are now all alone, but the truth is, he's not sure. Anybody could have seen them slipping inside the preacher's quarters.

Which is why Bob moves quickly through the back hallway, past the galley kitchen with its reeking refrigerator and festering drain, through the living room with its peach crates and newspapers stacked nearly to the ceiling, and finally into the bedroom that smells of old liniment and stale fabric permeated with the traces of ancient cigarette smoke and cooking grease. The brownstone has had a checkered history—before the outbreak belonging to an elderly shut-in, and then commandeered by a succession of the Governor's goons.

"I knew he had something up his sleeve," Bob is saying as he kneels by the bed on creaking, arthritic knees, "but I never thought it would be as god-awful loony as this. You might want to sit down."

"Bob, is this really necessary?" Lilly says, standing over him, observing with hands on her hips and a sour look on her face.

"Just give me a second." He grunts as he yanks the enormous duffel out from under the bed, the clinking sound of glassware accompanied by the rasping noise of carpet threads tearing under the weight. Bob rises to his knees and unzips the thing. He pulls one of the beakers out and shows it to Lilly. "Get a load of that," he says. "Go ahead, take a closer look . . . just don't spill it."

"What the fuck?" She takes the beaker from him and reads the label. "Hydrogen cyanide?"

"You see this shit most of the time in the form of a gas," Bob says, levering himself back up to his feet, fishing for a handkerchief, rubbing his sore neck. "Comes in liquid form and crystals as well. Smells faintly of almonds. Goes well with Kool-Aid."

"Bob, you don't know if this is—"

"Blow the wax out of your head, Lilly!" The abrupt spike in the volume of his voice makes her jump. He needs to get through her thick skull quickly, they don't have much time, and Bob has an overwhelming feeling right now of being watched. He drills his gaze into her. "Jonestown, Jim Jones—ring any bells?"

"Bob, slow down—"

"I saw Saddam Hussein use this shit on the Kurds in northern Iraq back in '93. It can shut down the oxygen production of a person's cells in a matter of seconds, and you kick in less than a minute. It ain't pretty. Trust me on that. You choke out on your own throat tissue."

"Bob, stop!" She puts the beaker on the floor and then holds her head with both hands as though it might crack open. She closes her eyes and holds her head, and she looks down. "Stop . . . just stop."

"Lilly, listen to me." He goes over to her, gently takes her by the arms. "I know you're just trying to do the right thing by everybody. You're a good gal. Never asked to be no politician, never wanted to be no hero. But now you gotta step up."

"S-stop . . ." Her voice barely registers. She can hardly utter a sound. "P-please just s-stop . . ."

"Lilly, look at me." He shakes her a little. "In less than twelve hours, these fruitcakes are going to turn this town into a mass suicide." He shakes her again. "Look at me, Lilly-girl! Now, I don't have a clue what all that ordnance is for, but you can bet your ass it ain't meant to celebrate the Fourth of July! I need you to get pissed and get with the program here! You hear me? Are you reading me on this?"

She crumbles in his arms, her emotions and exhaustion pouring out of her on a tide of tears and snot and grief. She cries and cries, and the sheer intensity of it—the convulsive sorrow gushing out of her in Bob's arms—is so disconcerting to him, so troubling and un-expected, that he doesn't even hear the person who has been watch-ing them all along, listening to their every word, now carefully entering the rear of the brownstone with a 9mm pistol poised and ready in his hand, the safety off.

TWENTY-ONE

Pressing her face into the smoky, moldy folds of Bob's flannel shirt, Lilly sobs with absolute unhinged abandon. She has never cried like this in her life. Not even at her daddy's funeral, even when she lost Josh last year, even in the aftermath of Austin's heroic sacrificial death outside the prison a few months ago. She shudders and keens and tries to breathe through the agony, but the pain is coming in waves—so amorphous and ill defined that she can't even pinpoint the source of it—like tremors passing through her bones. Is she crying for her lost dreams? Is she mourning the normal life that will always be just out of reach in this hideous world? She keeps hearing the old hymns that Harold Stauback sang that night when they all celebrated the sanctity of life and the future of Woodbury in the square, and now she hears nothing but the ugly drumbeat of a funeral dirge drowning that lovely gospel voice, drowning everything good and hopeful with its brute pedestrian clang, a broken gong, *a death knell.*

"Honey?" Bob's voice in her ear. "I know it's hard. I know you're hurtin' . . . but you gotta get your shit together for the sake of them kids."

Lilly lets out a pained, strangled breath and listens to what he's saying.

"You got to pull it together, girl. I can't push back at this all by myself. I can get Speed and Matthew on my side, maybe, David and Barbara, sure, maybe Gloria, but I need you, girlie-girl."

She nods. Her face is soaked. She hitches in an unsteady series of breaths and looks at him through the glazed membrane of her tears. "Okay . . . I'm . . . okay."

He pulls his handkerchief back out and dabs her eyes. "I heard them in the woods, they're doing it tonight and they ain't taking any prisoners."

She nods, wipes her face. "Okay. I'm sorry, sorry. Let me think."

"They're gonna be back for this stuff soon." Bob looks at her. "Are you okay?"

She nods. "Yeah, I'm good," she lies. Her head is spinning. She wipes her eyes again. "Just let me think for a minute." She gently disentangles herself from Bob's arms and begins to pace, back and forth, shooting nervous glances down at the duffel bag and its contents. "Think . . . think." She wipes her mouth. "How did this happen? How does something like this happen?"

Bob gives her a shrug. "Goddamn Holy Rollers, who knows what notions they get in their heads."

"But why take us with them?" Lilly's skull throbs as she paces, a splitting headache threatening to rend her head apart. "Why not just sacrifice themselves? What do they have against us?"

Bob watches her pace. "I don't think they see it as a negative."

"It's mass murder."

"No argument here. You're preaching to the choir, Lilly-girl."

"But why?" She threads fingers through the loose tendrils of hair that have come undone from her hasty ponytail. "Why now? Here? Why today?"

Bob sighs. "Who the hell knows what bugs crazy people get up their ass? It could be the summer solstice. It could be the tenth anniversary of who-the-fuck-knows."

Lilly feels the anger sparking in her like a flint striking. "What I mean is, why *now*—today—after the world's been like this for so long? Why not put everybody out of their misery back at the start of the Turn?"

Another shrug from Bob. "Like I said, you're gonna have to ask the monsignor."

Lilly gazes across the bedroom and sees the tarnished silver-plated crucifix lying on a cluttered bedside table. She goes over to the thing, stares at it, and suddenly, with one violent sweep of her arm, she wipes the cross and everything else on the tabletop onto the floor. The abruptness of the gesture makes Bob jump. Lilly's face darkens a shade or two. "Brotherhood of man, my ass!" she barks. "These are *Christians*? *FUCKING HYPOCRITES!*"

Bob stands back, watching, fishing in his shirt pocket for a hand-rolled cigarette. He's been cutting down on account of dwindling rolling paper supplies, but now he lights one of his last smokes with his Zippo and nods. "You're not wrong, Lilly-girl." He takes a drag. "Let it out."

"They're fucking liars!" She kicks the desk chair onto its side. "Fucking con artists!"

"Amen, Sister." Bob smokes and looks on with morbid satisfaction. "I hear ya."

"LIARS!" With one heaving shove, she overturns the desk. The contents of the drawers spill across the floor as the legs collapse, cracking apart. "FUCKING LIARS!"

Bob waits, smoking, as Lilly stands in the center of the bedroom, her fists clenched, her chest rising and falling. Her mind swims. She can't latch on to one single thought. She never wanted to be a leader, never asked to take over the reins of this town, never wanted anything beyond a normal life, a husband, a home, some children, maybe a little bliss. And now *this*? She put her ass on the line for these lying hypocrites—Reverend Jeremiah and his flock—she risked her life and the lives of her people, and now they're going to all be snuffed out in a blink? Without a fight? Without a struggle? Like votive candles being blown out after a service?

Lilly gets very still then. Her eyes burn. Her guts congeal and tighten. A singular, burning urge is building deep within her—a jagged emotion she's never before felt in this plague-battered world—*the need for revenge*. At last, Lilly says in a soft, measured, flat voice, "Bob, we're going to nip this shit in the bud."

Bob starts to answer when a third voice speaks up. "I'm sorry."

Lilly and Bob snap their gazes toward the far corner of the room.

Calvin Dupree stands in the doorway with his Glock gripped in both hands, raised and aimed at them, his face twitching with nervous tension. "I'm so sorry, Lilly," he reiterates in a quavering voice, his eyes welling with tears. "But nobody's going to stop this blessed event."

Lilly and Bob exchange quick glances. Neither of them has a weapon handy—that's the first thing that registers to Lilly—the .357 is out in the living room, sitting on the coffee table. Lilly's Rugers are back at her place. Nowadays, she rarely leaves her apartment without her iron, but today she left in a hurry, Bob dragging her out of there like the place was on fire, her thoughts racing, distracting her. Lilly looks back at Calvin and starts to say something when the second thing registers to her: *This is Calvin pointing a gun at them, her dear, sweet, lovable Calvin, standing before them like a crazed zealot, ready to kill for a madman.*

"Calvin, what are you doing?" Lilly stays planted right where she stands, makes no move to intercede or approach him. She merely looks into his eyes. "What are you doing? Seriously."

His hands tremble with anguish, the gun's muzzle shaking. "You d-don't understand, Lilly. I can help you understand. This is for the best."

"The best?" She keeps her gaze leveled at him. "Really?"

Calvin nods. "Yes, ma'am."

"This is how God wants you to behave? Pointing guns at people?"

"Easy does it, Lilly-girl," Bob warns from the other side of the room, and Lilly can't tell if it's a ruse or if Bob is sincerely worried that Calvin will shoot them.

"Meredith always said this wasn't the end," Calvin tells them with emotion strangling his voice. The barrel of Calvin's Glock stays aimed at Lilly despite his convulsive shaking and apparent palsy of his legs. "We know there's a paradise waiting for us. It's waiting for you as well." A single tear runs down Calvin's grizzled cheek. "Please trust in the Lord."

"The Lord we're fine with, Calvin," Bob interjects from his position on the other side of the brass bed. "It's your preacher we ain't too sure about."

Calvin's tears flow now, his face wet and glistening with them. "God brought this great man here to lead us out of this hell."

"What about your kids, Calvin?" Lilly can barely feel her fingertips as they dig into the balls of her fists. "You're going to do this to your own children?"

"They want to be with their mother." He lowers his head and lets the tears shudder through him for a moment. "I'm sorry . . . so so sorry . . ."

It happens in the space of a heartbeat: Bob takes two quick strides toward the gunman, and at the same time Lilly whirls toward the window, and Calvin sees both of them moving and snaps the gun toward Bob. "YOU THINK I'M JOKING?" Bob freezes. Calvin roars at him, "I WILL SHOOT YOU IN THE HEAD, I SWEAR ON THE SOULS OF MY CHILDREN!"

"No!" Lilly moves between the two men. "Please! Calvin, don't!"

"I WILL!" His anguish turns to madness, his eyes glassy with rage now. "I SWEAR I WILL!"

"We believe you!" Lilly tries to dial it down by lowering her voice. She holds her hands up. "We believe you, Cal. We do. Nobody needs to do any shooting."

Calvin hyperventilates and stares at each of them, one at a time, his eyes a tennis match, the gun's muzzle wavering. Bob has his hands up in surrender as well, his gaze glued to Calvin. Lilly takes a deep breath. Nobody says anything for the longest moment. The bottles of clear fluid nestled in the duffel bag on the floor gleam dully in the early-morning light seeping through a crack in the drapes.

At last Lilly says, "Calvin, is there any way we could possibly put the gun down and—"

The blast cuts her off midsentence, a photo-strobe-bright flash *behind* Calvin Dupree, as hot as the sun, the wasp sting of a small-caliber bullet taking a chunk out of the back of his head, tossing him forward as though a cable were yanking him off his feet.

His life flows out of him even before his body stops twitching on the floor.

A lurid, garish instant of time passes with nobody making a move, both Lilly and Bob just gaping, the soft trickle of blood dripping off Calvin's skull the only sound other than their racing heartbeats. Calvin lies facedown in a spreading pool of deep crimson. The back of his skull is ravaged by the ballistic damage of a point-blank-range blast—apparently fired from directly behind him—the vantage point somewhere in the living room.

Then Lilly hears a thud, someone out in the other room dropping a gun to the floor. The soft whisper of a child's crying can be heard.

Lilly glances at Bob, and Bob glances back at her with eyes widening.

"Oh, Jesus," Lilly utters as she charges around Calvin's body and plunges into the living room, where Tommy Dupree slumps on his knees in front of Lilly's .22-caliber Ruger. Dressed in filthy jeans and a Pokemon T-shirt, the boy softly cries. Lilly goes to him. "Oh, Jesus, Tommy, oh, God," Lilly murmurs, kneeling by the boy, putting her arm around him. "C'mere, c'mere."

The boy sobs into Lilly's shoulder. "I shouldn't have done it, but I had to."

"Sshhhhhh . . . Tommy." She strokes his damp hair. "You don't have to—"

"I heard what he said to y'all."

"Okay—"

"Ever since them dead folks came back, my mom and dad had been going a little more insane every day."

"Tommy—"

"I thought it would be my mom I'd have to do something about, though . . ."

"Sssshhhh—"

"She was the first one, started acting weird, said it was God's will, I was afraid she would hurt me or my brother or my sister or maybe even *herself*."

"Okay, okay, hush now." Lilly hugs the boy tightly, as Bob looks on with an anguished expression. Lilly's tears run in rivulets down her face "You don't need to explain, Tommy, I understand."

Tommy buries his face in the convolutions of her T-shirt. His muffled voice has calmed slightly. "I believe in God, but He ain't like no God they talk about." He shudders. "First, my dad said this plague was because we were being punished, and then he started talking in his sleep, asking God to take him, take him now."

"Okay, Tommy, that's enough." She presses the side of his face to her chest. "That's enough."

The boy pulls away, looking up at her through his scalding tears. "Is he dead?"

"Your dad?"

The boy nods. "Did I kill him?"

Lilly shoots another crestfallen glance at Bob, and Bob slowly nods. Lilly can't tell if Bob is nodding because he wants her to tell the child the truth or if he's confirming that Calvin Dupree is dead . . . or if he's nodding for some other larger reason, such as the fact that this was bound to happen so let's just deal with it. Maybe all of the above. Lilly wipes her tears. She looks at the boy. "Yes, sweetheart, unfortunately your dad . . ." She feels a paroxysm of sorrow rise in her so suddenly it takes her breath away. She can't look at the body behind her. She actually had grown to love this man. For all his faults, all his proselytizing and coarse backwoods philosophy, she loved him. She wanted to have a family with him. Now she looks down and utters the words as though they weigh a thousand tons. "He's gone."

Tommy doesn't respond, just lowers his head and silently cries for a moment, his tears dripping now from the tip of his nose.

Apparently Bob picks up a cue from this pause because he bows his head, turns, and goes back into the bedroom. He kneels and feels Calvin's neck for a pulse, gets nothing, turns, pulls a blanket from the bed, and gently—almost tenderly—lays the blanket over Calvin's corpse. Bob looks up at the twosome in the outer room.

The boy has stopped crying. He swallows back all the grief and looks up at Lilly. "Am I going to hell?"

Lilly smiles sadly. "No, Tommy. You're not going to hell."

"Do we need to shoot my dad again?"

"Excuse me?"

"Do we need to shoot him in the head so he doesn't turn?"

Lilly lets out a drained sigh. "Nope." She strokes the boy's cheek. "He won't turn, Tommy."

"Why not?"

"The wound is in his head."

"Oh."

Tommy has calmed enough now for Lilly to lead him over to an old broken-down armchair along the wall. She sits him down and says, "Buddy, I'm going to need you to just sit there for a second while I talk to old Bob."

Tommy nods.

Lilly hurries into the bedroom, where Bob is already pushing the duffel back under the bed. He grunts as he quickly checks the bag to make sure there are no signs of disturbance. "They'll be coming any minute," he says out of the side of his mouth to Lilly, speaking under his breath so the child won't hear him. "We gotta get outta here, gotta get this body out with us . . . wipe up the blood as best we can."

"He has a name, Bob." Lilly scans the room—the body, the boarded window, the closet—and she sees a plastic fuel container and a coil of rubber tubing by the foot of the bed. "What the hell is that stuff?"

"That's mine—I'll explain later—help me gather this shit up."

"You got a plan?"

"Maybe, I don't know. I'm sort of making this up as I go along." He gives her a look. "How about you? You got any brilliant ideas?"

"Not really." She glances out the bedroom doorway at the boy fidgeting in the chair. "All I know is, we have to get the children somewhere safe."

"Fucking Jesus freaks," Bob grumbles as he stuffs the fuel container and tubing into his knapsack. "They'll fuck things up every time."

Lilly feels light-headed, short of breath. She looks at the shrouded remains of Calvin Dupree and utters, "How did this happen?"

"Hey!" Bob grabs her arm, shakes her a little. "I need you sharp."

She nods, says nothing.

Bob pats her arm. "I know your heart is broken, Lilly-girl, but you need to stay with me, stay frosty."

She nods again.

Bob shakes her. "You understand what I'm saying? We need to get outta here *right now* before—"

A series of telltale noises suddenly interrupt from outside the boarded windows—bolt mechanisms on rifles clanking, voices calling out—and the sound of it makes Bob and Lilly go mannequin still.

TWENTY-TWO

The good and honorable Reverend Jeremiah Garlitz stands in front of the ramshackle brownstone, his shoulders squared off toward the front porch, the wind flapping the legs of his trousers and the tails of his threadbare suit coat as he cradles a 12-gauge shotgun in his arms, giving him an almost regal, Arthurian mien as he yells, "LILLY! BOB! WHOEVER ELSE IS IN THERE! PLEASE DON'T DO ANYTHING RASH! WE ARE NOT THE ENEMY! PLEASE ACKNOWLEDGE THAT YOU HEAR ME AND YOU UNDERSTAND!"

The preacher fingers the blue-steel trigger pad as he awaits a response.

Jeremiah has positioned his men on all sides of the building. Most of the male congregants are present and armed and willing to do what has to be done. There are only two absentees. Old Joe Bressler, the seventy-three-year-old retiree, has stayed behind the lines with the women of the church group as they prepare the sacramental food and drink in the back kitchen of the Dew Drop Inn on Pecan Street. Wade Pilcher, the leathery former cop, has been dispatched to the neighboring hills and bluffs above Elkins Creek to prepare the secret apparatus of the summoning.

It has been less than an hour since Calvin Dupree agreed to join the Pentecostal People of God, subsequently volunteering to serve as a mole amid the more recalcitrant residents of Woodbury. It pains Jeremiah greatly that he has to resort to this heavy-handed cloak-and-dagger routine, especially since he merely wants to give the good people of Woodbury a free ride out of hell and into paradise—an all-access pass to heaven—but so is the way of the world. As it says in John, chapter 2, verse 15: *Do not love the world or the things in the world, for all the world is passing away along with its desires, but whoever does the will of God abides forever.*

All of which is why Jeremiah has now positioned Mark and Reese on the east side of the brownstone, Harold and Stephen on the rear, and Anthony on the west. Each male parishioner has been issued a weapon from the Woodbury arsenal—currently a two-hundred-square-foot rats' nest of a storage locker in the rear of the Dogwood Street warehouse, the dwindling contents reflecting the town's dearth of ammo and firearms—the key to which Calvin had managed to steal from Bob's infirmary closet. Now some of the churchmen wield assault rifles, others high-powered semiautomatic pistols.

Jeremiah loathes human-on-human violence of any sort, but these are times that call for good Christian soldiers to follow Ecclesiastes's imperative that there is a time for peace and a time for war, and it is now a time to battle anyone who would try to stop the blessed deliverance scheduled for later this day.

At last, a shrill, crumbly voice issues from behind the boarded windows of the brownstone, so unsteady and shaky it sounds almost feral. "WE HEAR YOU!" Pause. "WE UNDERSTAND YOU'RE NOT THE ENEMY!" Pause again. "BUT WE ALSO KNOW EXACTLY WHAT YOU'RE PLANNING FOR TONIGHT!"

Another slight pause here, which makes Jeremiah go still, his stomach clenching as he looks off at each flank, each church member raising his weapon, ready to fire.

The voice continues: "I'M TELLING YOU RIGHT NOW THIS ISN'T GONNA HAPPEN!"

"LILLY, LISTEN TO ME!" The preacher applies his most convivial tone here. "WE HEARD GUNFIRE! WE DON'T KNOW IF ANYBODY'S BEEN SHOT OR IF YOU PLAN ON DOING ANY MORE SHOOTING, BUT THERE'S NO REASON FOR ANYONE TO GET HURT! WE CAN WORK THIS OUT—"

"ARE YOU KIDDING ME?" The voice from the brownstone hardens, sharpens like a knife. "NOBODY NEEDS TO GET HURT? DO

YOU THINK WE'RE IDIOTS? YOU WERE GOING TO TAKE EVERY LIVING THING DOWN TONIGHT! YOU WERE GOING TO POISON US WITHOUT GIVING IT A SECOND THOUGHT!"

"LILLY, IT'S NOT WHAT YOU THINK! IT'S STILL A FREE COUNTRY, EVERYBODY'S GOT A VOTE HERE! NOBODY HAS TO DO ANYTHING THEY DON'T WANT TO!" The preacher licks his lips. He's lying, of course. At this point, the wheels are in motion, and nobody is going to stop the machine. Plus, they can't risk someone gumming up the works, swaying the consensus, or weakening resolve.

Glancing over his shoulder, the reverend sees a few of the original residents about a block away—the Sterns, the woman named Gloria—coming out of their buildings and heading toward the commotion. The clock is ticking. Jeremiah knows he has to act quickly and decisively. As his daddy always said, best way to deal with a mischievous child is quick, harsh, but fair punishment.

Right now.

Jeremiah motions to Mark Arbogast, the lanky former bricklayer now standing guard on the east corner of the building. "Brother Mark! C'mere!"

Arbogast obediently leaves his post and trots over to the preacher.

"Change of plans, Brother," Jeremiah says, keeping his voice low as he motions to other men. "Everybody! Over here! Quickly! C'mon!"

The others appear around the far side of the building, their faces tense and twitchy as they rush over to where the preacher is standing.

Jeremiah nods toward the other townspeople now heading this way—the Stern couple, Gloria, and Ben Buchholz—about a block away and closing the distance. "We gotta contain this right now before it gets out of hand." Jeremiah looks at Arbogast. "Brother Mark, I need you to keep these townspeople back, keep them away from the building, tell them . . . tell them we're dealing with somebody who turned and broke into my place. You got that?"

Mark nods and then whirls toward the oncoming clutch of people.

Jeremiah turns to the other men, and he speaks very quickly and very clearly, explaining exactly what they're going to do and emphasizing the importance of speed.

Lilly hears a voice calling out for her from the rear of the brownstone and in her panic misidentifies it as the voice of her father. Everett Caul used to stand on the porch of their Marietta house and bellow his daughter's full name as though beckoning a family pet: *LILLLLLLLEEEEEEEEE CAAAAAAUUUUULLL!* Lilly remembers playing hide-and-seek with the neighborhood kids and hearing that clarion call echoing over the tops of oak trees, rich with the portents of a hot dinner, bedtime stories, and maybe a TV show or two before lights-out. But just as quickly as she found herself reveling in a flickering memory of her daddy, she now finds herself wrenched back into the here and now—the cluttered living room of a rundown brownstone in Woodbury, the sound of the preacher's voice cutting through the silence.

"LILLY?"

Both Lilly and Bob spin toward the sound of the voice—now coming from the back of the place in a disorienting game of Whac-A-Mole—as Tommy Dupree jerks off the armchair and springs to his feet. "What are they—? Why did—?" he babbles.

Outside the rear of the brownstone: "LILLY, CAN YOU HEAR ME?"

Lilly scoops her gun off the floor—the gun used by Tommy to kill Calvin—ejecting the Ruger's magazine and checking it. The clip is full. She sees Bob out of the corner of her eye spinning the Magnum's cylinder, peering out into the kitchen. Lilly goes over to Tommy and speaks very softly, "I'm going to need you to stay right behind me. Can you do that? Can you stay right behind me no matter what?"

He nods.

Outside, in the back courtyard, the baritone voice calls out again: "LILLY, I'M SO SORRY TO DO THIS TO YOU, BUT I'M GONNA NEED YOU TO GO AHEAD AND COME OUT THE BACK DOOR NOW."

Bob jerks his hand up, motioning for Lilly and Tommy to stay put, stay there for a second. He goes into the kitchen, his gun now gripped with both hands, Weaver stance, Israeli commando technique he learned in Basic at Fort Benning. Lilly watches from the living room. Bob's boots make crackling noises on the old linoleum as he shuffles over to the window, his gun poised and ready to rock. He peers through a crack in the boards nailed up across the broken pane, gazing out into the rear courtyard. He lets out a pained sigh.

"I'M REAL SORRY, LILLY," the voice calls out, "BUT Y'ALL GOT ONE MINUTE TO COME OUT WITH YOUR HANDS AND GUNS WHERE WE CAN SEE THEM!"

Lilly raises her .22 and nods at Tommy. "Stay close."

She scuttles across the room with her gun raised, through the kitchen doorway, and over to where Bob stands by the window. Tommy shuffles along behind her, holding on to the belt loop on the back of her jeans. His heavy, nervous breathing is audible in the silent kitchen. Lilly looks at Bob and starts to say something.

Outside: "THIRTY SECONDS . . . AND THEN WE'RE GONNA HAVE TO GO AHEAD AND COME ON IN."

Lilly whispers to Bob, "I got six rounds in the mag, I say we make a break for it."

Bob shakes his head, lowering his gun. "It ain't worth it, Lilly. They're gonna come at us from all sides, and they got them Bushmasters."

"What? What are you talking about?"

"Lilly—"

"You still got that speed loader, we can hold 'em off and make a mad dash for the wall. Regroup in the woods, take them down one at a time."

"Lilly, come on—"

The voice: "FIFTEEN SECONDS, LILLY!"

Lilly feels the moist, tight, terrified grip of the child against her tailbone. She hisses her words, the rage clenching her guts. "Bob, I'm telling you, the element of surprise will get us across that courtyard—"

Bob shakes his head. "No, trust me, we gotta throw in the towel."

"TEN SECONDS!"

Lilly looks at Bob. "I'm not gonna give up, I'm not going down without a fight."

Bob looks into her eyes, and for just an instant something resembling a smile crosses his deeply lined features. "I didn't say anything about giving up."

"FIVE SECONDS!"

Bob turns toward the back door, thumbs the hammer down on his gun, holds the .357 over his head, and calls out, raising his voice loud enough to be heard by the gunmen on either side of the building's rear windows: "Okay, you win! We're coming out! Don't shoot!"

Hours later, Jeremiah is philosophical about the whole incident. The momentary rebellion turns out to be a minor hiccup—a tempest in a teapot, as Jeremiah's grandmother used to call family squabbles—despite the fact that one of the faithful has fallen. Jeremiah is devastated that Calvin Dupree has given up his life prematurely. But in a way, it's a fitting tribute to the man's faith and bravery. He will enter paradise a few hours early.

By noon, the preacher has managed to contain the crisis, get the program back on track, and move closer to the final stages of the ritual.

Wade Pilcher returns from the hills and forests with good news. The remote devices have been set and tested, and the superherd has been located (the telltale dust cloud a mile east of Elkins Creek indicating its current position). Wade assures the reverend that the summoning will be ready when the time comes. According to the former cop's calculations, it will take the herd—once the signal finds them—approximately three hours to change course and cross the five miles of wetlands before reaching Woodbury.

That afternoon, at one P.M. Eastern Standard Time, a moment that will be memorialized later as a milestone in the epochal series of events that follow, the Reverend Jeremiah Garlitz returns to his brownstone, retrieves the heavy duffel bags from under his bed, carries the precious cargo across town to the racetrack arena, and descends the service stairs to the sublevels.

In the infirmary, the preacher finds Reese, Stephen, and Mark huddling in a pool of emergency halogen light in the corner of the room, drinking coffee from paper cups, softly chuckling at some joke. Next to them, the sacraments are boxed and stacked on stainless steel tables.

"*Hey!*"

The sharpness of Jeremiah's voice as he enters the sick bay startles the men. They look up from their coffee, their smiles lingering. "Brother Jeremiah," Reese says, his boyish face still full of good humor. "I thought you were coming down at three o'clock."

Jeremiah walks up to them, carefully sets down the duffel bags with a dull clank, and glowers at them with the utmost gravity on his handsome features. "There will be no joking around on this day, gentlemen. I don't want to hear any chuckling or giggling from anyone."

The men look stung, their smiles fading, their faces turning downward. Reese stares at the floor. "Sorry, Brother . . . you're right."

"This is a solemn day." The preacher scans their downcast faces. "Yes, it's also a joyous occasion, I admit that. But the time of laughter and telling jokes has come to an end, my brothers."

Reese is nodding. "Amen, Brother . . . amen."

"I want everybody to complete his tasks to the letter, we owe that much to the good people of Woodbury. Do you understand what I'm saying?"

Nods from all three men. Then Mark, the lanky former bricklayer from Tallahassee, speaks up. "Do you want all three of us in the service bays with you when you . . . you . . . *deal* with the traitors?"

"They're not traitors, Brother."

"Sorry, I didn't mean nothing by it."

Jeremiah offers a paternal smile. "I know you didn't mean any harm by your question. But the truth is, they're just doing what any of us would do if we thought somebody was threatening our loved ones."

Mark glances at the others, then back at the preacher. "Not sure I understand what you mean, Brother."

The preacher pats the younger man on the shoulder. "They're not bad people, they're not our enemy. They just don't realize the gift we're all about to receive. They don't see the wondrous glory in it."

Mark is nodding, his eyes already moistening. "You're right, Brother . . . you're so right."

Jeremiah kneels by the duffels, unzips the first one, and starts pulling out beakers. "And to answer your original query, Brother, yes, I want y'all to back me up in there." He puts one of the large glass containers on the stainless steel gurney against the wall next to the sacraments. He pulls rubber gloves from his suit pocket and puts them on. "The best way to put down an innocent animal is humanely and quickly. I want y'all to follow my directions exactly as I give them. Do you understand?"

Nods from the men.

Jeremiah points at the closest carton of freshly baked unleavened bread. "All right, it's time. Somebody hand me a small bite-sized piece of that host, and somebody else pour me about two fingers of this liquid into one of them paper cups y'all are drinking from."

TWENTY-THREE

The huge, battered garage-style door shrieks up its rusty castors, and they enter the first vestibule—a grease-stained former service bay directly underneath the deserted concession stands. They flip on the battery-powered camping light sitting on a stack of spare tires by the door, and a dull yellow glow illuminates two hundred square feet of leprous, oil-spotted cement floor, a single figure bound and gagged to a folding chair in the center of the musty-smelling, airless chamber.

Jeremiah approaches first, a purple liturgical scarf thrown around the shoulder pads of his dusty suit. The other three men follow on his heels with deferential, shell-shocked expressions, holding the sacramental items in their arms like courtesans in some royal harem. "'Wash me thoroughly from my wickedness,'" Jeremiah recites as he approaches the subject. "'And cleanse me from my sin.'"

Lilly moans under her duct-taped gag, her eyes bugging out in terror when she sees the paper plate on which the piece of bread and cup of poisoned liquid sit. She starts tugging at her restraints, shuddering in the chair, making a horrible keening noise that's muffled by the tape, her sweat-soaked top stretched taut by the plastic shackle binding her wrists behind her back. She burns her gaze into the preacher and shrieks something inaudible behind the gag.

Jeremiah turns to his minions and softly yet quickly and firmly says, "Have the host and the blood of Christ ready on my signal, and pay no attention to what our beloved sister might say when the tape comes off, because it will be Satan talking at that point, and Mark, you move behind her, and on my signal bend her head back just like we practiced on the dummy back in Jacksonville."

The other men get into position behind Lilly's chair as Lilly wriggles and strains and convulses against the bondage and screams garbled profanities beneath the gag. The chair squeaks and shimmies across the floor with her powerful convulsions and writhing movements.

" 'Make me a clean heart, O God," Jeremiah intones as he nods at Reese, the plate holder, to hand over the sacraments. " 'Deliver me from bloodguiltiness, O God, and my tongue shall sing of Thy righteousness!' "

Another nod to Mark, as he moves around behind Lilly's chair, and a nod to Stephen, and a final entreaty to the Good Lord: "Accept this young sister into your fold, O God, and deliver her to heaven!"

Mark, the strongest of the three, moves in behind Lilly and wraps his hands around the bottom of her chin and yanks, as Stephen rips the tape from her mouth.

"OKAY, LISTEN TO ME! PLEASE! I'M BEGGING YOU! YOU DON'T HAVE TO DO THIS! GIVE ME ONE CHANCE TO MAKE MY CASE! I RESPECT WHAT YOU'RE DOING! DO YOU UNDERSTAND WHAT I'M SAYING? DON'T DO THIS TO ME! PLEASE! WAIT—!"

In that terrible instant before Jeremiah stuffs a half-dollar-sized piece of soda cracker into her mouth, she realizes that she is going to die and it's all over and it will come at the hand of this insane zealot, and how ironic, how fucking ironic, that it comes *not* at the hands of the walkers but a man supposedly of God, and she realizes instantly that she doesn't give a fuck about irony, she just wants to live, and her voice suddenly tumbles into a cascade of ululating cries, deteriorating quickly into a garbled sob.

"P-PLEASE! OH PLEASE! OH PLEASE! PLEASE! PLEEEEEEEE—!"

They lodge the host in her mouth, the strong, unyielding grip of the bricklayer behind her wrenching her jaws open and shut around the morsel, violently massaging it down her throat. She chokes and coughs and tries to gag it up, but the peristalsis of the human digestive system, starting with the throat and moving down the esophagus, will involuntarily—as the church members have learned in their research—accept the food in this situation and digest it no matter how much the subject consciously fights it.

The strong barbiturate has been added to the dough before baking.

The clear, odorless liquid comes next. Lilly wretches and writhes in the chair, trying to expel the host, as Jeremiah takes the paper cup off the plate. " 'According to the multitude of Thy mercies,' " he prays aloud as he leans down and quickly tips the liquid into her mouth, which is again forced open and shut by the bricklayer. " 'And do away with all mine offenses, forever and ever . . . amen.' "

Lilly coughs and sputters and jerks, and Jeremiah stands there, waiting patiently, until he is certain enough of the cyanide has gotten into her system. She finally collapses in the chair—either from exhaustion or from the fast-acting toxin—her muscles going slack, her head lolling forward.

Jeremiah hears something very faint—almost like a death rattle—coming from her throat.

He leans down and whispers, "Don't fight it, Sister." He strokes her cheek with great tenderness. "You'll be with God soon . . . and you can tell Him all about it."

He nods at the others, and they follow him out. Before slamming down the garage-style door, the preacher sticks his head back in the cell.

"We're right behind you, Sister."

The door bangs shut.

Minutes later, it doesn't occur to Lilly that she should be dead already.

She lolls forward in the chair, unaware of how much time has passed, a drying crust of something on her lips, the room spinning. Did she throw up? She peers down into her lap and sees no traces of vomit. The crotch of her jeans looks damp. Did she wet herself?

She sits back in the chair, her wrists burning from the plastic restraints. Her gag lies on the cement floor in front of her—a wadded, crumpled piece of duct tape. She blinks. She feels dizzy, nauseous, chilled . . . but alive. What the hell is going on? She tries to wrench her hands free when she hears the muffled cries of Tommy Dupree coming from the service bay next to hers.

The walls are eighteen inches of mortar, rebar, and reinforced cement, so the sounds coming from next door are very faint and completely dampened by the infrastructure. Lilly has to concentrate on the noises, straining her ears, in order to make out what's happening.

She can hear two voices, one of them the high-pitched shouting of the boy. The sounds of a struggle come next. Lilly hears the squeak of a metal folding chair, the droning voice of the preacher, and then silence. Footsteps moving across the room.

The deep thud of the garage door banging down makes her jerk with a start.

She takes deep breaths, in through her nose, out through her mouth, swallowing back the horror. She wriggles her wrists, trying to keep the feeling in her hands, fighting the pinpricks of numbness setting in. Her stomach roils. One thing is certain: She doesn't seem to be passing over into the afterlife as promised.

She's not dying.

What the fuck?

The sound of another garage door going up makes her jump.

She hears Bob's gravelly voice letting out a series of muted obscenities, the crackle of tape being ripped off his mouth, the praying, the sounds of struggle, more praying, and then . . . silence again. Footsteps. The booming thud of the garage door shutting.

Then Lilly hears the footsteps of the mercy killers receding down the corridor.

A moment later, a shroud of silence descends upon the sublevel.

Lilly tries to breathe through the terror. The silence is unbearable. It's a leaden, pervasive, primal silence—the silence of the tomb—and Lilly starts to panic. Is she hallucinating all this in her death throes? Are Tommy and Bob gone already? Is she actually dead and having one of those brain glitches that mislead a victim into thinking she's actually okay when her guts are about to spill out at any moment?

She tries to breathe as evenly as possible and get a grip on her emotions when she hears another sound coming from behind the wall between her and Bob.

At first, she thinks it's merely the sound of Bob collapsing—a dull thud and a metallic clunk—as his chair tips and he slams down. Then she realizes she's actually hearing a dragging noise crossing the

238 | Jay Bonansinga

neighboring service bay. Bob is moving. He's dragging himself, perhaps while still shackled to the chair, toward the door.

What the fuck is going on? Lilly focuses more intensely on her shackles. She feels a wet sensation, which she assumes is blood from the constant wriggling and tugging at the restraints. One of her wrists begins to slip through its plastic cuff, the greasy lubrication from her own blood allowing it leeway, and she works it and works it, when all at once a sharp, metallic squeak makes her start.

The noise comes from Bob's cell, and it has the effect of waking Lilly up. She calls out to him, "Bob!?"

"Coming, goddamn it!"

The raspy, whiskey-cured voice—barely audible behind inches of stone and ancient steel lath—reaches down into her soul. She's not dreaming, and she's not hallucinating. She actually hears Bob's cranky, croaking bullfrog of a voice behind the wall. "Just hold your horses for a second!" the muffled voice admonishes her.

"Hurry!" Lilly gets one hand free of its shackle. Her wrist is deeply gashed from the frantic tugging, a thin runnel of blood creeping down her forearm. She can hear the adjacent garage door squeaking open on rusty tracks, followed by shuffling footsteps.

She leans forward and tries to reach the rope binding her ankles to the bottom of the chair, but with one hand still bound to the chair it's impossible. "Bob, what's going on? What are you doing?"

"Getting the kid!"

The voice comes from the opposite wall, as the sound of a second garage door squealing upward on oxidized runners penetrates the stone barrier. Lilly's heart quickens. She can hear Tommy Dupree's voice—thank God, thank God. Lilly tries to scoot her chair toward the door.

A moment later, her cell fills with the ratcheting squeak of her door being heaved upward.

"Jesus Christ, what did they do to you?" Bob exclaims as he lurches into her chamber, followed closely by Tommy. "You need a goddamn tourniquet!"

"It's nothing, I did it to myself trying to slip the shackles." Lilly holds her hand up, blood sticky on her skin. "Get me loose, Bob."

He kneels, unfolds his pocketknife, and cuts her out of the wrist shackle and the ankle restraints.

She rubs her sore, oozing wrists while throwing a glance at Tommy. "You okay?"

He nods, evidently still in shock, his face as pale as wallpaper paste. "I'm okay, I guess. What did they just do to us?"

"I don't know, Tommy."

The boy frowns. "Wasn't them things they fed us supposed to be poisoned?"

"That's a good question." Lilly looks at Bob. "What just happened?"

Bob has already moved across the room to the stack of tires in the corner. He quickly rifles through a pile of rags, some stray candy wrappers, and a discarded box of shotgun shells. "Bastards took our guns," he grumbles. "They got every firearm in town now."

"Bob, did you hear what I just said?" She lifts herself out of her chair. The room is still spinning, and she has to brace herself on the chair back. "What the hell is going on? What was in that water?"

Bob mumbles as he scans the room, "Water . . . that's what was in it. Nothing but good old H_2O."

"Okay, I'm a little confused." She looks at him. "What are you talking about?"

He turns to her and sighs. "I replaced the cyanide with water this morning before I showed it to you—just to be safe."

She stares. All at once she remembers the plastic fuel container and the coil of rubber tubing that Bob had brought into the brownstone, sitting by the foot of the bed in Jeremiah's bedroom—a fuel container filled with water—and it clicks in the back of Lilly's mind, the moment when Bob flashed his little enigmatic smile at her right before they surrendered to the preacher's men, and Bob's whispered words that sank a hook into Lilly: *I didn't say anything about giving up.*

"Bob Stookey, you're a genius." She grabs the older man by the shoulders, grins at him, and leans over and kisses him on the cheek.

"Only one problem," he says, fixing his droopy, hound dog gaze on her, his expression as grim as a mortician. "Without weapons, we might as well fucking give up."

TWENTY-FOUR

The sun surrenders the day at approximately seven thirty that night, the light sinking behind the treetops of neighboring bluffs, shooting radiant orange beams through the feathers of cottonwood and mist as thick as gauze. It's a fitting sunset, a heartbreaking pastel elegy for the motley collection of souls now gathered on the edge of the speedway gardens—a total of twenty-three people standing hand in hand on the dusty warning track, faces upturned as though supplicating to God—some of them silently meditating, preparing themselves to leave one realm for another, others awaiting an unknown fate.

In addition to the ten members of Jeremiah's itinerant flock, there are twelve Woodbury residents—including, of all people, Ben Buchholz—who have joined the communicants for the final ride into oblivion.

According to rumors whispered among the more religious of Woodbury's citizens, Ben had his epiphany only hours ago—either a mystical conversion experience or a nervous breakdown, depending upon whom you ask—on the back steps of his apartment building on Pecan Street. Slobbering drunk, he slipped and careened down the stairs, and when he landed he was a different person. Jeremiah got to him first, comforting him and promising him eternal salvation and love. Ben broke into sobs, melting in the man's arms like a lost child who has finally found his way home. It was the same sales pitch that the preacher had proffered throughout the day to the most faithful of Woodbury's residents: "Come to our 'Mega Communion' tonight, seven o'clock sharp, with an open heart and a clean conscience, and you will be delivered from this hell. God will take your hand, and He will lead you into paradise."

Jeremiah sees it as a truthful statement, not the bait-and-switch tactic that Harold Stauback accused him of perpetrating on these people, the allegation leveled at the preacher late that afternoon during a private meeting in the infirmary. Voices had been raised. Now Harold is one of three members of the Pentecostal People of God who are conspicuously absent on this glorious night. The other two absentees, Wade and Mark, are off on an important mission in the hills east of town. But the absence of these congregants will not dampen the ecstatic mood that currently vibrates deep in the preacher's marrow as he ascends the steps to the makeshift podium.

The rippling sounds of whispered *amens* and throats clearing nervously fade as the reverend moves behind a stack of tires bordered with wildflowers and wooden crosses. A small radio mike is clipped to his lapel. The setting sun puts a halo of golden light around his coiffed hair, his eyes filling up with emotion.

"MY BROTHERS AND SISTERS . . . TONIGHT WE CLOSE A CIRCLE. WE ARE READY." His deep, rich, stentorian voice echoes out over the virgin soil and empty vestibules. His entire career—in fact, his whole miserable life—has been building up to this final sermon. Big Dan Garlitz would be proud. "WE HAVE—EACH AND EVERY ONE OF US—MADE PEACE WITH OUR MAKER. BROTHERS AND SISTERS, LET US PRAY."

Some of the Woodbury people exchange nervous glances. They had expected some kind of mass baptism, or perhaps a sort of group induction into the preacher's fold.

But now something seems amiss.

A mile to the west, in the high trees along Gainsburg Bluff, two members of the Pentecostal People of God crouch in the lengthening shadows, putting the finishing touches on the summoning.

Dusk has almost completely given over to night, and the drone of crickets and tree frogs engulfs Wade Pilcher and Mark Arbogast as they hurriedly fiddle with the knobs and switches of a small portable public address system—a relic from the old gospel revival shows, during which Jeremiah required amplification to reach the old folks on wheelchairs and mobility scooters in the back of the tent. About the size of a small dehumidifier, the battery-operated Heathkit PA system features a horn on top of a battered amplifier, and a remote receiver on the back that has just begun to blink green as the speaker starts to crackle with the sound of the preacher's voice: " . . . *AND ON THIS SACRED EVENING WE ASK THAT YOU ACCEPT EACH AND EVERY ONE OF YOUR CHILDREN GATHERED HERE TONIGHT INTO YOUR BLESSED DOMINION . . .*"

The ghostly, tinny voice of the preacher echoes out over the wooded knolls beyond Elkins Creek and Dripping Rock Road, swirling on the breeze like the call of a nighthawk. Wade and Mark glance at each other. Mark nods. Wade gazes out across the deep green patchwork of farm fields turning purple in the encroaching darkness. He raises his binoculars to his eyes and scans the surrounding landscape as the crackling hiss of the preacher's voice reverberates off the far hills, beckoning the horde like a dog whistle.

"O LORD, WE ARE READY TO TOUCH THE HEM OF YOUR GARMENT. WE ARE READY. ANOINT US WITH YOUR GRACE AS WE ACCEPT THIS SACRAMENT . . ."

The echoing amplified voice penetrates the neighboring hollows, the wooded gulleys, and the dense groves of pines where the ragged figures hunker in the shadows, chewing at the air and clawing at the void. The noise disturbs them and coaxes them until they begin following the voice, the sound of it a homing beacon, a clarion, a summoning . . .

". . . WE CAST OUR FATE TO YOU, O LORD, WE TAKE YOU INTO OUR HEARTS. HEAR OUR PRAYER, TAKE US TO THAT GOLDEN SHORE, COME AND TAKE US . . ."

In the distant woods, in the valleys and the hills, among the wreckage of deserted rural crossroads and from the depths of abandoned barns and grain elevators, more and more of the creatures are awakened, clumsily pivoting toward the sound, awkwardly climbing out of dry riverbeds and up muddy slopes, drawn to the promise of human flesh.

". . . WE ARE COMING, O LORD, WE ARE ON THE EXPRESS TRAIN TO PARADISE . . ."

Wade looks at his watch. Less than fifteen minutes before the next stage of the summoning needs to be rolled out. He nods at Mark.

Then the two men hurriedly gather their knapsacks and weapons, and hurtle down the rocky, untrimmed path that wends its way back toward Woodbury.

It is now seven forty-six P.M. Eastern Standard Time.

A hush falls over the racetrack arena as the preacher begins to softly weep. He doesn't make a big deal of it; he simply lowers his head and lets a single teardrop fall from the edge of his prominent chin as he continues: "THESE OFFERINGS, O LORD, REPRESENT THE FLESH AND BLOOD OF YOUR ONLY SON . . . SACRIFICED SO THAT WE MAY LIVE . . . A SYMBOL OF YOUR LOVE."

Behind the preacher, Reese and Anthony appear in the shadowy mouth of a vestibule, each holding a stainless steel tray from the infirmary, each tray laden with sacraments like party favors.

Jeremiah feels the tension in the air tightening, and he channels it with the aplomb of a master conductor coaxing a performance from a symphony. "NOW, AS WE EACH COME FORWARD, ONE BY ONE, TO ACCEPT THE FLESH AND THE BLOOD OF CHRIST, WE REJOICE IN OUR LOVE OF YOU, O LORD, AND YOUR PROMISE OF EVERLASTING LIFE IN PARADISE."

Some of the veteran church members move toward the front of the warning track now, their hands raised in the universal gesture of a true believer filled with the spirit—the gentle wave overhead, face turned downward in reverent ecstasy. The others fall in line behind them, single file, hands clasped in front of them as they await the morsels.

"LET US REJOICE, BROTHERS AND SISTERS, AS WE EACH ACCEPT THE SACRIFICIAL HOST, IN THE NAME OF GOD THE FATHER, THE SON, AND THE HOLY SPIRIT . . ."

Jeremiah moves down the risers to the edge of the infield, the two tray carriers converging on him, holding the poisoned offerings for his inspection.

"WE NOW GIVE OUR LIVES OVER TO YOU, O LORD," Jeremiah sings out in his musical baritone voice, as he turns to a tray and plucks

244 | Jay Bonansinga

the first wafer of tainted unleavened bread. "IN HONOR OF ALL OUR LOVED ONES WHO HAVE FALLEN, WE ACCEPT THIS COMMUNAL HOST."

The first communicant steps up to the edge of the bleachers.

Old Joe Bressler, the seventy-three-year-old retiree who helped the women of the church group prepare the sacramental food and drink in the back kitchen of the Dew Drop Inn, now stands trembling on arthritic knees before the preacher. The man's deeply lined face cants upward. He closes his eyes and opens his toothless mouth, his upper dentures stained and foul smelling. Jeremiah places the host on the man's tongue, and Joe closes his mouth around the morsel and gums it for a moment before swallowing it.

The smile that appears on Joe's face speaks volumes. Here is a man who ran a grocery store for forty-three years in Tallahassee's tough Frenchtown area, who looked the other way when the poor kids from the neighborhood came in to steal diapers and formula, who ran off counterfeit food stamps for some of the local mothers, who was married to the same woman for almost fifty years, childless, and yet devoted to his Ida, and the love he had for her lasted right up until the day she turned and he had to stove her head in with a garden hoe. The smile that creases this weathered, parchmentlike face is a smile of release, a swan song from a man who has lived the fullest life one could imagine.

Jeremiah smiles back at the man, exultant in the knowledge that the strong barbiturate will knock the old codger out before the cyanide fully kicks in, sparing the man any pain in his last moments.

"Hallelujah, Brother!" Joe exclaims, a crumb of cracker still clinging to his liver-colored lip. "Praise the Lord!"

Jeremiah pulls the old man into a warm embrace and whispers to him, "You'll be the first to touch the hem of his robe, Brother." Then Jeremiah turns to the other tray, takes one of the paper cups, and hands it to the man. "Down the hatch, Joseph."

Joe knocks back the tepid fluid that he expects will finally bring his long, full life to a close. He hands the empty cup back. "God bless you, Brother," Joe says with tears welling up in his eyes.

He steps aside and heads back to his place on the warning track.

The next congregant steps up.

The Dupree children—Lucas and Bethany—are the sixth and seventh in line.

The signal is supposed to come from Lilly. She hides behind one of the gigantic load-bearing pillars in the upper stands on the opposite side of the racetrack. She is supposed to fire off a single shot at the appointed time, which will cue the rest of her little band of insurgents to engage the crowd. Drenched in sweat, pulse pounding in her ears, she tries to breathe normally and stay calm as she watches the proceedings. She can see the preacher on the other side of the infield, down on the edge of the warning track, conducting his ritual in the dying light, giving the crackers and the drinks to each of his subjects as the drone of voices offer *amen* and *hallelujah*. Lilly has seen documentary footage of Jonestown, has read about suicide cults down through the years, but she would never have expected the real thing to appear so . . . *still*. So *tranquil*. Even the children seem delighted to accept this symbolic communion amid this horrible plague. Maybe it's some kind of twisted version of mob psychology. Or perhaps it's simply what happens when people are beaten down by a plague this horrible for this long. The truth is, Lilly has no idea how many of these congregants are even *aware* of the suicide pact.

Now Lilly grips her crappy .45 semiauto pistol with white-knuckle nervous tension and simmering rage. Her anger—tempered by the unresolved grief of losing Calvin—is exacerbated by the pitiful quality of her new gun. The weapon was scavenged that afternoon in a frantic search of the ruins of the burned-out National Guard station. Bob found it in a previously undiscovered underground bomb shelter, along with some military-grade shotguns and extra rounds of ammunition. But Lilly has no idea how long the guns were down there or if this piece of junk even fires properly. She has eight rounds in the pistol and one additional clip with ten extra rounds in it, and that's it.

The rest of the insurgents are positioned at key junctures around the arena with minimal firepower. David Stern and Speed Wilkins have the only fully automatic assault rifles in the group, while Gloria Pyne has her trusty Glock, and Barbara Stern her .38 Police Special—neither handgun very effective from a long distance. Matthew and

Bob each have a shotgun—Bob sporting a 12-gauge, and Matthew a 20-gauge scattergun—neither weapon necessarily designed for long-range applications. All told, their meager arsenal is not much of a match for the firearms and ordnance the church group has amassed.

All of which is why Lilly—despite her fog of rage—has convinced her team to hold their fire unless absolutely necessary. The plan is to wait for the moment Jeremiah and the others realize nobody is shuffling off this mortal coil as planned, and both the barbiturate and the poison seem to be neutralized and ineffective—*that* will be the optimum time to intercede. Maybe Jeremiah will see the failure of the poison to do its work as an act of God. Maybe he'll interpret it as a sign. But in his confusion, he'll be more manageable. He'll listen to reason.

Lilly is thinking about all this when she notices a couple members of the church group are missing. The cop—what's his name? Wade? And the dude from Panama City—Arbogast, Mark Arbogast. Lilly had gotten to know both of these men during supply runs, and she liked them. They were solid, simple, small-town men with simple values. But for some reason, their absence is making Lilly nervous. In fact, she starts searching the far reaches of the stands, looking for them, when she hears a commotion down on the infield.

Raised voices echo on the wind, a few of the parishioners arguing with each other. Lilly snaps her gaze toward the preacher.

In the distance, Jeremiah has come around from behind his makeshift lectern and descended the bleacher steps, and now he angrily pushes his way through the crowd, feeling people's foreheads and looking closely at their eyes with the hectic attention of an overworked nurse. His expression is hard to read from this distance, but it looks as though he is pallid with shock, and people are yelling at him. It's difficult to hear the exact words being spoken, but it seems as though Jeremiah is responding at the top of his lungs, "*It's not His will! It's not! Something's wrong! You should be going to sleep! You should all be going to sleep!*"

Lilly gives the signal—a raised hand, a fist, and then a quick yank downward.

Instantly she sees a flash of movement down on the portico along one side of the infield, about a hundred feet from where the preacher is now weaving through his congregation, trying to figure out what has happened to his poison.

Speed Wilkins lurches out from behind one of the columns, raises the muzzle of his AR-15, and fires a controlled burst into the sky.

TWENTY-FIVE

For one surreal moment, most of the parishioners simply gape in thunderstruck silence, some of them raising their hands as though being robbed. Some of the male congregants go for their guns, but the other rebels—Bob, David, Barbara, Gloria, and Matthew—all come out of hiding then, with weapons raised, each firing off a single round into the air in order to get everybody's attention and to warn off any would-be heroes. The salvo echoes up into the dark heavens.

Lilly calmly walks out to the edge of the mezzanine balcony a hundred and fifty feet from where the preacher now stands paralyzed, staring up at her as though seeing a ghost. Lilly holds her gun hand up, her voice projecting like an actor in a Shakespearean play. "Jeremiah, I'm sorry . . . but this can't happen!"

"What did you do?" His eyes fill with absolute, unadulterated terror. "Oh, dear Lord, what in God's name did you *do*?"

"We switched out the poison with water!" She takes a deep breath. "Now it's time for you to—"

"YOU HAVE NO IDEA WHAT YOU'VE DONE!" He screams this at her, his face suddenly a mask of abject horror. "YOU HAVE NO EARTHLY IDEA!"

"Calm down," she calls back down to him, speaking sharply as if to an unruly pet. "Shut up for a second and listen to how this is going to go down!"

"HOW THIS IS GOING TO GO DOWN? HOW THIS IS GOING TO GO DOWN?" He looks around as though he's about to tear his hair from his skull. The whole arena is silent. He looks at his watch.

He looks back up at Lilly, and his eyes practically glow with dread. "YOU HAVE ENSURED THAT WE WILL ALL DIE A HORRIBLE, PAINFUL, HELLISH DEATH—!"

"Calm the fuck down!" Lilly thumbs the hammer back on the .45 and points it at him. "You've manipulated these people long enough. This is our town and we're not going to—"

The first explosion cuts off her words, rocking the stands and ringing in the rafters with a resonant boom of thunder. Lilly instinctively crouches down. What the fuck? She senses a flash and a shockwave of heat off her left flank, and she whirls toward the east.

The second explosion comes from the northeast corner of the barricade, a strobelike flash, followed by a resounding boom, which sends shards of timbers and a mushroom cloud of debris heavenward.

Lilly's heart skips a beat, her breath clogging in her throat as she realizes what's happening. But *why*? Why would they knock down the town's fortification—especially if they were bent on self-destruction through poisoning? It makes no sense. But Lilly quickly realizes that there's no time to figure it all out because Bob is spinning toward the makeshift altar with his muzzle raised as people scatter in all directions.

Then Lilly sees the preacher lunging toward one of his minions—the man named Anthony—who holds one of the stolen AK-47s. All at once, Jeremiah has an every-man-for-himself look on his face, and he has snatched the assault rifle from the grasp of his disciple and is snapping the cocking mechanism back with a single jerk.

"LILLY, GET DOWN!"

The voice of David Stern from behind her sends a warning alarm down Lilly's spine and drives her to the ground as the air lights up with a barrage of high-velocity rounds, which strafe the upper balconies of the racetrack in gouts of sparks, dust, and ringing shrapnel.

In time, Lilly will put the pieces together: That second duffel bag full of ordnance that Bob had mentioned, the one that Stephen had carried—this was earmarked all along to clear a pathway, if not a barricade like the one in Woodbury then perhaps the side of a building or the windows of a warehouse or a citadel. The idea was to let in the horde of undead only *after* the members of the church had taken their own lives and the sacrificial grounds were littered with freshly deceased bodies. The stampede of walkers would then descend upon the Pentecostal People of God and consume them in some warped inversion of Holy Communion. Somehow, in Jeremiah's scrambled, through-the-looking-glass worldview, to be devoured by the horde would consecrate those who sacrificed themselves. Perhaps, Lilly reasoned, if Jeremiah's fractured logic were extended, the process of communion, sacrifice, and consumption would bring the apocalypse to an end.

If only . . . if only . . . if only, Lilly finds herself thinking as she ducks behind the pilaster amid the snapping ricochets of high-velocity bullets sparking off the upper stanchions.

More of the armed congregants have followed their preacher's lead and begun to fire at the rebels. The rest of the bystanders begin to scatter in all directions, trampling seedlings and rows of new vegetables, trying to find cover or routes of escape across the infield. The air inside the arena lights up, crackling with gunfire of all varieties, calibers, and velocities. A few of the adults rush to gather the children and yank them out of the line of fire, but the cordite and smoke and particulate rise almost instantly, turning the racetrack arena into a fogbank.

In a hail of bullets strafing the upper decks, Lilly curls into a fetal position behind the column, covering her head as debris rains down on her, forgetting that she has a gun still gripped in her right hand. She can see blurry movement in her peripheral vision on either side of her, and she catches glimpses of Bob, Speed, Matthew, Gloria, David, and Barbara each diving for cover behind cross beams, empty bleachers, and support columns. In the chaos, Lilly feels a fist of rage clenching her guts, and she rises to her feet, jacking the cocking mechanism on the .45 and peering around the edge of the column.

She sees the faint shadow of a figure wearing a suit jacket, standing near the makeshift altar, spraying bullets up at the cheap seats with an AK-47. *He's lost his mind now,* she thinks, *he's finally slipped his gears and has gone completely psychotic.*

"IS THIS WHAT JESUS WOULD DO?!" Lilly wails down at him as she fires off three quick bursts, two-handing the antique Smith & Wesson, the muzzle roaring loudly in her ears, making them ring and spitting blowback on her cheek. She misses the preacher by a mile.

Another volley of high-velocity rounds answers her fire, ringing off the girders above her and spraying the stands around her feet.

She jerks back behind the column, thumbing the hammer instinctively, calculating the odds in her traumatized mind. She coughs a lungful of cordite and dust. She's fairly certain there are three, maybe four shooters down there with assault rifles. If she can coordinate her blasts with the other insurgents, maybe they can pick off the gunmen one by one. But what about collateral damage? Where are the children? Lilly peers around the column and gazes into the nebula of pea soup, the arena so foggy with dust and debris now it's difficult to make out anything but bleary silhouettes of figures scattering in all directions. Every few seconds, another salvo of gunfire crackles and flickers in the dust, pinging and sparking off the bleachers.

"YOU FUCKING ARROGANT, SANCTIMONIOUS HYPO-CRITES!" Lilly shrieks over the din of screams and intermittent blasts. "IS THIS WHAT JESUS WOULD DO?" An enormous blast booms next to her, and she jumps back with a start. "FUCK! FUCK! FUCK! FUCK!"

Matthew Hennesey stands in a swirling miasma of dust off her right flank, about thirty feet away, pumping shells into his shotgun's chamber and firing one at a time, crazily, without much thought or precision, in the general direction of the altar, bellowing some string of profanities at the top of his lungs each time he fires—gangster-style—a series of words and threats that Lilly can't quite decipher. She starts to shout something at him when a barrage of return fire slices through his midsection and sends him pinwheeling backward over empty bleachers, the shotgun flying out of his hands, a gout of bloodred tissue spewing from the exit wounds in his back as he lands supine on a bench.

"MATTHEW!" Lilly crawls on her hands and knees across the thirty-foot gap to the fallen man. "OH, SHIT! OH, GOD! MATTHEW, HOLD ON!"

The former bricklayer from Valdosta lies faceup, draped over the metal bench, blood streaming from his mouth, coughing, trying to speak, his gut ravaged with bullet wounds, his organs already starting to shut down. He's a big man, but he seems to shrink before Lilly's eyes as the life drains out of him. She manages to get to him right before he winks out, cradling his head.

"I'm sorry I wasn't much help—" he says, and coughs up blood and chokes and tries to put his dying thoughts into words. "I need you to—I need you to go ahead and—I need you to—to—so I don't—"

"Ssshhhhhh," Lilly comforts him. Without much forethought she says, "Close your eyes, Matthew. Just close your eyes and go to sleep."

He closes his eyes.

She puts the muzzle of the .45 against his temple and turns her face away.

David and Barbara Stern have been in rough scrapes together since the plague broke out . . . but nothing like *this*. At the moment, David is dragging her along the chain-link barrier on the south side of the arena, choking on the smoke, trying to stay low as the crackle of crossfire buzzes and zings over their heads. The only thing David has going for him at the moment is the fact that he's one of the few people down in the fogbank of dust with a fully automatic assault rifle. On the negative side of the equation, he has lost track of his comrades, has no idea who he should be shooting at, can smell the telltale stench of the horde closing in, and can't get his pain-in-the-ass wife to move.

"We can't just leave them!" Barbara wriggles in his grasp, trying to tear herself away. Her gray tendrils of hair hang down across her sweat-damp face. "David, stop! We have to go back!"

"Gloria's got the kids, Babs! In case you didn't notice, the wall's down, and we gotta get inside . . . or we're gonna end up somebody's dinner!"

"Goddamn it, I'm not leaving her with those kids!" Barbara finally tears herself free, pivots on her tennis shoes, and charges back toward the dust cloud.

"Why did I have to marry this woman?" David asks himself somewhat rhetorically as he starts after her. He jacks the cocking mechanism on his AR-15 and catches up with her within seconds. "Barbara, stay low! Get behind me!" He moves ahead of her. "Keep your head down and—"

A single burst of automatic gunfire from the opposite side of the arena interrupts.

The Sterns duck while errant blasts ricochet off gantries above them, but through it all they keep moving along the chain-link barrier toward the southeast corner of the infield. They can see the small cluster of little people slipping into the mouth of a vestibule fifty feet away, being led by a small, stocky woman in a visor.

Barbara calls out to her. "Gloria!"

The woman in the hat pauses, turns, and peers around the edge of the vestibule. "Get your butts in here already!" she shouts. "What the hell are you doing?"

The Sterns duck-walk another forty feet or so and then plunge into the cement passageway, both hyperventilating with nervous exhaustion. The darkness and musty smell of wet cement and the body odors of a half dozen children immediately engulf them. The high ceiling drips with condensation, a single cobweb-covered EXIT sign dark and powerless. The children—ages five through ten—huddle against one leprous wall, some of them softly moaning, trying to be brave, stifling tears.

The passageway extends another hundred feet of ancient concrete before opening out onto the dark, deserted gravel lot on the south side of the arena.

"We gotta get these munchkins somewhere safe ASAP," Gloria Pyne announces to the Sterns, stating the obvious. Each adult can smell the darker odors on the night breezes teasing at the vestibule opening. The faint stench of rotten meat, infected tissue, and black mold has risen to the point of making eyes water and stomachs heave. The distant chorus of feral growling noises has already begun to echo over the tops of neighboring trees.

"All right, let's take them across the—" David Stern starts to say, when all at once an enormous clap of thunderous noise comes from outside the far mouth of the passageway—a sound not unlike a massive redwood keeling over in the forest, slamming down so hard it shakes the ground—and all heads snap toward the north and the general direction of the damaged, still-burning barricade.

The air swells with a wave of chirring, snarling, watery yawping noises.

TWENTY-SIX

The herd shambles into town from three directions—north, east, and south. If viewed from the sky, the slow-motion infestation might resemble a steady, incessant assault on a giant organism by an invading army of cancer cells. They pour through the smoky ruins of the barricade down near Folk Avenue and spread out across the train yard, bringing the infection of their stench, their yellow eyes scanning the property ravenously, arms outstretched in the darkness like those of a deadly, psychotic chorus line. They push in from the woods, entering through the blown sections of wall near the intersection of Pecan and Dogwood, seeking warm flesh, brushing against each other in their communal hunger, each and every one of them growling in unison, creating a rising drone like a great turbine engine turning faster and faster. They trample the burning, fallen segments of barricade across Durand Street and unfurl like a riptide across the vacant lots, oozing down sidewalks and pushing into the town's square. The incredible stench spreads inklike through the darkness, invading homes through open windows, permeating the back alleys and alcoves and cul-de-sacs, the odor so powerful it clings to the skin of those few humans now scattering for cover, screaming in terror, frantically seeking shelter.

On the north edge of the town square, Speed Wilkins tries to outrun a cluster of walkers latching on to his scent, but he inadvertently gets surrounded when he takes a wrong turn at the old live oak in the center of the grassy square. He gets pinned down by three separate waves of the things converging on the square and he has only ten rounds left in his AK-47 but he still tries to shoot his way out. Big mistake. In the time it takes him to spray the leading edge of the walkers coming toward his right flank—heads erupting like rotten melons bursting, ragged figures doing the boogaloo death dance in the torchlight—he not only uses up the last of his ammunition but also gives the row of monsters coming up behind him an opportunity to reach him unscathed.

The gun clicks empty at the exact moment a huge male in a scorched, fire-ravaged hospital smock pounces from behind him and sinks its black teeth into the nape of his muscular neck. He screams and drops the useless weapon. He whirls, but it's already too late. There are so many of them, the very act of heaving the big male off his back draws another dozen or so from the other direction like leeches, clamping their jaws on his arms and legs and shoulder blades. He fights valiantly, but the sheer number of them—the raw inertia of their weight and volume—finally drives Speed to the ground.

At this point, three separate groups of humans pass within shooting distance of Speed as they charge across the center of town, frantically seeking refuge, firing willy-nilly at the converging horde. Jeremiah and two of his minions—Reese and Stephen—are fleeing in tandem, blasting away with small arms, when they notice Speed being devoured under the tree. The former football player lashes out blindly as the walkers feed on his legs, his throat already breached and gushing. Passing within fifty feet of the feeding frenzy, Reese pauses for one horror-stricken moment. It occurs to him that maybe he should try to intercede—maybe that would *truly* be the Christian thing to do—when suddenly he feels an iron-tight grip on his arm. "C'mon, Brother, he's gone!" Jeremiah drags him away. "There's no time, c'mon!"

As the preacher and his disciples race off into the darkness, the walkers swarm Speed, tearing into him, rooting for his organs, ripping open flesh and snapping tendons like ribbons on a package. Speed is still conscious when the second group passes within earshot.

David Stern, with his AR-15 blazing, leads the group of six children—along with Gloria and Barbara bringing up the rear—toward the shelter of the courthouse. When David sees the grisly feeding going on, he turns and yells at the kids, "Everybody look at me, eyes up here! Eyes on me, look at me!" He backs toward the courthouse as quickly as he can on his arthritic joints. "That's good! Keep moving and keep your eyes on me!" As they vanish around the corner of the building, searching for a back way in—the front steps already crawling with walkers—the third and final group of survivors passes within view of Speed.

By this point, Speed is barely conscious, clinging to life as the walkers chew through his midsection, slurping at his entrails as wild dogs might root through a dung heap rife with kibble. Still possessing his vocal cords, Speed manages to let out one last cry of both defiance and rage—an inarticulate bellowing moan, his body shuddering in its death throes, an old-school jock going down for the count with his pride still intact—which reaches three other humans racing across the southern edge of the square. Lilly sees the horrible scene first, but Bob and Tommy Dupree don't see it until Lilly has come to a complete stop. Bob whirls toward her and demands to know what the fuck she's doing and has she lost her mind, but all Lilly can do is stare at the feeding as she raises her .45 and draws a bead on her friend, murmuring on a breathless whisper, "Go easy, Speed . . . rest in peace."

The blast takes the top off the young man's skull, bringing blessed darkness and closure to another one of Lilly's faithful friends.

In less than an hour, the superherd overruns the town. Later, in the aftermath, survivors will ponder the phenomenon and speculate on the factors that might have attracted so many of them to a single place. Ostensibly drawn by the amplified sound of the preacher's voice, the horde very possibly could have doubled in size after the noise and light of the explosions—visible from at least a mile away—effectively drawing even more of the creatures from the pockets and enclaves of neighboring farms and villages. Regardless of the explanations, however, by ten that night, the lumbering army of undead had infiltrated every sidewalk, every side street, every storefront, every vacant lot, every doorway, and every square foot of real estate Woodbury has to offer.

Most members of the Pentecostal People of God eventually get their death wish fulfilled—albeit in a much less humane fashion. Three of the women—Colby, Rose, and Cailinn—are attacked indoors, in the back of the Dew Drop Inn, where they had originally baked the sacraments used in the ritual. Apparently, a pack of walkers got in through a service entrance in the rear and devoured the women right on the kitchen floor.

Joe and Anthony don't even make it out of the racetrack arena. The first wave of walkers streams in through the vestibules, surprising the twosome as they try to get out through one of the passageways.

Wade and Mark perish outside the fence when one of the explosive devices goes off prematurely, injuring both men and making them sitting ducks when the walker army finally arrives. Other members of the church, as well as a significant number of longtime Woodbury residents, die while trying to flee the second wave of walkers that pours into town after devouring Wade and Mark.

Now only Bob, Lilly, and Tommy remain out on the streets, pinned down, isolated, out of ammunition, huddling in the shadows of an enormous culvert.

They've been hiding in this gigantic sewer pipe for thirty minutes or so, ever since the throngs of walkers got too thick, blocking their escape route and chasing them into the pipe. About six feet in diameter, lined with mossy herringbone bricks, and puddled down the center with at least three inches of stagnant water, the huge stone pipe reeks of brackish sewage. Bob believes it connects up with the deeper tunnels of the Underground Railroad, but unfortunately, the far end of the pipe is blocked by a waffling of iron bars, designed to keep raccoons and larger vermin out of the sewer. The mouth of the culvert—its opening half buried in the Georgia clay—opens out onto the abandoned train yard, which currently teems with walkers of all shapes, sizes, and states of decomposition.

"Bob, c'mon," Lilly whispers to the older man, who crouches near the culvert's mouth, scraping at the floor with the blade of his Swiss Army knife. "At this rate, Tommy will be done with puberty by the time you cut through that fucking thing."

"Very funny," Tommy whispers from behind Lilly. The boy is sitting against the iron screen inside the pipe, his *Pokemon* T-shirt looking as though it's been fed through a wood chipper. The boy is a marvel to Lilly—the toughest, nerviest child she has ever known—traumatized by killing his own father, beset with the tragedy of his mother's suicide, and yet still fighting to live, his little chin jutting defiantly, his sweaty, freckled face furrowed with courage. She could use about three dozen more Tommy Duprees. "What's down there, anyway?" Tommy asks Bob.

"A way outta this mess," Bob mumbles, working and scraping that dull blade down into the pipe's seam with the persistence of a prisoner trying to tunnel out of Sing Sing. "Most new municipal water pipes are made outta PVC," he explains while grunting with effort, worrying and digging at the notch, "but these older suckers around these parts, they're made of cement and mortar."

"Bob—" Lilly starts to break in, a wave of goose bumps coursing down her back. She just got a big blast of walker stench wafting across the mouth of the pipe, a mixture of rotting fish guts and festering shit, and now she sees shadows moving toward the culvert.

Bob is oblivious, obsessed with breaking through the drainpipe's floor. "The trick is getting through the first layer of composite," he mumbles.

"Bob, I think we better—"

A figure appears in the mouth of the pipe, a huge male walker completely burned to a crisp, with half his abdomen torn open, his entrails hanging out.

Tommy cries, "LOOK OUT!"

Bob whirls and raises the knife. The walker's eyes roll back in his skull, sharklike, as it pounces on Bob, going for the fleshy wattle of his neck. The old medic is lightning quick for a person his age, and he manages to simultaneously jerk back and bring the short blade down into the walker's forehead.

The blade sinks, fluids gushing around the hilt, and the walker sags.

Bob spins toward the others. "Noise is gonna draw more of 'em!" Tommy and Lilly exchange a heated glance. Bob wipes the blade on his pants and nods toward the far end of the culvert. "Try kicking out the bars! Do it together! Give it another good—"

Movement blurs behind Bob, cutting off his words, making him spin around as dark, ragged figures converge on the sewer pipe. Tommy lets out a startled yelp. Three creatures pounce on Bob—two females and a male—blackened mouths working busily, noxious breaths puffing out of them with each snarling growl. One of them goes for Bob's face, but Bob kicks out at it with all his might, knocking the creature back against the rim of the culvert's maw. At the other end of the drainpipe, Lilly frantically searches for something to use as a weapon while Tommy madly kicks at the waffling of wrought-iron bars.

All at once, an enormous cracking noise spreads across the inner liner of the culvert, sounding almost like ice breaking, as the walkers swarm Bob, and now Bob is yelling obscenities at them, slashing with his pathetic little knife. They pile on him, their weight pressing down on the spot already weakened and compromised by the constant notching of Bob's knife. Lilly screams as the floor starts to cave in. She reaches for Bob, grazing the sleeve of his shirt, grabbing for his hand, but it's too late.

In one great, heaving, swirling eruption of dust and noise, the floor of the pipe collapses.

The horrible din drowns Bob's cry as he plunges into the darkness below, the monsters clinging to him, the mass of flesh and blood and teeth vanishing in the dark beneath the train yard. A huge battering ram of a thud rattles the understructure as Lilly crawls to the edge of the jagged hole now encompassing half the length of the culvert. She tries to see into the miasma, but she can't make out a thing in the dust-choked darkness. She makes a futile attempt to call out for her friend, but she can hardly draw a breath, the dust is so pervasive now, clogging her throat and stinging her eyes. She hears something giving way down below like the wrenching of timbers on a ship, and then a great rupture of water that sounds like a jet engine.

"Lilly!"

Tommy's voice yanks her attention back to the culvert.

Lilly rears back, falling onto her ass. She blinks and looks up as though snapping out of a daze. She sees the look in Tommy's eyes.

"Lilly, listen to me," he says. His eyes glow with adrenaline and panic. "We have to get out of here—right *now. RIGHT NOW!*"

Lilly sees that the mouth of the culvert is relatively clear, the closest walkers visible in the distant darkness along the train tracks about fifty yards away, scores of them dragging along the rails as though pursuing a commuter train that will never come. Lilly wipes the tears from her face and finds an inner reserve of strength for the sake of the boy, for the sake of the town, for the sake of all those who have sacrificed themselves . . . but mostly . . . *for Bob.*

She rises to her feet, sniffing back the pain and the shock, and takes Tommy's hand. Then, in one leaping stride, they both vault over the hole in the floor and plunge into the night.

TWENTY-SEVEN

On the other side of town, outside the wall, on the edge of a wreckage-strewn parking lot, three men hang upside down in an overturned SUV, the engine still rumbling, the rear wheels still impotently turning.

Partially conscious, bleeding, the man wedged behind the steering wheel still wears his trademark suit coat and is only dimly aware of the other two men in the upside-down vehicle. In the backseat, Reese Lee Hawthorne lies twisted and unconscious on the ceiling, still breathing shallow breaths, his hoodie soaked in blood from deep lacerations down the back of his skull. On the front passenger side, Stephen Pembry dangles, also unconscious, tangled up in his shoulder strap, his assault rifle still warm and smoking on the ceiling. When the wave of walkers closed in on the car from all sides and ultimately shoved it over onto its roof, Stephen Pembry was firing wildly through his shattered window.

Now the man behind the wheel struggles to stay conscious, blood streaming down his body, dripping off the top of his head onto the SUV's ceiling like a stubborn leaky faucet.

Jeremiah Garlitz never thought he would die this way—in an overturned stolen car, engulfed by hundreds, maybe thousands of walking corpses, bleeding out slowly while the multitude scrapes back and forth across the vehicle's windows, leaving trails of blood and bile smudged on the glass. The preacher always figured his death would be much less ignominious—perhaps even glorious and noble—but now he must face the fact that God wants him to die like this: a wounded animal in this upside-down SUV.

"Why, Lord? How did it come to this?" he utters through cracked, blood-crusted lips.

Outside, the shuffling of myriad feet—many of them shoeless and blackened with rot and lividity—mill around the SUV. Stirred by the muffled sound of the preacher's voice, the dead people rub up against the windows and quarter panels, radiating the stench of the grave. Through the cracked window glass the smell is unbearable, the odor of the devil, the scent of degradation and sin and weakness and rot and evil. The preacher has to gasp for breath—a puncture wound in one of his lungs making breathing a chore—and he fixes his bleary gaze on the ragged, dripping figures brushing back and forth outside.

He closes his eyes and tries to summon all the love in his heart for his dear Lord Jesus Christ, his savior, his guiding light, and he tries to ask for forgiveness for his many sins, and he prays that his passing will come quickly, and he tries to cross over calmly, peacefully, in a blessed womb of holy spirit, but something intrudes on the moment. The noise of the throng, the collective howls and groans of the beasts, a noise like metal tearing, resonates through the overturned vehicle, setting the preacher's teeth on edge, pounding in his skull and his sinuses, flaring white-hot in his eyes, tormenting him, torturing him, taunting him.

"WHY? WWWWWWWWHHHHY?!"

Deep in the recesses of his brain, way back in the secret chambers behind his consciousness, in the dark room where his secrets and skeletons lie in shadows, the source of his pain takes the form of a box, a small metal container with an even smaller door embedded on the top. He sees this box in his mind's eye right now, as the throngs build outside, drawn to the sound of his screams. He sees a small handle on the side of the box. The SUV begins to wobble as the horde presses in on the sides. The handle on the box turns. The throngs push up against the left side, the SUV listing violently. The handle on the imaginary box turns faster, a tinny, off-key lullaby coming out of it. The horde presses in on the right side, the vehicle tipping the other way. The tune to "Three Blind Mice" warbles out of the invisible box.

The wave of walkers rams into the opposite side with so much force
that suddenly, in one massive spasm, the car flips over onto its wheels.

The imaginary jack-in-the-box pops open.

The rear tires find purchase.

A little marionette of Satan springs out of the box in Jeremiah's
head.

The SUV lurches forward through a wall of walking dead, bowling over hundreds and hundreds of moving corpses as the preacher
grips the steering wheel with blood-slick hands and stomps the ac-
celerator to the floor. The rear wheels fishtail back and forth across
the gore-slimy pavement as more and more bodies are churned
under the vehicle, and the preacher begins to laugh in unison with
the tiny puppet of Satan in his imagination. The other two men loll
and flop limply as the SUV grinds through a sea of guts, and Jeremiah
roars with laughter now, his injuries growing numb and cold. The
raven-black Escalade mows through an ocean of walkers, tossing wakes of tissue and bile and brain matter up across the fenders
and hood, washing the windshield with offal and bits of organs and
shards of bone and blood the consistency of silt, and the preacher
laughs so hard it becomes ridiculous as he bursts through the last
few rows of undead and skids across the access road north of town.
And even as he's careening off into the darkness, free of the horde at
last, free of his past, free of the yoke of religion, he can't stop laughing at the meaninglessness and absurdity of it all.

He laughs and laughs all the way to the county line, then turns
south and heads into the void of night, thinking about survival, sin,
and settling scores.

They don't hear the voices until they turn the corner at Main Street
and charge north through the reeking darkness toward the town
square. Lilly uses a splintered length of wood from the breached wall
as a bludgeon, and she clears a path through the mob as she goes,
frantically lashing out at the backs of skulls or fending off attackers
by knocking their legs out from under them. Tommy is barely able
to keep up with her, swinging his own makeshift club, flailing at
the hungry horde with wild abandon. Every few moments, one of the

larger walkers lunges at the boy and Lilly has to pause to spin around and impale the thing's cranium on the business end of her bludgeon. In this laborious fashion it takes them over five minutes to cross the distance between the culvert and the square.

By the time they reach the grassy patch of land forming the town square, the number of walkers inside the safe zone seems to have doubled or even tripled. They are so profuse now that they stand elbow to elbow across portions of the sidewalk and the tree-lined square. Lilly has to kick over a garbage can along the curb just to distract enough of them to clear a path to the courthouse steps. But once she drags Tommy up the walk and reaches the stairs, she immediately sees the front entrance standing wide open, the huge double doors swinging in the wind.

Inside the dark foyer, litter scuttles across the parquet floor and the silhouettes of upright corpses stumble drunkenly back and forth. Every few seconds, one of their pasty-white, mottled faces catches the moonlight, a mouth gaping with feral hunger. "Great. GREAT! GREAT!" Lilly comments as she pulls Tommy back down the walk toward the street. "FUCK! FUCK! FUCKETY-FUCK!"

She decides to head east, and just as she starts dragging the boy behind the courthouse building she hears the faint sounds of voices calling to her—barely audible under the roar of walker noise—and she pauses for only a moment to glance behind her. She can't see anybody in any of the adjacent windows, nobody on the street but walkers, the sidewalks devoid of human activity. The place has given itself over to the throngs, and it makes Lilly's stomach clench with dread and desolation. She doesn't hear the slender female walker approaching from behind until Tommy screams.

"LOOK OUT!"

Lilly turns just as the walker pounces at her, knocking her off balance. Lilly sprawls on the pavement, wrenching her spine and hitting the back of her skull on the cement. She sees stars. The female falls directly on top of her, dead flesh hanging in strips off a mummified face, teeth exposed by receding black lips. The moonlight refracts off the creature's milk-glass eyes, its jaws snapping like castanets, when all at once the air lights up with the flash of a high-powered rifle.

The blast vaporizes the back of the female's skull, sending a saucer-sized disc of cranial bone heavenward and making Lilly duck down and cover her head. The walker collapses lifelessly to the pavement as Tommy rushes to help Lilly up, when the sound of the voices pierces the din once again: "Up here! LILLY! UP HERE, GODDAMN IT!"

Both Lilly and Tommy gaze up at the night sky, and they each see the source of the voices outlined in the moonlight.

A group of ten or twelve survivors huddles on the roof of the court-house, clutching each other on a narrow decorative rotunda at the base of the capital dome like lost pigeons. David Stern still has his AR-15 propped against his shoulder, the muzzle smoking from the direct hit on the female. Barbara Stern and Gloria Pyne hold on to half a dozen children, including Lucas and Bethany Dupree. Behind them, perched on a lone gable, sits Harold Stauback, the Voice of Valdosta, the man with the golden vocal cords, his dapper silk shirt practically in shreds.

"AROUND BACK BY THE SERVICE ENTRANCE!" David motions wildly toward the rear of the building. "THERE'S A FIRE ESCAPE LADDER!"

Lilly grabs Tommy and charges around behind the building before an approaching cluster of walkers can reach them. They find the oxidized rungs of an ancient iron ladder hanging down in the shadows. Lilly helps the boy up first, and then she hurriedly scuttles up the ladder behind him.

Once Lilly reaches the rotunda ledge, David and Tommy help her pull the ladder up—surrendering the streets of Woodbury to the dead.

TWENTY-EIGHT

The light of dawn illuminates the town gradually, revealing the siege in painful, excruciating stages. First, the horizon over the train yard warms up with a faint gray light, revealing just enough of the neighboring vacant lots and fallow fields to see the area abounding with figures. Initially appearing as moving blankets of shadows, the gathering light begins to show the countless bobbing heads jockeying for position along the tracks, down Main Street, and along the storefronts and condos of Pecan and Durand Streets. It looks like a convention in hell, a Mardi Gras of the dead, as the biter horde fills every nook and cranny, mills along every side street, loiters in every alcove. The sun-blanched lawns along Flat Shoals Road, once tidy little plots of land bordered by picket fences, now crawl with moving cadavers. Even the arena gardens are standing room only—the errant corpses trampling through the precious vegetable crop, aimlessly circling the warning track, and crowding every vestibule. Some of the walkers even trudge back and forth up in the stands, restlessly wandering between bleachers as though by muscle memory, as if looking for lost children or forgotten purses. Here and there stagger brittle, scorched specimens—victims of the big burn a few weeks ago—trailing ash and spoor behind them. The collective droning lamentations rise up like crashing waves, and the combined stench of the multitude hangs in the air like an invisible fog—an ocean of feces, pus, and tar.

In fact, the smell is so overwhelming that most of the survivors clinging to the capital dome of the courthouse building have taken off articles of clothing in the humid Georgia heat and wrapped them around their noses and mouths like makeshift biohazard masks.

"I have to go pee!" Lucas Dupree informs Gloria Pyne on one end of the narrow rotunda. The boy has a piece of shirttail tied around the lower part of his face, so his meek little voice is muffled and almost inaudible in the winds. The ledge is less than three feet wide, but, mercifully, someone thought of installing a small decorative guardrail that winds around the entire circumference. The railing has prevented numerous accidents with the children, as some of them have tried to scale the dome in order to see over the tops of the neighboring woods and maybe send an SOS to whoever might be out there.

"Let him do it around back," Barbara advises from a few feet away. She sits on the ledge between Bethany Dupree and one of the Slocum girls, a damp rag in her gnarled hand, the breeze tossing her wild gray curls. She turns to Bethany and says, "Open wide, sweetheart."

Bethany leans her head back and Barbara squeezes a few drops of water from her bandanna—sopped up from the dew that's collected on the roof tiles—into the little girl's parched mouth. The child's lips are so dry, cracked, and chapped they're starting to bleed. The girl swallows the water and looks at Barbara. "That's it, that's all the water I get?"

"That's it, I'm afraid," Barbara says, throwing a worried glance across the rooftop at her husband, who sits shirtless and cross-legged on the ledge, his head wrapped in a makeshift turban of fabric ripped from his chambray shirt. His rifle is cradled across his lap as he stares longingly off into the distant hills.

David Stern knows they're in deep, deep trouble, and when he turns and looks at Lilly, who sits next to him, he sees the anxiety on her face as well.

"We'll figure something out," she murmurs, speaking more to herself than anyone else. After a day and a night on the roof, her fair skin is already beginning to burn, her neck and cheeks as pink as boiled lobster. She stares at the far northern reaches of Main Street, making note of the scores of monsters trampling the delicate flower bed she planted in front of her building, and feels a sinking sensation that's almost breathtaking. For some reason, those flowers getting stomped is more of an indicator of doom than anything else she has seen from up here.

Tommy sits next to her, compulsively whittling a stick with Harold Stauback's pocketknife, a bandanna wrapped around his nose and mouth. The boy hasn't said much since they ended up on the roof, but Lilly can tell by the glint of pain in his gaze that he's hurting inside.

Harold stands behind the boy, bracing himself on a copper gutter tarnished with a patina of weather and bird droppings. Even holding a handkerchief to his mouth, his belly distended above his belt, Harold has a rakish, dapper air to him. He has done more to keep their spirits up than anyone else, casually singing folk songs and gospel tunes, telling anecdotes of growing up the son of a sharecropper in Florida, and entertaining the kids with magic tricks. But even Harold is starting to show the fatigue.

Gloria takes Lucas around the ledge to the back of the rooftop.

The little boy stands at the top of the fire escape, unzipping his Oshkosh overalls and gazing down at the crowd of cadavers milling about the loading dock area. The wind tosses litter across the scarred pavement as the monsters awkwardly pace, rubbing against each other, so tightly packed that they look like a school of ghastly fish. Some of them hear noises from up on the roof and tilt their nickel-plated eyes up at the child.

The kid proceeds to urinate down upon the creatures.

Gloria watches, her expression grim and distracted. Dehydration has thinned and weakened the boy's stream, but he has enough liquid to get the walkers' attention. The monsters snap their feral gazes up at the sky as though baffled by the sudden rainfall. Unsmiling, the boy watches the urine pattering off the tops of their ragged heads, trickling down their emaciated forms. Apparently the child finds no humor in it, no pleasure, no mischievous charge.

Just morbid fascination.

They hear the noises later that afternoon. Harold is the first to register the sounds, whirling around toward the trapdoor embedded in the side of the dome, instinctively pulling his .45-caliber Smith & Wesson and pointing it at the door. "What in the Sam Hill is that?" he says, the muzzle of his revolver trembling slightly.

Lilly springs to her feet, David hauling himself off the ledge and bringing the barrel of the AR-15 up. The others back away on either side of the ledge, staring at the congealed ancient trapdoor. The kids are particularly petrified by the banging and squeaking noises coming from inside the building, echoing up the staircase inside the hatch. Can walkers climb stairs? Nobody is quite sure what the answer is to that one, but what they *are* certain of is that most buildings in town have been breached and infested by the dead.

"Everybody just take it easy," Lilly says loud enough to be heard above the wind. "It's probably nothing."

"It doesn't sound like nothing," Gloria utters, holding one of the younger children against her chest, the child's eyes radiating terror.

"Them things can't climb steps, can they?" Harold's rhetorical question hangs in the wind like a toxic gas.

"Some of them things managed to climb the speedway bleachers," Gloria counters.

"Everybody stay calm." David points his rifle at the door, nodding at the rusted, oxidized, fossilized brass handle. "Even if they get to the top of the stairs, they'll never get that door open."

The muffled noises intensify as they rise closer and closer to the roof: shuffling, creaking footsteps climbing toward the inner door. It's impossible to tell if it's a single walker or a dozen of them shambling up the iron risers. Lilly stares at the brass knob. The service door hasn't been used for generations. Embedded in the side of the dome, mossy with barnacles of age and bird shit, the door once served janitors and workmen when the courthouse was enjoying its glory days. "Barbara, just in case," Lilly says, throwing a glance across the ledge at the gray-haired matron, "why don't you take the kids around to the back of the roof."

Barbara and Gloria do as instructed, slowly ushering the half dozen little people around behind the dome. Even Tommy sheepishly hands Lilly the pocketknife and goes with the kids, gladly leaving the business of dealing with the attackers to the adults.

Meanwhile, the noises have risen to the point of being only a few feet away. Scraping, shuffling sounds move awkwardly behind the door, and then pause, and then a loud thud makes everybody on the roof jerk with a start. "David, be ready to fire controlled bursts," Lilly says in a flat, terrified monotone.

"Got it." David moves in tight, holding the muzzle only inches away from the door.

Another thud makes the door shudder and sends a puff of plaster off its hinge.

"Make every shot count," Lilly says, standing next to Harold. She has no gun but that doesn't stop her from holding Harold's knife aloft, poised for action.

Harold grips his .45 with both hands, aiming it at the door.

Thud!

"Ready . . . set . . ."

The door bursts open, and a deeply lined, haggard face peers out at them. "What the hell are you people doing up here . . . sunbathing?"

"Oh, my God," Lilly utters breathlessly, struck dumb by the twinkling eyes staring back at her.

Bob Stookey's hair is greasier than ever, his denim sodden with filth as though he's been crawling around a tar pit or an archaeological dig for the last week. He grins at the others and his eyes gleam with emotion in folds of crow's-feet. "You people ready to come down from here, or should I go get some Coppertone and join you?"

TWENTY-NINE

They have a million questions for him, and he assures them there will be plenty of time to answer each and every one of them, but right now he has to figure out a way to get twelve people past the walker-infested first floor to the service elevator shaft, and then down the treacherous access steps to the sublevel, and then through the secret door into the interconnecting passageway, and finally into the main branch of his beloved Underground Railroad tunnels.

Barbara and Gloria keep the kids as silent as possible by playing let's see who can be completely quiet for the longest, the winner to be awarded a year's supply of cherry Kool-Aid—and Bob uses an age-old diversionary tactic of throwing a burned-out lightbulb across the courthouse foyer, the sudden noise of the shattering glass loud enough to draw the walkers away from the bank of elevators in the rear of the building for a crucial minute or two.

They barely get every last person down the service steps before the creatures catch wind and start lumbering after them. Bob stabs a crowbar through the eye socket of the closest biter, slams the doors to the elevator shaft in the faces of a dozen more, and then climbs down behind Harold into the darkness of the sublevel. It takes another ten minutes to pass through the connecting passageway and reach the main tunnel.

Along the way, Bob leads the group through six inches of stagnant water rife with festering garbage and slithering things that elicit a howl of terror from a different child every few minutes as the water bugs or miscellaneous vermin brush past their exposed ankles.

"My hand to God," Bob says to Lilly as he leads the group around the corner of intersecting tunnels lined with slimy brick, the moldering walls flickering in the distant orange light of torches. "When I fell through the floor of that culvert, I actually experienced the luckiest break of my miserable life."

"And that would be what?" Lilly asks, unable to stifle her grin, still giddy and reeling from the emotional roller coaster of discovering her friend alive. Her tattered T-shirt is now so filthy and sweat stained it has transitioned from light blue to toilet-water gray, and she feels the old claustrophobia tickling at her nerve endings, making her scalp crawl, but it's buffered by the sheer joy, relief, and gratitude for something finally going their way. She realizes that Woodbury as a community—her dream home—may be gone, but the only things that really matter in a community are the people, and she still has a good group of people by her side. The others walk behind her, the children exhausted and yet spurred on by fear and anticipation, David bringing up the rear behind the group with his AR-15 cradled in his arms.

"I fell right on top of them sons a bitches, cracked one of their skulls right off the bat."

"Get outta town, you did no such thing."

"Lilly, I would not shit you," he says, grinning at her. "After all, you're my favorite turd."

She gives him a good-natured punch in the arm. "Watch the language in front of the kids."

Bob shrugs. "I'll have to work on that." Then he lets out a chuckle and keeps walking. "Anyhoo . . . one of them bastards got his skull crushed underneath me, and I managed to get that little old knife in the noggins of the two females pretty dern quick." His smile fades. "Not even sure I knew what I was doing . . . was kinda on autopilot there for a while."

"I can imagine." Lilly sees another bend in the tunnel ahead of them and something glowing beyond it. A fire? Torches? Oddly, it looks almost incandescent. "So how did you get from there to here?"

Another shrug from Bob. "I don't know exactly. I guess I been studying that damn land survey so much in the past month or so I kinda memorized the dern thing. I took off running through the sewer, and it was probably a blessing in disguise that I got lost."

"How do you mean?"

"All of a sudden I started noticing things that looked familiar, tributaries of the sewer that seemed to crisscross the main conduit I been working on for weeks. Anyway, I found my way back to the main branch." He points up ahead. "It's up here just a piece, not much farther now."

He leads the group around the bend, and about fifty yards away, Lilly sees a dusty cage light hanging down on a heavy-duty cable. The light glows. "Wait a minute," she says and pauses. The others stop and stare. Lilly can't believe what she's seeing. "How did you do that?"

Bob gives her another shrug. "Good ol' American ingenuity."

The section of tunnel transformed by Bob's handiwork and ingenuity over the last five weeks spans nearly the length of a football field, and is about eight or nine feet wide, maybe seven feet high—a long, narrow chamber of crates, propane tanks, and small appliances that recalls an enormous galley on a giant submarine. The walls have been adorned with maps, corkboards, and art prints, and a patchwork of carpet remnants and secondhand rugs runs down the center of the floor in order to make the space homier. At regular intervals, card tables and pedestals have shaded lamps on them, their sixty-watt bulbs glowing genially over stacks of books and magazines taken from the library. The cumulative effect of the space is cozy, inviting, and maybe even a little surreal.

Upon closer scrutiny, however, it's the technological touches that truly impress Lilly and the other adults as they slowly enter the sanctuary and gaze in wonder at the metal housings along the walls containing small generators, which are softly rumbling, their exhaust pipes retrofitted from furnace ducts and channeled upward to ventilation shafts in the stalactite ceiling. Here and there, a few strands and bundles of electrical cords run down the walls like vines, connecting up with duplex outlets, and every hundred feet or so a portable fan circulates air. For the longest time, Lilly is speechless. At last, she takes Bob by the arm, as the others collapse onto trundle beds and armchairs, and the kids start inspecting the shelves on which rows of canned goods, cereals, and various nonperishable treats like beef jerky and vitamin water are neatly arrayed.

Lilly leads Bob to the end of the tunnel—the terminus point marked by a wall of chain link, freshly painted a bright Rust-Oleum blue—and she speaks softly, almost under her breath, so that the others won't hear. "When did you do all this?"

Bob gives her another one of his customary shrugs. "I guess I did most of it while them Holy Rollers were taking over the place, but I didn't do it all by my lonesome." He jerks a thumb at the others. "Dave and Barb helped me round up the machinery, wire the place up, figure out the ventilation and exhaust systems. Gloria was sorta my interior decorator, I guess you could say."

"It's incredible, Bob." Lilly gazes at the shadows of the deeper tunnels on the other side of the cyclone fencing. "This will definitely tide us over until we can get the town back from the walkers."

Bob awkwardly looks at the ground, licking his lips and choosing his words carefully. "Yeah, um . . . we should talk about that."

Lilly looks up at him. "What's the matter?"

Bob takes a deep breath. "Woodbury's gone, Lilly-girl."

"What?"

"It's as gone as a wrecked ship on the bottom of the ocean."

"What the hell are you talking about?"

He gives her a paternal pat on the shoulder. "It's the way of the world nowadays, Lilly. You lose a place to them shit bags, you move on."

"That's ridiculous." She looks back at the far recesses of the tunnel. "We can rebuild the town, clean up the place, start over, give these kids a place to grow up."

He holds her by the shoulders until their gazes lock. "This is our new home." He has never looked as serious as he does right now. "Woodbury has turned, Lilly."

"Bob—"

"Listen to me, it's turned just as sure as one of them things up there used to be an ordinary person . . . the town has turned. Them things are *inside* the buildings now, they're everywhere. It's goddamn Chernobyl up there. You ain't gonna be cleaning anything up, Lilly, or rebuilding anything, it's gone . . . dead and gone."

She stares at him for a moment, words failing her. "I . . . I can't even breathe down here." She looks back through the fence. "How am I gonna live in this sardine can, Bob? With my condition?"

He puts his arm around her. "Lilly, we got a truck load of Xanax, Ambien . . . Valium, even. And when we run out, we can move around the county underground without risking our asses, and we can find *more* drugs. And supplies and medicine and food and whatever else we need, for that matter."

"Bob, I can't—"

"Yes, you can." He gives her a friendly squeeze, another reassuring pat. "You're Lilly Caul, and you can do pretty much anything you put your mind to."

She doesn't say anything, just stares at him for another moment.

Then she turns and once again gazes out at the dark reaches of the tunnel.

Through the screen of chain link, way out in the depths of the main tunnel, in the grainy darkness, like ghosts, the other tributaries branch off in opposite directions, the legacy of fleeing slaves, calling out to Lilly, a dark heritage of pain and suffering and loneliness and desolation, a low rumble of voices from the grave, whispering from long ago: *Run . . . run away . . . run for your life!*

Lilly senses a response forming deep inside her, a secret voice, *felt* more than heard, triggered by fight-or-flight instinct.

She'll stay.

And fight.

"An excellent companion to
THE WALKING DEAD.
Something no fan will want to miss."
—Examiner.com

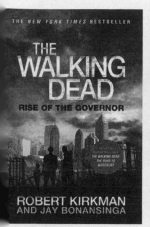

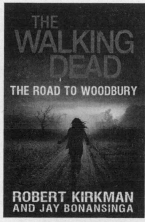

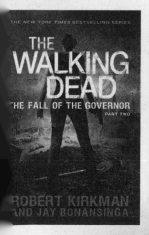

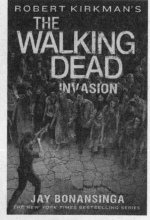

AVAILABLE OCTOBER 2015

St. Martin's Press THOMAS DUNNE BOOKS St. Martin's Griffin